From Amazon readers' reviews...

Beyond Beautiful

"Bornstein is able to convey to the reader the beat of the music, and the perfection of the musicians and song writers. She has the ability to reveal a progression of growth from a shallow one dimensional character to caring, sensitive, believable personalities creating an empathy with the reader."

"You will fall in love with the characters in this book! If you love Aerosmith, rock music, or are just a romance novel enthusiast you will love this book. I can't wait to see what will happen next in this trilogy!"

"Completely and thoroughly enjoyed this book. I loved the feeling of being "a fly on the wall" and getting a behind the scenes/backstage pass into the personal lives of these characters. I am a shameless romance novel fan and this has it ALL. Anyone who loves rock-n-roll, suspense and ROMANCE should definitely pick this up!!!!"

"A well balanced mix of romance and suspense keeps this absorbing plot moving from page one to the final climax, leaving the reader eager for the upcoming sequel."

Sweet Emotions

"...provides romance, drama, thrills, and chills. It is the whole package: the ability to feel like the characters are alive can only be attributed to Jan's ability to write so well. This book is one of those books that once you start reading you feel like you are a part of all the action taking place. A really good read."

"Jan captures the essence of the flow of energy from stars on stage to the audience and back to the synergy of the performers. Bornstein shows remarkable insights into the conflicts experienced by those in the rock music industry. She has an incredible understanding of the team effort of musical groups, the tensions, the hours of practice to perfect a song arrangement or producing a unique sound... "

"Whether you're looking for entertaining reading, romance, action, suspense, or for something that you can sink your teeth into, Jan Bornstein's writing meets them all with a multifaceted plot and charismatic characters as unique and individual as the popular well-known rock stars competing in the world of music today."

The Song Trilogy

Beyond Beautiful
Sweet Emotions
Deuces Are Wild

Deuces Are Wild

Jan Bornstein

back channel press
portsmouth new hampshire
www.backchannelpress.com

DEUCES ARE WILD
Copyright © 2008 by Jan Bornstein
ISBN 13: 978-1-934582-09-1
ISBN 10: 1-934582-09-3

THE SONG TRILOGY
www.janbornstein.com

BACK CHANNEL PRESS
170 Mechanic Street
Portsmouth, NH 03801
www.backchannelpress.com

Printed in the United States of America

Cover artwork by Matthew Pippin
Cover design by Cecile Kaufmann
Book layout by Nancy Grossman

Library of Congress Control Number 2008933618

Dedication

For everyone who contributed and supported me throughout this journey.

Acknowledgements

I want to express my gratitude to Cecile Kaufman and Matthew Pippin who once again made my ideas come to life for the cover of this final book of the trilogy.

To Aaron Bornstein for all the time, effort and help he's given me right from the beginning.

To Deidre Randall and Blueline Publicity for all their help and hard work in getting my writing recognized. To Back Channel Press for their continued guidance and support in the publication of all three books.

Finally, I owe everything to my wonderful editor, Nancy Grossman, who once again worked hand in hand with me on this book. She took my dream and, with time and perseverance, enabled me to bring this trilogy to my readers.

Chapter 1

ROCK STAR JENNA BRADFORD TENNY quietly hummed the melody of "Long-standing," the song that had won her a Grammy award only a month and a few days earlier. When she came to the song's bridge, she softly, unconsciously mouthed the lyrics:

> *Cuz our love's longstanding,*
> *It's as old as the hills and as ancient as the sea.*
> *Our love's longstanding.*
> *Its gift to the world will be of you and of me...*

As she sang the final few words, Jenna lowered her lips to ruffle the fine, dark hair atop that little "gift to the world," the almost impossibly small Zachary Matthew Scott Tenny, who stirred, stretched, then rearranged himself as he fed, one tiny hand reaching up and sliding into the cleavage between her swollen, sensitive breasts. "Typical male," she whispered, smiling, "copping a feel, Mr. Cool, like I'm not supposed to notice? I've met your type before."

At first distressed by having to leave her baby in the neonatal intensive care unit when she had recovered from his traumatic premature birth, Jenna had come to treasure the hours she spent in the NICU, quietly holding, nuzzling and feeding her so longed-for first child. She was often the parent earliest to arrive in the morning, clocking numerous hours of "skin time" with Zach before reluctantly returning him to the care of his devoted team of doctors and nurses.

"A chip off the old block," murmured a most familiar but unexpected masculine voice behind her. A far larger hand slid its way down into Jenna's cleavage, slipping an index finger under the tiny hand already resting there; miniscule fingers closed reflexively around it. "Easy, there, champ. That's one of your daddy's most important piano fingers, you know."

Scott Tenny's world was also music; little Zach's mom and dad were rock stars of equal magnitude. Scott had exhibiting signs of his own father's talents as a pianist long before he'd shown up for his first day in elementary school; it was quickly obvious that Scott's future would be music. It certainly wouldn't be academics. He'd survived a tumultuous childhood defined by attention deficit disorder long before the term had been invented. From the beginning, there had been little similarity between his father's piano style and Scott's; Scott was born to play rock ' roll. For years he had been the lead singer of the internationally famous Blacklace.

Scott drew his son's diminutive hand back into more G-rated territory. "That kind of behavior leads to Oedipus complexes," he said with mock sternness to the oblivious infant. "Enough of that, young man. Daddy's watching."

"Do you think we need to be looking into psychoanalysts for him already?" Jenna laughed.

"Any son of mine can't get started early enough," Scott chuckled. "And we probably should be getting him enrolled in his first twelve-step program while we're at it. BMA – Breast Milk Anonymous." As if he agreed, Zach wriggled again, relinquishing the breast and releasing his grip on his father's finger with a soft burbling and pursing of his lips. Scott reached down to quietly rub his little son's back. "Poor guy. Addiction's a bitch."

DRIVING HOME FROM South Shore Hospital, Jenna was pensive. Scott reached over and took her hand. "How are you doing, little mother?"

Jenna sighed. "I'm fine till the postpartum hormones kick in. It's like someone throws a switch, I swear. I'm okay while we're there. It's when I have to leave that world and step back out into this one – "

She gestured randomly at the late afternoon winter landscape as Scott dodged in and out of the rapidly building early evening traffic. "While I'm at the hospital, I'm completely focused. Out here – I feel lost. It's not that I'm not busy enough. It's not that everyone doesn't try to help keep me preoccupied. I almost wonder if it wouldn't be better to have a little more alone time to let myself adjust."

"I was wondering how long it would take for you to get to that point," Scott said, nodding sympathetically. "Everyone means well…"

"One little item, and then I'm going to suggest – *insist* – that Mom and your dad head back to L.A.," Jenna said firmly.

"Item?"

"Event, actually."

THE 'EVENT' WAS A belated birthday party for Scott, and as birthday parties went, this one was going to be one for the record books. Celebrations this year had disappeared into the vortex of Zach's difficult birth, Scott's birthday falling as it did less than a week after the baby's unexpected arrival, but Jenna had spent many of her unrushed hours in the NICU, rocking and planning a very special party worthy of a very special man, this man she'd allowed into her life and heart.

Aiding and abetting her in her thinking were her mother, her step-sister Kristin, Jeremy Sandborn, Scott's lead guitarist and his wife Carrie, Jenna's best friend. Jeremy had promised to take an active roll in the preparations as well. The fact that Kristin was back in L.A., pursuing her acting career which had taken a giant step forward with her recent acceptance into the Actors Studio, only helped facilitate the West Coast part of the planning. This marriage was bicoastal – Scott's career had taken off and remained based in Boston. Boston had accepted and embraced Jenna, a native Angelino, with amazingly rapidity by New England standards.

"The venue *won't* be Blue Skies," Jenna had decided almost immediately. They'd already held a number of events, both small and large, at the restaurant Jeremy and Scott had bought into more than a year ago now, including their wedding reception the previous Christmas Eve. It was time for a change of scenery.

"Where?" was Carrie's first question. Jenna decided Boston. Carrie did the footwork and was back a day later with an eclectic list of possibilities, everything from hotel rooftops and university reception rooms to galleries and museums across the city.

Overwhelmed, Jenna put the selection to her mother. Linda Huntington Bradford Tenney – Scott was still adjusting to the fact that Jenna's mother was now both his step-mother and his mother-in-law – chose the Spanish Cloister of the Isabella Stewart Gardner Museum. Looking at the pictures, Jenna had to agree. The opulent formality and scale of the space fit her mood to perfection. None of Blue Skies' checkered tablecloths for this party. This was going to be an elegant, fancy dress affair. "The hardest part will be getting Joe and Scott into tuxes," Jenna laughed.

"Not my Joe," Linda corrected her. "Lately he seems to be looking for excuses to dress. Don't know what's gotten into the man. He hasn't been the same since the wedding. Just when you think you know what you're marrying."

Jenna's eyes met Linda's for more than a moment, then sought Zach's eyes, who lay peacefully in her lap. Comfortable with the tangle of tubes hooking him up to the pulsing equipment arrayed about them, she picked him up gently and held him close, rubbing his back. Her mind resisted thinking about her father, screen star Robert Bradford, dead now almost two years, she realized – and his multiple betrayals which she was still working to assimilate. She much preferred thinking about how happy her mother was with her new husband.

Carrie and Jenna set to work drawing up a guest list. "The entire extended Blacklace family – that goes without saying," Jenna said. "Kids too." Carrie started listing everyone who played in Scott's band and their significant others: guitarist Dan Clark and his girlfriend Jill; backup guitarist Jeff Aquino, his wife Denise and their fifteen-year-old son Travis; drummer Tim Knowleston and his wife Paula; and newcomer Ryan Ellis, who played keyboards, sang backup, and put a blushing smile on Kristin's face. At the bottom of the list, Carrie included Jeremy and herself and their sixteen-year-old son Aiden.

"And then my band," Jenna said. "They've agreed to come out on the condition that we find studio time while they're here. We've got several new pieces in progress and there's just so much they can do without me. Mark and Nadia Newsom." Mark was Jenna's lead guitar. "Tom and Rena Jacobs." Tom was her drummer. "And Bob Roskowski and Dane Sturdevant." She had to spell the last names of her bass and specialty guitarists. "Bob's bringing Angela Tay – they're pretty much of an item these days. Dane says he's coming by himself, but let's save an extra place next to him. I have an idea."

"You playing matchmaking?" Linda chuckled.

"You're a fine one to talk, Mother," Jenna grinned. Linda's role in encouraging Scott in his pursuit of her hard-to-get daughter were by now family lore. "I doubt I'd be holding this little guy if it weren't for all your hard work." Linda acknowledged her complicity with a wink.

"Okay. Managers," Carrie prompted Jenna. "Strang, on our end." Eddie Strang had managed Blacklace for more than thirty often arduous years.

"And Brian Mason for me. He'll be bringing his girlfriend de jour. My publicist, Bella Sutton. And Philly Argo's coming – he's my record producer. And all the Blacklace guys – Bella will love finally getting to meet Stanley." Stanley Havlik, Scott's publicist, had done plenty of phone work with Bella, managing the flow of information about their respective clients, who had been dubbed "Boston's Cinderella couple" early in their relationship. If Cinderella and Prince Charming had had a pair of publicists like Bella and Stanley, the Grimm Brothers' fairy tale would have read quite differently.

"And family," Jenna went on. "My baby bro told me last night he's going to be able to make it." Chris Bradford, a rising film studio executive, carried his life in his suitcase and practically lived on airplanes. "Jim and Sue can make it too." Jim Bradford and his wife, both professional campaign managers, lived their lives in parallel maelstroms of politics. Jenna had never imagined this marriage would work; the fact that it had she attributed to prolonged periods of work-related separation. They wouldn't have lasted a year in nine-to-five jobs. "And Kristin's coming out next week. She doesn't want to miss one bit of the action."

"Scott's family?" Carrie asked.

Jenna reported that Scott's daughter Laurel and her husband Rick Kalman would be there, along with the youngest invited guest, their twenty-month-old son Luka. Jenna couldn't help but smile at the thought that the tiny preemie in her arms was Luka's uncle. Missy, Scott's older daughter, and her fiancé Alex Calby, wouldn't be able to commit till the last minute. Theatrical technicians, both were subject to the never-ending demands of Broadway.

"I talked to Annie last night," Linda volunteered. "She, Mark and Nancy will be here. Joe's trying to track down David – he's got it in his head it'd be a great surprise if he could produce him." Annie, Scott's only sibling, and Mark Fitzgerald hadn't seen their wayward son for almost five years. While her husband and their daughter had learned to live with Annie's controlling ways, David never could. He'd hit the road right out of high school. Occasional postcards, usually to Nancy, but also to his Uncle Scott or Grampa Joe, painted a pointillist picture of a young man in search of himself.

"How many does that make?" Jenna asked.

Carrie did a quick tally. "Forty-two, if you include the four maybes."

"Okay, let's include Big Bob and Little Bob." Big Bob O'Halligan, Scott's tour manager, stood six foot three. Bobby Malatesta, Big Bob's intern from Berklee College of Music, was only a six-footer. "They'll both bring dates."

"Forty-six," Carrie said.

"And Paulie, of course. Paulie and Sarah." Paulie Gattonucci had been Blacklace's recording engineer for fifteen years. "And an invitation to Matthew Caine," Jenna said, more to herself than to Carrie.

"That makes forty-nine," Carrie said, then looked up as she added him to her list. "Matthew Caine. The L.A.P.D. guy?"

"The guy who saved my life. And Zach's," Jenna murmured, nuzzling her baby. "Oh, how I wish you could make it fifty, little Z."

ONE WALL OF THE Spanish Cloister at the Gardner Museum is dominated by a tremendous John Singer Sargent oil of a flamenco dancer in a white skirt and heavily fringed black shawl, with guitarists and spectators lined up in chairs along the wall behind her. Jenna seized on the image as the central theme of the party.

"This bash is going to be about anything but rock 'n roll," she decided. "Enough with sound checks and amps. We're going castanets and acoustic for a change." Carrie went ahead and lined up a mariachi band and a troupe of flamenco dancers to entertain. Cards featuring prints of the Sargent painting went out as invitations; guests were encouraged to study the painting and dress accordingly.

THE EXOTIC, BLACK-HAIRED lead dancer who came clicking and stomping her way through the hall to the head table could have been Sargent's model. Heads turned and followed the tall, lithe woman as her flounced white satin skirt trailed and twirled, leaving them hypnotized in her wake. Head and shoulders thrown back arrogantly, the dancer's pale skin seemed only the whiter for the blaze of fiery red lipstick that defined her sensuous lips. She needed no prompting. She reached out a graceful hand as her eyes locked on Scott's, drawing him from his seat like a powerful magnet.

Scott had gone all out when he'd been told about the theme for the party – he'd rented a full-on flamenco dancer's outfit – high-waisted tight black pants, and a ruffle- sleeved white shirt that he wore unbuttoned to the top of those tight pants under a tiny, bright red jacket. It wasn't much of a stretch for him to adapt his normal stage gyrations to the blistering choreography of flamenco. Lifting her skirts, the sizzling señorita matched him, move for move. Even as he kept pace with the dancer, his eyes sought out and held those of his wife, as if she was his dance partner, not this Spanish beauty. Jenna blew him a kiss, then began to clap in rhythm with the guitars. Soon the entire room was clapping in unison, providing the most primitive form of percussion for the age-old scene. The net effect was riveting.

One by one the male dancers invited the male guests to join them to one side of the dance floor, teaching them the moves of old Andalusia, while the female dancers drew the female guests to the other side to demonstrate and share their art. With a little practice, the more confident sought out partners. Couple after couple paired off until few were left to watch.

Scott and Jenna had no trouble adapting to each other's moves. Not touching, moving with magnetic precision, they matched each other step for step, until Scott took Jenna by the hand and drew her around him into his embrace. Lost in each others' smoldering eyes, they moved gracefully across the floor, first overtaking their parents, who seemed oblivious to the presence of anyone one else in the room, and then Bella and Stanley, whose minds never strayed far from business.

"I guarantee you I can have a photo of you two dancing on the front page of the morning's L.A. Times," Bella brayed, a pair of bright red flowers tucked behind one ear. She pulled off the patterned shawl she wore, brought it sweeping around before her, then like a bullfighter, shook it smartly to bait Stanley.

"I'll have them on the eleven o'clock news in every time zone tonight," Stanley countered nonchalantly, raising his clapping hands as he sucked in his gut and moved past by her with tiny, crisp percussive steps. Dropping his hands to his sides to his hips, he threw his head back, spun and danced tightly in place, refusing to move until she finally capitulated and swept dramatically to his side.

Spinning around him, Bella whispered something in his ear, then drew back with a triumphant cackle. "Try topping *that*, Stanley Havlik!"

Stanley considered her, smiled devilishly, did a pirouette, then bringing his hands up to clap rhythmically by his ear, he whispered into *her* ear.

Bella backed off and stood in one place stamping her feet while buying time to think. Then she moved in tiny pairs of steps back to his ear, whispered again and pulled back to see the effect that her newest strategy engendered. Stanley pursed his lips, looked impressed, nodded several times, then brought his hands down to clap them at her in applause.

"You're gal's good," he conceded to Jenna, then bowed his head to Bella in courtly concession.

"Heck, anyone can get headlines in Boston," Bella snorted. "If you can do it in *L.A.*, you can do it anywhere!"

Chapter 2

❋

LIFE SETTLED DOWN, as much as life ever could for two rock stars with heavy touring and recording schedules – and a premature baby receiving round-the-clock care in the hospital. Scott struggled to find his focus as he and the rest of Blacklace started serious rehearsals for their summer tour. When Jenna wasn't at the hospital with Zach, she was either working on her own music or rehearsing with Scott and the band.

She had no plans to perform for several months at the least; the baby was her first priority and his prognosis was still of great concern. Signs of progress were measured in micro-units – fractions of ounces and inches, heart beats per minute, points on the Apgar chart, percentages of oxygen in the bloodstream.

Emergencies developed and were dealt with. Zach had already recovered well from the first operation of his young life, a surgical tying off of a blood vessel that bypasses the lungs during pregnancy, then normally closes shortly after birth; in Zach's case it hadn't and was flooding his lungs with blood. A brief episode of intraventricular hemorrhaging – bleeding into the ventricles, the open spaces in the brain – was another heart-stopper, though the nurses kept assuring Jenna that a "grade one bleed" was almost to be expected and posed no long-term threat to the baby's future brain functioning.

Recurring bouts of jaundice led to frequent rounds of phototherapy in his incubator. "Definitely a future rocker," Scott decided upon first encountering the sight of his son, a miniature spa mask covering his eyes, lolling comfortably in the midst of all his viper's nest of tubes under a purple neon glow, looking like a scene from a big-budget science fiction movie. Sliding an arm around his weary wife, Scott rubbed her back. "Don't you worry, Baby Blue," he said calmly. "Our boy's gonna be fine." In fact, Scott was anything but calm. Wanting to be as supportive of Jenna as he could be, he bottled up his fears and frustrations. Like champagne under pressure, it was only a matter of time before he blew his cork. He took out his frustrations, as he always had, on his band.

MAY MERGED INTO JUNE as tensions built. Jenna put as much time in with them as she could manage, but found herself wracked with guilt and anxiety every hour she spent away from Zach, and it showed. Songs weren't coming together. Videos had to be reshot because nothing was quite working. Black-lace was scheduled to take to the road in mid July; an album had to get finished and into stores well before their first major show of the summer in San Francisco. A trio of local shows in early July, in Boston, Providence and Manchester, New Hampshire, had been lined up to work out the last wrinkles. Jenna had no plans for going on tour with Scott; she even had issues about just performing in the local shows. With the never-ending demands of their daily lives, they'd had little time for each other.

Scott was able to control his temper in front of Jenna – he owed her that much – but he was rapidly driving his band members to the brink of mutiny. Stress before tours was nothing new to any of them, though Ryan Ellis, the youngest and newest member of Blacklace, was still trying to get used to it; this would only be his second tour with the group. By the end of his first, he'd adjusted fairly well to Scott's eccentricities, but he was young and his skin was still thin. Drawn to vulnerability, Scott had taken to picking on Ryan on the last tour, and he was back at it again as rehearsal after rehearsal devolved into shouting matches. Jeremy was getting tired of playing referee.

Cornering Scott one afternoon, he finally addressed the problem head on. "What the fuck's eating you?" he asked point blank. "You've been acting like a first class ass. I was thinking things might mellow with Zach's arrival, but it appears I was wrong. Far from it." Scott tried to push past him, but Jeremy grabbed his arm and pinned him against the wall.

"Take your hands off me," Scott hissed angrily, struggling to get free of Jeremy's iron grip.

"When you come clean," Jeremy said quietly. "I'm your friend, your bro, man. Talk to me. It feels like a tornado's about to come rippin' through the studio. It's no wonder nothin's working – everyone's got one eye on the exit at all times. What the fuck's your problem?"

Scott stopped resisting, threw his head back, closed his eyes and let out a prolonged sigh. "Shit," he moaned. "Everything. Nothing." He brought his head down, opened his eyes and looked his best friend straight in the eye. "Everything," he said finally. "Everything the fuck is wrong."

JEREMY SENT EVERYONE HOME, threw Scott in his car and drove the two of them over to Blue Skies. The parking lot was well on its way to capacity when they pulled in, which did much to improve both their moods. Making their way to the door, they could pick up the heavy beat of Devil's Opera Box, the local band that had been consistently drawing a good Wednesday night crowd since they'd started playing there three months earlier.

Ann Westover, one of their partners in the bistro and lounge, was han-dling the door and greeted both her associates warmly. Less than a mile from Scott's house and rehearsal studio, the Blacklace family had long considered the friendly restaurant, originally known as 'Ann's Place,' their favorite hangout; many locals did. Since Jeremy and Scott had come in as investors, Blue Skies had expanded, now serving up live music nightly along with even better cuisine, and had been turned into a virtual museum of Blacklace memorabilia.

"Busy!" Jeremy yelled over the din, giving Ann a thumbs up and a grin.

"These guys have really caught on," Ann yelled in response. "The crowd gets bigger every week. Word of mouth."

"Best kinda advertising," Jeremy nodded. "Hey, rather than subject ourselves to constant interruptions, would it be okay with you if we just pulled up a couple of chairs and ate in the manager's office? We've got some business to work out."

"Sure, sweetie. What would you like?" she asked, showing them the specials. "The osso bucco's to die for."

"Sounds great," Jeremy said.

"Me too," Scott agreed. "And a couple of salads. That'll do us fine, hon." Jeremy hoped the 'hon' meant Scott was mellowing out.

OPENING THE DOOR TO the manager's office, Jeremy ushered Scott in, then didn't waste any time making it clear this wasn't a social visit. Before they'd even sat down, he launched into Scott, picking up where he'd left off back at the studio.

"Okay, come clean, asshole. What's eating you? Talk to me."

Scott dropped into a chair. Hunching over, elbows on knees, he took refuge behind the long dark hair that spilled over his face. His hands, clasped as if in prayer, came up to covered his mouth. Propping his chin on his thumbs, he stared into space before finally lowering his head into his hands with a groan.

"Talk to me," Jeremy repeated, quieter this time.

Scott sighed. You've had a kid," he said, not looking up. "You must remember what it's like."

"Back in the Ice Age, but yeah, I remember, sort of. You do forget eventually, believe it or not."

"What I remember of Missy's infancy I remember through a drug-induced haze. Of course I never even knew Laurel existed till she was five. But Zach's a whole different story anyway. The hospital..." His thought trailed off.

"That's gotta be so hard, man," Jeremy said compassionately.

"For Jenna more than me," Scott said quickly. "But, yeah."

"It's not just Jenna that's taking the emotional hit here," Jeremy pointed out. "Let me guess. It leaves you feeling helpless, Zach's future being a question mark. Having to put your faith in his doctors...in God."

"Yeah," Scott mumbled. "Helpless – powerless..." Again, his thoughts trailed off into painful territory. "You know, you could have all the money in the world and you wouldn't have one more degree of control over the outcome than I do right now. I so wish I could spare Jenna the fear, the pain..."

"Of course you do, Scott. We all do."

"At the same time – and I know this is gonna sound so fuckin' selfish, man – we haven't been able to spend any kinda time alone. Fuck – we haven't made love since the baby was born. Plus, she pumps milk every two hours all night long, but she won't let me near her breasts, either, they're so sore. Everything's a mess." This all came out in a self-conscious rush. "Jesus, that sounds so lame, but – it's drivin' me fuckin' nuts."

Scott jumped to his feet and started a random pacing of the cramped office. "I mean, the little bit that we *are* alone, all she thinks about is the baby." He stopped and faced Jeremy. "Don't get me wrong. I think about him too but she's at the hospital every day, sometimes *all* day. I can't remember the last time we just sat and held each other."

Jeremy nodded. "I hear you, bro. I gotta tell you, Carrie's worried about you and Jenna too. It's not your imagination. She sees it. Just the other day, she was saying how worried she was, that it can't be good for either of you."

Scott sat down again and looked over at his musical partner of thirty-some years. "At least I'm not crazy," he said, gratefully.

"No, you're not crazy – but that doesn't give you the right to take it out on the rest of us. You gotta get on top of your temper, man. Time's runnin' short, and I swear, you don't watch out, Ryan's gonna bolt. He's had it. And you know that'd come back to bite you, big time." Scott didn't need to be reminded.

"I know," he mumbled. "There's probably some Freudian term for it, takin' out your frustrations with your wife on your wife's half-sister's boy-friend." Scott snorted in self-contempt. "I'm such an ass."

"Look, bro, why don't you make plans to take Jenna out somewhere," Jeremy suggested tentatively. "Go to the hospital, *together*, tomorrow. Take her out somewhere afterwards. Talk to her. Somewhere neutral – away from home, away from the hospital, away from all of us. Let her know how you feel."

Scott crossed his arms, then raised one hand to massage his temples. Finally, he looked up at Jeremy. He had just said, "You're right," when Ann came bustling in with their dinner. Jeremy smiled quietly to himself. Those were words from Scott he rarely ever got to hear.

UPON OPENING HIS EYES, Scott found only a note for him the next morning on the empty side of the bed where he'd hope to find his wife. Jenna had been asleep when he'd gotten in; apparently she had already left for the hospital, with plans, the note said, to return home mid-afternoon. Mid-afternoon found him sitting at the kitchen counter, waiting to waylay her when she came through the door.

"Babe," he said, opening his arms to her. She dropped her shoulder tote of baby paraphernalia to the floor, shrugged out of her hat, coat, scarf and gloves, pulled her cell phone from her pocket to check it quickly for messages and finally came into his outstretched arms – to give him a quick peck on the cheek. "We gotta talk," he said in response to the quick peck.

"Jeez, I don't have time to talk right now, honey," she said, already pulling out of his embrace as she spoke. "I've just got enough time to get a couple of really important things done for the shelter, but then I need to get back to the hospital." Jenna had been the moving force behind the establishment of South Shore First Step, a small but rapidly expanding community shelter for abused women and their children one town over. Before Zach, First Step had been her baby.

Something in Jenna's tone of voice pushed Scott over an edge he had never realized was so precariously close at hand. "You don't have the *time*?" he exploded. "*Make* the fucking time. *Now!*" Jenna immediately pulled clear of his grasping arms and backed away from him, astounded.

Grabbing his head with the two hands she'd rejected, Scott immediately regretted his words. "Jenna, Jenna! I'm so sorry! I just want – need – to know what the hell's going on here. We've hardly had a moment alone, we don't talk to each other, you're always at the hospital. You rarely even ask me to come along with you. We haven't made love since before the baby was born."

Scott was furious with himself as all his frustrations came pouring out – this wasn't how he'd meant to talk to her, the words he'd been carefully rehearsing for the last hour. It certainly wasn't the heart-to-heart conversation Jeremy had suggesting the night before. The only thing he could give himself any credit for was honesty, which he finally gave in to. There was no starting over.

"Okay. Listen to me. Frankly, I've gotta tell you I'm damn frustrated about the whole situation. We need to talk about what's going on. I have a plan for tonight and I want you to listen to it. You and I go to the hospital, *together*; I'd like to see my son, too. Then we go out for a nice dinner and maybe take a walk on the beach. And *talk*."

Jenna started to interrupt him, but Scott put a finger to her lips. "No, wait," he said, determined to get everything off his chest. "We've lost touch with each other. I know life since Zach's been crazy, but we've never experienced a disconnection like this before, even when we were fighting about something. We barely kiss each other these days, let alone make love, and I gotta tell you – I miss it, honey. I miss *you*. Please – tell me what's going on."

Jenna did listen, and as she listened, her anger, tinged with fear, was replaced with realization and regret. She hung her head, nodding. "God, you're right, honey," she finally said, looking up at him, her expression completely altered by guilt. "I miss us too, and it's mostly my fault."

Scott started to protest, but just as he had, she held a finger to his lips and continued. "I've been so consumed with the baby. He's been my morning, noon and night, and you're right, I *have* left you out. I guess I just assumed you'd spend as much time with him as you wanted to. It never occurred to me to ask you to join me, to plan to spend time with him together. I never meant to leave you out, or make you feel left out. I'm truly sorry. I love you so much. That hasn't changed, but it certainly has gotten lost in the shuffle. And you're right – we haven't spent any time together, for the two of us. *We*'ve gotten lost in the shuffle. We'll do what you've planned. We need to do it."

Reaching out to him, she welcomed him into *her* open arms. "You could be a little more polite about it, though," she whispered in his ear, then let her lips find his.

SCOTT SLID AN ARM around Jenna's waist as they entered the constantly humming world of the NICU and headed for Zach's incubator. As they threaded their way through the orderly ranks of identical incubators and all their attendant monitors and machinery, Jenna pointed to one that now sat empty. "Jade went home today!" she exclaimed, as pleased as if it had been Zach himself who'd been discharged. "I was here when they left. The entire staff was in tears. She was such a miracle baby."

"I can't wait for that day for Zach," Scott said. "Our own little miracle man." As they reached Zach's clear plastic world, he gave her a squeeze. Zach was awake, as if expecting them. Scott relinquished his hold on his wife to reach in through one of the portals to give his son a tickle. "How's it goin', my boy?" he murmured.

Lifting the cover of the incubator, Jenna leaned over and gently picked up the baby whose hands instinctively reached for her. Zach was still a featherweight; it would be four more weeks before her original due date. His birth weight of one pound fourteen ounces had practically tripled, Jenna had been told that morning, but he still was a precious tiny thing, and it still took more than a moment to adjust to that reality every time either she or Scott visited, no matter how recently they had last been with him. As she pulled him close, his initial squirming ceased and his little body relaxed. He knew where he was.

"MY SWEET, I COULD watch you breastfeed all night," Scott said contentedly, smiling over at Jenna who was rocking gently in one of the many glider rockers in the room off the NICU set aside for nursing. Fidgeting about on a rolling stool, he slid it up to her and beat out a rhythm on the arm of her chair with a couple of pencils he'd dug out of his jacket pocket. He started humming. Before they left, they'd worked up the tune and first verse of a rock lullaby for Zach.

Dinner was at a little Italian restaurant in the North End of Boston which Jeremy had highly recommended, and it more than met their expectations. In a quiet corner made all the more intimate by the flickering candle on their table, they decided to sample their way through an extensive offering of appetizers rather than order entrees, saving room to split a slice of 'cassata' that Jeremy had said they mustn't miss a Sicilian specialty comprised of thin layers of sponge cake and sweetened ricotta flecked with citrus peel, candied fruit, almonds and chocolate shavings, iced with a sheet of almond-rich marzipan.

Scott held Jenna's hand as they took their time making their way through the delicious confection. Jenna halved the last bite and ate her half. Scott halved *his* piece and ate his. Jenna halved the morsel that remained and again ate her piece. Scott scooped his up on his fork and insisted that she pop it in her mouth. Then he kissed her.

IT WAS RELATIVELY WARM for a Massachusetts May night. Scott turned up the heat and rolled down the windows so they could enjoy the bracing breeze as they drove back home to the mellow beat of *No More,* the acoustic album they had released together after the tour they had taken on the road almost a year ago now, just the two of them, to shine a spotlight on the subject of abuse. The proceeds of that tour and album had made up the down payment on the hundred-year-old farm house and piece of property that had become the abuse shelter known as South Shore First Step. The tour had won them a Grammy humanitarian award.

Before they got all the way home, Scott pulled off the main road and headed down to a little beach that he knew they would have to themselves at this hour on a May night. Parking at the end of the road, he pulled a flashlight from the glove compartment. With its aid, he found the trail that ran through a quarter-mile of woods and down to the beach beyond.

Winter had littered the narrow trail with fallen limbs and windblown detritus. Shining the light ahead of them, they picked their way though it all carefully, and were glad when they broke free of the woods and out onto the open stretch of dunes where the clear roar of the surf and the smell of the salt air hit them simultaneously.

Turning off the flashlight, Scott took Jenna's hand and the two ran slogging through the sand, their way now easy to see under a clear sky and a quarter moon. In a bowl formed by the dunes that protected them from the wind, Scott pulled Jenna down, into his arms, to his hungry lips. The night fell still and the world fell away as they rekindled and fanned the flames of their faltering passion. Before long, they had it blazing anew, its flames once again flaring to the heavens.

Chapter 3

❋

THE DIFFERENCE IN REHEARSAL the next day was quickly obvious to all. It took a few hours for everyone to trust it, but eventually their guard came down and they regained their familiar stride. No one recognized the change in mood more than Ryan. Scott joined him several times as they sang, looking him square in the eye. Clearly encouraging Ryan, he was finally working with him, not against him as he seemed to have been doing for the past several weeks.

Jenna rehearsed with them for more than an hour in the early afternoon. Her mood was buoyant and infectious. Grins replaced grimaces; jokes started circulating. Dan, the merry prankster of the group, let the wise cracks fly, most if not all referencing Scott's recent bad behavior in one way or another. Scott laughed harder than anyone.

Within a week they were back in the studio and finishing up the album that had been giving them such headaches. Scott decided to call it *Good Grief.*

JENNA WAS CONTEMPLATIVE as she and Scott headed into Boston for the first of the three pre-tour warm-up shows. The Fleet Center (which would always be affectionately referred to by Boston old-timers as the Garden) was home base for Blacklace; all pre-tour shows started there and were always a guaranteed sellout. The Good Grief Tour was no exception.

This was the first time she would go almost a full twenty-four hours without seeing Zach. She had left a more than adequate supply of breastmilk behind for him, and she knew he would receive almost as much physical attention from staff as he would have from her, but she felt herself tethered to him by a strong, invisible umbilical cord that stretched adequately between the hospital and home, but with greater and greater tension the further north they drove.

Jenna closed her eyes, breathed deeply and set herself the task of letting go of the distressing image of a baby blue bungee cord stretched to its snapping point. In its place she visualized that cord growing thinner and more elastic with every mile, until it was merely a durable thread sagging in the ease of its stretch, comfortably allowing her as large a radius of movement as she needed. At the other end of this fine, stretchy thread, she envisioned Zach enjoying a kids' sleepover, he and his tiny friends, no staff responding to sudden emergencies, no parents hovering anxiously, just a lot of happy, healthy, tiny little kidlets lobbing tiny little handfuls of confetti and singing at the tops of their tiny little lungs, rocking the NICU till the break of dawn.

JENNA'S PRE-SHOW ROUTINE was complicated by her need to express breast-milk before going out on the stage; it wouldn't do to have leaking breasts in front of twenty thousand fans. The little manual breast pump she'd brought with her struck her as clumsy and inefficient when compared to the hospital's hi-tech pumping apparatus.

"We're on," Scott yelled in to her as she tried to maintain a zen-like calm while she continued her pumping.

"Take your time. Stretch it out with chatter," she called back to him. "I'm barely halfway through the second breast."

"Get a move on, sister," he said, but there was no pressure in his voice.

"You can't rush this, dammit," Jenna retorted in genuine frustration.

"Need help?" he joked.

"Go out there and sing, singer man," she laughed back at him. "Go give 'em your all. I'll be out when I'm good 'n ready, and not a minute sooner, I'm afraid."

SCOTT GAVE THEM HIS ALL, and then some. The first time he'd performed since the removal of a polyp from one of his vocal chords the preceding January, he felt a surge of electricity race through him as he charged out onto the stage. Ripping off the long red, orange and green scarf tied loosely around his neck – which but for a scrap of a tank top, left him naked to the waist – he held it up like an Olympian's flag as he took a victory lap out the catwalk and back, bathed in the adrenalin rush that only a live audience like this one could provide. The roar that greeted him made the past six months' of dread, despair and exasperation vanish the way a bad dream does when one wakes in the arms of his lover. He was back.

Perhaps the hardest thing he'd ever had to do in his life, Scott had followed his doctor's orders to the letter during his period of recuperation, slowly building his voice back to full volume. Recording had been no prob-lem; Paulie had been able to supply what Mother Nature wasn't ready to let him have yet, and he could have allowed Ari Lakhdur, the tour sound man, amp him up to full power if need be, but he was having no problems at this point. Who knew what damage six weeks on the road would do, though. He knew he still had to pace himself.

But not tonight. Tonight was for Boston, and the hometown audience would get every last decibel he had to give them.

JENNA COULD HEAR THE crowd's approval grow stronger and stronger with each song Blacklace sang. By the end of the second number, she'd completed her maternal chore and packed away her milk on ice. Not back in shape from pregnancy to her complete satisfaction, she chose a low-cut, glittery purple jumpsuit with a long cowl that fell strategically across the bit of bulge that still remained. Checking herself from all angles in the mirror, she finally accepted what she saw with a little nod. Her enhanced cleavage more than made up for the yet conspicuous tummy. "You definitely still have work to do, woman," she said sternly to her reflection. "Too much time in that glider and not enough in the gym." A little more mascara and a flip of her hair, and she was ready to go.

Which was just how Jeremy introduced her. "Okay, Boston, put 'em together for the mother of the year, your favorite and ours, Ms. Ready to Go herself – Jenna Bradford Tenny!" The house went dark, only Scott standing illuminated in a pool of light, as Tim's drums revved up a welcome for her. A second spot picked Jenna up at the edge of the stage and followed her as she fought her way through a virtual wall of noise into the open arms of the man she loved.

Bending her backwards, Scott engulfed her in a rehearsed kiss that rocked the rafters. Then he swept her up off her feet and into his arms. However, this move they hadn't rehearsed; Jenna knew she had no choice but to just go with it.

The band broke into an unfamiliar opening tune, chords that gave nothing away as to what song was to come. Slowly, maddeningly, as Scott carried Jenna like a bride over a threshold, crossing the stage to the main mike, the chords began to morph into something tantalizingly almost recognizable. Just as Scott set her down lightly in front of the mike, they finally stopped teasing and launched full bore into the intro to "Ready to Go." Scott gave Jenna another, almost chaste, little kiss, then the two turned to the mike and got to down to work, each taking alternate lines.

> *Take me to bed. I am ready to go.*
> *Take me to heaven. I'm ready to go.*
> *Take me this minute. I'm ready to go.*
>
> *Take my hand, take my heart. Ready to go.*
> *Gratitude, thankfulness. Ready to go.*
> *Take care, my lover. I do love you so.*
>
> *Here is my hand – I can give it to you,*
> *Cuz here is the heart I have given to you.*
> *Hand and heart, mine to give – take them in yours.*
>
> *Please take my heart, dear – it's already yours.*
> *Please take my heart, love, because I am yours.*
> *Take my hand, take my heart. Ready to go.*
> *Gratitude, thankfulness. Ready to go*
> *Take care, my lover. I do love you so...*

As they started the final verse, Scott positioned himself behind Jenna and wrapped her in his arms. Dragging out the last word, "so…" he turned her to him and they kissed as if they were alone on a deserted island, six hundred miles from the nearest shipping lane.

Finally coming out of the kiss, they moved to opposite sides of the mike, looked deep into each other's eyes and returned to the first verse. This time, Jenna sang the first line and Scott echoed it, then the second and its echo, and the third. The lights dimmed on Scott's final, quiet "I'm ready to go…"

BACK HOME THE NEXT morning, Scott brought a tray laden with fruit, bagels, cream cheese and lox, and a pot of coffee into the bedroom, set it on the bottom of the bed, then went back down to get the morning papers. Jenna, roused by the aroma of garlic-rich bagels, pulled on a short, velvety thick pink robe, left the sash suggestively untied and climbed back into bed. One look at her had Scott dropping the papers on a nearby chair and moving the breakfast tray. Only after their sexual appetites had been satisfied and Scott had hollered "uncle," did they move on to the more mundane demands of the morning.

Scott spread cream cheese on bagel slices as Jenna tore through the pile of papers, looking for reviews. They weren't hard to find. The first page of the entertainment section of all three papers featured commentary on the previous night's show. Photos and a review took up an entire half page of the *Boston Globe*. The reviews were uniformly enthusiastic. All three spent several inches on Scott's voice; all three agreed he'd come back from his surgery at full strength and voice range.

Only one had the audacity to suggest that Jenna's choice of costume could only be attributed to a need for postnatal camouflage. "Never has an audience seen so *little* of the beautiful Ms. Tenny as they did last night," was columnist Agnes Deutsch's catty remark.

"So little!" cackled Scott, gleefully sliding over to kiss her on the neck and caress her slightly rounded belly. "Only *I* know what you really look like, my sweet. *They* can imagine anything they damn well please. Your secret's safe with me, babe."

PROVIDENCE PROVIDED FOURTEEN thousand fans an unforgettable evening, and Manchester's Verizon Center gave more than eleven thousand the last chance to see Jenna and Blacklace at their pre-tour best. From then on, Jenna's presence with the band would be occasional and unadvertised, and had been clearly publicized as such. If anything, the unpredictability of her performing had helped, not hurt, ticket sales. The fans apparently welcomed the opportunity to play rock 'n roll roulette, hoping to be one of the lucky ones who'd be able to brag that they'd caught one of the rare shows that included her that summer.

JENNA HAD NO TIME TO lounge around the morning after Manchester to read reviews; she had an early appointment with her obstetrician/gynecologist.

Scott had just returned from the local newsstand with a copy of the *Union Leader* as she was heading out the door.

"I'll see you at the hospital at eleven, hon," she said, giving him a quick kiss. "Please don't be late. We're meeting with the entire team."

"I'll be there," Scott assured her. "And give Julia my love."

Jenna did. As her OB/GYN for the past two years, Julia Williams had been at Jenna and Scott's side through more than one catastrophe. First it was the loss of another man's child as the result of a horrific car accident; Jenna had been pregnant when she and Scott had gotten together. Then it had been the miscarriage of a child of their own the following winter. And she'd been there when Zach had been born – and Jenna had almost died. Julia knew both of them in ways few ever could, or would want to.

Dressing hurriedly after her exam, Jenna went down the hall and joined Julia in her office. Copies of sonograms were spread across her desk.

"Julia, tell me, please," Jenna said before she'd even taken a seat, "what are my chances for carrying another pregnancy anywhere near term?"

Julia was equally forthright. "Based on your history, Jenna, I am not at all sure that a full-term pregnancy will ever be possible for you. Honestly, hon, I have to question if you will even be able to carry another child to viability." Julia gave her a moment to digest the unhappy piece of information before reaching across her desk and laying her hand over Jenna's before adding, "I wish I could be more optimistic."

Jenna looked down, trying to compose her thoughts. Then she looked back up at her doctor. She turned her hand and squeezed Julia's.

"But I *can* try, right?"

"You can try. But I have to suggest that you not try getting pregnant for at least a year. Give your body time. It's been through so much."

Jenna left the office fighting tears.

IT TURNED OUT THAT Jenna was the one who was late for the hospital meeting. She'd made it down to her car in reasonable control of her emotions, but when she'd gotten in and pulled the door shut behind her, she was overcome by a profound sadness the likes of which she had never experienced. She had no choice but to let her tears flow until they finally slowed of their own accord.

Taking a moment to try to repair her makeup, she finally pulled away from the curb and into the flow of traffic. She made her way across the city as efficiently as possible by slipping off onto side streets to avoid traffic jams building ahead. At least she was getting good at that, she thought to herself with grim self-satisfaction. Boston was a nightmare for non-natives.

Slipping into the meeting, she hurried over to the vacant seat beside Scott, sat down and took his hand. Glancing at her, he could tell something was wrong. He gave her a quick kiss. "Is something the matter?" he whispered.

"Later," she whispered back, then addressed the assembled doctors and nurses. "Please forgive me. I had an earlier appointment and it took longer than I'd expected to get across town."

"No problem, Mrs. Tenny. Let me backtrack," said Dr. Van Dusen, the neonatal pediatrician who headed up the team. "We'd just been telling Scott that basically Zach's doing well – very well, indeed. He's gaining weight. His respiratory system has improved markedly and he should be totally independent of any need for oxygen soon. As you know, he recovered remarkably well from the surgery – no complications, no problems. He took it right in stride."

"And his cranial ultrasounds continue to be fine," added the neurosurgeon who'd performed the surgery, who was sitting at the far end of the table. "No signs of any further problems in my department."

"The CT scans of his digestive tract," offered the pediatric gastroenterologist, gesturing to ghostly black and white images on one of the light boxes in the meeting room, "show slow but steady improvement. Intestinal function is consistent for a child at thirty-seven weeks. Everything is continuing to develop just as it should, right on schedule. I foresee no problems in terms of digestion."

"We're still doing metabolic screens on a daily basis, with particular attention to the thyroid and pituitary numbers," said the pediatric endocrinologist. "The rest are definitely what I want to see. And thyroid and pituitary aren't that far off."

"And on a less clinical note, I just have to say that Zach's just a joy to work with," volunteered the head of nursing. "A sweetheart. He may look fragile, but he's one sturdy and determined little guy. You've got quite a boy there, a real survivor. And I've got to say, Jenna, you are to be commended. You are one of the most devoted, dedicated moms I think I've ever worked with."

"If everything continues going well, I think we're looking at a mid-July discharge," Dr. Van Dusen said with a smile.

"I'M AS HUNGRY AS he was," Scott said, giving Zach a kiss on the top of his head before Jenna tucked him back in his incubator. "How about a bite downstairs in the café. For hospital food, it ain't bad. If we go somewhere food critic-approved, you'll just have to fight your way back here afterwards."

"I've had worse at some five-star restaurants I can think of," Jenna agreed.

Lunch was ordered before Scott brought up what Jenna had been avoiding since she'd hugged Zach goodbye. "So what was bothering you when you arrived? I could tell something had – has – you upset."

Jenna looked down, bit her lower lip, sighed, then looked him straight in the eyes. Before she could open her mouth, he reached across and took her hand. "What did Julia say? What are the odds?"

"Not good." Tears began to glisten in her eyes. "Full term would be a miracle, from what she said. She's not even sure… She wants to do some tests. And – she doesn't want us trying at all for a year. Oh, Scott…" Her thoughts were in total disarray.

"Hon, a year's not all that long. It'll give Zach time to really get on his feet – literally," he added, chuckling. "A year's not the end of the world."

"I know. I guess I'm hearing my biological clock chiming midnight. I'm so afraid I'll never have another child."

He squeezed her hand. "Baby, hang onto this thought: if you do, it will be a gift; if you don't, it wasn't meant to be. You have Zach. And you have me," he added, holding her with his eyes. Jenna found herself smiling through her incipient tears. Reaching over with his free hand, he wiped away one that had escaped and was flowing down her cheek. Then he brought her hand to his lips.

"Look, she didn't say you couldn't for sure, am I right?" Scott asked, optimistically. "Let's not get ahead of things. You'll have the tests and we'll see what happens from there. You know what we need? Since we're not having the big July fourth at the lake get-together this year, why don't you and I, just the two of us, take an overnight and head north? We need some time alone together, especially with Zach coming home soon. Besides I'll be leaving; it's going to be a long haul till I'm back."

Jenna was amazed at how easily she was able to say yes. "Can we go tomorrow? Is that too soon?" she blurted out. "They've got plenty of milk stored at the ICU."

"And I'll be happy to help you pump," Scott grinned. "Always wanted to try my hand at dairy farmin'."

Chapter 4

JENNA AND SCOTT MADE the normally two-and-a-half hour drive up to Sunapee, New Hampshire, in just a little over two hours; the only thing that slowed them down, once they were clear of Boston, was holiday traffic in the little lakeside town itself. They arrived just a few minutes after noon.

Radar detector activated, Scott had used the trip to test what he could expect from his new sleek black Mercedes G-class SUV. To celebrate the positive reports from the hospital and Zach's imminent arrival home, he'd dropped a bundle for the "family car" of his fevered imagination. He'd never owned what he jokingly referred to as a sedan in his life, and as sedans went, this one was a doozy: German-engineered and Austrian-built, the exterior looked like an indestructible cross between a Jeep and a Hummer. The interior was wall-to-wall luxury.

Scott eased his way down the lake house driveway, threw the vehicle into park, killed the engine and jumped out. Two hours sitting in any one position was about his limit; this was a man who needed to move. Hustling around to the back of the car, he grabbed out their bags and was halfway to the front door before Jenna had collected up her things and climbed out. She took a few deep, restorative breaths of pungent pine and stretched in the warm, dappled sunlight before she was ready to go inside.

THOUGH SCOTT AND JENNA couldn't be there because of Zach, Jeremy, Carrie and the rest of the Blacklace family had used the lake house over Memorial Day weekend, six weeks earlier; it had been shut up since then. It never took long for the interior to revert to its empty-house mustiness. After dropping their bags at the foot of the staircase, Scott and Jenna went room to room, throwing open windows and doors, gathering up odd glasses and cups that had never made it back to the kitchen as they went.

"Oh, it is such a joy to be back here," Jenna exclaimed, finally taking a moment to step out on the screen porch overlooking the lake.

"And such a joy to be sharing it with you – just you," Scott added, coming up behind her, smothering her in a bear hug, punctuated by a lick and a kiss on the neck. "I know that sounds selfish, but I gotta admit, babe, there are times when I want to stand at the top of the steps and holler, 'Everybody get outta my house!' Not really, but you know what I mean."

"Oh, yeah," Jenna said, relaxing back against him reflexively and rocking in his arms. "I know exactly what you mean. It does tend to get a bit crazy."

"A bit," Scott chortled. "Like Shibuya at rush hour."

"Shibuya?"

"Tokyo's answer to Times Square."

"Hmm…never done Tokyo."

"You should. We did Japan a few years ago – right before I met you. It's one place in the world that's actually faster-paced than me."

"This is *not* the place to the talking about fast-paced," Jenna reminded him gently.

"Not even a fast run upstairs and a quick jump in the sack before lunch?" Scott whispered seductively. "What's the matter, Mother Tenny? Can't keep up with your old man's fast-paced appetites anymore?"

Jenna made a point of beating him up the stairs.

THE JOINT WAS JUMPING at Tiny's, the third-generation dinner with the lakeside view that Scott had been frequenting since he was a kid; Scott had grown up in Sunapee. He and Jenna had made it a tradition to stop by every time they made it up to the lake since the first time they'd come up together two years earlier. Jenna had quickly been accepted by sumo-wrestler-sized Tom Correlli and his petite wife Sally as one of the regulars.

Tiny's had originally been named Correlli's, but the founder, Tom's grandfather Tony Correlli, had been such a small man that he had quickly been renamed 'Tiny' by the locals. His son, Tom's father, was hardly larger and had finally given in to tradition, having a new sign painted that put 'Tiny's' officially on the map. People today who knew no better just assumed the name referred to Sally.

Tom and Sally were delighted to see them again. Sally hugged Jenna, and Tom gave Scott a pat on the back. "We hear congratulations are in order," Sally said with a wink to Jenna. "We've been following the baby's progress in the paper. How's he doing? If you're up here, I assume things are good?" Jenna filled her in on the latest report as Sally ushered them to a table.

"You look at the menus – there's some new stuff this year," she told them, "while I go get you some water and a little something special. Be right back." And she was, with two glasses of water and a package wrapped in blue baby wrapping tucked under her arm. She set the waters down and gave the package to Jenna with a kiss.

Jenna pulled a card from under the bow and handed it to Scott, who opened it and read, "A little something for the next generation of Tenny bad boys – from a Correlli bad boy and his Missus." Unwrapping the present, Jenna found a lacey black hand-crocheted baby blanket within.

"Oh, Sally – it's fabulous!" Jenna exclaimed.

"Dear God, I just get more jealous of my son every day," Scott chimed in. "This is just too perfect, hon. Perfect!"

"I went to work when you told us you were expecting last fall, well at least when the season wound down. I wasn't half finished when Zach made his untimely but well publicized appearance, so I went into overdrive to have it ready by Memorial Day. It's been waiting for you ever since. May he love it so much he wears the darn thing to rags."

"Blacklace blankies – we're going to have to add them to the rest of the Blacklace merchandise," Scott laughed.

"I can't wait till Zach's old enough to sit here in a highchair and thank you in person, Sally," Jenna said. "You guys are the best."

BACK AT THE HOUSE, Scott took Jenna's hand and led her down the windy path to the lake shore. They went out to the end of the short finger dock, sat down at the edge, pulled off their shoes and dropped their feet into the still chilly July water. Jenna shivered at the momentary shock; Scott put an arm around her.

The lake was buzzing with boating traffic – Fourth of July week brought with it an explosion of motorboats and jet skis. Those with kayaks, canoes and sails tended to savor the peaceful early-morning hours on the lake, then put in at smaller, quieter area lakes later in the day.

"Zach is so gonna love this," Scott said, looking out across the lake while playing with the skinny strap of a lime green camisole Jenna was wearing.

"He already does," she laughed. "Playing with my straps, silly," she added in response to Scott's puzzled expression.

"I mean playing on the lake – *silly*," Scott retorted.

"I know you do. I was just having some fun with you." Jenna smiled, wrapped an arm around him and dropped her head on his shoulder. "What a place to grow up," she mused. "What a lucky little kiddo."

"I can't believe we haven't been here since last October. My God, so much has happened since last October." He shook his head in amazement. "Our folks getting married. *Us* getting married."

"You and Annie burying the hatchet. Don't forget that," Jenna added.

"Yeah, and we couldn't done it without you. You get all the credit for that miracle. Who'd have ever thought…"

"I'll take credit for figuring out how to make it happen, but you two took it from there," was all the credit Jenna wanted.

"And Zach," Scott continued. "And all that that entailed. God. When I think of all the ways that could have ended in catastrophe."

"Don't. Just think forward. No more backward. It's over, it's done, and our lives are in front of us, all three of us. At the least – maybe more," she added quickly, almost superstitiously not wanting to jinx the outside chance that, someday, God willing, she *would* be able to give Zach a brother or sister to grow up with.

"Maybe more," Scott repeated. He moved his hand up to run it through her long, rich brunette waves, then bent down and kissed her. She returned his kiss with interest.

AS THEY MADE SUPPER, Jenna in the kitchen and Scott on the grill, they planned the next day, determined to maximize every minute of their brief stay

"Want to go riding?" Scott asked as he rubbed herbs all over a couple of racks of baby back ribs.

"Horse or bike?"

"Something tells me you'd prefer horse to hog," Scott said diplomatically. He'd happily spend the entire day on the Harley he'd left up here the previous October, but he knew her tolerance for the machine was limited to quick jaunts only. She wasn't biker lady material – that she'd made clear to him the day she was introduced to his pride and joy, a 1980 Low Rider. Down deep, motorcycles scared her.

"Ya know – I bet you'd love the bike if I got a sidecar for it," Scott ruminated. "Road trip! We could get a micro-helmet for Zach!"

"Over my dead body," Jenna said succinctly.

"Ooooo-kay," Scott backtracked. "How about something a little more sedate, in that case? Anyone for antiquing after we go horseback riding?"

"You're just full of ideas, Mr. Activities Director," Jenna said, surprised.

"I happen to love antiquing," Scott disclosed. "Old stuff in general. Doesn't have to be fancy, just old and interesting."

"Oh, you do, do you? Well, it just so happens so do I," she told him.

"Great. Just no wisecracks about collecting *me*, okay?"

"Never crossed my mind, old man."

THEY ATE DINNER on the deck as the sun went down. Afterwards, Scott cleared the dishes and insisted on cleaning up the kitchen. When he was finished, he found Jenna sitting in front of the fire with a faraway look in her eyes. Sizing her up, he reached down, took her by the hand, and led her out the front door and up the path to the road.

"And where might you be taking me, may I ask?" she said.

"Down to Cobbies for an ice cream cone."

"You clever boy. Now why didn't I think of that?"

"Your mind seemed to be wandering elsewhere, my sweet. Someone has to think of practical matters, after all."

"Amazingly, I wasn't thinking about Zach, if that's what you mean," Jenna said with a smile. "If you want to know, I was thinking about what it's going to be like, with you on the road and me basically a homebody. I have no clue when or how much I'll be able to join you. So much depends on when they tell us Zach can travel."

"I want you two with me as much as possible while we're on the road. I know it's no life for anyone, much less a brand new family like us, but damn, I hardly got to see Missy as a baby, we were touring so much in those days. I want to watch my son grow and discover the world around him. I want to show him things. I want to *be* there."

"You're gonna be the best dad a kid could ever want. It may be an unconventional upbringing, but it's the love that counts. And *that* he's gonna get plenty of. He's going to be the center of the universe," Jenna said dreamily, then came quickly back to reality. "The center of a totally chaotic universe. Our lives are going to be like so turned one hundred eighty degrees upside down."

"That's part of why I want to do as much goofing off as we can tomorrow, before we head back. The last of the 'just us' time," Scott said, almost wistfully. "Things are going to be different when Zach comes home. Very different."

"Everything's going to be different," Jenna sighed. "And so much depends on who we end up with for a nanny. I've narrowed the field to four. God, it's such an important decision. I like them all. Great women, great credentials – all four of them have worked with preemies. You've gotta help me with the decision."

"You know I'll pick the hottest one," Scott laughed. Jenna pretended to haul off and slug him. "Just kidding, just kidding!" he said, throwing his hands up in mock defense. "Don't worry, babe. I'm taking this as seriously as you are. We'll make it priority numero uno when we get home. We're getting down to the wire."

"The hottest. I swear," Jenna laughed. "You sure *better* be kidding, mister."

"Scott's honor," Scott said solemnly, holding up his right hand, index and pinkie fingers raised. Jenna grabbed him around the waist, pulled him to her and kissed him hard, once, twice, three times. "Okay, okay," he surrendered. "*You're* the hottest."

"Damn straight I am, and don't you forget it, hotshot."

"No, m'am," he said, catching up her hand again and kissing it as they continued down the road. "I'll make sure to remember *that.*" As they rounded a corner, Cobbies came into view.

"Can I tell you something?" Jenna asked in all seriousness. "Oh, God – even though I've worked with Zach so much in the NICU, I still feel damned intimidated about taking full responsibility for him."

Scott squeezed her hand. "You're going to be fine, babe. You'll settle into routines before you know it. Just watching you with him now, I have no doubt."

"Yeah, but that's with never less than a half-dozen nurses handy, to help if anything goes wrong. That'd give anyone confidence."

"Actually, I've been thinking maybe it'd be a good idea to hire a nurse for a while, a night nurse at least, as well as a nanny," Scott said. "People have to sleep. I know you'd sleep better, what sleep you'll be able to get. I know *I'd* sleep better, wherever I was, knowing things at home were fully covered."

"I'd been thinking the same thing. Maybe full-time nurses for the first week or two. It's an extravagance, but I just want to know I've really got things under control. Oh, man. I can handle a crowd of twenty thousand – but this one little half pint's got me shakin' in my boots."

"One day at a time, Mum. One feeding at a time, one burping at a time."

"One diaper change at a time," Jenna said, taking up the theme. "One diaper rash at a time. One ear infection at a time. One …"

"Okay, okay. Enough, or you're gonna scare yourself to death," Scott laughed.

"Can't we just raise him in the NICU, till he's ready for college?" Jenna moaned.

WANDERING BACK DOWN the road with double-dip cones already dripping in the hot July night air, Jenna felt like a schoolgirl – then immediately found herself wondering if it was the last time she'd feel this way in her life. It felt like the weight of world, not the five-odd pounds Zach would weigh when he came home, was settling itself down on her shoulders.

Then she stopped herself. Jenna Tenny, she told herself sternly, you've gotta just shove those heavy thoughts to the back burner, girl, and make a conscious decision to simply enjoy the rest of the time we've got up here. Relax.

"Holy shit. Take a lick of this," Scott exclaimed, stopping in his tracks and holding his cone to her lips. "If you thought the strawberry shortcake was over the top, you gotta taste the marzipan chocolate."

Jenna had to agree. "That may be the winner so far. But taste my bottom one." Scott ran his tongue around the base of her cone, slurping up a good sampling of her fast melting banana fudge. "Whaddya think?"

"Whew, that's a winner too. I don't think there are any losers on their menu," Scott decided as he hurried to consume more of his before it simply melted away. Jenna finally gave up and tossed the remains of her cone into the woods. Scott eventually had to follow suit; it was getting to be too much of a mess. Licking their fingers clean, they finally joined hands again and jogged the rest of the way back to the house.

FLIPPING ON THE television, they settled into the couch and each other's arms as Scott "performed on the remote," as he put it. And he did, switching channels to a rhythm in his head that Jenna kept trying to guess.

"It's 'The Hard Way,' right?"

"Nope."

"The Harley song?"

"Nope."

"'Outta My Way'?"

"Nope."

She waited and really studied the progression of changes. "I got it. I got it!" she exclaimed. "It's 'Drivin' It Home.' No question."

"Can't believe you don't even recognize your own song," Scott grinned.

"Mine? Oh, shit. I figured it was one of yours. Okay." She focused on the rhythm again. Suddenly, she laughed. "I get the message. I'm 'ready to go,' too, babe," she said huskily.

Scott jumped to his feet, reached down and swept her up in his arms. Reaching up, she put her arms around his neck and dropped her head on his chest. "I love it when you go all Rhett Butler on me," she moaned dramatically.

"I'm gonna make love to you all night long, Ms. Scarlet," he replied, heading for the stairs. "You can make love to me tomorrow. Tonight, it's all for you, my love."

Chapter 5

❋

OVER JENNA'S PROTESTS, Scott kept his word, or at least a good part of it. Maybe they didn't make love *all* night long – they drifted in and out of sleep and sex until the sun rose, as if there were no boundaries between the two instinctual states – but he did insist that it be all about her. Every time she tried to take the offensive, he stopped her instantly, first with verbal reminders, then with a raised finger. Finally, all it took was a cautionary look. Taking a completely passive role in bed was a novelty for her. "I guess you *can* teach an old dog new tricks," Scott eventually whispered in her ear.

"Who you calling a dog? Much less an 'old' dog?" she roared back. But she remained lying as he'd positioned her, flat on her back, legs spread, arms at two and ten o'clock. "I feel like I'm posing for da Vinci. A female version of the guy that proves all the proportions or whatever he does," she giggled.

"Vitruvian Man," Scott whispered in her ear.

"Oh, baby, I love it when you talk dirty to me," she whispered in his.

BUT WHEN THE SUN spread a glow around the edges of the window shades, the tables were turned. As Scott rose up over her to make love yet again, Jenna surprised him by pushing him back, springing up and assuming the dominant position. "Now it's *my* turn," she said, kneeling above him with a wicked grin. "Now you are *my* victim, you poor man. Now you are in *my* power."

"Help! Help!" Scott barely whispered. Jenna lip-read the words more than heard them. "Somebody help me!"

"No one is going to come to your aid, my pet," she assured him. "You can whisper all you want. There's no one for miles to hear you."

Scott's hand reached blindly for the bedside phone. "Sorry, pal. I cut the phone lines." He pretended to look wildly around him for some way to defend himself. She blocked him as he lunged for a sheet; grabbing a corner, she tore it off the bed and cast it to the floor. "You're mine, all mine," she laughed diabolically.

Perhaps it was the role, perhaps it was the product of a night of playing passive, but Jenna suddenly felt a torrent of liberating feminine power surge through like she'd never experienced in her life. The man she loved lay beneath her, waiting impatiently, growing before her in tumescent anticipation of her hands, her lips. She loved this! She drew out the moment, savoring his ragged breathing, holding back, devouring him only with her eyes. Shoulders thrown back, milk-gorged breasts on full display, she was a vision to behold, particularly from Scott's pinioned vantage point.

Slowly, she brought her lips down to his. As his arms came up to hold her, she took them by the wrist and pinned them down to his sides. As his tongue attempted to enter her mouth, she forced it back and explored his mouth with hers. As his groin rose in a futile attempt to find its ultimate goal, she drew her pelvis up and away from him, teasing him, enticing him, then released one wrist to place a firm hand on his washboard-flat belly. "You better lay still, mister, or you can wait here all day," she said huskily. "We're on *my* time table, not yours, big boy." Her hand remained until he settled back down, then returned to his temporarily liberated wrist.

"Yes, m'am," he groaned.

Then, unhurriedly, she allowed her lips to return to his. This time he waited for her tongue to enter his mouth. She let go of his wrists; his arms lay where she'd positioned them. She rose up and looked down into his flaming black eyes. "Good boy," she smiled sweetly. Then she went to work in earnest.

Trailing her long hair and fingers and breasts over his chest and upper body, she dropped her lips wherever she found herself, on his neck, on his belly, on his ear, on his side, on a nipple. And wherever her fingers and lips dropped, they stayed and explored, and her tongue explored as well. Soon his groans were growing real, not theatrical.

Then she pulled back and moved on down his body, again sweeping her full head of hair here and there – and there. And again, touching and kissing and trailing her tongue wherever she was – in his naval, around almost behind him to nibble at one of his cheeks, across his groin.

And then she took him in her mouth. And stayed there. And explored and tantalized and played and labored, and before long brought him to climax. And just as he did, he reached over, against all the rules, and brought her to climax as well. For a second, she thought about stopping him. Then it was out of her control.

BOTH SCOTT AND JENNA lay on their backs, staring at the ceiling fan as it whirred silently above them, waiting for their gasping to return to something like normal. "Oh my God, babe – do you realize what you just did? Man, that took my breath away."

Jenna was quiet for several moments. Then she said, her voice hushed with wonder and amazement, "And I didn't panic. It was – it was like I'd been doing it all along. Like it was something totally normal. Like – like I'd never had a problem with it in my life. Like none of that stuff had ever happened to me. Do you know what this means?" she finally said, turning to him, her eyes wide with disbelief.

"That I can look forward to more?" Scott said warily, afraid to trust in this completely unexpected breakthrough.

"That I've turned a corner, maybe? That I've put that behind me? That I've gotten free of that bastard? Malone's had a choke-hold on me my entire life, like even from the grave."

Scott needed no reminder who she was referring to: Peter Malone, neighbor and "friend" of the family, who'd molested Jenna at the age of twelve; a good portion of that molestation had consisted of forced oral sex. Malone had died not long after the adult Jenna had put a bullet in him, almost two years ago now. She'd born the psychological scars of his abuse for more than twenty years.

"Oh my God, Scott – I think I've finally broken clear of him."

"Man, this is unbelievable, baby," Scott whispered, pulling her close. "But let me tell you, if it never happens again, I'm okay. That was just incredible – I can go to my grave a happy man. Not that I'd *mind* if it happened again," he teased her as he reached out and started tickling her. Squirming from his arms, she grabbed the nearest pillow and brought it pummeling down on him. Tackling her, he quickly reversed their positions and pinned her down. "That was damn sneaky of you, Baby Blue. I'm not gonna forget that," he laughed.

A little more tickling and he went serious. "Jenna, honey, I can tell you one thing: being away from each other for almost three months is definitely not going to work. No question, I'm going to be making a lotta trips back home in between shows. We've gotta find out if and when Zach can travel. I don't care if we have to hire a whole team of doctors and nurses to come along with us, just as long as we can be together. I don't want to miss all that time away from him *or* you."

THE DRIVE TO LAKE VIEW FARM, a few miles from the house, put both in a reminiscent frame of mind. The place loomed large in their short history together, though they'd only been there twice. The first time, when they'd just stopped by to see the facility, had been a disaster; Jenna had slipped on ice and brought on a miscarriage. The second time, they'd rented a couple of horses – and Scott had proposed to her.

Making their way along the road that hugged the lake, they approached a cutoff that led to the house where Scott had grown up. "Want to stop by the place and see what's been done since we were last here?" Jenna suggested. Scott's father had finally sold the family home two years earlier.

"Ya know, I don't think I want to," Scott said. "Maybe when Zach's old enough to appreciate it, I'll bring him to see his family roots, but I really don't feel a need to keep going back." They sped past the turn-off and were soon winding their way down the pine-lined drive to Lake View and its own private world of barns, paddocks, riding rings and trails. Jenna's heart registered mixed emotions when the main barn's old red cupola came into view.

FIFTEEN MINUTES LATER they were trotting side-by-side out to the dusty trail head.

After a mile or more under the cool canopy of tall oaks and giant maples, they emerged into a broad, open field – a knee-high sea of wind-blown grass bordered by disintegrating stone walls. "Look at this," Jenna cried. "It's so beautiful."

"Probably farmed land, at one time," Scott surmised.

"Race ya!" Jenna challenged him. "To that old wreck of a gate over there." She pointed to the skeletal remains of a gate at the farthest corner of the huge field.

"You're on!" Scott shouted. "On your mark, get –" And he took off at a dead gallop without looking back.

"Hey, that's not fair!" Jenna wailed as she spurred Zappo, the big dappled Appaloosa she was riding, into action. With ground-covering long legs, he overtook Augie, the compact black Morgan that Scott was on, about three-quarters of the way across the field. Jenna was able to pull up at the gate, wheel Zappo and face Scott several strides before he and Augie arrived at the finish line.

"Damn, there's gonna be no living with you now!" Scott laughed. "Come on." Turning, he led the way over the remains of the rock wall and back into the woods. With the temperature hovering at ninety, the shade provided welcome relief. Cantering along, the wind in her hair, Jenna couldn't remember feeling so happy, so carefree – so *free* – in years. Maybe ever.

COMING TO THE BANKS of a stream, Scott pulled up. "Let's let the horses get a drink," he suggested, throwing a leg over the saddle and sliding off. Jenna did the same. The horses needed no encouragement.

"Guess you *can* lead a horse to water," Scott laughed. Leaning up against a tree trunk, he reached for Jenna with his free hand and pulled her to him. "Come here, beautiful," he said with a wink.

Jenna melted into his embrace, sliding her one free hand up and behind his head, drawing his lips down to hers. Scott's free hand set to exploring under her tank top, gently caressing her breasts. "Oh, baby," he whispered. She could feel him growing hard against her. Losing herself in the moment, she reached for his straining zipper.

Scott quickly raised his head and surveyed the area. The woods were quiet but who knew how long they'd remain so. But a nearby outcropping of rock would provide all the cover they needed; wading, they led Augie and Zappo downstream and around behind the crags and boulders. A heavy limb at the water's edge made a convenient hitching post for the horses. In total privacy, they made love amidst the rocks.

"AFTERWARDS, AS THEY SAY in the romance novels…" Jenna laughed as they started pulling themselves back together. "Oh, man!"

"Now this is the way I remember us," Scott said happily, pushing his hair back out of his eyes. "But, now – oh my God, even better…and better…"

Jenna, completely blissed out, could barely move. "Oh, yeah, doll. I remember this version of us too," she murmured, looking over at him. Reaching for him, she pulled him to her and kissed him yet again.

"More?" Scott said, dazed, mesmerized, but just as he spoke, the sound of horses approaching set their horses on edge. Augie half reared, setting Zappo to jigging nervously. Both started tugging on the reins Scott and Jenna had rather casually double-looped over the branch.

Pulling up his jeans with one hand, not out of modesty but simply so he wouldn't trip on them, Scott lunged for the reins, which in Augie's case were about to come free. He caught Augie's reins but one foot, connecting with a slick patch of slime on the rocks, and went out from under him. At the same moment, Augie gave another sharp pull. Scott landed at good way out from shore, up to his waist in cold water. He let loose a resounding, "Oh, shit!"

Getting back to his feet proved to be difficult; the slime was everywhere and Augie, who was also having trouble keeping his footing, continued to buck and rear out in fear. Jenna caught Zappo's reins easily, then quickly turned back to help Scott struggle to his feet. "Can you toss me his reins?" she called to him.

"Won't work," Scott said, quickly gauging the distance and viability of the idea. "Find a branch or something."

The current wasn't particularly swift; Augie was upstream from him, so hanging onto him easily kept Scott from slipping any further downstream. Regardless, he found he couldn't make any headway back to shore on his own. And to his embarrassment, he now had an audience. Three little girls on ponies were lined up where he and Jenna had first stopped to let Augie and Zappo drink. Grimacing, he gave them a casual two-fingered wave, then turning his back to them, got his jeans properly buttoned and zipped as inconspicuously as he could.

Jenna retied Zappo, far more carefully this time, went scavenging and quickly returned to the shore dragging a long limb behind her. Angling it out a little above him, she let the current carry it to within Scott's grasp.

"Something tells me we'll be stopping by the house before we go antiquing," she said, trying to suppress a giggle as she helped him the final few steps out of the water.

AFTER A PIT STOP for Scott to change, they got back to work making the most of their day, buying the ingredients for lunch and picnicking by a waterfall, then stopping into a musty, roadside antique shop.

They'd had so much fun, amusing each other with items that caught their eye, that Scott pulled off at the next antique shop, and the one after that. "This is more addictive than scag," Scott laughed as they pulled up in front of a barn that had been converted into a group shop, with aisle after aisle of stalls rented by small-time dealers.

"Okay, but this is it," Jenna said. "I want to be able to stop by the hospital on the way home tonight for one feeding.

"And you shall," Scott assured her. And she did.

A FEW MORNINGS LATER, the phone rang early and Scott reached over to answer it. When he realized it was the hospital calling, he whispered the fact to Jenna and sat up quickly. Alarmed, Jenna grabbed for a robe.

"Yes, Dr. Van Dusen. Good morning. Yes. Oh, my goodness – wow! Shit!" Scott exclaimed happily, forgetting who he was addressing. "Excuse me, I'm just so wicked excited, doc. We'll be there as soon as we can be. Oh, okay. Thank you. Thank you *so* much!"

Before he could hang up, Jenna was already out of bed. "Zach's coming home today!" Scott yelled at the top of his lungs, jumping out of bed himself. "They want us there at eleven." He and Jenna grabbed each other and half hugged, half jumped for joy.

"But – but – I haven't even settled on a nanny yet!" Jenna gasped. "This is more than a week early!"

"Start with nurses. Call the NICU back – they'll have recommendations," Scott suggested." I've gotta finish putting the changing table together."

The three hours before they presented themselves at the hospital, an empty carrier in hand, were a blur of deliriously happy, if chaotic, action.

Chapter 6

✺

JENNA FOUND HERSELF trembling as she held her baby in her arms. Everything up to now had been a dress rehearsal. This was for real. Zach was coming home. A nurse would be at the house waiting for them when they got back, but knowing that did little to settle Jenna's suddenly disconcerted nerves. Who was this fragile being she held? How was she going to cope with all it would take to keep him alive, much less help him thrive?

Jenna kissed the tiny bundle in her arms on the top of his little blue hat, then looked up at Scott. The tears in his eyes triggered her own. For a brief instant, they felt alone, just the three of them, momentarily oblivious to the sea of well-wishers around them. Nurses, doctors, specialists and orderlies had come to see their little patient and his celebrity parents off.

"I want to take advantage of this special moment to thank you all," Scott said as the throng quickly hushed to hang on his every word. "Every one of you has played your part in bringing our precious son to this day. I feel like we're standing on the summit of Mt. Everest, Jenna and I, we're so fit to bust, bringing our boy home with us. But we never would have made it to the summit without you guys – our guides and Sherpas, all you pros. Our gratitude knows no bounds. Thank you."

Silence, smiles, nods and tears quickly gave way to a round of applause more intimate and personal than any either Jenna or Scott had ever received.

Juggling Zach, Jenna raised a hand to interrupt the clapping. "I need to say something. I know you do this, day in and day out, but for us, suddenly finding ourselves in your world, the past four months has been the experiencing of a slowly unfolding miracle. If you hear us performing a song that sounds like it has something to do with this miraculous world of yours anytime soon, believe me, it's dedicated to you, every single one of you. You're doing God's work. Thank you so much." Again the gathering applauded.

"Jim – Dr. Van Dusen," Scott said, singling out the head of Zach's team, "we want to give you this to further your work with babies like ours." He fished a check out of his back pocket, gave it to the doctor and gave him a heartfelt hug.

Van Dusen's eyes popped as he glanced at the six-digit figure scrawled on the check. "Scott, Jenna – this is *so* generous of you. Trust me, it will be put it to the best possible use, every penny of it. You have *our* gratitude."

"We're blessed to be in a position to be able to help," Scott said humbly. "And we're blessed to be taking Zach home today. May every little one in there get to go home with his or her grateful parents too," he said gesturing to the door to the nursery.

"This will go a long way to help," Dr. Van Dusen said, waving the check in the air. "Now, go, and God speed."

SCOTT AND JENNA HAD, for once, completely forgotten the fact that news – any news – about celebrities travels, and it travels relentlessly and it travels fast. They'd walked into the hospital in relative anonymity – everyone on staff knew who they were and were long used to seeing them in the halls. Few visitors noticed them, much less recognized them.

Exiting the building was another matter. Someone had tipped off the press that Scott and Jenna Tenny were there to bring their miracle baby home that morning. By the time Scott, Jenna and Zach reached the front door, the sidewalk outside was a roiling sea of reporters, cameras and microphones.

"Shit," Scott said through clenched teeth. "Who's gonna do the talkin'?"

"You take it," Jenna said without hesitation. "I'll do the smiling. I don't want anyone poking mikes at Zach."

"Okay, here we go," Scott said as the doors automatically slid opened.

THEY MET THE SAME phenomenon at the foot of their gated driveway; the reporters and paparazzi were visible from far down the road. Again, it gave them time to strategize. Jenna, sitting in the back seat beside the infant carrier, was clear on one point: her window would, again, remain shut. The rear window glass of the SUV was tinted dark, allowing for a good degree of privacy.

NEWS TRAVELS FAST among friends, too. When they finally made it to the house, they found that almost the entire Blacklace family had already arrived to welcome the new family home. Close to a dozen vehicles lined the drive way, spoiling any idea of a surprise, but that didn't dampen the enthusiastic welcome they received as they clattered through the mudroom and stepped into the kitchen. Zack squirmed in surprise as a cacophony of welcomes greeted him.

Stepping from the happy pack of welcomers, a young woman in multi-colored teddy bear scrubs signaled for everyone to tone it down. "Hi," she said to Jenna as she smiled down at Zach. "I'm Elizabeth Hardy. I'm here till seven."

"I'm Jenna, and this is our boy. Zach, Elizabeth. Elizabeth, Zach." She took one of Zach's little hands, put it to his mouth and helped him blow Elizabeth a kiss.

"He's already a ladies' man," Scott interpreted for his son.

"Chip off the old blockhead," Jeremy kidded.

"I'll blockhead you," Scott shot back as Carrie pressed a mug of coffee into his hand. "Thanks, hon," he said. "Much needed."

"You guys are gonna run on the stuff for the next year," Jeff assured him.

"Years," chimed in Denise, an arm around their son Travis. "Right, kid?"

"I'll teach Zach the ropes," Travis volunteered. "Hey, Zach, say 'no.' Come on, you can do it. 'No.' Say, I want a raise in my allowance.' 'I.' 'Want.' 'A.' 'Raise.' 'In.' 'My.' 'Allowance.'"

Zach let out a perfectly timed little screech.

"Thatta boy! High-five!"

Scott stepped in to play puppeteer with Zach's right hand. When it interfaced with Travis's hand, he looked up at Travis and held Zach's hand in place. "Would you look at how much bigger your hand is than his," he marveled.

"Yeah. Like, wow," Travis said, surprised. "Dude, you got some serious growin' up to do!"

EVERYONE DRIFTED FROM the kitchen into the great room, where a big sign hung from the rafters: WELCOME HOME, ZACH!!! Carrie, who was holding the baby at the time, pointed up for him to appreciate her handiwork. "That's for you, little guy," she whispered.

"Man, he's tiny," Aiden said, who was hanging over her. Waggling a finger in front of Zach, he was delighted when the baby made a couple of futile swipes at it, then latched on and held it tight. "Hey, look at that!"

"He's gotcha now," Carrie laughed.

"Can I hold him?" Aiden asked. Carrie glanced over to see Jenna's reaction to the teenager's request. Jenna smiled a nod, then sipped on her coffee while she watched Carrie transfer the baby carefully into his arms, all under the ever-watchful eye of Elizabeth.

Aiden stood stock still, suddenly turned to stone by the awesome responsibility he had just assumed. "Zach," he whispered. "Hey, Zach. It's me, Uncle Aiden. Man, it's gonna be fun, watchin' you grow up. Hey, maybe *we'll* have a band some day. I play guitar. You can be the singerman, just like your pop. D'ya like to sing?"

Zach seemed to burble a string of nonsense syllables in response.

"Not bad!" Aiden said. "How about like this?" And he reproduced Zach's sounds perfectly, except with a suggestion of a tune to them.

"And so the collaboration begins," Jenna commented. "I wonder how long it'll be till they'll start fighting over it."

SCOTT APPEARED AT Jenna's elbow. "Your mom," he said, giving her a quick kiss and the phone.

"Mom! How are you?"

"Forget me. How's my grandson?" came Linda's take-charge voice.

"He made the trip home like a trooper – and he got his first taste of our friends, the press," Jenna said, disdainfully.

"Oh, honey, that's so unfair," her mother said sympathetically. "We never had to cope with the kind of attention you two are subjected to today. And now Zach. God, there ought to be a law."

"Just try enforcing it," Jenna harrumphed.

"So – it sounds like a party."

"It'd be an even better party if you and Joe were here. And the rest of the crew."

"Kristin's here. You want to speak to her?"

"Absolutely."

"Give our boy a kiss for me. And here's one for you," Linda said and made good on her promise, resoundingly. The next thing Jenna knew, Kristin was on the phone.

"Sis! How are you?"

"Fine. Scared!" Jenna admitted. She could smile as she said it, but there was nothing comforting in the fact.

"I bet you are. You're finally a stay-at-home mom."

"With a husband who's going off on tour in a matter of days. And, okay, with a nurse, twenty-four seven, for a while anyway."

"That's like so smart," Kristin said. "You're no slouch in the smarts department, big sis. You gotta send me a picture of Zach in his crib, okay?"

"You'll have it, hon," Jenna promised her. "Complete with the awesome mobile you sent him. It's the last word!"

"Nothing's too good for my – good grief, I can never get this right. What is he anyway?" Kristin mumbled, fishing for the right terminology. "My – half-nephew?"

"Enough of this 'half' shit," Jenna said. "And I mean it. You're my sister. He's your nephew and you're his Auntie Kris, which makes him one lucky guy."

"Just another reason why I love you," Kristin said with a grin that Jenna could hear on her end of the three-thousand mile connection.

"Speaking of love, baby sis," Jenna said, her voice changing to a light-hearted, questioning tease. "Um – there's this glum sorta guy? All by himself? In this middle of all these crazies? It's wreckin' the party. You wouldn't like to maybe talk to him, would you? He sure looks like he could use it."

"Ryan?" Kristin giggled.

"The same," Jenna laughed.

TWENTY MINUTES LATER the phone rang again. Scott pulled out his cell and headed down the hall to find a quieter spot to talk.

"Hey, big Daddy!" came a duet of voices, unmistakably those of Missy and Laurel, each on their own extension. Then the two launched into a pair of tangled monologues from which only a few phrases made it out intact.

"Yeah, we're at Laurel's," Missy said.

"Luka says, 'Be cool, Uncle Zach.' I'd put him on the phone but he'd like totally hog it," Laurel said. "It's his new favorite toy."

"How're you hanging in there, Dad?" Missy asked.

"Hey, we just got home. Ask me Friday," Scott chuckled.

"You're laughing now," Laurel said. "I *will* check in with you on Friday."

Scott was just assuring them both, "Everything's under control," when Aiden, Travis, Tim and Jeremy came noisily shambling down the hall, bouncing off the walls, playing keep-away with a basketball. "Well, *almost* everything's under control," Scott laughed when he could be heard again.

A FEW HOURS LATER, Scott and Jenna, with Zach asleep in her arms, finally closed the door on the last of their well-wishers, Scott with a grin that hadn't left his face the entire time. Turning to plant a kiss on her, he found Jenna stifling a yawn. "Hey, babe, you're bushed. You need a nap. Hand him over," he said, reaching for Zach. "I'll have Elizabeth put him down."

"Okay," Jenna said reluctantly, her fatigue trumping the automatic protest of her mother hormones. She put the slumbering infant gently in his arms and pressed her lips to his forehead, then gave out a long sigh of exhaustion. "What a day," she whispered. "And what a long time coming. It feels like a year since he was born."

"It *has* been," Scott whispered back. "More than a year. A lifetime."

"Will it ever feel normal?" Jenna wondered aloud. "Will we ever take him for granted? Get mad at him? Wonder why on earth we ever had a kid?"

"Think Aiden. Think Travis. If you really want a reality check, think *me*," Scott said soberly, shaking his head as he looked down into the face of innocence.

JENNA, STILL HALF asleep, wandered back into the living room an hour later to find Scott with Zach burbling in his lap, bright-eyed and very much awake.

"This little guy's waiting for his double soy cappuccino grande with breastmilk, hold the soy, hold the java," Scott riffed, getting up from his chair. "How about I make you the cappuccino and you take it from here."

"How long's he been awake?" Jenna yawned, taking Zach and hugging him.

"Ten minutes or so," Scott said. "I just wanted to spend a little guy time with my son, and let you sleep a little longer," he smiled. "But when he tries to figure out how to get milk outta this washboard chest, it's definitely your show."

Jenna unbuttoned her blouse and put Zach to her breast, which he took greedily, then settled into the corner of the couch with him.

"Anything with that cappuccino?" Scott asked, lingering, mesmerized by the sight of her nursing. "Can I tempt you with a white chocolate ginger biscotti?"

"Ummm…that sounds fantastic."

Scott continued to stand staring back at her. "Not half as fantastic as you look right now," he finally said, shaking his head. "You're one damned beautiful woman, but you are *so* beautiful like that. Oh, God, how can I leave this? And for what – to go out on the fuckin' road yet again. If I thought I used to get lonely on the road, shit, that'll be nothing compared to what this is going to feel like."

"Language!" Jenna laughed, covering the tiny ear Zach had turned to the world. "It won't be for long, hon. We'll be underfoot before you know it," she went on dreamily. "Maybe even as soon as he's had his two-week exam."

"Get him a tutor. It can't be soon enough."

THE FOLLOWING SEVERAL DAYS were a blur of rehearsals, interviews with the final four contenders for the job of Zach's nanny, moments of quiet and hours of barely contained pandemonium. One thing Jenna couldn't help but notice: Scott didn't thrown one of his way too typical pre-tour tantrums all week. Zach seemed to serve as a governor on his temper.

"Okay, it's decision time," Jenna said decisively, after they'd said good-bye to the fourth of the potential nannies. "Who do you think?"

Sitting back on a kitchen stool, Scott crossed his arms, splayed a hand across his lower jaw in contemplation and started tapping his forefinger unconsciously on his cheek. Jenna pulled a legal pad towards her. It was covered with notes.

"Okay. I'm going to say that Evelyn seemed too awed," Jenna said tentatively. "Did you get that?"

"I wasn't sure what I was getting, but I think you've put your finger on it," Scott said, nodding. "Too many questions about us, not enough focus on Zach?"

Jenna nodded. "And the least experience with preemies. I was much more impressed with her the first time around, but she was the first I met with. My standards have gone up. I'd say she's definitely third runner-up."

"Second runner-up, in my book, would have to be Martine," Scott chuckled. "I give you credit for putting her in your top four. I should think you would have disqualified her just on the basis of the French accent and the miniskirt."

"She wore a pantsuit last time," Jenna said dryly. "I saw the French as a plus. I have to say, I started having second thoughts when she came through the door. You have enough temptation in your life," she grinned. "You'd have to move your rehearsal space to Boston, to keep everyone at work and out of the nursery."

"She could be distracting," Scott had to admit. "And, God, think of the social implications. Every kid with a single dad would want to come over and play. We'd have to hire a social secretary for *her*."

"Her credentials are impeccable," Jenna said, glancing at her notes again. "She's only worked with two families – a total of five children – in her eleven years as a nanny. She's loyal. You wouldn't believe how some of them bounce around. I think they see being a nanny as a way to see the U.S.A."

"Which is a plus for Nicole," Scott said. "She's seen the world. She the most settled of the bunch. She's older. She has kids in college."

"I don't know," Jenna said, then sat biting her lip and staring at the table, deep in thought. Finally she looked up. "This may sound frivolous, but I wish she smiled more. She's so – serious. It's not like I'm looking for Mary Poppins. I know caring for children is serious business – but there's something almost grim about her. She's all business. I don't see much fun in there. It feels right for now, for the first year maybe, but I have trouble picturing her down the road."

Scott was nodding. "Maybe *she's* third runner-up."

"Maybe."

"Which leaves Ellen."

"And she's no slouch," Jenna said and started ticking off her qualifications. "Forty, four families – three really. Not going with the people who were transferred to New Zealand is understandable. Midwestern, solid citizen, but with a really delightful quality to her, don't you think?"

"She'd fit in here," Scott said, fishing for words. "I can see her here with no trouble. I think you and she'd work well together – I was seeing a real give-and-take when you got into the thing about travel."

"I see flexible. I see adaptable. I see smart," Jenna nodded. "I see easy."

ELLEN STARTED THE DAY Scott left. The night before was a frenzied combination of Scott's packing – a chore he always put off till the last minute – and Jenna's putting finishing touches on the rooms that she'd rearranged for Ellen. The house had three guest rooms, two of which shared a bath. They'd decided to turn those two into a bedroom/sitting room suite, wanting Zach's nanny to feel every bit as comfortable and at home as possible.

When all was done and they'd kissed Zach goodnight, left in watchful care of his night nurse, they retired to their bedroom and closed the door behind them with a pair of matching sighs that made both of them laugh. "Come here, beautiful," Scott said. He opened his arms and she slipped into them and threw her arms around his neck. They kissed tenderly and long.

SCOTT GOT UP EARLY, to make love to Jenna one more time, to down a cup of coffee, and to spend some "serious skin time with his son," as he liked to refer to it. Ellen had already arrived and was in consultation with the day nurse who'd come in at six when Scott came wandering into the nursery. "Looking for my boy," he said. Zach was lying on his back staring up at the colorful mobile above his head which was turning to the tune of "Doe, a Deer."

Scott reached in and brought Zach out in one smooth, practiced motion. "Gotta come up with a line of mobiles that play rock songs," he whispered in Zach's ear, then hummed a few bars of "Drivin' It Home." Zach's eyes locked on his.

"Back in a bit," he told Ellen and the nurse. "We're going for a walk before I have to leave."

Clad only in jeans, Scott held Zach, clad only in a diaper, and headed out for a stroll, out around the old barn that had been converted into a studio, across the lawn to the tall trees and hedges that provided shade and privacy for the sprawling property.

Coming upon an old apple tree that was just beginning to form fruit, Scott took Zach's little hand in his and had him heft the tiny round green orb. "That, Zach, is going to grow into a bigger green apple and then, one day, it's going to be a big *red* apple," he told his son. "Just like you're going to grow into a little boy, and then into a bigger boy, and then one day into a man."

He found it wrenching, returning Zach to Ellen's waiting arms.

"OKAY, BABE, BACK in two weeks," Scott yelled over his shoulder, his parting words before he jumped into Jeremy's taxi-cab yellow Explorer. "I love you. I love you both." Jenna, standing in the doorway with Zach wriggling in her arms, burst into tears. She was going to miss Scott terribly.

Chapter 7

※

TWENTY MINUTES BEFORE it was time to head out for Zach's first check-up since leaving the womb of the NICU, Scott strode in the door. He'd chartered a flight out of Love Field in Dallas, but even charters had been grounded as a cold front ushered a phalanx of thunderheads through the region; a half dozen tornadoes had touched down in southern Oklahoma and north Texas, one less than two miles from the runway he'd be departing on. They'd made the appointment in the afternoon, in anticipation of just such problems.

DR. MELBA TUCHMAN, as a consulting pediatrician, already knew Zach well; she'd seen him weekly while he was in the NICU and was part of the decision-making concerning his episode of intraventricular hemorrhaging; pediatric neurology was her specialty. Her style was comforting, both for babies and their anxious parents.

"Okay, open up wide for Dr. Mel," she cooed to Zach, slipping her pinky finger in the corner of his mouth to trigger a reflexive reaction. His tiny mouth opened on cue. Eyes glued on hers, he let her poke and probe without fuss. He was equally complacent about her listening to his heart and lungs, but drew a line at her eavesdropping on his ticklish belly. His flailing arms quickly tangled in her stethoscope; a little fist closed around tubing and yanked one earpiece right out of her ear.

"How am I supposed to tell your mommy and daddy that you're fit to travel if you keep confiscating my equipment, little guy?" she joked with him, gently prying his grip loose, setting things right and continuing with her exam. As she tapped, patted and prodded, she kept a running commentary going with Jenna and Scott.

"How's he sleeping," she asked as she turned Zach on his tummy.

"Fine between feedings," Jenna answered.

"Duration?"

"Oh, twenty, maybe twenty-five minutes at night. And he usually falls asleep before he lets go. Most of the time I can put him back to bed without waking him."

"And frequency?"

"He's pretty consistent," Jenna said. "Between two and a half hours and three. He's got me trained – I wake up at about two and a half and go in to see where he's at. He's usually awake and thinking about it."

"Me, too," Scott piped in. Jenna grimaced.

SITTING IN THE PEDIATRICIAN'S office, Zach in his father's lap studiously scrutinizing Dr. Mel's credentials on the wall in front of him, Jenna and Scott got the news they wanted to hear. "He's really doing well," the doctor summarized her findings. "Excellent weight gain. His blood work is where I want to see it. Lung and heart function are amazingly good. What a trooper you've got there," she said, enjoying being able to have good things to report. "I wish all my preemies could do so well. This child is blessed."

Scott and Jenna smiled at each other; Scott winked. "And travel…?" Jenna asked, holding her breath for the answer.

"I see no reason why he can't, but I wouldn't make it a habit, if you can avoid it. Kids need stability in their lives, even at this young age. Just because *we* can't remember being infants doesn't mean nothing's going on in there," she said, pointing to Zach's cranium. Scott tousled the fine dark hair that covered it. "And the less air travel the better."

"No problem," Scott assured her. "I'm actually thinking about investing in a motorhome for us."

What a great idea," Jenna said, surprised. "When did you come up with this?"

"Ideas don't come much fresher – it just hit me this morning as I passed an RV lot on the way to the airport. Home away from home," Scott said, and Dr. Mel nodded.

"And Georgie can drive it," he said in an aside to Jenna. "He's driven limos longer than these things. He'll love it." Georgie Del Guercio had been Blacklace's chauffeur since 1991.

JENNA AND SCOTT dropped Zach at home, leaving him in Ellen's care, then jumped back in the car and headed for an RV dealership Scott knew a few towns over. "And if they don't have anything we like, I know another place over near Randolph," he'd told Jenna as they drove. The next fifteen minutes were spent creating a list of criteria for the vehicle.

They pulled up the driveway four hours later with a forty-foot 1999 Country Coach in pristine condition, with three slideouts and less than twenty thousand miles on the engine, and honked the horn. Ellen appeared at the door, Zach in her arms, and stood there shaking her head in amazement.

"Wow and wow again," she said as she stepped aboard and took in the gleaming surfaces and plush upholstery. "I've been on some pretty fancy yachts that couldn't hold a candle to this!"

Scott activated the living room slideout. Ellen stood beside him, mesmerized, as its hydraulics allowed the space to expand quickly and silently before her eyes. "That's your bedroom, actually," he explained, pushing another button to demonstrate a pair of ceiling-mounted curtains, rich velour up to the five-foot level, then scrim above for ventilation, that drew shut automatically to provide more than enough space and privacy. Ellen was delighted with the arrangement.

"For now, Zach can travel in his playpen/bassinet. I'm going to rig up something to immobilize it, both in the living room –"

"The lounge," Jenna corrected him, drawing the word out grandly while gesturing around the space in imitation of the star-struck salesman who'd sold it to them.

"The *lounge*," Scott imitated her perfectly, gesture and all, "and back in our bedroom. Can you be ready to leave tomorrow?"

"You bet," Ellen said enthusiastically.

"SORRY ABOUT HAVING TO make it a working dinner," Scott apologized as he and Jenna slid into a back booth at Blue Skies for a quiet meal together before going back to the pressures of the road. Ann had met them at the door with a file folder of checks needing either his or Jeremy's signature. "And there's a carton of fan mail in the office," Ann had added with a grin. Scott had smiled self-effacingly.

"The downside of being part owners," he mumbled as he started looking through the paperwork. "This won't take long."

"Don't worry about me," Jenna smiled. "Actually, you do that and I'm going to go say hi to Bob and Sandy." Bob Underwood and Sandy Blackstone manned the bar. "I want to see what you did with the photos of me, if you must know."

"Such vanity," he said, smiling at her appreciatively.

The bar was a showcase of Blacklace memorabilia. Jeremy had finally brought up the fact that even though she'd been singing with them off and on for the past two years, there was no sign of Jenna amidst the myriad photos of the guys. Jenna's only request had been that they not end up in the men's room. She took their word for it that none did.

THEY WERE HALFWAY through dinner – linguini with clam sauce for him, a lighter veal picante for her – when Jenna suddenly started feeling nauseous. Without explanation, she quickly excused herself and hurried to the ladies' room. Fortunately, it was just a few steps down the hall from where they were sitting.

After throwing up all of the meal she'd enjoyed so far, she emerged shakily from the stall and sat down quickly to give the dizziness that had accompanied the nausea time to recede. She sat there, rocking herself gently, feeling perfectly miserable. That's all I need, she thought to herself. A case of the flu and a six-hundred-fifty mile drive to Cleveland tomorrow. All the luxury in the world ain't gonna make that fun.

A knock on the door was quickly followed by Ann's head peering around the door as she opened it. "Are you okay, honey?" she asked Jenna. "Scott was worried about you. He asked me to come see."

"I'm okay. I just lost my dinner, unfortunately. Don't tell anyone in the kitchen," she hastened to add. "It wasn't the food. It was great. I think it's the flu. I've got a killer headache."

"Let me get you something for the headache, at least," Ann offered. Jenna smiled gratefully.

"ARE YOU OKAY?" Scott asked her anxiously when she finally returned to the table, looking far paler than she had ten minutes earlier.

"I'm okay now. I was thinking flu, but then I decided it may just be that I'm nervous about traveling with the baby. Don't worry about me. I'll be fine."

Jenna sipped a cup of tea as Scott finished his meal. When she got home, she drew herself a warm bath, stepped into the Jacuzzi tub, turned on the jets and slid down till her chin was at water level. She closed her eyes with a sigh.

JENNA WOKE UP the next morning feeling better. At ten o'clock the, the "ZT Express" was ready to pull out. Zach, for whom it had been named, lay on his back, eyes wide, taking in as much as he could see from the confines of his bassinet. When Georgie revved the giant Caterpillar engine, sending shuddering vibrations through the chassis of the motorhome, Zach blinked several times in quick succession, then grinned happily and opened his eyes wider still.

"That's my boy," Scott said with a crooked grin. "You've definitely inherited the big motor gene." Then he went to join Georgie in the passenger's seat.

After Georgie had eased the big RV onto the interstate, Jenna brought Ellen a mug of tea and sets hers on a side table with a selection of current magazines to keep them occupied. Then she took Zach from the bassinet, settled into a leather recliner, brought up the footrest, opened her blouse and put Zach to her breast to nurse.

"Welcome to motherhood in the twenty-first century," she chuckled to Ellen.

"I'll take this any day over hotels," Ellen said, stretching out on the couch comfortably. "Being cooped up with a baby on a rainy day in any hotel room in the world is my idea of eternity. And I've been there. The folks I worked for from Detroit traveled endlessly. Hotel rooms, restaurants, airplanes, baggage claim, customs, security checks – it was a nightmare with three kids – one square in the middle of his terrible twos." She rolled her eyes at the memory. "I was thrilled when they broke the news to me that he'd been transferred overseas. Paris I might have gone for, but Auckland, New Zealand, was out of the question, and they knew it. They were so apologetic. It was easily the happiest day of my life."

"Not the day *we* hired you?" Jenna teased her.

"Okay, the second happiest day," Ellen laughed. "I won't kid you – I was thrilled to get this job. And I haven't had the first reason to regret it, either."

"You will," Jenna assured her. She had explained Scott's volatile temper clearly to all the applicants during the interview process. "Things are mellow enough right now. I seriously doubt there's any reason to believe they'll stay that way."

JENNA FOUND EXCUSES to neither rehearse or perform with Blacklace for the entire first week of their time on the road together. Her primary focus, she told Scott and had him relay to the rest of the band, was in being sure that Zach and Ellen were adjusting well to their new routines. "It's also to be there for you at the end of a hot night of struttin' your stuff out there," she'd teased him provocatively.

So far she'd been able to keep her problems from Scott. Touring was stressful enough – he certainly didn't need the extra worry, she decided. Late in the first week, she'd confided in Carrie, who had been able to come along with Jeremy for the current leg of the tour while Aiden was in Colorado visiting his grandparents.

"I just wished I felt better," Jenna sighed. "This could be so much more fun if I only felt normal."

"Fun, schmun," Carrie said. "I'm concerned about you. You don't *look* well."

"It'll pass," Jenna had said, without much conviction. It sure didn't feel like it was passing.

"Chicken soup," Carrie prescribed.

BY WEEK TWO, it was clear to Carrie, at least, that all the chamomile tea and chicken soup in the world wasn't going to cure her best friend's ills.

Jenna had made it through her rehearsals with the group and had committed to performing that evening. Carrie had managed to corner her in her dressing room half an hour before they were scheduled to take the stage at the big outdoor amphitheatre of the Verizon Music Center, just outside of Indianapolis.

"Honey, you look worse than I've seen you all week – and that was pretty bad," she said. "Are you sure you should be singing tonight?"

"What a friend," Jenna griped at Carrie's reflection in the mirror. Then her focus returned to the job in hand: attempting to hide the bags under her eyes with the application of a creamy, yellowy-beige concealer. The circles seemed to be growing one shade darker every day.

"Friends tell friends when they look terrible," Carrie disagreed, "and you, my dear, look terrible. If you feel half as bad as you look, it's amazing you're even sitting here. The guys may not notice it but I sure do. You've gotta level with me."

Jenna looked up at Carrie's reflection, put down the brush she was using to apply the concealer, and suddenly sagged. "Okay, no, I don't feel great," she admitted. "But it's not going to stop me from singing. It's been almost six months since the last time I sang with the guys. I'm excited about starting again. Don't worry – I'll be fine. I'm just a little nervous. Really."

Carrie shook her head and shot Jenna a look that said, "Sorry, sister. I don't believe a word you just said."

THE SHOW THAT NIGHT came off well; no one in the audience would have believed that Jenna hadn't been on a stage for the past half year, if they hadn't read it in the gossip rags and fanzines. But the second of their two-night stand in Indianapolis was another matter altogether.

Jenna had felt lethargic, border-line nauseous and light-headed all day. Two naps, one short and unsatisfactory, the other profoundly deep, had made little difference. It took all the energy she could muster to simply pass herself off to Scott as okay.

As it turned out, she'd barely seen him other than for a quick, twenty-minute lunch. He'd been preoccupied with the band for the greater part of the day, working up an entirely new version of "Outta My Way." The only elements they'd left alone were its searing lyrics and unrelenting rhythm. The music was entirely new.

Tim, in his unofficial role as band bookie, had gotten a pool going on how long it would take, in five-bar increments, for the Indianapolis audience to catch on. The bidding had taken less than fifteen seconds. Scott bought in at ten bars. The song had gone platinum in 1996; any Blacklace fan knew these lyrics cold. Tim was even more optimistic, buying in at five. Jeff quickly took fifteen; Dan, shaking his head, went for twenty; Jeremy grudgingly took twenty-five. He knew there was no way he was going to win. Ryan, the reticent newcomer, found himself stuck with thirty.

AFTER HER SECOND NAP, Jenna sat sipping on a cup of tea and staring out the window at the gently rolling landscape, a patchwork quilt of fields and parking lots as far as the eye could see. "You feeling any better," Ellen asked with concern, returning from putting Zach down for a nap in the darkened back bedroom.

"Not really," Jenna admitted. "But it doesn't matter. I'll be okay tonight. I've felt worse and turned in rave-review performances." She smiled, then returned to staring out the window. "I swear it's the spotlights," she mused. "They're wonder drugs. You stand there in the dark feeling like an under-dressed, over-madeup piece of shit. The spotlight comes on and the adrenalin kicks in. Adrenalin can get you through damn near anything."

THE SPOTLIGHTS AND ADRENALIN cocktail she was relying on, it turned out, never got a chance to prove her right or wrong that night. In the backstage dressing room, making final adjustments to the skimpy gold lamé slip of a dress she was wearing, Jenna was suddenly hit with a rolling shockwave of nausea that made her break out in a sweat and sent her running for the sink.

Clinging to the cool porcelain afterwards, waiting for the room to stop spinning, she looked up and caught a glimpse of herself in a mirror that wasn't rung with makeup lights. By God, Carrie was right, she thought to herself with a groan. She did look terrible. What was wrong with her? Her skin had clearly gone white under her makeup; the net effect, under this unflattering light, was a sickly shade reminiscent of mushrooms. When she could, she headed for a sofa in the corner and draped herself across it like it was a Victorian fainting couch. The effort made her feel like she'd just run a marathon. A moment later, before she'd been able to catch her breath, Scott walked in without knocking, as he always did.

"What in the hell!" he exclaimed. "Jenna, you look horrible. What's wrong with you, honey?"

All of a sudden it hit her. She looked up at him. "Oh, my God, Scott," she gasped. "I – I think I'm pregnant. That's gotta be it. That's why I've been sick these past few weeks. It hadn't crossed my mind till just this minute. But – I can't be... Julia said –"

"Julia said," Scott took over Jenna's faltering thought, "that nursing would provide natural birth control for – what? Six months, I think it was."

"That's what I remember," Jenna agreed. "But I think she also said something about it being some percent for sure. I don't remember the percent."

"Me, either," Scott admitted. "Of course, if you are, it really doesn't matter what it was."

"Yeah," Jenna said, contemplating that reality. "Man, she's not going to be happy, if it's the case. I'm not supposed to be getting pregnant."

"If you are, we'll deal with it," Scott said decisively.

Jenna sat up slowly, tentatively, feeling her way.

"Why don't you just stay here and rest," Scott said. "I'll tell everyone you're sick and can't perform."

Jenna disagreed. Standing, she took a deep breath and squared her shoulders. "No, I'll be all right. The worst is over. It's only a few songs."

"You're sure?" Scott said dubiously.

"I'd tell you if I weren't."

"You sure about that?" he asked her point blank. "Well, you damn sure haven't told me you've been feeling sick for weeks."

"I didn't want to worry you, hon."

"Oh, so now I have to be protected from worry," Scott said slowly, anger beginning to simmer behind his eyes.

Jenna took another deep breath and held her hands, folded prayer-like, to her mouth. "Not now, Scott, okay?" she said, shaking her head. "This isn't the time." The two locked eyes, and Scott quickly understood that this was a fight he'd lose.

"Okay, okay. But don't do anything –" He started to say 'stupid,' but caught himself before he stepped on *that* landmine. "Foolish," he substituted. That seemed to sit okay.

Scott and the band would open with three songs before Jenna was scheduled to join them. She used the time to regroup, adjust her makeup, then slip into a lotus position in an effort to put everything out of her mind and find her focus.

Rising as she heard the band nearing the end of the third number, she experienced another slight wave of dizziness and grimaced, but her frown instantly changed to a smile at the thought of the possible – probable – cause of her discomfort. Another baby! she thought happily. Too bad what Julia might think.

SHE WAS ON HER WAY to make her entrance when the entire backstage started spinning and Jenna's world went black. A crew member standing a few strides away from her ran to where she lay, quickly assessed the situation and called out for help, just as Scott was coming around the corner to escort her on stage.

"Oh Christ," he exploded. "I knew this was gonna happen. Help me get her into the dressing room."

By the time they'd gotten her back to the sofa, Jenna had come to.

"What – what happened?" she asked, dazed.

"You passed out. That's what happened," Scott informed her. "I told you it wasn't a good idea for you to be singing tonight."

"I'm sorry – but I feel better now," Jenna said, then couldn't help adding, "Mister I-Told-You-So."

"I don't care how great you feel, you're not going on," Scott decided. "We can't have you passing out on the stage. You're not on the marquee – they don't know you were gonna sing. You just lay right here until we're done." Jenna started to protest. "No arguments this time," he stopped her, shaking his head.

"Okay, okay. You're right," she finally said with reluctance. "I'll stay here." At a stern, questioning look from Scott, she added, "Promise."

"We've got three days before the next show," he said, going into planning mode. "First thing in the morning we're chartering a plane and going back home, and getting you in to see Dr. Williams." Kissing her on the forehead, he turned and left her and headed back to the stage.

Jenna lay back with a moan. She had to admit she felt terrible, terrible enough that arguing simply wasn't an option.

"BY THE LOOK OF THINGS, you're about six weeks," Julia Williams confirmed Jenna's intuition. "The three of us need to talk after you get dressed."

Jenna joined Scott in Julia's office. "It was that weekend in New Hampshire," she said ruefully. "I shoulda known. It always happens when we go there." Scott took her hand just as Julia entered her office, sat down behind her desk and sat, hands folded, shaking her head at the two of them.

"Okay," she said, addressing Jenna first, "I'm still concerned about your being able to carry a child to term – more so after my exam just now. We won't talk about the year I'd suggested. We'll just deal with the situation in hand.

You will need to be monitored closely. It may even require that you be put on strict bed rest." She looked to Scott.

"Do you have any idea how far Jenna can carry the pregnancy?" he asked.

"If everything goes well, maybe six, maybe seven months."

"And for now?" Jenna asked. "I mean, what can or can't I do?"

"It's mostly can'ts, I'm afraid," Julia said sympathetically. "Nothing strenuous. No touring. You'll need to limit your stress level as much as possible. I'll need to see you more frequently, and absolutely regularly, of course. The next six weeks are critical to the overall outcome."

"I'LL JUST FLY HOME, as often as possible, in between shows," Scott said as they slipped into the traffic streaming along the Storrow Drive on their way home. Neither would have admitted it, but they were both still reeling from the reality of Jenna's condition.

"I don't want you making extra trips," Jenna objected. "You'll be exhausted. I don't want to be the cause of that. Maybe I can come out and join you every once in a while, even if it's only to sit in the hotel room. I refuse to let things between us get out of control like I did after Zach was born."

Scott turned his fears and frustration on himself. "If I didn't want to fuck you so damn much, none of this would have happened, dammit."

"You certainly don't need to blame yourself," Jenna interrupted, chuckling grimly. "I was an entirely willing participant, as I recall. You get back to the tour and we'll see each other over Labor Day, and hopefully sooner. And maybe I'll be able to go back with you afterwards. One thing though: please, *please*, I don't want you telling anyone yet. Especially Mom and your dad. I'll decide when we do that. Promise?"

He promised.

Chapter 8

GEORGIE DROVE THE ZT Express back to Massachusetts and pulled it in next to the four-car garage that housed Scott's treasured collection of two- and four-wheeled vehicles. Jenna came out to greet him feeling utterly defeated. It showed.

"Hey, cheer up, Mrs. Tenny," he told her. Jenna had originally insisted he address her by first name, like he did all the guys, but since she and Scott had married, he'd taken the more formal approach, and in spite of Jenna's best efforts, it had stuck. "You're pregnant again!" he said heartily. "It's time for celebration, not moping around. This rollin' playpen's going to see plenty of time on the road, don't you worry for a moment that it won't." Jenna smiled in spite of herself.

SCOTT MADE IT HOME for Labor Day weekend break, though most of the band stayed put in Vancouver where they'd played three shows, flying their families and significant others out to join them there for the next several days.

Back east, Scott, Jenna, Zach and Ellen headed up to the lake for a rare quiet family holiday. Scott spent hours in the woods with Zach, introducing him to the natural world he'd grown up with. "The only difference," he whispered in his son's ear, "is that I just wandered in anybody's woods. One day, these paths, that boulder, those trees, this beach will all be yours." Zach looked up at him in what Scott took for amazement. "Hey, I'm not shittin' ya, kid – really," he'd laughed.

A sunrise paddle in the canoe provided the peak moment of this brief Sunapee getaway. Scott stepped into the boat just as the first beams of sunlight broke over the horizon; Jenna and Zach were already reclining in pillowed comfort in the bow of the boat. As they paddled quietly, Jenna lay Zach across her lap, trailed his hand in the water and helped him toss sparkling droplets into the air. Every handful was followed by a fit of mother-and-son giggling.

After enough of that game, Zach grew restless and suddenly broke out in painfully heart-wrenching sobs. "Snack time," Jenna smiled as she turned him over, opened and pulled aside her orange canvas life jacket and drew him to her breast. As was his custom, Zach wriggled and squirmed until he'd latched on and was feeling secure and cozy. When he'd settled down, Jenna drew the life jacket around him, lay back and closed her eyes. It was all Scott could do keep from bursting into tears, the sight was so beautiful.

WHEN THEY GOT back home, Jenna had a check-up with Julia. Every thing looked good, considering, and Julia gave her permission to accompany Scott out to rejoin the band in Los Angeles. Jenna was thrilled. "But you know the rules," Julia admonished her.

"Nothing strenuous. Nothing stressful."

"Right."

Jenna thought for a moment. "Can I perform, like a little?" she wheedled. "If I just stand there and don't move? Just sing? I never get to sing for my family, and they're all going to be there for a change."

"Well – I don't know. Would you characterize singing as stressful for you? It certainly would be for me," Julia said, smiling ruefully.

"No more stressful for me than doing a Pap smear is for you, I'd imagine," Jenna countered.

"Well, if you put it that way. Okay. You can sing – you be the judge of if you're overdoing it. But you stay out there for a week, at the very least, before you and the baby get on a plane again." That part would be a pleasure. Jenna and Zach would be staying on at Linda and Joe's after Blacklace departed for Denver.

"WELL, WOULD YOU look at this little man," Joe cried, taking Zach out of Jenna's arms after giving her a welcoming hug. "Come give your grampaw a hug, boy. All I gotta say is," you look a lot more like a human baby than you did when we first met you."

"Joe!" Linda scolded him. "What a way to talk about my daughter's son!"

"He may be your daughter's son," Joe conceded, "but he's every bit my son's son, too, ya know. Which gives me the right to comment on anything I darned well please. Take these ears, for instance," he said, his finger tracing the little pink shell of one ear. "Tenny ears. No question. Not that you ever get to see Scott's, under all that hair. But ya gotta admit…" he said, holding Zach ear-to-ear with himself. He was right. They were perfect matches in all respect except size. "Laurel's got 'em, Missy's got 'em. Even little Luka's got 'em," he said proudly.

Linda took her grandson from her husband's arms. "Come here, you poor little thing," she whispered. "Let me tell you how beautiful you really are."

"He's not beautiful," Kristin protested as she gave Scott a hug of welcome. "My nephew's *handsome*," she insisted. "Hand him over," she told Linda. "It's about time we finally met." Linda gave up Zach to her reluctantly.

Within a few minutes, Jim and Sue had pulled up the driveway and Chris wasn't far behind. "You look fabulous, sis," Chris said, holding Jenna at arm's length and nodding at what he saw. "Motherhood becomes you."

"I look like hell, but I'm getting used to this mother gig," she acknowledged, feeling a bit guilty. She'd sworn Scott, as well as the entire Blacklace family, to absolute silence about her pregnancy. She didn't want her mother breathing down her neck every minute of their visit. The new baby would remain as much their private business as possible, until she'd made it to five months, she'd decided.

"You didn't tell us this was going to be a Bradford family reunion," Scott said as they finally all made their way inside. "This is great," he said turning back to his father just in time to catch Joe shooting Linda a wink. "What? What's going on?" Scott asked Joe, who instantly became the picture of innocence, leaving Scott nowhere to turn but to his mother-in-law for enlightenment.

"Oh, it's nothing," she dismissed him. He looked dubious. "No, really," she insisted, which made Jenna was curious. How well she knew that I've-got-a-secret look on her mother's face. But neither Linda nor Joe could be talked into admitting to anything.

Everything became clear half an hour later, when Laurel, Missy and Luka came bursting out onto the patio where the rest were relaxing and catching up. "Su-pwise!" Luka yelled on cue.

Zach squirmed in Linda's arms to find the source of another child's voice. "Oh, you know that's a baby too, don't you, you clever boy," she said. "Luka, come over here, dear. Come and say hi to your Uncle Zach."

"Hi, Uncle Zach," Luka said dutifully, then pulled a squirt gun out of his pocket and 'shot' his Uncle Zach square in the middle of his round little belly. Zach loved it.

THE FOLLOWING NIGHT Blacklace was headlining at the Hollywood Bowl. Pure electricity was crackling through the heat of the August night air by the time the warm-up act, the tightly choreographed East L.A. rappers Jamma G, had existed the stage. Every seat in the place contained a fan eager to be entertained. In spite of some steep ticket prices, the famous eighty-year-old outdoor amphitheatre was bursting at its invisible seams.

As usual when Jenna put in an unannounced appearance, the band opened with a few songs on their own, then found a way to spirit her on stage without the audience being aware of it. Tonight, the stage went totally dark and the crowd drew in its breath, creating sufficient silence to allow the distant drone of a helicopter to enter their collective consciousness. Several moments later, a light came up behind the unmistakable silhouette of a woman, a tall, thin, spectacularly well endowed woman with a mane of dark hair. No one wondered who it was. Jenna gave a characteristic toss of her hair, brought a mike to her lips and the din of the screaming spectators instantly drowned out any thought of low-flying helicopters.

Launching into "Panic Button," a huge Jenna B hit from 1999, the song took on an entirely new sound with the addition of the six distinctive voices that made up Blacklace. Ryan brought his signature falsetto into play, providing a top line that slid in just beneath Jenna's gritty contralto; Dan underscored it all with his growling low baritone. From the constant outbursts of applause, it was clear that the synthesis was a crowd-pleaser.

Scott stayed out of sight through the first verse, then wandered into view from back behind the drums, causing yet another wave of screaming to rise to meet the star-studded night sky. Coming up behind Jenna, his arms snaked around her bare midriff as he pulled her tight up against him and kissed her on the side of her neck. It was all she could do to keep singing. He spent the next verse driving her mad, finally joining her on the bridge. From that point on, they sang the rest of the song to each other, oblivious to both the band hard at work behind them and the seventeen thousand fans – family included – arrayed before them. Jenna sang another song, almost exclusively solo, then reluctantly left the stage to Blacklace for the duration of their first set. She knew she had to pace herself.

BY THE TIME SHE rejoined them during the second set, the audience had shouted itself hoarse, begging for her to return. As determined screams of "Jenna, Jenna, Jenna" rent the air, Scott finally threw his hands up in mock surrender, went off stage and brought her back with him. "Okay?" he growled into his mike. "Are you happy now?" There was no question just how happy Jenna made this crowd.

Jenna put an arm around Scott, commandeered the mike from him and waited for the noise to quiet down. "Hello, L.A.," she grinned with a wave and set the thundering applause off all over again. "I gotta tell you, it's so great to be home." Again, she waited out the clamor her words produced. "I just wanted to thank you for giving Blacklace such a warm welcome. They're pretty near and dear to me," she said, then counted off a one-two-three-four. Tim picked up the tempo on the drums, Ryan came in on the keyboards with a noncommittal set of chords, then Jeff, Dan and Jeremy came in on guitars one by one. And still no one in the audience had a clue what song was coming. And then they launched into the combined form of "To Be Loved by You," a song Scott had written for Jenna, and "I'm Ready to Go," a song Jenna had similarly written for Scott.

As they sang, they strolled out the catwalk into the audience, arms around each other, as casually if they were alone in the woods. When Scott sang, Jenna laid her head on his shoulder; when Jenna sang, Scott alternately devoured her with his eyes and peppered her with kisses. When they got to the end of the runway, just before the song came to an end, they both seemed to suddenly realize where they were, as if just noticing for the first time the mob of fans surging around their feet. Hands reached up eagerly to them, pulsing in rhythm with the music.

Without letting go of each other, Scott and Jenna reached down and started squeezing hands, Jenna going for a male hand to her left, Scott for a female to his right in an effort not to unbalance themselves. They'd managed this feat several times when Jenna felt Scott suddenly stiffen and quickly pull back, drawing her along with him. Startled, Jenna looked into the audience seeking a cause but could find no clue. Scott wheeled her around and started propelling the both of them back up the catwalk to the stage.

AFTERWARDS, AS THEY left the stage for the last time, arm in arm, waving as they went, Jenna finally had a chance to ask for an explanation.

"What?" Scott asked, feigning ignorance. "What do you mean?"

"Something made you turn and bolt," she insisted.

"I just realized we needed to get back to the stage before the song ended. That's all," he said. "I did *not* want to be out there in the middle of all those people when the clapping started." Jenna pondered the thought, then let it go.

SCOTT LEFT WITH THE band the following day, and Jenna and Zach settled in for a good, long, satisfying visit with Linda and Joe. She was even able to get one-on-one time with her mother, with Joe, with both of her brothers and with Kristin. Like many luxuries in her fast-paced world, this special time came as a mixed blessing. It was hard enough keeping the secret of her pregnancy from the family as a unit. It was almost impossible to keep it under individual scrutiny.

"You look tired," her mother had observed almost daily since she had arrived.

"Are you okay?" Jim has asked. "You seem – dragged out or something"

"Is it me, or are you looking mumsier than usual?" Kristin had remarked, then responded skeptically to Jenna's offhand, "Oh, pu-leeze."

The only one she couldn't fool was Adella, her mother's long-time housekeeper, who had all but raised Jenna herself. Jenna had never been able to keep a secret from Adella. Fortunately, her dear Adella knew how to keep a secret when asked to.

SCOTT AND THE BAND ricocheted from L.A. to Tucson, to Salt Lake, to Seattle, to Denver. Their longest layover in any one city was three days.

Scott, who normally grew more and more restless, erratic and aggressive on tour like this, had been behaving oddly since they'd left L.A. His behavior was the subject of speculation when he was out of earshot. One afternoon in Seattle, Jeremy finally dragged him out to a coffee shop and confronted him. "Is it my imagination, bro, or are you a bit on the quiet side since we left California? Missing Jenna and the baby?" he suggested.

"Plenty," Scott said, then went silent.

"*But*…" Jeremy tried to cue him. Scott didn't fall for it. "Okay, then, how about *and*…?" Scott rolled his eyes. "Look, Tenny, *some*thing's eating you. Don't try to pretend it isn't," Jeremy insisted.

Scott put his elbows on the table, lodged his chin in his palms and started rubbing his eyes. "Tour's getting' to me, I guess," was all he was willing to allow.

"I've seen tours get to you," Jeremy countered, shaking his head. "This isn't that."

Scott studied the opaque surface of his latte. "That ain't tea, ya know," Jeremy finally observed dryly. Scott looked up. "You won't find your future in there, dude," he said. "Talk to me."

Scott sighed, picked up the cup and took a long, time-buying swallow of the rich brew. "I got a problem," he finally mumbled.

"Surprise, surprise," Jeremy commented.

"A groupie."

"Oh?"

"A stalker-type groupie."

"Ooooh." Jeremy sat up. This was a subject that rock stars had to take seriously. "You've told Lund about it, right?" Pete Lund was the head of security on the road.

"No."

"Scott..."

"It's – it's problematic."

"Well, yeah. Stalkers are problematic by definition. Why haven't you told Lund?"

"Because – okay, but this is between you and me," Scott said in all seriousness. "*I* will decide what I tell Lund and when – agreed?"

"Yeah, but I shouldn't," Jeremy nodded, reluctantly.

"It's, um, delicate. I have some history with this broad."

"You've got history with a thousand broads."

"This is history I don't think Jenna could handle."

"Oh." Jeremy sat thinking about this. "How – serious is the stalker part?"

"I don't know. I've just been seeing her at like every show for a while now."

"Which is why you've been in such a hurry to get out of places."

"Yeah."

"And why you told the crew to stop putting in the catwalk?"

"Yeah."

"Jenna's a big girl. She knows about groupies getting to be problems."

"She's seen a picture of this broad and me, taken when we played Chicago last year, and she went totally ballistic. When I finally got a chance to explain it to her, I – lied about it. I don't know why, I just did. The thing that really ticks me off is that I really didn't have to lie – I'm not even sure *why* I did. But I did."

"So you just come clean with her. She'll understand."

"Not while we're on the road. I don't want her sitting at home blowing it all out of proportion. She will. It's hard for her, her at home, me out here. She doesn't say so in so many words, but I know it drives her fuckin' crazy."

"So why doesn't she come back out and join us again. I know it's a bit problematic, with Zach and all, but I thought the motorhome was a great solution. Get her back out here."

"It's not that simple," Scott said. "I'd explain it, but – that's a secret too. That one's Jenna's, not mine," he hurried to add as Jeremy rolled his eyes.

"Too damn many secrets," Jeremy said, throwing his hands up in despair.

JENNA PASSED HER quiet days with songwriting and Zach. She barely left the house. But she did have one errand she didn't want to delegate to Ellen. Scott, due home in a few days, had asked her to stop by Blue Skies before he returned, to pick up any mail that had come in for him. Suffering from cabin fever, she decided she'd time it to make the errand double as a dinner outing.

"It looks like it's going to be a quiet night," Ann had told her when she called to say she was coming by. "I'll join you for dinner if it stays that way." Jenna was pleased at the prospect of non-baby conversation.

ANN HAD BEEN RIGHT. It was a quiet night at Blue Skies. Since live music had been added to the menu, any night without a band seemed quiet indeed.

"I'll be free in five," Ann told Jenna when she arrived.

"I'll stop and say hi to Sandy. Come get me when you're ready," Jenna suggested, and headed into the lounge.

"Hey, how ya doing, sweetheart?" Sandy asked. Taking a stool at the bar, she leaned over it and gave him a kiss. "The regular?" he asked her.

"Great," she responded, but just as he turned to pull her a tall club soda and lime, she felt a sudden, fairly strong pain in her abdomen which grew by quick degrees until she had to grit her teeth against it. She stood, but the pain only worsened. With a silent groan, she felt behind her for the chair to sit back down again. Abruptly the pain doubled in intensity. She screamed aloud, grabbed her belly and fell to the floor.

Sandy and Ann both arrived at her side at the same moment. "Oh, God, help me," Jenna managed to say. "The baby..."

"I'll call 911," Sandy said quickly. Ann stayed at her side.

"Jenna," she asked. "'The baby'? Are you pregnant again?"

"Yes, but I'm losing it," she grunted, tears rolling freely down her cheeks. "Please, my – cell's in my pocket," she said, indicating her right pocket with a nod of her head. "Call Ellen. Tell her what's happening. Ask her to call Scott." The ambulance had arrived before Ann could finish delivering Jenna's message.

SCOTT ARRIVED FOUR hours later. The first person he saw as he hurried into the emergency room waiting area was Dr. Williams. "Julia," he said, "how is Jenna." Julia's face told him before Julia could.

"She's okay, but she's lost the baby, Scott. I am so sorry," she told him compassionately. "She's still asleep, but you can go in and sit with her. I'll be back in a while to check on her."

Jenna woke to the sound of his footfalls. "Scott," she whispered raspily, fighting her way clear of anesthesia. He reached for her hand and she looked up at him, then tears came. "I lost the baby, Scott," she cried. "I am so sorry."

Sitting down next to her, he brushed the hair from her face. "Don't apologize, babe. It wasn't your fault. I don't know how much more of this you can take. Let's get through this, then we need to talk and make some serious decisions."

"How'd you get here? What about the tour?" she asked, trying to make sense out of the chaos.

"When Ellen got me, I grabbed a charter. I told Jeremy to can the rest of the tour. We can reschedule later. He's taking care of everything. I'm home." He stayed with her through the night.

JENNA WAS DISCHARGED early the next afternoon. On the way home they barely spoke to each other, both harboring their own guilt. Ellen and Zach met them at the door. Scott reached quietly for Zach; it had been almost three weeks since he had seen his son.

Jenna looked at Scott and his son. He may be the only child I will ever be able to have, she thought, burst into tears and ran for the bedroom.

Scott handed Zach back to Ellen and quickly followed. He found her sprawled across their bed, sobbing hysterically.

"Jenna, honey, is it the baby or is there something else?" He gathered her in his arms and started murmuring the words he hoped she needed to hear. "Babe, I don't give a damn if you can't have another one. After all you've been through since I met you, I don't want to watch you go through any more. You've lost three babies, and almost lost not only Zach but your own life as well. Do you know what I fucking went through when I heard you almost died? None of this has been easy on me, either. You don't know what it's like to have to stand by and watch you in pain, time after time. I love you. I love Zach. I love my two daughters and my grandson. I'm happy and content with all that. If you can't have another baby, it won't bother me. Please believe that." He went quiet, then added, "I'm gonna get a vasectomy."

Jenna suddenly squirmed free of him, jumped up and bolted for the door. He called after her, asking where she was going. "Just leave me the hell alone and don't talk to me. I'll be in one of the other rooms."

Angry, he went after her. Her found her down the hall just about to go into a guest room. She looked back at him "I asked you to leave me alone for a reason, Scott," she said accusingly. "I don't want to say things I may regret."

"Say whatever you have to," he said quietly.

Jenna stood in thought for a moment, then started slowly. "It's all about you. What *you* felt, what *you* want or can live without. How *I* feel, what *I* want

– that doesn't matter to you. It's the same old thing: whatever Scott wants and to hell with everyone else – in this case, me. Well, now that I know how you feel, I need to figure out if I want to live with that. So get the hell out of my way and leave me the fuck alone." She entered the bedroom and slammed the door in his face.

Scott left the house, jumped on his motorcycle and took off. Jenna sat and cried.

Chapter 9

✳

SCOTT PULLED THE Harley into the garage in the low light of late afternoon and headed for the back door. He noticed Jeremy's Cherokee parked beside Jenna's little Miata as he rounded the corner of the garage. Ellen was fixing Zach's supper when he came through the door. "Where's Jenna," he asked her.

"She took the baby and left a little while ago," Ellen said over her shoulder. "She didn't say where she was going or when she'd be back."

"That's odd," Scott muttered. "Her car's still in the driveway. Is Jeremy here?"

Ellen shook her head. "I don't think so. I haven't seen him." Now he was really puzzled.

He called Carrie to see if she knew anything. "No, but Jeremy went straight over to your house when he got in. That was at least an hour ago," she told him.

"Yeah, his car's here. Look, I'll let you know what's going on whenever the fuck I figure it out," he said and hung up.

FINDING NO ONE BUT Ellen when he'd arrived earlier, Jeremy had gone over to the studio to make use of the time till either Scott or Jenna showed up. Stepping into the creative disarray of the rehearsal space, he found Jenna sitting at the piano, Zach on her lap.

"What's up, little mother?" he asked Jenna kindly. Jenna turned to him, tears running down her cheeks. "Jenna, honey," he said, dropping his lanky frame on the piano bench next to her and putting a big-brotherly arm around her. "Where's Scott?"

Jenna hung her head. "We had a row. He took off on his bike. Which is fine by me – he's the last person I want to be with right now," she cried. She told him some of the more damning details of their spat. "He can be such a self-righteous prick."

"Hey – cut the boy a *little* slack," he said. "He's gone through hell. Look, *you* know what it's like to stand there helpless; you had to do enough of it with Zach. Scott's been through it, over and over, with both you *and* Zach. It's taken a lot out of him."

"You're just sticking up for your best friend."

Jeremy pulled back and made her look him in the eye. "Let's get one thing straight: I consider both you *and* Scott my best friends. Okay?" She nodded, mollified, touched. "Look, hon, I've been there with him, each time you were in the hospital. I know the pain he's been through, but mostly it was pain for what was happening to you. When he heard you almost died with Zach, he actually went to a bar and almost picked up a bottle."

"No!" Jenna couldn't believe it.

"He never told you because he didn't want you blaming yourself. He could barely hold it together – but he knew you and Zach would need him, so he made himself stop and got himself to an AA meeting. He's been going to them regularly ever since, especially while we've been out on the road."

Jenna shook her head in sorry amazement. "Oh my God, Jeremy, I had no idea," she said. "I – I didn't want to hear what he was saying to me. Thank you for telling me all this," she said, putting a hand over his. "I'm gonna go find him and apologize."

Gathering Zach, she headed for the door.

"Jenna," Jeremy called to her as she went. She turned back to him. "I'm sorry, about losing the baby."

"Thank you," she said quietly, and left the studio quickly as tears welled afresh.

JENNA HURRIED OUT THE door of the studio and almost into Scott's arms. "Where the hell have you been?" he asked angrily. "I've been worried sick about you."

"Let me take Zach into Ellen. We need to talk. I didn't mean to worry you, honey, really I didn't."

Jenna came back out and the two went and sat on a knoll with a panoramic view of the Atlantic Ocean spread out before them. Scott sat first, giving Jenna the option to find her own comfort zone. She chose to sit right beside him. They both sat silent for a few moments, staring out at the cloudless horizon.

"I've caused you no end of worry since we've been together," Jenna said, finally breaking the silence. "I was over in the studio when Jeremy came in. We talked. He told me things I didn't know anything about – and should have. About the night Zach was born, the AA meetings." Scott's sigh confirmed Jeremy's account.

"We're in trouble, Scott," Jenna said plainly. "I'm afraid of what's happening to us, and it's not just recent – it's since Zach was born. Look at the things we've said to each other. God, I know you worry about me but I'm not ready to hear anything about not ever having another baby. This whole thing is a mess. I don't know what to do." Tears started to flow again. "And of course I'm this hormonal wreck again, too," she wailed.

Scott wrapped his arms around her. "Babe, neither of us could love it more if we could have another baby, but not if it means putting your life in danger. Zach needs a mother. I know what this means to you, really I do. I'll make you a deal," he said finally.

Jenna looked up. "A deal?"

"We go see Julia again and have a serious conversation about all this. Really lay it all out. Maybe get a second opinion. Really understand it all, the physical, the emotional, everything. We'll make a decision based on the facts. Whatever that means for us." He looked at her as she weighed his words. "Deal?"

She closed her eyes, then started nodding. "Deal," she agreed, then laid her head wearily on his chest.

SCOTT WENT AND FOUND Jeremy fooling around on his guitar. "Bro," he said by way of greeting. "I owe you one." Jeremy looked up, not sure what Scott might be referring to. "Bringing Jenna, uh, up to speed on the state of my insanity."

"Hey, I hope you're not angry, my telling Jenna – "

"Have no fear. You've just saved us a fortune in therapy," Scott said surprisingly lightly. "Look, what I know *I* need is some music therapy. We've been dicking around about pulling another album together. Let's really get on it. We've got a good chunk of time till the holidays and a good chunk of half-boiled songs in the works. Let's focus. Whaddya say we nail it before the holidays?"

Jeremy strummed a succession of chords as he chewed on the idea. "Do-able," he finally said. "I've been playing with this idea…"

JENNA SUGGESTED THAT Ellen take the night off, wanting Scott and herself to have an evening alone with Zach. Five minutes later, Ellen hurried out the door to catch a movie. The two adults spent the next hour and a half on the floor, experiencing their son's world first hand. Language was reduced to baby babble as they rolled and scooted and flailed about, exploring crevasses beneath couches and reaching for anything that dangled off a table. Jenna found herself having to play dual roles, one as an equally curious six-month-old and one as Mother, trying to keep as many foreign objects out of Scott's mouth as out of Zach's.

After they'd finally put Zach to bed, the two of them went out on the porch and got comfortable on the porch swing, Jenna curled up with her head in Scott's lap. Subject matter ranged from plans for the new album, to the upcoming holidays, their parents' anniversary and their own.

"And you're definitely part of the album, in case you were wondering" Scott told her, smiling down at her and playing with her hair. "I'd like to see this one as a real collaboration. You have equal standing with everyone else."

"You mean, as in no standing whatsoever if it's not what you want to hear?" Jenna asked sweetly, only half teasing.

"I mean, as in collaboration. If I stop listening, you have my permission to pour a Gatorade over my head. For which I hereby swear," he said in mock seriousness, his left hand raised, "I will *not* kill you."

Then he grew serious. "I love you, Baby Blue," he whispered. "My heart breaks for you." He leaned down, kissed her gently and set the swing rocking. Silently, he stroked her hair as he looked out to sea. By the time he next looked down, Jenna was asleep in his lap. It had been a very long and stressful day.

Scooping her up, he stood and carried her lithe form inside. Half-waking, Jenna slipped her arms up around his neck and settled in for the ride. A few minutes later, they were naked in each other's arms. Exhausted, they held each other close until they both fell sound asleep.

THE NEXT FOURTEEN DAYS in a row Scott, Jenna and the rest of the world-class talent that made up Blacklace clocked no less than six hours a day in the studio. Carrie dropped by a few times and was blown away by what she was hearing. Jeremy and Scott still had their arguments, but Jenna brokered compromises like a diplomat. They got back to work so fast that Dan started complaining.

"Hey, man, I count on this shit for a few extra coffee breaks a day," he groused at one point as he hurried back, donut in hand, to what he referred to as the 'driver's seat' of his drum set. "Things sure are different since this Mrs. Tenny chick came aboard." He always follow such sentiments with a wink to Jenna. He too had his diplomatic side.

But all the hard work was producing quality product, music that everyone agreed was every bit as good as – and in a couple of cases, better than – any of their best. Inspiration sparked inspiration as they played with each other's ideas, expanded them, shrank them, juggled them, turned them inside out and stood them on their ear. They reworked their own songs; they played fast and loose with old blues standards, metal and rap. Nothing was off limits. They swapped instruments, tried new combinations of instrumentation, new vocal registers. Scott put one of Jeremy's guitars in Jenna's hands and overruled her protests. "Just mess around," he insisted. She did, and found she enjoyed the occasional break from singing, diving deep into the music with the guys, leaving Scott to do the vocal heavy lifting.

They decided to break with tradition and swap out their usual New Years Eve Boston blow-out for a hometown show the weekend before Thanksgiving – which is to say, Scott decided and no one objected.

And no one questioned – at least not within Scott's hearing – his not wanting to tour at all before the first of the year. Dan weighed in as the rest of the band contemplated all the unexpected changes in the usual scheme of things. "Hey, look, did it ever occur to any of you – maybe he's finally like *slowing down*, as in, you know, uh – aging? Like the rest of us are…"

Dan ducked in time as Jeff grabbed a nearby guitar by the neck and swung it at him like a baseball bat. "What the fuck? You callin' *me* old?" he accused Dan point blank. "You callin' Tim and Jeremy old? You can call yourself old all you want in the privacy of your own fucked up universe, but you keep that kinda talk to yourself, hear? You got a shitload o' balls callin' *me* old, my brother."

Ryan, half the age of the youngest of the rest of Blacklace, walked away from the fray and busied himself at the keyboard, improvising a medley of lines from "When I'm Sixty-Four," first in the style of Mozart, then Scott Joplin, then into a freewheeling jazz variation. He quickly switched to the Blacklace hit "On the Floor," rendered in the style of Bach, when he saw Scott walk back in the room.

IT WAS WITH HEAVY hearts that Jenna and Scott walked into Julia Williams' office a few days later. After giving Jenna a thorough examination, Julia sat down with them to go through her recommendations and answer all their questions.

"Okay, this is how it is," she said, sitting behind her desk, her hands folded in front of her. "You can start having intercourse again. But Jenna, you must *not* attempt to get pregnant for an absolute minimum of six months. You just can't. Longer would be better yet. You simply *have* to give your reproductive organs time to fully recover and heal. If you want to try and carry another baby – *you have to give it time*." She gave emphasis to every word and let the thought sink in completely before continuing.

"Then I would want you to see a reproductive endocrinologist/gynecologist. You say your mother also has a history of miscarriage. My guess is that the problem is a luteal phase – the time between ovulation and menstruation – defect, or maybe an immune function disorder. We've already ruled out anything structural. There are answers, but you aren't ready to start down that path yet. In the meantime, I want you back on birth control – today – and I do *not* want any more "I goofed" appointments, okay? I don't want to see you one day sooner than six months. Can you two promise me that?"

Jenna and Scott both soberly agreed.

AFTER THE APPOINTMENT, Scott suggested lunch, followed by some shopping. They wanted to get Linda and Joe something for their upcoming anniversary; Thanksgiving would be celebrated in L.A. again this year. Scott and Jenna would have Christmas at home and celebrate their first anniversary with their east coast family.

Over lunch, Jenna broached what she feared might be a difficult subject: she wanted to start singing with her band again after the holidays.

"This is new," Scott said, surprised. "When did this idea come about? I – I think maybe we ought to sit down at home and talk about it in detail. There's a lot involved. I don't think we should tackle it over lunch." At least he didn't object outright, Jenna thought to herself, relieved. That's a good sign.

"Okay," she said, agreeably. "Let's stay in and make dinner tonight. Some time with Zach, and then we'll have plenty of time to talk about it afterwards. A nice fire…"

Scott grinned. "Think that'll soften me up, eh? Careful. It might have just the opposite effect."

"I'M THINKING ABOUT just doing a few shows here and there for starters, building back up gradually to doing a full-fledged tour. What do you think?" she asked Scott. The two sat side-by-side on the couch, Jenna's feet up under her, Scott's on the coffee table, the first fire of the season crackling before them.

"With your band versus Blacklace because…" Scott prompted her.

Jenna turned to him as she considered her answer. "Because I like performing on my own as well. I guess it's an identity thing – I was Jenna B before I met you. Sometimes I find myself wanting to – I don't know, I guess revisit Jenna B, as this new version of me, the me that's changed and grown with Blacklace and marriage and motherhood. I'm not skipping out on Blacklace – I want to keep a foot in both worlds, yours and mine." She took his hand in hers.

"Where you get to make all the decisions?" Scott ventured.

"There's that," Jenna conceded, playing with a knotted rope bracelet he was wearing, "but it's a lot more than that, Scott."

"Brian's not pressuring you, is he?" Scott asked.

"Not a bit. We've had a long talk about it, though. Look, this is for *me*, something I have to do. I've learned so much, watching you guys take music apart and rework it. I want to see what Mark and the rest of my guys would do with some of our stuff. My head's bursting with ideas. It's going to drive me crazy if I don't find an outlet for it. I know it's tricky, what with you on the road too, and Zach not even a year old and all…"

"Hey, we can make it work, babe," Scott said, sliding a hand up into her hair. "That's not the question. The question is really *why*, not how. I gotta say, I like your whys. God knows I understand what happens when your head gets going. I took you away from your thing. I can imagine how I'd feel if being with you meant leaving Blacklace behind. I couldn't do it. Obviously, neither can you. Nor should you. We'll work it out, babe."

"Your support means the world to me," Jenna said, putting her arms around him. "Aren't we being mature," she mused, "working through all this without a fight. Almost like – adults." Just to prove he wasn't being adult at all, Scott started tickling her. Then he set to kissing her.

"AND YOU'RE WEARING your patch, m'dear?" he asked as he drew her to him under the covers. She took his hand in hers and slid it around to her left buttock to prove it. "How delectably responsible of you," he whispered into her hair as he squeezed her butt and the all-important patch upon it, their bodies meeting skin-to-skin, eager to renew their relationship at its most primitive level.

With a quiet moan, Jenna rolled one leg over him and reared up, looking down at him through a tangle of hair. Swooping down, she reached behind him and pulled his head up to her, kissing him on the neck and then on the lips.

Laying him back down, she slowly slid her hands down both sides of his torso, her open mouth and tongue trailing close behind. It had been weeks, and she still didn't trust her new-found willingness to engage in oral sex, but when she reached his crotch, she found her earlier willingness had been supplanted by an unexpected, an almost impatient eagerness. Scott groaned with pleasure as she took him deep in her mouth. Before long she was groaning in the throes of her own ecstasy.

Time stood still, tides and nations rose and fell, seasons came and went and came again, as they continued their explorations into new territories and old. It was quite a while before Scott finally wrapped his arms around her and lay quiet. Jenna lifted her head, gave him a sleepy kiss, then curled up against his warm, lanky body and drifted off into deep, dreamless sleep.

WHEN JENNA WOKE late the next morning, Scott was gone. In his place was a note saying he'd taken Zach over to the studio so she could sleep in; he'd given Ellen the morning off. She was to just sit with her coffee and enjoy reading the paper. Jeremy would be joining him shortly, the note continued; the rest of the guys would be arriving later.

Jenna took her time getting up, enjoying the silence and a feeling of extravagant indulgence. She was glad Ellen wouldn't be back till the afternoon. It would give Scott more time with his son. He was so good with him. She loved watching the two together. Zach was at his happiest, laughing endlessly, when he was with his daddy.

But when she finally wandered out to the studio, she was dismayed that the first thing she heard, stepping through the door and into the sound-proofed space, was the all-too-familiar sound of Scott and Jeremy fighting. Her immediate thought was, not in front of Zach! She sighed as the residual glow of her peaceful morning vanished in an instant.

"No fuckin' way!" Scott was yelling, but to her relief, Jenna instantly recognized an exaggerated, joking tone behind the expletive. "Not *my* son!"

"Give the poor kid a proper start on a *guitar*, man. And not a Les Paul Jr. – the real thing," Jeremy said vehemently. "Get him one of the new Bob Marleys. I played one the other day. Man, it's goddam righteous."

"Nope. He starts on drums, like I did. And then the piano."

"The piano's for wimps. And like you're some kinda well-rounded musician? You're a motherfuckin' poster child for why you should start on a friggin' guitar. Uh, oops –" Jeremy looked up and noticed Jenna leaning against the door jamb, arms crossed. She grimaced, then took a few steps into the studio and found Zach sitting in the middle of a pile of tambourines, ratchets, rattles, other percussion instruments.

Scott held up a bead-covered rattle in front of Zach and said, "Cabaças. Can you say cabaças? We're just hashing out Zach's music career for him," he said, glancing guiltily up at Jenna, gauging her mood, having no idea how much she'd overheard. "What do *you* think he should play."

Jenna threw her hands up. "No way I'm getting in the middle of *this* discussion," she said, then had to laugh. "You guys sound like a couple of kids yourselves. Bad little boys, using bad language where nobody can hear you. But, not to be a prude or anything, guys – Zach *can* hear you. I'd really prefer his first word be mother, not motherfucker."

Sitting down next to the baby, she picked up a tambourine and held it out to him. "Tambourine," she said and repeated it as Zach babbled his own take on the word, then brought his hand slapping down on the drumhead of the instrument. Delighted with the jingling sound it produced, he proceeded to slap it again and again. Scott took his 'drumming' hand by the wrist and added a bit of rhythm to Zach's efforts. When he let go, Zach went right back to his previous random approach, grinning ear to ear. "We'll have to start calling you Mr. Tambourine Man, Mr. Zachary!" Jenna exclaimed, then picked him up and headed for the piano. "Time for your piano lesson, young man," she said firmly, entirely for Scott and Jeremy's benefit. They had her vote.

BEFORE THEY KNEW IT, the early Thanksgiving Boston shows finally rolled around. Jenna loved the fact that she was genuinely nervous as she counted down the days. For her, nervous equaled challenge, growth.

In this case, nervous also included playing the guitar on a stage for the first time ever, and not just in the Blacklace numbers they'd worked up; she'd agreed to take a solo, with guitar. She'd be playing a black vintage Stratocaster Jeremy had given her, a gift designed to encourage – or in his words, "totally shame" – her into doing more with it.

Dressed to go on, Jenna walked into the dressing room that Scott and the rest of the guys were sharing, in search of moral support. Wearing only the skimpiest of spangled black tops and a pair of thigh-high red boots that came nowhere near the hem of her red leather miniskirt, what she got were whistles and catcalls. "Can it! At ease! Down, boys, down!" she laughed.

Scott was on the floor relaxing slowly into a half lotus forward bend, his torso curling down over his one outstretched knee until his nose touched flesh. Staying limber and fit was an obsession that was easy for Scott to satisfy – he'd been born with "a hyperkinetic streak wider than Job's Creek," his father had once told her. She was disappointed when Scott showed her Job's Creek the last time they were up at the lake; she was expecting something much broader. Turning his head to one side to catch a glimpse of what had set the rest howling, Scott rested his ear on his knee and joined in.

"So what are *you* wearin', bro?" Jeremy called over to him from the other side of the room, where he was doing a set of slow-motion pushups. "It better be good or nobody the fuck's gonna *notice* you."

"Oh, they'll notice me," Scott grunted. "Hey, you look nervous, babe," he said, looking beyond the flashy costume, to the eyes of the woman he loved, as he pulled back into an upright position.

"Uh, yeah," Jenna admitted. "Just a bit. Maybe even more than a bit."

Rising, he barked a two-word order: "Everybody out." When the door closed on the last of the band and the grumbling had receded down the hall, he locked the door and turned to her. "Come here, baby," he said, his voice low and persuasive. "Let me calm you down."

EVERYONE AGREED: SCOTT was in rare form when he hit the stage twenty minutes later. Clearly, he was in a great mood and was out to have fun. When Jenna appeared after the now customary three songs, he went as crazy as the rest of the house did.

They opened their duo part of the show with their, by now, infamous version of Dirty Dancing, and what followed made that pale by comparison. Having no family in the stands, they gave their inner censors the night off. Unlike earlier versions, however, he kept the action as far back from the lip of the stage as the setup of instruments would allow. He'd seen his "groupie-stalker," as he'd come to think of her, in the audience almost as soon as he'd taken the stage. She had a name. Ashley West. At least that had been her name when he'd known her as a teenager. Who knew what name she went by now.

Finally, it was time for Jenna's solo. Walking slowly to the center mike, guitar in hand, she gazed around the floor and up to the rafters at the crowd of almost twenty thousand that filled the Fleet Center, still referred to by most as the old Boston Garden. The band started playing an intro for her, then one by one, got up and abandoned the stage. Ryan and Jeff had left and Jeremy was just going as she slipped the red leather guitar strap over her head and picked up the intro herself, both on the guitar and humming into the mike. Scott was the last to leave, after giving her a peck on the cheek and sauntering off with a wave at the crowd who had gone astonishingly quiet. They knew something big was coming their way.

She came to the end of the intro, then started it up again and spoke into the mike, her voice husky and intimate. "Boston, work with me here. I'm trying something...new." The audience exploded in approval, love and support. "Thanks," she grinned. "I needed that. Okay..."

She started in on a song neither Scott, nor the rest of the band – nobody on the planet, in fact – had ever heard. She'd written it as a teenager, originally for a composition course, and with an eye to performing it with Chick Cheeks, the all-girl band she'd sung with in college, but by the time it was finished, she'd decided it was too personal. She submitted another song for a grade and filed "Where Did You Go?" away with a lot of other painful memories.

She walked in the door like it was any old day.
She barely made mention that she'd been away.
She settled back in like nothing was changed.
She hardly acknowledged that we'd been estranged.

She walked in the door and back into my life,
Her children's mother, her husband's wife.
She settled back in, she took back her role.
She took back her place, but never my soul.

What the fuck, Mom, where did you go?
What were you thinking? I just gotta know.

I was twelve when she left, walked out of my life.
Pain, loss and terror tore me like a knife.
Two years of darkness, two years of grief.
You stole my childhood, dear Mother, you thief.

What the fuck, Mama, where did you go?
What were you thinking? I just gotta know.

Jenna's delivery grew more passionate and more self-assured with each verse. At the end of the second refrain, she played a verse on the guitar but talked directly to the audience.

"I wrote this song when I was a kid. My mother left us, for two years – you've probably heard about it. My life got pretty screwed up while she was away. I didn't know that when I wrote this, but it sure seems like my subconscious did. It's only recently that I learned the whole truth, that my father had gotten caught red-handed with a mistress and a child she'd had by him. To protect my father's squeaky-clean image, my mother took the fall for him. In all the years before his death, my father never set the record straight. Knowing now how terrible those two years were for my mother as well as for me, I've written a new verse. She's not here tonight but, Mom, this is for you."

Nothing, it seems, was as we had been told.
You were no monster, you were not stone-cold.
You too were a victim then, so long ago.
You were suffering too. Thank God I now know.

You too were a victim, Mom, so long ago.
You suffered too, Mom. Thank God I now know.

By the time she let the final chord die away, tears were running down her cheeks. She let the audience's earsplitting adulation and acceptance comfort her.

Chapter 10

※

EVERYONE MADE IT to Linda and Joe's by early afternoon, the day before Thanksgiving. A party for Linda and Joe's anniversary was scheduled for that night. Included in the gathering clan were Scott's older sister Annie, her husband and, for the first time in years, both of their children.

David had called Joe out of the blue a few weeks earlier, wanting to touch base with his grandfather; Joe had been the only family member David had been able to get along with once puberty had set in. Finding out his grandfather's phone number hadn't been easy. He'd called his sister at an hour when he knew his parents would both still be at the school where they worked – his mother taught sixth grade; his father was the principal. Nancy was thrilled to hear her brother's voice. He was at a pay phone. She had him give her the number and hang up, and called him right back. They talked for over an hour. She cried when they finally said goodbye.

When he'd called Joe, David had no intention of telling him where he was. He'd spent five years keeping well off his family's radar. At first all he was willing to admit to was that he was in California. "Well, it *is* a small world, isn't it?" Joe exclaimed. "Me too. I'm in Beverly Hills, of all places,"

"NO SHIT!" DAVID had blurted out. "God, that's – " He stopped short.

"That's what? Not far? A million miles away?" Joe said, playing a hunch.

"Not far," David admitted.

Joe changed the subject, not wanting to corner the boy. "So, what are you doing to keep body and soul alive, lad?"

"Driving a truck. For one of the studios."

"Hey, that's not a bad job. You old enough to drive?"

"Shit, Grampa, I'm twenty-three."

"No! You were just learning to walk…"

They bantered back and forth for a bit. "Man, I miss you, kid," Joe finally said. "I'd sure love to take you to Disneyland. Always meant to some day. Still could…"

"I could meet you there," David decided, which turned out to be step one to getting him to the house a few days later. After several visits, he volunteered that he had been living in Encino, just over the hill from Joe and Linda, for the past three years.

"Neighbahs," Joe had laughed, laying on the New England accent he tried to keep in check these days, "and we never even knew it."

It had taken every diplomatic trick in Joe's book to get David to show up for Thanksgiving.

THE FAMILY REUNION had been uncomfortable. When Joe had let Annie know that David would be there, her first response was, "Well, he certainly has some explaining to do."

Only Nancy could embrace her brother without an agenda. His mother gave him a brief, brittle hug without a kiss; his father put his hand out for a formal shake. Scott had welcomed him with open arms, much to Annie's dismay. She had spent most of David's youth trying to keep her degenerate brother and his overprotected nephew as far apart as possible, which had provided the only upside for her when David had left home – at least Scott would no longer be an influence. Joe had taken Annie aside after they'd said their initial hellos and recommended she give the boy space – "and plenty of it." Giving space wasn't her style, but she withered under her father's stern glance.

It had been so long since Scott had seen David that he almost didn't recognize his nephew. Annie had kept the boy clean-cut and well-dressed from the time he was out of diapers, as if he had to be ready for an Ivy League college interview at a moment's notice. The David of today was a tanned, sun-bleached, shaggy-headed California skater-boy, a young man clearly comfortable in his own skin. Scott threw one arm around him and the other around his niece, then introduced them to Jenna and her brothers and sister, and then to Zach and Ellen.

"Nancy and I know each other," Jenna said, giving her a hug before turning to David. "You I am delighted to finally meet. Don't you go vanishing again for five years." It was the icebreaker the day needed.

LINDA AND JOE HAD claimed they only wanted a small family gathering for their anniversary, but that idea had been unanimously overruled by their offspring, who hired a hall, arranged for a band and invited some close family friends, the couple were informed after the fact. No one let on who the band was they'd lined up.

David had grown up knowing the uncle he rarely saw was the lead singer for Blacklace; he couldn't remember ever not knowing this. There had been no Blacklace albums in the house, but he had a stash he'd accumulated on the sly over the years; he'd taken them all with him when he left home. He'd never been able to afford a ticket to see his uncle perform when they'd come to L.A., but the previous year, a friend had gotten him a spot on the local pickup crew that supplemented the army of roadies who traveled with the show, loading in and back out at the Staples Center. Part of him had wanted to try to get a message to Scott that night, but his need to stay clear of family had prevailed. So no one arriving at the party was more amazed or excited to find

Blacklace – minus Scott and Jenna – on the bandstand. "Oh, man. Blacklace! Somebody pinch me," David murmured, dazed at the reality. Uncle Scott reached around Jenna and did so. "Thank you," David deadpanned, then grinned.

Blacklace kept the music fairly tepid, playing the most relaxed versions of standard reception hall fare they could manage. They hadn't altered their normal dress for the occasion, though, so the end result was humorous. Jeremy played the role of emcee like a veteran standup comic.

After dinner was over, Jenna and Scott joined them on the stage. "Let's hear it for the band!" Scott said, grabbing Jeremy's mike as he and the rest of the band decamped. "While they're getting their dinner in the kitchen, we have a couple of ditties we want to sing for you," he smiled with a wink. "This is for you, Dad."

Jenna moved to his side with another mike in hand. "And for you, Mom. We love you both."

Scott stepped to the keyboard, slid the mike he was carrying into a nearby holder, sat down, adjusted the mike and launched into a jazzy intro to Cole Porter's "You're the Top." Altering the lyrics, he and Jenna painted a biographical portrait of both their parents that caught the audience off guard and immediately set them laughing, then quickly going quiet, not wanting to miss a line of it. After they'd "done" their parents, they went on with verses that included the rest of the family as well. David got a verse all his own. He looked delighted. His mother looked less than amused.

The song ended, and once the applause had died down, Jenna reached for a nearby guitar, then turned back to the audience. "Mom," she said softly into the mike, "I wrote this a long time ago and it covers a lot of historical ground between us. The last verse I wrote a month ago. I love you." And she proceeded to sing a G-rated version of "Where Did You Go?" She ended it with a final instrumental verse while motioning to her mother to join her on the stage. As she played the last note, Linda enveloped her daughter in a tearful hug.

When she could, Linda took the mike. "Oh, sweetie," she said, then had to collect herself and start again. "I so wish you'd never had to write that song. But I am so glad you could and you did. You are the most honest – and most forgiving – and most loving – and most lovable daughter a mother could ever wish for." They embraced again, then left the stage together.

Scott stayed behind at the keyboard, starting one familiar intro after another, until finally settling into the melody of the Blacklace song "Inappropriate Behavior." Then he spoke into the mike.

"Dad, I'm not gonna say this was written with you in mind." A chuckle rippled through the room, clearly defining who in the crowd knew the Blacklace discography. "But it could pass for a commentary on what you had to put up with, and what I hope we've put behind us. I'm going to dedicate this to all sons and fathers. And sons and mothers," he added, with a nod to his sister and nephew.

Thanksgiving Day, everyone pitched in to help with dinner preparations. Everyone from the band arrived together, with the sole, immediately conspicuous exception of Ryan. Jenna assumed he must be coming on his own, but as the four o'clock appointed dinner hour approached, she started to wonder.

Mashing potatoes, she picked up her bowl and sidled over to Kristin, who was distractedly chopping up carrots. "So, little sis, we've barely had time to talk. How are things?" she asked, intentionally posing an open-ended question.

"Well, the acting program's going really well," Kristin answered lightly. "It keeps me busy. And I love it," she quickly added. Then her tone changed entirely, going sharp and brusque, taking Jenna by surprise. "What you really want to know about is Ryan, so why don't you just come out and ask?"

"Whoa, Kris," she said, wide-eyed. "I don't know why you're using that tone on me, but I really don't think I deserve it. You know I care about everything that's going on in your life. Whatever you want to tell me is entirely up to you."

Kristin dropped the knife she was using amidst the chopped carrots, planted her hands on the counter, dropped her head and closed her eyes, swallowing hard, struggling not to cry. "I'm sorry I'm being a bitch," she said finally. "Ryan and I – we've – we've split up. The long distance relationship – just wasn't working. No," she stopped herself and her voice went steely cold. "That's not the truth. The long distance part was just an excuse. The truth is that he's got somebody else."

"Oh, honey, I'm really sorry. I had no idea. I haven't seen Ryan much to talk with him lately – it's all been work. Come to think of it, he's always running late, appearing at the last possible moment. Scott hasn't said anything to me either, so I doubt he knows."

Kristin covered her eyes as a sudden uncontrollable convulsion passed through her. Then she ran from the room. Jenna quickly finished mashing her potatoes, finished up Kristin's carrots as well, then went in search of her sister, but came upon Scott first. "Where's Zach?" she asked him. He and the baby had been inseparable all afternoon.

"His grandparents kidnapped him. I came out to the kitchen to see what you were up to, but it looked like you and Kristin were into something intense, so I left you two alone. You looked pissed. What was going on with you two?"

Jenna told him about Kristin and Ryan's split-up. Scott's quizzical look morphed seamlessly into one of guilt which Jenna could read easily. "You knew!" she said in amazement. "You've known and you didn't tell me. Why?"

Scott grabbed her hand. "Ryan told me, but we've all been so busy I completely forgot. Honest," he said earnestly. Then anger took over. "Hell, why didn't Kristin tell you? It wasn't *my* job to tell you."

"Honey, I'm not mad at you," Jenna said quickly. "Really. I just wondered why you hadn't told me. You're right – she should have. But her problems aren't going to become our problems," she added and gave him a hug. He responded with a kiss.

"Now, what about dinner?" he asked. "That's really what I came to the kitchen to find out about. I don't know about everyone else, but I'm ravenous."

JENNA HELPED KRISTIN pull herself back together. The two arrived at the Thanksgiving dinner table just as Joe appeared in the room with a new, old highchair for Zach. It had once been Scott's. Scott recognized it instantly.

"How in the…? Where did that thing come from?" he blurted out.

"Kept it when I moved out of the old place," Joe grinned. "Just had a feeling. When you're old and gray, you'll understand. You'll understand everything, in fact."

"You mean next week he's gonna understand *everything*?" Dan stage-whispered to Tim who was sitting next to him.

"Everything," Scott confirmed, having heard Dan just fine, "according to the expert here. And actually, that was last week, not next week. *Everything.*"

Which set the tone for the entire meal. Scott offered a prayer and thanks on behalf of everyone to their hosts. "Then let the games begin," he announced dramatically, setting the festivities in motion. Toasts were raised, praises sung, and plenty of bantering was passed with the peas and carrots.

When all was done, leaving everyone groaning, Ellen plucked Zach from the highchair and headed for the door. "We'll be back as soon as we get cleaned up," she said, holding him at arms length. "You look like a mixed-media collage, my little friend. We'll call you 'Turkey Dinner with All The Fixings,'" she decided.

Afterwards everyone congregated in either the study or living room, for coffee and more intimate conversation. Linda and Joe sought out Jeremy, Dan, Jeff and Tim, personally thanking each of them again for coming all the way from Boston, forgoing their own family Thanksgivings, to play for their anniversary party.

Heading out to the kitchen for more coffee, Linda found Jenna in the process of brewing another pot. "Great minds think alike," she laughed, then grew serious. "I have to tell you, darling, how much your song meant to me. I never knew you'd written that," she said, reaching unconsciously to push a stray lock of hair back behind her daughter's ear. "Why didn't you ever tell me?"

"I guess I was saving it for the right occasion, Mom," Jenna smiled and moved into Linda's outstretched arms for a hug.

"I love you so much, baby girl," her mother whispered in her ear. "I always have and I always will. Never forget that."

IT WAS HARD FOR everyone, saying their goodbyes that night or the next day. "Christmas is only a month away" became the mantra of the moment. They would all be gathering at Scott and Jenna's for what became the other mantra of farewell, "Sure hope it'll be a white Christmas!"

Scott gave David a special hug, whispering "Hang in, kid," in his ear as he did.

"I will," David told him. "On my terms."

"Only way," Scott reinforced the thought. "You can go along with want they want for you, but do it your own way." Annie had made an announcement, in the form of a toast to David the day before, that David would be coming back home with them, would be choosing a college and would be getting on with his education. His "little break," as she put it, after high school was over.

THE NEXT TWO WEEKS sped by like the landscape viewed from a car traveling at ninety. Jenna continued laboring with Blacklace on their album. They had gone into the studio the Saturday after Thanksgiving, and had been recording daily since then. In the midst of all that, she's managed to find time to work with Brian and Frank Kalkorian, her road manger, putting together a reasonably paced January-February tour of southern states only. She also had to coordiante with the individual members of her own band about the logistics of getting together again to rehearse in preparation for the tour. The unusually leisurely tour schedule was an easy sell. "Hell, everyone's calling it a paid vacation," bass guitar and keyboardist Bob Roskowski reported to her. It became the official name of the tour.

On top of all her musical commitments, the opening of the shelter was now just a week away, and couldn't come soon enough. The holidays brought out the worst in people, producing numerous victims of abuse seeking refuge. South Shore First Step would be a godsend to many in need.

Whenever they weren't in the studio, Scott and the rest of the guys were helping her out with last minute details. Carrie and the other wives had jumped in to help with supplies and setting up the rooms. The place was coming together beautifully and Jenna was more than satisfied with the results.

BLACKLACE WAS TAKING a break at nine o'clock one evening when Jenna got a call. Fishing her cell phone out of her pocket, she swallowed what she was eating, then answered. "It's Brian," she whispered to Scott. "You're joking, right?" she said into the phone. "Of *course*, I'll do it. Tell them yes." She hung up and took another bite of her sandwich.

"So?" Scott said impatiently. "Tell who you'll do what?"

"Oh, it's nothing," Jenna said, playing with him.

"No, it's not. I know that look," Scott countered.

"Oh, just another Grammy gig. They want me to be a presenter for this year's awards," she said off-handedly. The whole group's whooping and whistling almost drowned out the ringing of Scott's phone. Blacklace had been nominated for Song of the Year for "Something So Small," a song he'd written for Zach, during his earliest, most frightening days in the NICU, and recorded as a single. They'd be including another version of the song on the album they were almost ready with, as well. They had also been asked to perform.

"Oh. The Grammy's again," observed Tim, in his most been-there-done-that tone of voice.

A FEW NIGHTS LATER, Scott and Jenna kissed Zach goodnight, then bundled up to head off for the shelter's opening. As they stepped out the door into the cold night air, Jenna stopped Scott and pulled him to her into an embrace. "It just hit me. Tonight never would have happened without you," she said huskily. "I love you so much. I have so much to thank you for."

Scott was moved. He was also instantly aroused. "Oh, babe," he whispered, the second word coming almost as a groan. Jenna had no trouble following his train of thought. She pulled away from him and started down the steps.

"Remind me later."

"What?"

"To express my thanks," she smiled back at him, teasingly.

WHEN THEY ARRIVED at the opening, Jenna was pleased with the large turnout. The publicity committee had done their job well.

The house couldn't have looked better, and everyone in attendance was duly impressed. Reporters were all over the place, as were photographers, busy getting pictures of city officials, Jenna and members of the shelter board and staff. The guest list included a number of social service agency representatives, as well as an equal number of entertainers and friends. Needless to say, everyone from the Blacklace family was in attendance.

The evening was well underway when Harold Katzenbach, the mayor of Boston, took the podium. "I've been keeping an eye on this project," he opened his remarks, "ever since that little fundraiser you folks held in Boston last year." A chuckle passed through the room. Plenty of lot of hard work had gone into that "little" fundraiser.

"You've provided a remarkable model for other groups to emulate," the mayor continued on a more serious note, "a private nonprofit addressing a public need in a time when public funding cannot begin keep pace with demand. The moving force behind all this," he continued, pausing to indicate with a sweep of his hand that he was referring to shelter, not the party, "was Jenna Tenny, who needs no introduction." With that he gestured to her to join him at the podium. Jenna made her way through the applauding crowd, smiling and thanking everyone as she went. By the time she reached his side, she was fighting tears.

The mayor gave her a hug, put an arm around her, then continued. "Jenna Tenny embodies public spirit," he said. "She has taken personal tragedy and turned it to the public good. She exemplifies giving back, and serves as an inspiration to many in a position to use their fame to focus the public's attention on difficult problems. The South Shore is lucky indeed that Jenna has made this part of Massachusetts her home. Boston salutes you. And," he added, retrieving a check from his inside breast pocket, "Boston wants to help see your effort grow." He put the check in her hands, then gave her another hug and stepped back into the crowd.

"Oh, my goodness," Jenna said, turning to the microphone. "This is like winning a Grammy. Maybe better! Mayor Katzenbach, I can't thank you enough. We all can't thank you enough."

Then she turned her gaze on the crowd in general. "I can't tell you how important a night this is, for me personally, and for those who need our help. I want to share with you all that Shelly, our general manager, has told me she has already interviewed several individuals and mothers with children who will be admitted first thing tomorrow. The need couldn't be greater."

She went on to thank those, present or not, who had been instrumental in turning her dream into a reality. She ended on a sobering note. "If only there was no need, never had been a need, never will be a need for all that we've done and will be doing here."

WHEN SCOTT AND JENNA got home, she found herself too wound up to even think about sleep. The embers of a fire were still glowing, so Scott added two small logs and within minutes, they were curled up on the couch, watching sparks from the little blaze take wing and rise up the chimney.

They stayed up, talking about Christmas and their anniversary. Neither could wait to see Zach's reaction to his first Christmas tree. Most of the family were expected to arrive Christmas Eve; Linda, Joe and Kristin would be coming on the twenty-third.

Jenna lay her head back on Scott's chest. He reached down and pulled the throw on her lap up to her shoulders. As he wrapped his arms around her, she released a sigh of profound contentment. Scott ran his fingers through her hair, then looped one heavy strand around his hand and drew it out until he held the last inch between his thumb and forefinger. Using it like a paintbrush, he trailed it over the blanket and back up to Jenna's face. With a smile, she slid down until her head was in his lap and he "painted' her features. "Paint by numbers," he whispered.

"You're such a well-rounded artist," she murmured, then flinched as his makeshift brush tickled her nose. Reaching up to scratch the itch, she let her hand continue up to caress his cheek.

"Did I tell you how proud I was of you tonight?" Scott asked her, now applying an imaginary blush to her cheekbones. "The way you handled the mayor and all the rest of the muckety-mucks – it was like you'd been doing it all your life. *They* were impressed, that's for sure. But, heck, who isn't?"

Jenna puckered her lips and sent an air-kiss up to his. "Flattery gets some people nowhere. Flattery will get *you* everywhere, my love," she said suggestively.

"Me, flatter?" Scott protested. "Not in my repertoire."

Jenna smiled. "You're right," she conceded, then changed the subject. "So – how shall we celebrate our anniversary?"

"Ah, our anniversary. Anniversary numero uno. Don't you give our anniversary a moment's thought, babe. *That* I have completely under control."

She looked up at his eyes to see them twinkling merrily. "What? You've got a secret. Tell me!"

"Nope. You'll just have to wait and see..." he teased her, then brought his lips down to hers and kissed her deeply.

Chapter 11

LINDA, JOE AND KRISTIN arrived while Jenna was out doing last minute Christmas shopping. Ellen had offered to do it for her, but she had to do it herself, she'd told her with an I've-got-a-secret smile. Scott welcomed them and helped unload the rental car they'd come in.

"It's good Jenna's out," he said, letting them in on the anniversary surprise he'd planned. "I need your help on this. Jenna doesn't know it, but I've reserved St. Brigid's to renew our vows tomorrow evening. She's clueless. All she knows is that we're all going to Christmas Eve services, and then to Blue Skies for a family party."

Linda smiled. "Beautiful," she said. The simple word sounded like a benediction, delivered as it was in her low, sonorous voice.

"But I want her to wear her wedding dress, to make it complete. Needless to say, she's going to wonder why. Can any of you think of an excuse she might believe?"

"To capture as much of the memory as possible?" Linda volunteered.

"Perfect," Kristin agreed. "I'll help sell the idea."

"Sounds good to me. Let's just hope she falls for it," Scott said.

Joe stood there, shaking his head. "How am I supposed to compete with a romantic like you? You realize you've just raised the bar, my boy."

"And when did it become a competition?" Scott countered.

"When did what become a competition?" Jenna asked as she came breezing in, bestowing kisses as she came.

"Don't you worry your pretty little head," Scott said, planting a kiss on her nose. "In due course, my pretty. In due course."

OVER SUPPER THAT NIGHT, Scott and Jenna filled everyone in on their touring schedules. "But before we hit the road, we're taking a week alone, starting January first," Jenna said, relishing the thought.

"Right," Scott joined in. "A real rest-up. I've leased the house in Coral Gables again – the house we had last year for our honeymoon," he added, reaching over for Jenna's hand and squeezing it. "Time to bring our memories up to date." Zach, who was pulled up to the table in his highchair with the rest of them, started clapping.

"Sorry, Zach-o," Kristin addressed him from across the table, her tone serious. "You don't get to go. Can you say, 'alone'? Mommy and Daddy need to be *alone*." Zach's lower lip slid into a pout, as if he knew precisely what Kristin's words meant.

"Hey, there'll be plenty of trips for you, too, Z-Man," Scott told him, then held a baby spoonful of mashed potatoes in front of him. "Ready?" Zach giggled. "Open the garage door." Zach opened his mouth wide. Scott revved his engines and drove the spoonful right it. "Close the door now." Zach clamped his mouth shut, then when he was good and ready, chewed and swallowed. Scott revved his engine again. Zach threw his head back and his mouth flew open right on cue.

Jenna smiled.

BY EARLY AFTERNOON the next day everyone had arrived. As the day wore on, the men drifted out to the studio with Scott; Jenna and the rest of the women were in the kitchen, making early preparations for the following day's Christmas dinner.

It had been threatening snow all day. With December's early dusk came the first, huge snowflakes of what promised to be the white Christmas everyone was still holding out hopes for. Kristin grabbed Zach up from the floor where he was playing and ran him outside to see his first snowflakes firsthand. "Snow! Snow!" she said, over and over, as he grabbed for the magical apparitions that vanished every time he managed to catch one.

Jenna stood at the window peeling carrots and watching her sister and her son, hypnotized by the sight. Linda came up behind her. "It's time to be getting ready for the Christmas Eve service, isn't it?" she asked innocently.

"Right," Jenna said. "In a sec. I'm almost done with these."

Jenna finally bagged up the carrots, washed the knife and cutting board and turned to her mother. "Ready."

The two headed upstairs. Linda lagged behind on purpose, wanting Jenna to enter her own room before Linda would have proceeded down the hall to the guestroom she and Joe were sharing. She was exactly where she wanted to be, just at the door of the master bedroom, when Jenna cried, "What the…?"

She stepped into the room. Jenna was just unpinning a note fastened to the front of her wedding gown which hung in all its understated elegance on a closet door. The white silk shoes she'd worn with the gown a year ago this day sat on the floor beneath it.

"Mom?" Jenna said, looking up when she heard Linda behind her. "Do you know anything about this? Why is my wedding dress here?"

"What does the note say?" Linda said.

"It says, 'Let's relive the memory.' Scott didn't sign it, but no question it's his handwriting."

"What a beautiful idea," Linda said, playing her part in the charade. "What better way to recapture as much of the memory as possible."

"It'll feel like Halloween," Jenna protested. "Or being on stage."

"It's a beautiful, romantic gesture. Who cares what anyone thinks, sweetie?" Just then Scott walked in, wearing a tux. Jenna stood there, dumbfounded, staring back and forth between the two, who she suddenly realized were co-conspirators.

"This is a set-up!" she laughed once she'd caught on.

"It's all yours," Linda said to Scott as she exited

"Hey, baby. I had Kristin get it out for you. Surprised?"

"I couldn't be more surprised," Jenna said. "But why didn't you just say something to me about it?"

He went over to her and gave her a kiss. "Just get dressed. I'll be in the living room waiting for you."

When he left Linda came back in, dressed and ready to go, and offered to help Jenna get ready. Humming the Wedding March as she patiently buttoned Jenna into her gown, she stepped back to see the overall effect when she was finished. For once, she was entirely pleased.

"What is going on?" Jenna asked for the fifth time.

"Stop asking questions. Go to Scott."

Scott and Jeremy were standing in the living room when she came in. Scott couldn't believe how she looked. "I swear you're more beautiful than the day we got married," he said as he took her in his arms and kissed her gently. Then he held out her warmest coat for her. Jenna slipped into it, still shaking her head.

Scott, Jenna, Jeremy and Linda all left for the church in Jeremy's car, Linda in the front passenger seat, Scott and Jenna in the back. "Where are Carrie, and Joe?" Jenna asked.

"All will be revealed soon enough, my love," Scott said. When she continued to question him, he kissed her. The minute he stopped, she started to ask again. He kissed her again, this time for as long as he could before he needed to come up for air. She got the point and didn't say another word.

SCOTT TOOK JENNA in his arms and kissed her once again just as they turned the last corner and pulled into the parking lot of St. Brigid's, keeping her occupied so she wouldn't notice how empty it was.

Jeremy walked Linda into the church, while Scott took his time walking the short distance with Jenna. Just as they got inside the door, he told her to wait a moment, that he'd forgotten something in the car. As she stood waiting, Carrie and Kristin appeared, dressed as they had been for the wedding. That's when she finally noticed how quiet the church was and realized what was going on.

"Scott planned this, didn't he?" she gasped. "I don't believe it! I had no idea. How long have you all known?"

"He started planning it over a month ago, but he kept it to himself till Thanksgiving," Carrie told her.

"Leave it to Scott to come up with something new and different," Jenna laughed. "What wouldn't that man do?"

Carrie hugged her. "When it comes to you there's nothing he wouldn't do."

Jenna turned around to see her brother come out from the church office and walk over to join Carrie and Kristin. "Well, sis," Jim said, "Do I get to give you away again? Are you ready to remarry your husband?"

Jenna could only nod as tears started to flow. Suddenly music filled the tiny space and Kristin led off the procession, followed by Carrie. Jim offered Jenna a handkerchief. She mopped her eyes, tucked it back in his pocket, then took his arm and they too set off down the aisle.

Reverend Bob, Scott and Jeremy waited at the alter as Jenna came down the aisle. Locking eyes with Scott's, her tears came again. When they reached the altar, Jim passed her hand into Scott's. Scott turned so they faced the minister.

"When you first joined hands and hearts here last year, you could not know where life would take you, what life held in store," the Reverend began. "You promised to love, honor and cherish one another through all things. One brief year has brought you both blessings and trials. As you come before me today to reaffirm your wedding vows and as you reflect back over the year since you first spoke them as husband and wife, do you now reaffirm the vows you took last year?"

"I do," they both said in perfect unison.

"I LOVE YOU SO MUCH," Jenna said, wrapped in Scott's arms.

"And I love you so much, babe," he whispered into her ear. Everyone had headed over to Blue Skies except for the two of them. They had stayed behind for a few private, emotional moments.

"Scott, I can't thank you enough for making this anniversary so special," Jenna said. "We've come through heaven and hell this past year. We've given each other our fair share of worries."

"That's for damn sure," Scott agreed.

"But I have all the faith in the world that we'll be fine," Jenna said with conviction. "As long as we have all our love, honesty and trust in each other, there shouldn't be anything we can't get through." They embraced and kissed. Then and only then were they ready to go to Blue Skies.

TO ACCOMMODATE AN entire gathering of the Bradford/Tenny/Blacklace clan now required the larger of the two function rooms at Blue Skies. A few strategically positioned potted plants, a "Private Party" sign and José, a beefy dishwasher willing to play bouncer for the evening, gave them all the privacy they could want.

Scott barely sat still the entire evening, and Zach was on his hip most of the time as he swooped in and out of conversations, pulled an extra chair up to join in for an exchange of greater duration, or just danced his way around and around the room.

At one point José signaled him over. "Somebody gave me a note for you, boss," he said, handing Scott a piece of paper that had been folded and refolded numerous times until it was a small as it possibly could be. Scott dropped it in his pocket, deposited Zach with Ellen for a few minutes and retreated to the men's room to read it. For no good reason, the sight of it had sent a chill through him. His radar was up.

He had the men's room to himself. Withdrawing and unfolding the paper, a single piece of standard, letter-size printer paper, he couldn't shake his foreboding. When it was completely unfolded, he laid it on the counter and smoothed out the myriad creases. One entire side of the page was covered in a loose, feminine scroll.

> *12/24/02*
> *Hey, Scotty-boy,*
>   *Knew you'd be here celebrating your anniversary. Checked a few sources, here and in L.A. No question, you stayed home for the holidays. You look positively bitchin' in your tux, lover. Jenna in a wedding dress, though – isn't that a bit over the top?*
>   *Of course, it's <u>our</u> anniversary too, which I'm sure you haven't forgotten, right? That Christmas Eve party, when you were home on vacation from that school they sent you away to, when I was in 9th grade. You, me, Dave. Man, <u>I</u> haven't forgotten it, I can tell you that. And neither has Dave – we were comparing notes a while back. He thinks it's pretty shabby the way you treat me whenever we see each other when you're on tour. Come to think of it, so do I.*
>   *Anyway, just wanted to wish you – and <u>me and Dave</u> – a very happy anniversary, honey. You know I'll always have the hots for you. See ya soon – you can't stay home forever.*
>   *Mega love – Ashley*

Just then, Tim came banging through the door. "Hey, bro," he said. "Great party. Congratulations. Can't believe it's been a year already." Refolding the note, Scott looked up at him. "Are you okay, man?" Tim asked. "You look like you've seen a ghost."

Scott turned to look at himself at the mirror. All the color had drained out of his face. "Actually, I have, Brother Timothy," he said to Tim's reflection, then turned and walked out the door.

When the party was over and it came time to leave, Scott had Jeremy bring his car around to the back entrance. He and Jenna exited the building through the kitchen. He'd told her he just didn't want to go through the autograph thing.

THEY WERE THE LAST to get home. The immediate family who were staying overnight with them had reconvened the party in the study to keep the noise down; Jenna had given Kristin the job of making sure that happened. Scott, however, had other plans. Rather than head down the hall to the study, Scott tried to drawn Jenna towards the stairs.

"Let's just let them keep partying," he said, pulling her close to him. "I want to get to the rest of the anniversary celebration, upstairs," he whispered into her ear, following the thought with his tongue.

"Oh, man," she whispered back, "you sure are one hell of a salesman. We can't be rude, though. Just for a few minutes."

"Ten, max. Think they'll notice if I just suddenly throw you over my shoulder and walk out?"

"I'd hope they would," she laughed, put an arm around him and headed the two of them down the hall and into the study.

"Well, here's the happy couple," Joe's voice rang out above the rest.

"Happy anniversary," everyone cheered them yet again.

"Holy shit!" Scott exclaimed. "Jenna!" His eyes had been instantly drawn to a stunning photograph hanging over the desk that hadn't been there five hours earlier, a photo of Jenna and Zach taken at most a month earlier. The trees in the background were bare, the leaves on the ground no longer vibrant with the palette of October.

Jenna sat on the ground smiling straight into the lens, in jeans and a heavy, warm fisherman's knit sweater, leaning back against the trunk of a massive weeping willow. Zach half-stood in her lap, in a turtleneck, hooded Red Sox sweatshirt and a pair of tiny jeans cut to accommodate the contours of a diaper, completely engrossed in the curtain of slender branches that swept the ground all about him. The picture was taken on a windy day. Jenna's hair was wildly, marvelously disheveled.

Jenna already had her arm around Scott. He slid his arm around her, then moved his hand up and into her hair. In a matter of seconds, it looked just like her hair in the photo. Then he kissed her. Then they said goodnight.

LATE CHRISTMAS MORNING, after all the gifts had been opened and all the pictures had been taken, Jenna stood by the tree, smiling down on Scott playing with both Zach and Luca. Laurel came and stood by Jenna.

Jenna reached over and took her stepdaughter's hand in hers. "Beautiful sight, isn't it," she murmured.

"I'm so happy that Daddy can spend time with Luka," Laurel mused. "We never had this, him and me."

"I know, Jenna said quietly. "He's told me so many times how much he regrets not being there as you grew up. Both you and Missy, for different reasons. Missy was pretty young when her mom and your dad split up. All I can say is, I'm so glad that you all have finally been able to come together as a family."

Laurel squeezed Jenna's hand. Her eyes still fastened on her father and her son, she said, "and I'm glad you and Daddy have Zach. This is his chance to be there from beginning." Then she turned to Jenna. "You know, I don't think I've ever told you this, but I am so glad you've become a part of the family. I've never seen Daddy as happy as he's been since you came into his life. He loves you with every breath in his body."

"And I feel the same," Jenna said, humbled by the intensity of Laurel's words. "Thank you." The two embraced, pulled back, then hugged again.

The tender moment was cut short by a sudden cry. "Look! Hey, look!" Scott exclaimed. "Wouldja look at that!" Zach was standing, hanging onto the raised edge of the coffee table, looking every bit as surprised and pleased as his father. He swayed, clung desperately, fell back on his bottom, then set to work pulling himself back up the leg of the table until he was upright once again. Steadying himself carefully this time, he turned and looked around the room, as if he were the ruler of all he could see. "Merry Christmas, Zachary Matthew Scott Tenny," Scott beamed. "Step one to independence!"

Jenna found herself praying that Scott – and she, too – would be able to be there to witness and celebrate every milestone of Zach's life like this. The lives of rock 'n roll musicians didn't lend themselves naturally to 'being there.' This, she knew, would take planning, synchronicity, luck – and the occasional miracle.

THE FOLLOWING MORNING was total chaos. Linda and Joe would be staying on until the end of the week for some serious grandparent time with Zach before he and Ellen went down to Florida to join Scott and Jenna. Everyone else had either left the night before or were in the process of decamping now. Separate stacks of suitcases, duffels and shopping bags full of gifts represented family units headed for cars, trains and planes.

The hardest goodbye for Jenna and Scott was Zach. Their arms felt empty and their hearts ached as they headed off to the airport.

Conversation on the plane south constantly returned to one aspect or another of the dual problems of touring and parenting. Pulling out copies of their schedules, they laid them side by side and negotiated who'd have Zach when. "Let's face it," Scott finally said, frustrated by the complexity of coordinating, "the reality is that we both want him 24/7. The reality is, we can't. There are two of us and there's only one Zach."

"Okay," Jenna said. "Time to get pragmatic. What's best for Zach? Where are the greatest number of stationary days in our schedules." For all her talk of pragmatism, Jenna couldn't help occasional bouts of tears as she faced the reality of separations, but she made herself work through them. Passing a highlighter back and forth, they marked off the rare three-day and, rarer yet, four-day layovers that would have to pass for stability until their schedules merged in Los Angeles for the Grammies. Fortunately, their itineraries dove-tailed reasonably well. Painstakingly, a schedule for Zach and Ellen's comings and goings emerged.

"Georgie's gonna put a shitload of miles on the ZT Express," Scott said as he folded up their paperwork, stowed it away, then took Jenna's hand in his and brought it to his lips. "Okay. That's done. Now, my love, it's time for us."

By the time Ellen appeared at the door with Zach in her arms six days later, Jenna and Scott had put their time alone to every self-indulgent use possible, stretching their imaginations in a hot blooded collaboration designed to satisfy the corporeal five senses – and untold incorporeal senses as well.

TWO DELICIOUS DAYS shared with Zach, in the pool, on the beach, in the hammock and all over the huge beach house, were the icing on the cake. They also left Jenna and Scott feeling like they'd gotten to know every square inch of the sprawling Coral Gables rental from Zach's point of view on the floor. As time for his departure grew nearer, Scott found himself jealous of the extra three days Jenna would have there with Zach, before she too had to leave.

Torn as he said his final farewells before climbing into a limo that would take him to the airport, Scott held and hugged Zach, returned him to Ellen, held and hugged Jenna, then reached for Zach one more time. With Zach still in his arms, he gave Jenna another hug, then turned to step into the car.

"Whoa there, mister!" Jenna laughed. "I'll have the Feds on you before you leave the city limits. Hand him over." Scott gave up Zach with a crooked grin. Then he reached in his pocket and pulled out an envelope.

"Not to be opened till I've left the city limits," he said with a wink, kissing her as he tucked it into the waist of the sarong she'd tied over her little bikini bottom.

Jenna didn't wait. She and Zach waved him off, then as the limo pulled out of the driveway, she pulled the envelope back out and opened it. Inside was the deed to the house.

Chapter 12

❋

THE MORNING AFTER Scott's departure dawned spectacularly Florida-in-the-wintertime gorgeous. The sun had already woken Jenna, who was stretching luxuriously when the phone rang at five past seven. Her hand didn't have to stretch much further to pick up the receiver. "Mornin', babe," she purred; who else would be calling her at this ungodly hour.

"Personally, I'd prefer to keep the relationship businesslike, if you don't mind," came the unmistakable voice of her manager.

"Christ, Brian, don't you ever sleep? It's gotta be…" – she glanced at the clock – "…four in the morning out there."

"Can't make money in my sleep, Jenn," Brian said matter-of-factly, unperturbed. "Can't juggle the schedules of one full-time and four part-time bands like yours." Brian's pointed choice of the words "part-time" stung. "Nobody else's manager's sleeping. Nobody's else's – "

"Okay, okay. I get it," Jenna stopped him. "What can I do for you this bright and beautiful morning, oh good manager of mine? Doubt you called to chat."

"Chat – yeah, right," Brian responded scornfully. "I've got your schedule for after the Grammy's worked out – last piece of the puzzle materialized last night. I was able to slot you into the Dodge Theatre in Phoenix – great little mid-size house. Fifty-five hundred. So, I've got you El Paso, Austin, Albu-querque, Tucson, Phoenix, San Diego, ending up back in L.A., all in a tidy little leisure package, couple days here, three days there, slow-mo, just the way you want it, with the break to see your folks. Then it starts another swing further north. I'll fax the schedule over. I need your okay by noon. Bella's chompin' to start doing the publicity thing. You do have a fax down there, right?"

"Yeah, I've got a fax," Jenna sighed. She loved performing, but she hated it when the business end of it intruded into an otherwise unscheduled day. "You'll have your okay." She started to say goodbye, but as it always was with Brian, heard the dial tone before she had the word out of her mouth.

She hung the phone up, rolled back over and sighed. Bri thought he had the hardest part of the job. *She* had to make this schedule jibe with Scott's. She left a message for him at his hotel, asking the receptionist not to deliver it until ten. She knew he'd be sleeping in. Blacklace had played Columbia, South Carolina, last night; tonight they'd be in Little Rock.

JENNA, ELLEN AND ZACH had just settled into a routine when Jenna's band descended on the house, which easily absorbed four more musicians and two wives.

Jenna commandeered the media room for rehearsal space, then they all got down to the job of working up sets, combining the best of their older material with a good balance of fresh songs they'd been putting together long-distance, through the wonders of modern technology. Now they'd have the luxury of fine-tuning these new songs together, in real time. They'd be playing their first show in Orlando in five days.

Zach couldn't get enough of watching his mother rehearse. At one point, when Ellen had needed to go out to run a string of errands as quickly and efficiently as possible, Jenna had brought his playpen into the rehearsal room and put him in it, praying he'd cooperate. Normally never happy for more than a few minutes in a playpen, he'd cried when Ellen had come to retrieve him, more than an hour later. The next thing they knew, he was begging to get into it – as long as it was in the rehearsal room and his mother was singing. Percussive instruments became his favorite toys. "We're gonna have to sign him on," Tom, her drummer, joked. "He's got an agent, right?"

They'd started rehearsing at nine. Half an hour later, Scott's call came through as expected. Jenna told the band to take a break.

Running out to the kitchen and grabbing the schedule Brian had sent her from the fax machine, she had Scott pull his out so they could compare notes. Sitting down on a stool at the counter, she spread her schedule out in front of her and found a pen.

"Okay," she said. "I get three days in L.A. after the Grammies."

"I have two."

"Great. And we both have the two before – that's practically five full days we can all be together. Okay, then Brian's got me basically going up the west coast – some back-tracking, but –"

The conversation suddenly came to a halt as Jenna absorbed the implications of the dates that had been scheduled in March. "Oh, no," she moaned. "He's got us in Vegas for Zach's birthday."

"You can't do that. We agreed we'd be home, together, for Zach's birthday. In Boston."

"I know. I know," Jenna concurred. "Oh, crap. I know that was a particularly tight set of dates for him to swing. He's going to go ballistic."

"Whoa," Scott said, a noticeably sharp edge to his voice. "He works for you, not the other way around, remember."

"God, Scott. I know that."

"You don't sound like it."

"I'm not allowed to say what I'm thinking?"

"Zach comes first. Remember? That was our basic, number one assumption. You do remember that, right?" Scott said bluntly.

"Hey – I don't need a lecture on this," she responded in kind. "I know what we agreed to. I just know what Brian goes through. I know how hard he has to work to make things happen the way I want them. I ask a lot of him. This was my fault – I never told him we had to be home for March fifteenth. There's no reason he should have known that. Excuse me for feeling a little guilty here."

"He'll deal with it."

"Of course he'll deal with it," Jenna sighed in exasperation. "But, the reality is, Zach's only turning one. He wouldn't know if we celebrated his birthday a week later, or a week earlier, for that matter…"

"His birthday is March fifteenth," Scott said adamantly. "We celebrate it March fifteenth. This is how it starts. A little slippage here, a little fudging there. Either we say we're going to do something or we don't."

"What are you running for, Father of the Year?" Jenna found herself saying, then immediately regretted her words. "Hey, honey – I'm sorry," she quickly said into the sudden silence that she knew represented Scott growing angry. "That was uncalled for. I know you want to do what's best for Zach. And you're right – you're right." She didn't want to irritate him. Life was hard enough on the road. "I'll call him right now."

"You do that," Scott said tersely. Jenna bridled at his wording it as a direct order, but swallowed her annoyance, the bulk of which she knew she should rightfully be aiming at herself. She felt like a fool for not telling Brian; on a rational level, she knew she never reacted well when she felt this way. The last person she should be taking it out on was Scott.

ON THE OTHER HAND, the last person Jenna wanted to tell that she had to change plans was Brian. He never took such news well. As Jenna looked him up in her contact list on her cell, her thumb paused and hovered over the 'dial' button. She felt trapped between two huge, angry, male egos – and one tiny, fragile, almost-one-year-old, male ego as well. Both of the adult egos, of course, claimed to have nothing but her best interests at heart. Glancing out the window, the tropical paradise that was Florida in January seemed to recede into the far distance.

She set the phone back down on the kitchen counter, propped her elbows on it and dropped her face into her hands. Massaging her temples and breathing deeply, she worked to quell her frustration. She needed to speak with Brian from a place of calmness, tranquility. She felt anything but.

Finally, she put the call through. With any luck, he'd be out and she'd be able to leave a message with Angelique, she thought as the number started to ring.

No such luck. "Yeah." Brian always answered his own phone if he was in the office. "Speak ta me."

"Bri, I –" Jenna started.

"You'da faxed it back if everything was okay," Brian said. "So this spells trouble, right?" Jenna sighed.

JENNA'S "PAID VACATION TOUR" and the Blacklace "Yeah, Yeah, It's Us Again Tour" met up, as planned, in Atlanta to put on a trio of mega shows at the Philips Arena, for a total of sixty-six hundred screaming fans. Ashley West made all three shows. She probably wasn't the only one, but she was the only one Scott looked for and spotted every time – and studiously ignored. She didn't stand out in the crowd – her behavior differed in no way from the rest of the writhing mass of humanity that washed up at the foot of the stage every night. He always pinpointed her position before going to the opposite end of the stage to reach down and grab a few hand to shake. On the third night, he had to watch helpless as Jenna, working the other end of the stage, unknowingly reached down and gave Ashley's extended hand a warm squeeze.

After the concert that night Scott made love to Jenna, ferociously if quietly, all night long.

THE LAST MORNING of their sojourn together in Atlanta, Scott got up early and went to get Zach from Ellen for a little private family time before he'd be heading off with Blacklace – and his son. He had no illusions as to how hard this separation would be for Jenna.

Holding Zach close, he tiptoed back into the master bedroom, whispering a quiet 'shhhh' into Zach's ear. Zach smiled broadly, a willing co-conspirator. When they got to Jenna's side of the bed, Scott slid one hand under Zach's belly. Securing him with the other across the baby's back, he swooped him down, airplane style, until his baby lips hovered a fraction of an inch above one of Jenna's ears. "Give Mommy a kiss!" Scott told him. Zach knew exactly what was expected of him. Jenna came awake to the startling sound of a big, resounding 'mwwaaahhh' ricocheting through her inner ear. Her day started with laughter. It ended with tears, as she waved Scott, Zach, Ellen, Georgie and the ZT Express goodbye for the next ten days.

Scott had taken her back to bed and held her close, a few minutes before he had to leave. "Use this time," he'd murmured in her ear.

"I won't know what to do with myself!" Jenna wailed. He stroked her hair, then trailed a hand slowly down her backbone.

"Rest, babe. Indulge yourself. You've earned it. Kick back. Spend a day at a spa. Go shopping. Get hour-long massages every day – twice a day. God, babe, you need a break. Use the down time you have between shows well."

"At least I won't be wondering what you're doing with *your* down time," Jenna was able to joke through her tears, running her hands along either side of his face, tracing its contours, as if she was memorizing its angles and texture with her fingertips.

"No problem there," he smiled. "Zach will make the perfect chaperone. But that's why I say you should rest, babe. You'll need to be rested up. By the time I get back, man, am I gonna be one love-hungry motherfucker!"

"I swear," Jenna laughed. "Is that *all* you think about? Poor Scott. My poor, sex-starved husband."

"You *don't* want me comin' home sex-starved? You *want* me to take advantage of everything that's thrown at me, night in, night out?" he teased her.

"And I suppose you think you're the only one with temptations?" Jenna countered coyly.

"Oooo – the old 'two can play that game' game, eh?" Scott pursued the thought, wiggling his eyebrows suggestively, a wicked gleam in his eye.

Jenna found herself uncomfortable. This wasn't territory she wanted to explore, in jest or otherwise. She wasn't naïve. The temptations of the road were all too real.

When she checked into her hotel room in Memphis that afternoon, she found two dozen pink roses waiting for her. The card with the simply said, "Rest."

Chapter 13

JENNA HAD PLENTY OF touring experience under her belt when she'd first met Scott. She'd experienced her share of lonely hours. She'd stared at her share of strange patterns on unfamiliar ceilings. She knew those moments when the thought of another midnight supper with the band was more than she could stand.

She also knew the exhilaration of performing before thousands of fans. On this tour, for the first time in her career, she was also experiencing something she'd only heard about over the years, from Brian mainly: how easily a performer could lose her fan base. Fans could be fickle. Fans could be lured away by the next Jenna B. For the first time in years, she saw posters outside venues she was playing without Sold Out stickers plastered across them.

She responded to this new state of affairs the only way she knew how. She gave each and every audience one hundred and ten percent, both on stage and afterwards. She stayed to sign album covers, she did local radio shows. She wooed them back, one precious fan at a time. She worked. No politician ever worked harder for a vote.

More than once, she overheard – or was told point-blank – that Blacklace plus Jenna was simply a better buy.

SHE ALSO MOURNED. It had always been hard being separated from Scott. The combination of his and Zach's absence was wrenching. She called Ellen several times a day and had ten minute "chats" with her son that consisted of motherly discourse, lullabies and nonsense songs. Zach held up his end of these conversations with a happy stream of baby babble. In the middle of one call, Jenna swore she heard the word "Mama."

She called Carrie for moral support. "That's what best friends are for," Carrie had assured her after she apologized for taking up so much of her time on the phone. "You get lonely, kiddo, call. I'm not goin' anywhere." Carrie was so easy to talk to. She knew life on the road. Jenna didn't have to explain anything, nor did Carrie try to dismiss any of Jenna's very real frustrations and pain.

Her conversations with Scott were far more complicated. For one thing, she never knew which Scott she'd get – the happy, self-satisfied, convivial Scott or the frustrated, controlling, implacable Scott. She had no way of knowing if he'd just come fuming from a fight with a band or crew member, or if he'd just come in bouncing off the walls after catching a great, post-concert, late-night show. His moods, always volatile, seemed to be exacerbated by the simple fact that she too was touring.

He loved having Zach along – that part was going fine, he assured her every time they spoke. The two of them spent a great deal of the daylight hours on the road between shows in the front passenger seat of the ZT Express, Zach in Scott's lap ("Yes, *under* the seat belt," Scott had assured her), surveying the highway as it unrolled before them. Zach was now saying "Dada" quite regularly, Scott informed her. He also could say something remarkably like "Ellen," and had his own version of "Georgie" that cracked everyone up.

Every conversation invariably grew intimate as it drew to a close, and the tone of the intimacy also served as a barometer of Scott's moods. When he was in a good mood, his words were gentle and kind, thoughtful, introspective, tender. When he was glum, he became needy, recasting their separation as willful deprivation; the source of his blues he often identified as Jenna's need to go off on her own. When he was angry, his fantasizing could be blunt, egotistical, demanding, sometimes downright vulgar. Jenna treasured the good moods and tried to improve the glum ones. The angry ones she cut short, then tried to let go of them as quickly as possible. She knew from experience that Scott did.

THE TWO BANDS CAREENED all over the map. At the ten-day point, Jenna flew to St. Louis to spend a couple of days with Scott, perform one show with Blacklace, then have Georgie drive the bus down to Nashville so she could rejoin her band.

Jenna sighed inwardly as she hurried past the first of many Blacklace posters she saw hanging outside the twenty-two thousand seat Savvis Center. "Sold Out" had been stenciled across all three show dates in a garish day-glo red.

Feeling Scott pick her up, whirl her around, then set her back down and wrap his arms around her quickly put all thoughts of her own personal frustrations out of her mind, however. Jenna found the entire band on stage, working their way, one performer at a time, mike by mike, through sound checks with their road engineer. When she walked on, Scott signaled to a woman about Jenna's size who was sitting on a bench. "You can go," he called over to her. "Jenna's here now. Thanks for your help, dear." The woman waved, stepped off the stage, gathered her cleaning supplies and got on with her work. Playing body double for Jenna hadn't been half as exciting as she'd hoped it would be.

"Okay, now gimme kick, snare *and* hats," Ari Lakhdur's voice emerged from Tim's monitor. Relaxed behind his drum kit, Tim set up a beat with the bass drum, then added a quick series of rolls and flams on the snares, starting soft and building to a crescendo that ended with his sticks raining down on a pair of fifteen-inch hi-hat cymbals. Grabbing a brush, he tickled the cymbals back down to a whisper, then took the brush to the snares for a whole range of sounds from them.

Satisfied with Tim, Ari started working with Jeremy, Dan and Jeff and the spectrum of guitars each would play in the course of a show. Scott took Jenna off to one side. The two settled on a pair of tall stools, then wrapped their arms around each other again. Jenna set her lips to work depositing little kisses up and down his neck.

"Jeez, babe," Scott groaned. "I couldn't have missed you more. If we didn't have fifty witnesses, I'd rip the clothing right offa ya, right now."

"My sentiments exactly," Jenna chuckled for his ears only. "Damn sound checks. You're running late."

"I know. One of the trucks didn't get here till almost ten. It's amazing we're as ready as we are. Fuck – I just want to take you across the street to the hotel. I've got us a room over there, babe – privacy. I decided we deserve it. I just want – "

"Stop torturing yourself, hon. We're stuck here till Ari turns us loose."

IT TURNED OUT TO BE almost two hours before Ari finally did turn them loose. As soon as Jenna could be spared, Scott told her where she could find Zach and Ellen. The ZT Express was parked in a private lot in the midst of a battalion of eighteen-wheelers.

Jenna banged on the door of the forty-footer. "Ellen, it's me," she yelled. Immediately, Ellen appeared at the door, Zach in her arms.

"Mama!" Zach shouted at the top of his lungs.

ZACH WENT DOWN FOR a nap just about the same time Scott was finished up with sound and equipment checks. Grabbing Jenna by the hand, they dashed out the door, through the back hallways of the arena, out a side door and across the street to a side entrance of the hotel that opened right into the lobby's main elevator area.

As luck would have it, there was only one person waiting for the elevator. As bad luck would have it, the one person was an entertainment reporter for KDNL, the local ABC affiliate. They bartered a later, exclusive interview in exchange for an hour of immediate gratification.

Scott slipped a key card in the door of Room 2814. Sweeping Jenna up in his arms, he carried her in, then kicked the door shut behind him. She ran her hands up his chest, then locked them behind his head. His lips came down on hers while one hand found her top button, then the next one down, and the one below that. He'd completely unbuttoned her blouse before he laid her across the king-sized bed. Dropping down beside her, he drew open her blouse, then let his hand slip where it would until it found its way to her bra.

"Oh, you clever girl," he said. "A front closing bra. Just another reason I love you so," he said, snapping the tiny clip open with one hand as his lips followed his fingers.

The show that night came close to qualifying for an X rating.

JENNA AND SCOTT toned their act down the following day to take Zach to the zoo. Rather than deal with autograph hunters, they arranged a private tour; the fact that it was a weekday in February would help as well. An unseasonably mild warm front was moving through, in advance of what forecasters were describing as a succession of cold fronts, bringing with them a string of snowstorms predicted to completely shut down the Midwest. Traveling by plane, Jenna, Scott, their bands and entourage would be safely in L.A. before the first of the storms could hit. Georgie had pulled out early that morning.

Their guide, an elderly gentleman in khaki and a pith helmet who introduced himself as Greeley – "like the expedition," he'd told them with a wink – had been asked to put together a tour specially geared to Zach's age and attention span. Meeting them at the entrance at the appointed time, he took in his exotic charges like he was encountering a new species of wildlife. Clearly, his area of expertise wasn't rock 'n roll. Unflappable, however, he kept his bemusement to himself, ushered them briskly into a waiting golf cart, took the wheel and set off.

Greeley had chosen the most visually intriguing of the zoo's inventory of more than twenty thousand animals for Zach's kid-friendly safari. Their first stop was home to a small herd of zebras and half a dozen giraffes. Greeley took them right in. He even let Zach feed a young giraffe a handful of leaves. "Giraffe," Scott said, holding Zach up to make his offering of greens to the ten-foot youngster.

"'Raffe," Zach burbled. "'Raffe, Dada!"

"A sentence!" Scott marveled. "That's your first sentence, Zach!"

"Phrase," Greeley observed dryly, obviously a stickler for detail. "That would be a phrase. He would have to include a verb for it to qualify as a sentence."

"I stand corrected," Scott said good-humoredly.

"Now here's a question," Greeley said with a twinkle in his eye. "Is a zebra white with black stripes – or black with white stripes?"

"Oh, man, this has to be a trick question," Scott laughed, then really looked at the closest specimen. Jenna shook her head; she didn't have a clue.

"Okay – I'm gonna guess," Scott said. "They're black right around their hoofs, and their hoofs are black – I'm gonna say black with white stripes."

"Bingo!" Greeley grinned. "If you shaved them, you'd find their skin is black. A herd of zebras is known, by the way," – he reached over and covered Zach's ears – "as a harem." He pointed out which were the stallion, his mares, and their younger offspring.

Scott started nodding with obvious enthusiasm. "Don't go getting any big ideas," Jenna whispered in his ear. "You're my stud and *my stud only*, mister."

THEY ARRIVED IN L.A. late in the evening, two days ahead of the Grammys, and rang Linda and Joe's doorbell with a sleeping Zach in their arms. He woke up to find his grandparents making a fuss over him. When Linda started to give him to Ellen, however, Zach rebelled, reaching tearfully instead for his mother. Jenna took him, then she and Ellen brought him upstairs together. "Daddy and Mommy will be right here," Jenna told him as they walked past their guest room to the room beyond, which he and Ellen would be sharing.

Zach woke up to the sound of birds the next the morning. Scott woke up to the sound of banging at their door. Quickly jumping out of bed in the hopes that Jenna wouldn't waken, he opened the door to find Zach sitting on the floor, kicking at the door with his feet. Ellen emerged from their room at the same moment.

"I'm so sorry," she whispered to Scott, reaching down for Zach. "We went downstairs for an early breakfast. When we came back up, I set him on the floor to play and started straightening up. I turned my back for a second, and in a flash, he was out the door and on the prowl."

"That's okay," Scott whispered back as he scooped up his son and gave him a kiss. "I take it as a compliment." He smiled. "Jenna will too. Take some time off. Go for a walk. It's a beautiful morning."

Scott brought Zach into their room, stood him at the end of the bed and helped him stumble his way down to the other end where his mother lay sleeping. When he got close, he pulled his hands out of Scott's and lunged at Jenna, who woke to giggles and cries of "Mama, Mama!" Reaching up, she pulled him into her arms and under the sheets. Scott climbed back in on the other side of the bed, and Jenna sandwiched Zach between the two of them. Their feet intertwined, they played like children themselves with the tangible product of their love, this miracle baby who'd beat immeasurable odds to arrive at this moment in time.

After a half hour of fun and games, Zach yawned, setting both his parents yawning, as yawners will. Jenna started crooning a lullaby, Scott hummed in harmony, and before long, the three of them had fallen back asleep, Scott's arm around Zach, his hand buried in the tangles of Jenna's long hair.

KRISTIN ARRIVED IN TIME for a late morning brunch. As soon as the dishes were cleared, Scott headed for the piano. Joe and Linda announced that they were kidnapping Zach and shooed Jenna out of the house. "Spend some time with Kris," Linda suggested. "She misses you."

Jenna went and found her sister curled up in the corner of a couch in the living room, just finishing up a quick phone call. "Come for a walk?" Jenna suggested, reaching a hand out to her. Kristin took it, stretched her legs out and rose to her feet. "Let's hop in the car and run up to Mulholland Drive."

"Cool," Kristin grinned. "I'll get some shoes."

Twenty minutes later, they'd crossed over the San Diego Freeway and continued along Mulholland until they got to a section that was raw and undeveloped. Pulling over to park, they got out and crossed over to the other side of the road. The view: in one direction, the haze of Los Angeles; in another, Pacific Palisades, Topanga and the Pacific Ocean sparkling in the distance. Jenna let out a long sigh. "Oh, I do miss this sometimes." Then she turned to Kristin. "How are you, little sis?"

Kristin didn't answer immediately. Jenna gave her time. The two started walking along the shoulder of the highway. "I made the right decision, coming back," Kristin finally said. Her words, emerging slowly, were carefully chosen. "It cost me, but it *was* the right decision."

"Classes are going well?"

"Fabulously. I am learning so much," Kristin said, this with greater animation. "The people I get to work with, that's what it's all about. They're great. Even the difficult ones, the prima donnas – they can be royal pains, but you still learn from them."

"Are you seeing anyone?"

"God, that's such a lame expression, 'seeing anyone.' I'm seeing you right now. Call it what it is: dating, in love with, whatever."

"Okay, are you dating anyone? Shacked up with anyone?"

"That's more like it," Kristin grinned. "I've been dating some, but nobody special. I guess I'm still getting over Ryan." She drooped as she said it.

Jenna took her hand. "But you did make the right decision. You know what? Our father would have been proud of you. You'd have made him happy. He was disappointed that none of the rest of us followed in his footsteps. You got the acting gene."

Kristin smiled a crooked grin. "Ya think?"

"I know," Jenna said firmly. "It's written all over you."

"So what about you, big sis?" Kristin asked. "How's it going, touring and being a part-time wife and mom?"

"It's hell," Jenna said without hesitation. "It's hard, it requires the coordination skills of a flight controller, and it's painful beyond belief. Amazingly enough, I think I'm getting used to it. I guess you can get used to damn near anything, if you have to. I have to tour. My fans seem to have the shortest attention span on the planet."

"You're so good with Zach. You're a great mother."

"Thanks," Jenna smiled. "Mother love, mother hormones – powerful shit. You constantly find yourself doing things that made you cringe when you saw other mothers doing them – the babytalk, the coochicoo stuff. It comes outta your mouth like a second language you never knew you knew. Weird." They laughed, then Jenna went quiet. "It's hard to believe he'll be a year old next month," she said almost wistfully. "When you're with him daily, time crawls. The minute you're away, it flies."

"Any thoughts of having another?" Kristin asked. "I know you had a hard time having Zach…"

"Thoughts! It's an obsession. It's not clear if I can, though. We can't even try right now. It's driving me crazy. Scott doesn't want to see me go through any more, and I can't blame him – I know it's been hard on him too. For now, we're following doctor's orders. I just hope we can get pregnant again. I *so* hope it. But – if it doesn't work this time, that's it. We won't try again."

JOE AND LINDA threw an impromptu party for both bands and their assorted wives and girlfriends that night. The next day would be taken up with Grammys in one way or another, from daybreak till the earliest hours of the morning.

"Well, you sure look a lot happier than the last time I heard your voice," Carrie said as she and Jeremy arrived, giving Jenna a hug. "Man, I'm glad to see you happy."

"I don't think I could have gotten through that leg of my tour without you," Jenna groaned. "How am I gonna go back out there? No, I told myself I wasn't going to even think about it this week. I'm here. I'm happy. I'm tickled to death to be doing the show tomorrow night. Nervous, of course, but thank God I'm not filling in for Scott this year."

"Yeah, he sounds great," Carrie said. "What a scare that was. You'd never know now. Do you know what category you're presenting?"

"Won't till tomorrow."

"What are you wearing?" Carrie asked just as Kristin appeared at her elbow.

"Hey, yeah, what *are* you wearing, sis?" All three retired to Scott and Jenna's room, where they spent the next half hour playing dress up.

By the time they got back downstairs, it was immediately obvious to Jenna that Zach needed to get to bed. He'd been having a great time, what with all the attention he was getting from every quarter, but by now he was overtired and overexcited.

Jenna made her way over to break up a wrestling match between Jeremy and Zach. "Ding! End of round four! Time for bed, Z-Man," she said as she reached down for him. Zach let out a scream the likes of which she'd never heard, then burst into tears. "Oh, my, it's *definitely* bed time," she laughed, but her laughter was cut short when he swung and hit her, hard. "Whew. No way, Zach. No!" she said, catching his hand before he could strike at her a second blow.

Within seconds Scott was at her side. Grabbing Zach, he roughly pinned both the boy's hands so he couldn't repeat what he'd just done, making Zach cry just that much harder. "Zach!" he yelled. "What the – " He stopped himself before he could anything more. A moment later, Ellen appeared, equally alarmed.

"I've never seen him hit *any*one," she said, taking him from Scott. "Zach, what are you thinking? *No hitting*," she said sternly, then in a softer but still firm voice said, "It's time for bed now. Say goodnight to Mommy and Daddy." Still crying, clinging to his anger, Zach refused silently, turning away.

"Take him on up. We'll be up in a few minutes," Jenna said, shaken.

By the time they entered his room, Zach's sobs had subsided to residual sniffles. When Jenna leaned down to kiss him, his hands only went up to touch her, to reassure himself that she still loved him, that she was still there for him – not try to hit her again.

Scott looked down at him in his crib, then finally reached down and touched his son's hand. Zach wrapped his little hand around his father's and held on. The two stayed that way, eyes locked, until Jenna gently suggested they ought to let him get to sleep.

IT WAS LATE WHEN Jenna, Scott, Linda and Joe closed the door on the last of their guests. "Phew!" said Linda, turning to survey the chaos left in the evening's wake.

"I'll help, Mom," Jenna volunteered. "In fact, you go to bed. We'll clean up."

"To the contrary, sweetie," Linda declared, shaking her head. "You're the ones who need your beauty sleep. You have a big day tomorrow. Go."

Scott was unusually quiet as they got undressed for bed. "I can't believe what Zach did to you tonight," he finally said, climbing into bed. "I sure hope he doesn't make it a habit."

"It was just being the center of all that attention. He kinda reminded me of you, actually," she said lightly, "throwing a tantrum when he couldn't get his way."

"Oh, and you never get angry when you can't have your way?" Scott bristled. "So, every bad thing he does is gonna get blamed on me now?"

"Whoa! I was only kidding." But she found that what he'd said, or rather, the way he'd said it, irritated her. She got into bed and uncharacteristically turned her back on him. Scott moved close to her and put his arm around her.

"I'm just tired, and upset at what he did," he whispered into her ear by way of apology. "I know he's too young to understand, but it still bothered me when he hit you like that." Jenna rolled over and faced him.

"There's more to this then you're saying. Do you want to talk about it?"

"I just overreacted." His kiss said "subject closed." Jenna didn't believe him for a minute.

SCOTT WOKE EARLY and lay there watching Jenna sleep. Reaching over, he kissed her on the forehead and she woke. "I'm sorry. I didn't mean for you to wake up," he said quietly. Jenna pulled him to her and kissed him, gently, then with growing passion. Then she let her lips wander where they would. Before long they were making love, for Jenna fueled by distress and concern, for Scott by guilt and remorse.

Afterwards, Scott brushed the hair out of her eyes and looked at her. "You were right last night," he said. "There was more to it. Did you happen to notice how quiet my father was when all that stuff was going on with Zach?"

"No. Why?"

"What Zach was doing was a rerun of things I did as a kid – only they ended up with my father hitting me. I don't remember anything from when I was Zach's age, of course, but Annie's told me it had started by the time I was that old. I was always getting in trouble for something. No slap on the hand, either – he'd really let me have it. When I saw my father looking at me last night, I knew he was wondering how I'd handle Zach. That's why I lashed out at you. I shouldn't have. I'm really sorry, honey."

"I knew there was more to it," Jenna admitted. "I'm just sorry you kept it in for so long. You've told me that your father was hard on you, but you never said anything about him hitting you. Is that why your relationship was strained for so long?"

"It was a factor. Don't get me wrong – we've resolved all of our differences. I just couldn't help thinking about it when all that was going on last night."

Jenna lay quietly in his arms, thinking about her father-in-law.

"You were pretty quick to compare Zach to me last night," Scott interrupted her musings. "And you're probably comparing me to my father now."

"No, but yes, I was thinking about him."

"It's gonna hit you at some point," Scott said, with suddenly growing agitation. "You're gonna start wondering if I won't turn out to be the same kind of father as he was. Hell, *I* wonder. I just hope the hell I won't be."

Jenna was shocked to see him so upset. "For someone who has all this faith, you certainly seem to have forgotten about it. Well, I haven't forgotten mine. I guess it'll have to be enough for both of us till you get yours back. I know you'd never hurt Zach, or me, for that matter."

Scott sat up, crossed his arms and hunched in on himself. "Oh really? Maybe you shouldn't be so sure. You don't know what was going through my mind. I do. I almost did hit him," he said almost in a whisper. "But I caught my father looking at me. It stopped me cold. Jenna, I was terrified." He covered his eyes and shook his head slowly.

"Oh God, Scott, I'm so sorry you went though all that alone." She pulled him back down to her and wrapped him in her arms. "Honey, you've stood by and helped me deal with everything I've had to go through, and it's only made our love stronger. Let me ask you this: why do you think I'd react any differently?" She took his face in her hands and kissed him. "There's more, isn't there," she whispered, a statement, not a question.

Scott hesitated, then forced himself to speak. "You may never feel the same way about me again once I tell you, but yes, there is. When I married Missy's mom, we really loved each other. Things were going real good for Blacklace. I thought I was the best thing that had ever happened to rock 'n roll. I was knee deep in women, drugs, booze.

"I was still into all that when I married Nancy. When I wasn't high, things were great between us. There wasn't much we wouldn't do for each other. But when I was high, I got violent with her. Half the time I didn't know what the hell I was doing and there's a lot I don't remember, but she had pictures to prove it. That's the rest of the story, Jenna. And it scares the shit outta me. It's a proven fact: I am capable of violence." He started to get out of bed, but Jenna grabbed his arm.

"Don't you dare get out of this bed and walk away from me," she said, pulling him back. "Answer one question: why do you think this happened now? You've had plenty of reasons to hit me since we've been together, but you haven't. And why Zach and not me? Or have you had these feelings about me too?" Scott shook his head, but held a hand up. He couldn't speak.

"Scott, think about it," Jenna continued. "It really isn't that hard to figure out. In a way, it's almost like what happened to me. An event triggered a memory. That memory caused a reaction. Zach hit me and it triggered the memory of your father hitting you. You may have approached Zach with the thought of hitting him, but on the way you came face to face with reality – your father. You realized what you almost did and at that moment you hated yourself for it." Scott started to speak, but she put a finger to his lips. She had more she knew needed saying.

"Honey, you didn't hurt your son and I don't believe you ever will. I think what happened scared you to death and that alone will keep you from hurting him. As for the other part of the picture, the past – what you did to Nancy – is the past. You're not that wild, off-the-wall drug maniac you were back then." Jenna stopped and looked deep into his eyes. "I love you. I know that you would never hurt your son, or me. You are no longer that person. I have no reason to fear you."

Looking into her eyes, Scott was awed by the love he still saw there. "I thank the Lord for you and your love, Jenn. I was so afraid you wouldn't be able to feel the same about me, about us, if I told you everything."

Jenna just shook her head. "You *really* need to get that faith back, babe," she said once again.

Chapter 14

✵

JENNA AND SCOTT heard Zach's voice and a banging on the door. "Mama! Dada!" Scott got up and headed for the door, then hesitated and turned to Jenna. "Maybe you should let him in?" he said tentatively.

"Don't you dare do this, Scott Tenny," Jenna fumed. "You open that door and let your son in." Still hesitating, he heard Zach call out for him again. Squaring his shoulders, he turned and opened the door. Zach was kneeling on the floor, his fists raised to pummel the door yet again. Immediately he reached for his father. Scott scooped him up, hugged him tightly and brought him over to Jenna. She smiled at Scott, then reached her lips up to give Zach a good-morning kiss.

"I have to get a shower. You stay with Daddy, little Z," she told Zach. Climbing out of bed, she winked at Scott, then trailed a hand across his shoulders as she brushed past him. Looking back, she blew kisses to both her men.

ZACH WAS SITTING IN Scott's lap mooching a second breakfast off his father's plate when Linda and Joe came into the kitchen. "Hi, Mom," Jenna said, coming over to give Linda a kiss. "Joe," she nodded as he sat himself beside Scott and Zach. Adella looked up, pulled out two mugs, quickly filled them and brought them over. "Cup of tea for the lady," she murmured in her heavy-accented English, setting one in front of Linda, "and cup of Joe for the Joe." Joe grinned as she put his down with a flourish.

Linda smiled at Scott and Zach. "You're so good with him," she said to Scott.

"He gives Zach a lot of love and tries spend as much time with him as he can," Jenna said, then went on to detail their schedules. "I'll have him for the next two weeks, while Scott's in Canada, but then I'll be leaving him with Scott for the following two weeks. It's hard on him and us too, so we try to spend as much time with him together as we can when we're all home. All I can say is, thank God for Ellen. She's the stability in his life, the common factor."

Joe put a hand on Scott's shoulder. "He's a good father," he said nodding, looking up at Jenna.

Jenna watched Scott's expression as she answered her father-in-law. "He sure is. And I'm sure he got it all from you." Linda's brow furrowed at the touch of sarcasm in Jenna's voice. Scott, in the middle of explaining the day's plans to Zach, missed it.

JENNA AND SCOTT headed over to the Staples Center. Crowds had already filled the bleachers out front, craning for a glance of their favorite performers.

Hurrying inside, they arrived in the midst of a noisy gathering of famous names, their agents and managers, not to mention producers and technical people lined up ten deep, needing answers to production questions. Somehow, in the midst of the chaos, Jenna was able to spot her manager. Waving to him, she caught his eye. Brian raised his arm and pointed to a central meeting point.

"Wanna know what category you're presenting?" Brian shouted over the din when they finally got together. She nodded. "They had you doing fem pop vocal group, but Madonna's sick and they had to do some last-minute swicheroos. I heard some changes were going to be made so I put you up for this one. I guess the brass listened." He handed her the line-up. She was down to present the Grammy for best song.

"Are you kidding?" Jenna said and laughed. "Talk about potential role reversal!" Scott had placed the Grammy for Female Pop Vocal in her hands the year before. "Oh, thank you, Bri – this is great. Don't tell anybody. If Blacklace wins, I want it to be a total surprise." She gave him a hug and an air kiss, the industry standard.

"My lips are sealed," Brian promised. "I knew you'd love it."

IT WAS A GORGEOUS February L.A. afternoon. Limo drivers pulled into and away from the Staples Center like pilots practicing touch and go landings. Jenna and Scott emerged from one limo hand in hand as the rest of Blacklace poured out of the next, and Jenna's band and entourage from a third, to the screams of fans in the stands. Jenna waved to them graciously; with over twenty years of Grammy red carpets to his credit, Scott was a bit more offhand. They took their time, however, working the bleacher crowd as they readied themselves to run the gauntlet of reporters.

They were just about to turn and make their way in when one fan screamed, "Yo, Scotty!" at the top of her lungs. Scott didn't have to look; he knew exactly who it was. Jenna's eyes were drawn to a woman atop the bleachers, jumping up and down, long red hair flying wildly, a hand-lettered sign held high over her head that read, "Scott Tenny's My Man!" She looked like a street walker on her way to work. Jenna was about to turn when she suddenly knew she'd seen that face before. Gripping Scott's hand harder, she whispered out of the corner of her mouth, "I know that woman. From some-where. That face. That hair. That *body*. That – she's the woman in that news clipping, isn't she?!"

"Who knows, babe. She could be anybody. Not our problem. Let's get inside," Scott said through clenched teeth and a mechanical smile. Turning to her, he only had eyes for the beautiful woman beside him, Jenna in gauzy emerald silk, in what could barely be defined as a gown – yes, it had a neckline, and a hemline that trailed the ground, but it had very little in between. Sliding a hand around her waist, its velvet skin bared to his touch, he ushered her away from the crowds.

Scott was as much of an eye-catcher as she was, in a '60s-vintage purple satin Nehru-collared tux, the jacket unbuttoned and flying, no shirt but a rainbow of scarves also flying, the pants belled and impossibly low-cut.

Several presentations had been made before Sheryl Crow stepped to the podium and announced the second of the five Best Song nominees. A few measures of bass guitar and drum intro reverberated through the darkened theatre before a light came up on Blacklace, Scott and Jenna side by side, holding hands. Whispering into their mikes, they took turns singing a haunting version of "Something So Small," the rock lullaby Scott had penned for Zach. If the applause that followed was any indicator, they had another winner on their hands.

Back in their seats, Scott whispered to Jenna, "So when do you do your thing?"

"Patience! Soon enough," she teased. He'd been trying to get her catego-ry out of her all afternoon. Shortly, she gave him a kiss, excused herself and slipped backstage, long in advance of her place in the presentation line-up, just to maintain the mystery.

Finally, the loudspeaker announced, "Ladies and gentleman, to present this year's award for Song of the Year, here is the multi-Grammy award winning Jenna B. Tenny."

Scott had already experienced his first surge of adrenalin simply realizing it was time for the Best Song award. That Jenna was the presenter produced a quick second surge. Watching her cross the stage to the podium bathed him in what could only be described as lustful pride; judging from the comments around him, the audience was equally mesmerized by the sight of her. In motion, her gown looked like a confusion of gossamer green sea grass.

"A little bit of role reversal from last year," Jenna murmured huskily into the mike before settling into the prepared text on the teleprompter. Those with a good memory chuckled. Clutching the envelope, she made her way through the perfunctory remarks and list of nominees, until she could finally say, "…and the 2003 Grammy for Rock Song of the Year goes to … yes, it *is* a total role reversal! Blacklace, Scott Tenny, songwriter, for 'Something So Small.' Yes!"

Within moments, Scott was at the podium, the rest of Blacklace ringed behind him, his arm around Jenna, holding his Grammy up to the crowd. "Without this woman," he told the audience, "this song *sure* never coulda been written. My beautiful and loving wife, Jenna – thank you!"

THE NIGHT WAS YOUNG when the awards were over, giving them plenty of time to do a little party hopping before returning home for the family festivities. Missy had flown out that morning from New York for the big night; Laurel couldn't make it because of a four-day modeling gig in the Bahamas. "Excuses, excuses," Scott had kidded her when she told him he'd have to get through the awards without her. Otherwise, most of the family was there and already celebrating when Jenna, Scott and many of their entourage pulled in a little after ten. They walked in the door to an outburst of cheering and clapping.

Linda came over and gave Jenna a heartfelt embrace. "You both make me so proud, sweetie," she said, then turned to include Scott in the hug as well.

Joe joined them, his congratulations starting with Scott. Jenna watched the interaction between the two closely; after Scott's revelations the night before, she couldn't help but look at Joe in a new light. When he reached over to welcome her with a hug and a hearty "you must be very happy for your husband," she flinched reflexively, unintentionally. Realizing what she'd done, she attempted to make it look like a shiver.

"I'm thrilled for Scott," she said, "but I'm also freezing to death in this scrap of a dress," she added laughing. "I'll be right back." Scott followed her out of the room and cornered her in the hall.

"What just happened, when my father hugged you?" he asked her point blank.

"Quite honestly – I don't know," Jenna said, meeting his questioning eyes. "Was he aware of it? Did he say something to you?"

"No, but I wouldn't be surprised if he noticed. Was it about what I told you? Honey, if it is, then you gotta listen to me: let it go, for the family's sake. It's ancient history. It's over and done with." Scott took Jenna in his arms and just held her.

"I'm sorry, hon," she said after a moment pulling herself together. "Look, let's talk about this later. This is your night. God, the *last* thing I want to do is spoil it for you. Let's get back to in there. Don't worry, I'll get on top of it." And she did.

What with all the guests, and the post-party comparing of notes and sharing of moments with Joe and Linda that lasted another half hour, it was close to two before Jenna and Scott were able to retire, exhausted, to their room. Closing the door behind him, Scott said a quiet, "Come here." Jenna looked up and had to laugh at the theatrically lascivious way he was licking his lips. "I've been dying to figure out how the hell that gown works all night."

THEY DIDN'T WAKE till noon. Scott opened his eyes first and just lay there, hypnotized, watching Jenna's breasts rise and fall in the narcosis of sleep.

Finally, he couldn't stand it any longer. He kissed her forehead and she opened her eyes.

"Fuck!" she mumbled. "You woke me up from a really good dream..."

"Oh, yeah?"

"Oh, yeah. This tall, handsome guy was making love to me and…"

Scott stopped her with a kiss, then asked her, "Could he kiss like that?"

Jenna thought about it. "Better, actually," she finally said, having fun with this. "You see, he just loved to French kiss, kisses that went on forever and ever..."

Scott grinned cockily. "You mean like this?" They were more than a minute coming up for air.

"Okay, maybe I have to take that back," Jenna said in mock seriousness. "Maybe he wasn't as good a kisser after all. But…"

Scott bent down and gently licked at a nipple, then looked up. "What else did he do with his tongue?" he asked her, then ran it over her breast and back to the nipple he'd started with.

"Well…he dipped it in a hot cup of coffee and then did that," she riffed, "and then into a glass of ice water…"

Her teasing was cut short by a knock at the door.

"Sorry to bother," came Adella's voice, "but Meester Jeremy is here to see Scott. He says very important."

Scott groaned.

They got up and threw some clothes on, then went down to the kitchen. Jeremy was sitting at the counter, nursing a cup of coffee. "What's so important you had to come all the way out here?" Scott asked.

"If you had your fucking cell phone on, I wouldn'a had to, asshole. Everyone's been trying to reach you, 'brother.'" He spat the last word out like it tasted rancid. "*Rolling* Stone wants an interview, like in" – he looked up at the kitchen clock – "twenty minutes. The number here's fuckin' unlisted."

Jenna poured a cup for herself, and one for Scott in a travel mug and handed it to him without a word, then retreated to the other end of the kitchen. She'd never seen Jeremy so angry. She prayed it wouldn't turn into a knock-down-drag-out.

"I didn't have my phone on because we just woke up. What the hell's eating you, anyway?" Scott barked.

"Well, soooooorry," Jeremy muttered. "Didn't get any fuckin' sleep last night, then I get woken the fuck up to track you down. Why the hell didn't you give somebody the number here and save all of us a lot of trouble? Just go get dressed and let's get this over with, so some of us can get back to bed."

"Hold your horses. I'll go like I am. If he don't like it, that's his problem," Scott said. He grabbed a jacket, took all the time in the world kissing Jenna goodbye, then headed for the door Jeremy was holding open for him with ever-growing impatience.

Georgie gave Scott a little salute as he jumped in the open door of their waiting limo, while Jeremy went around, opened and climbed in the other, then took a seat as far from Scott as it was physically possible. Scott threw his head back and eyed the ceiling; Jeremy turned and stared out the window. The silence lasted for several blocks.

Finally Scott couldn't contain himself any longer. "You don't come into our folks' house using language like that."

"I wouldn't have had to if your fuckin' phone was on. Don't try blaming this on me. You've got your head so far up your own spectacular front man's ass, you don' give a shit if you inconvenience anybody else. What the hell *were* you thinkin', anyway? You were probably too busy fucking Jenna to think about anything else."

That was all Scott needed to hear. "What the hell was there to think about? How was I supposed to know we'd have an interview on short notice? For your information – as if it was any of *your* damned business – I wasn't fucking my wife. We *were* goofing around. Maybe you should try it sometime. It might help your disposition."

That thought was still stewing when Georgie pulled up in front of Jerry's Famous, the Ventura Boulevard deli to the stars. Dan, Jeff, Tim and Ryan were already there. "They sure look happy," Jeff said out of the corner of his mouth to Tim. "Hope this doesn't turn into a fiasco."

"You guys better not start on me. I've already had enough from him," Scott said derisively, hooking a thumb in Jeremy's direction. "Let's just get this over with." They went in and were given a table for eight, Scott and Jeremy again sitting as far from each other as they could. The free-lancer writing for *Rolling Stone* was the last to arrive.

Everything stayed civil for the next hour. When all was said and done and the reporter had left, they all got ready to go; some would be heading east immediately, some the following day. "What are your plans?" Dan asked Scott.

He looked over at Jeremy. "I m going to go fuck my wife," he said sarcastically.

Jeremy dropped his head, then looked up. "Hey, look, I'm sorry I said that, all right? I told you before, I was tired and aggravated. Can we just move on?"

Scott stared at him, then sighed. "Yeah. Sure," he finally said. As everyone got up, he sat quietly for a moment, doing some soul searching, then he too stood up, went over and gave Jeremy a lighthearted punch on the arm and a grin.

"Aw'right," said Dan. "Another hatchet buried. Somebody should follow you two sons'a bitches around with a metal detector. They could sell 'em on eBay."

THE NEXT MONTH went by in another well-orchestrated blur. Jenna took Zach along for the first two week, and her concerts went smoothly. Ticket sales had picked up after the Grammys. She and Scott met up for another "Zach swap," as they were now calling it, in Philadelphia, and did two shows there together.

Scott immediately spotted Ashley West at the first of the Philly shows, in spite of the fact that she was now sporting platinum locks instead of red. Jenna had decided to only sing three songs with them, so he quickly improvised some off-the-cuff choreography to keep her preoccupied – and away from the end of the stage that Ashley seemed to have staked out as her private domain.

The next morning, he sat down with Pete Lund, his head of security, laid the whole problem out for him, and the two came up with a plan. A half dozen plain-clothes guards, mostly female, would 'contain' Ashley from now on, whenever she was observed anywhere near the stage. No one would approach her, but neither would they let her out of their sight or let her get too close.

The new security detail was in place in time for the second show. Scott was hard pressed to pick out guards from fans, but it was clear than Ashley was tightly hemmed in at the far end of stage left; any thought of moving to another spot in front of the stage was hopeless. Scott's job was to wrangle Jenna without *her* being aware of it; she was free to roam stage right and never noticed a thing. At Scott's request, Lund met with Jenna's security people, outfitted them with photos and put them on alert as well, just in case Ashley should decide to follow her around for a change.

Before she knew it, Jenna was kissing Scott and Zach goodbye and heading back off on her own tour. She was getting used to what she had starting thinking of as her 'non-mom' time, learning to value it the way second-time-around camp moms all do.

But March twelfth couldn't come soon enough, the day she'd get back home. Linda, Joe and Kristin would arrive the following day in preparation for Zach's birthday party. Laurel, Luka and Missy would come up by train two days later, the morning of his birthday, an occasion Jenna at one time couldn't even allow herself to hope for. But his one-year checkup had gone brilliantly. His pediatrician couldn't have been more pleased. Not only had he made his one-year milestone birthday at all – he'd hit all the one-year developmental milestones as well. He'd more than made up for time lost in the womb.

SCOTT CAME UP BEHIND Jenna and wrapped his arms around her. "What must kids think of first birthday parties?" he asked her, marveling at the chaos. Luka was trying to teach Zach the birthday ropes, helping him rip wildly into the pile of presents that grew with the arrival of each new guest.

"Wow! A pirate ship!" Luka exclaimed as he pulled a brightly-colored plastic brigantine from a big box. "Say 'pirate,' Zach! Oh, and a pirate hat," he added, pulling a three-cornered hat out and putting it on, "and a sword! Wow, wicked cool!" He pulled of the hat and piled the pirate booty in Zach's lap, then moved on to tackled another present.

"I should be getting the cake ready," Jenna said, laughing.

"Wait a bit longer," Scott said.

"It's getting late."

"Just wait a little longer."

"Why?"

"Just be patient." Jenna had just turned to look at him quizzically when the doorbell rang. Scott released her to go and answer it. "I'm fixing the cake," she said the minute she was free.

"Go right ahead. I'll get the door." He knew who it was; he'd sent their late arrival an invitation via Kristin a month earlier. Pulling the door open, he found Lt. Matthew Caine, detective, L.A.P.D., standing on the step, looking around, surveying the acres of lawn that overlooked the Massachusetts shoreline and the Atlantic beyond.

Scott opened the door. "Hey, Scott," Caine said with a friendly grin.

"Hey, Matthew!" he said enthusiastically, clapping him on the back. "Come on in. I'm so glad you could make it. Let's go lay the surprise on Jenna."

"Who's at the door," Jenna shouted out from the kitchen.

"Come see for yourself," Scott called back to her from the living room. A towel in hand, she came in, tossed it aside and threw her arms around the late arrival.

"Oh my God, Matthew Caine! It's *so* good to see you. What brings you here?"

"If it wasn't for this guy, there might never have been a birthday," Scott said emphatically. "He deserved to be here and celebrate with us."

"Absolutely," Jenna said. "Let me get your coat. You look like you're dressed for the Arctic," she teased him as Matthew shrugged out of an oversized blue parka.

"Blood gets thin in L.A."

"It's practically spring here," she laughed. "Zach, come here," she called. "Come give your Uncle Matthew a big hug and a high-five!" Zach pulled himself upright and toddled over to his mother, looked up at the stranger towering above him, hid behind Jenna's legs, then peeked out again. Matthew squatted down on Zach's level.

"Hey, little guy," Caine said. "I couldn't be gladder to see you." Looking up at Jenna, he said, "He's sure your kid – he looks like you, Jenna. He's got your eyes." He winked at her. Reaching in his back pocket, he pulled out a tiny present. By now an old hand, Zach didn't need Luka's guidance anymore. He grabbed at the gift and tore into the wrapping. Inside was an L.A.P.D. badge.

"Wow! A policeman's badge!" Luka said, running up to see.

"Yeah, and it's gen-u-ine. The real deal," Caine assured the three-year-old.

His eyes wide, Luka grabbed it out of Zach's hands. Zach immediately set up a howl. Laurel, who saw what was happening, quickly interceded, taking it from Luka and returning it to Zach, who's wailing stopped as abruptly as it had started.

Jenna smiled her appreciation, then turned to the rest of the group. "Time for cake," she announced. Everyone scrambled back to the table and took their places. Ellen swung Zach up in his highchair while Scott carried in an extra chair for Caine. Luka climbed up and shoved Joe aside to sit next to Zach.

"Oh, so it's musical chairs, is it," Joe laughed and went and took Luka's seat.

Jenna emerged from the kitchen carrying the cake with it's single candle and set it in front of Zach. Everyone sang a verse of "Happy Birthday," then Scott jumped in with a second verse he'd thrown together the night before.

> *Happy birthday to you,*
> *You little kangaroo*
> *You may have had a hard start*
> *But you've really sailed through.*

Everyone cheered as Zach looked at the cake and candle, his eyes wide with awe. "Blow the candle out," Scott told him, but Zach didn't comprehend the concept.

Luka kneeled up in his chair, tapped Zach to get his attention, then did a perfect pantomime of what was required. "Blow," he told Zach, then showed him again, blowing just enough air to make the flame dance but not go out.

Zach formed his mouth in a perfect O and stared at the candle.

"No, *blow*," Luka repeated patiently, and demonstrated by blowing a healthy gust into Zach's face. "Blow!"

Zach got it and blew back in Luka's face. "No, at the *candle*," Luka sputtered in frustration. Reaching up, he turned Zach's head to face the candle and held it there. "*Blow!*" he yelled. Zach blew. When everyone exploded into applause, he clapped too.

"JENNA," CAINE SAID when the party was over and the wrapping paper had all been cleaned up, "could I speak with you for a minute? In private?"

Jenna looked at him quizzically, then over at Scott, who'd appeared at Caine's elbow. "I'd like Scott to join us," he added. "He knows about it already."

"About what?" Jenna asked, when they'd closed the door of the study.

"Why don't you sit down," Caine suggested.

"I'll stand." Her eyes kept darting back and forth between his and Scott's.

"This has something to do with Billy Malone, doesn't it?" Jenna said, anxiety in her voice belying an outward appearance of calm.

"Yes," Caine said, nodding reluctantly. Look, I don't want to spoil the party, but the District Attorney's making his case against him. You'll be called to testify," he told her. His words hung in the air until he went on. "The charges include attempted kidnapping in your case and attempted murder in Scott's case. And they've added conspiracy to murder," Caine said. "You're a material witness. As is Scott."

"A conspiracy charge?" Jenna asked, confused. "He acted alone."

"It's the best way to get him put away for a *very* long time, and we've got plenty of evidence, believe me. I'll do everything in my power to make this as painless as possible for you," Caine said sympathetically, "but your testimony is crucial."

"Dear God," was all Jenna could say. Her eyes glazed over as she relived the horror of the day after Zach's birth.

"I'll be going," Caine said. "I'll get my coat and say goodnight to your folks. You two need to be alone. I'll let you know if I learn anything new. Hey, I'm sorry." He gave Jenna a hug goodbye. "Zach's one great kid – with two great parents," he added.

Jenna tried to thank him, but her heart wasn't in it. Whether it would put him away for years or life, the thought of facing Billy Malone in court was devastating.

"I'll have to tell the story of the abuse and the rape again," she moaned once they were alone. Scott tried to put his arms around her, but she turned away from him and wrapped her own arms around herself. "I thought it was over," she said, her voice going flat with pain. "Now I'll have to have to relive the whole damn thing, all over again. And it'll be back in the papers and all over the news, all over again. We were able to keep some of it under wraps when it happened, but we won't be able to this time. We won't have any peace. Family and friends'll be hounded too. The press'll just eat this up."

Picking up a glass on the table next to her, she held it for a moment, staring at it but not seeing it. Then, suppressing the scream that so wanted to escape her, she suddenly flung it at the fireplace. Shards of glass flew in all directions.

"What the fuck…?" Scott cried.

Jenna just stood there frozen. "I'll tell you the fuck," she finally said. "Will this never end? Will it ever be truly *over*?" She dropped to her knees on the floor, bent over double and rocked, sobbing, her arms still tightly holding herself.

Scott was quickly at her side. Pulling her close, he held her, murmuring in her ear, until her sobs and quiet moans finally ceased.

A few minutes later there was a soft tap at the door. "It's me," came Linda's voice. "Can I come in?"

Jenna rolled her eyes, then nodded grimly and Scott said, "Sure."

One look at the broken glass all over the place and Jenna on the floor in Scott's arms told her at least half the story. "Matthew didn't come all the way out here just to celebrate Zach's birthday, did he," she said. It wasn't a question.

Jenna looked up. "Nothing much gets by you, does it, Mom," she said ruefully.

"Except for the sound of smashing glasses, I guess," she said, taking in the extent of the damage. "You're going to have to come back out to L.A. to testify, right?"

"Yeah," Jenna sighed.

"It had to happen sooner or later," Linda said pragmatically. "I knew this day was coming." She sat down on the floor alongside them, and gently pushed Jenna's hair out of her eyes. Jenna found her mother's usually annoying habit oddly comforting.

"If the DA calls me as a witness, I won't have any choice but to testify," Jenna said, shaking her head. "Scott either. It's going to be a media frenzy."

"It'll be months, babe. You don't have to worry about it till then," Scott told her.

"Scott's right," Linda said. "There's plenty of time to plan, and we'll deal with it when we have to. We may be able to keep a lot of it from the press. We all have connections. This is when you use them."

Jenna looked at her mother, shocked. "Mom – you're amazing," was all she could say.

Chapter 15

✺

JENNA WENT TO HER next appointment with her OB/GYN without Scott. She didn't even tell him that she'd scheduled it. If the news was bad, she knew she would need time by herself to face and absorb that reality. A lot of time.

Jenna lay on the examining table, keeping up a nervous chatter while mentally holding her breath. Her hands, which would have normally laid at her sides, were held prayerfully, unconsciously to her chin, as Julia examined her, taking breaks from time to time to consult the results of several tests and scans that she had ordered in anticipation of the appointment.

Before long, the two women sat once again facing each other over Julia's desk. Jenna's eyes, roaming the small room as she waited for Julia to finish making some notations, suddenly came to a picture of herself and Zach, tacked to a bulletin board. She took heart from the fact that Zach, *so* tiny when the picture had been taken, was so big today.

Finally, Julia set down her pen and nodded. Jenna didn't dare form the question that was trying to force its way out, but finally had to: "Can I? Can I get pregnant again?"

"You can try," Julia said, simply.

"Can I carry a baby to term this time?"

"That's doubtful. But I think you can carry a second child longer than you carried Zach. I'm pretty confident that you could make it to thirty-two weeks."

Jenna felt her spirit soar like a balloon, up and over the city of Boston.

JENNA PULLED UP THE drive, left her car in the midst of the rest of the band's cars parked helter-skelter all over the place, jumped out and ran for the studio.

Scott and Jeremy were at the piano, Scott standing over the keyboard trying out melodies as Jeremy sat on the bench trying out lyrics and scribbling in a notebook. Dan, Jeff and Ryan were working as a trio in front of the drum kit, developing harmonies for a song that seemed to have nothing in common with what Scott and Jeremy were busy composing; Tim was riffing to their beat. How anyone could think in the resulting muddle was anybody's guess. It was as if Pablo Picasso and Jackson Pollock had gotten together to sing "Row, Row, Row Your Boat."

Jenna burst through the door, saw Scott and crossed the room to him in a few long strides. Draping herself around him, she planted a huge kiss on the back of his neck, unselfconsciously wrapping a leg around his as she did. "Hey, baby," she said loud enough for everyone to hear.

"Boy, somebody's horny today," Tim said for Dan, Jeff and Ryan's ears only.

"What in the –" Scott sputtered. "Can't you see we're busy here?"

Jenna, whose mind was on reproduction, plain and simple, was hardly prepared for such a cold response. Backing off, stunned, she turned and fled before her frustration could begin to find words to throw back at him.

Jeremy was equally stunned. "What the fuck's wrong with you?" he said to Scott, staring after her as she slammed the door. "How the hell can you treat a woman as fine as Jenna like that?" Scott was already wondering the same thing.

"Be right back," he said, heading quickly for the door. "Or maybe not," he said over his shoulder.

"Take your time," Jeremy said, "asshole."

BY THE TIME HE got to the house, Jenna was already up in the bedroom, where she'd thrown herself across the bed, sobbing uncontrollably. Scott could hear her clearly from the bottom of the stairs. Taking them two at a time, he came into the room warily, then laid down next to her, wrapped himself around her and pulled her close. Slowly, he began massaging and kissing her pain and her fury away, murmuring apologies for what he'd inadvertently caused in her ear.

"Babe, the last thing I ever want to do is make you crazy like this," he whispered. "I love you. I – I know there's no excuse for it, but we'd been working on those damn lyrics for hours. We'd just had another one of our World War III arguments about it, and I was just plain fuckin' pissed off. I didn't mean to take it out on you. I know it's no excuse but it's the best I can do right now." Jenna turned to him and wrapped her arms around him, still crying. Unbuttoning the shirt he was wearing, he grabbed a corner and used it to wipe away her tears.

When she could speak at all, Jenna managed to get out an apology of her own. "I'm sorry, too," she said, choking on her words. "I know what it means to be stuck on a song. It's the pits. Its –" But then she burst into fresh tears.

"What is it? It's more than that, isn't it."

"Yeah, well, sort of. I mean, I've got some great news."

"It sure doesn't look like great news."

Jenna cracked half a grin through her tears. "It is. It really is, babe." Blowing her nose on his shirt, she sat up, wrapped her arms around her knees, rocked herself a couple of times, savoring her great news, and then smiled at him like the sun breaking through thunderheads.

"Dr. Williams says I can get pregnant again!" she announced jubilantly. "We can get right to work on it, and Hawaii will be *the* perfect place!" Their birthday present to Zach, and their break-from-touring present to themselves as well, had been a ten-day trip to the island of Kauai. They were leaving the next day.

"Oh, God, and I go overreacting about being interrupted," Scott groaned. "And in front of everyone. Jesus, can you forgive me? No – wait," he said, jumping up from the bed and reaching for her hand. "Come with me."

Mystified, she took his hand. "Where are we going?"

"You'll see." He led her right back to the studio. When they came through the door, he put his arm around her. "Everybody, listen up. I've got something to say." Everyone turned to see what the commotion was now.

"Look, I want to do this here because it includes all of you too," Scott said with a sincerity they hardly recognized. "I was a real jerk and I really hurt Jenna. I want to apologize to her, and to all of you, for how I acted just now."

"You don't need to apologize to us," Dan said quietly. "It's really up to Jenna to forgive you. She's the one you hurt."

Jenna looked at the floor before she raised her eyes up to Scott's. She realized Dan was right – her reaction wasn't just because of her heightened emotions relating to a possible second pregnancy. She *had* been hurt, hurt and humiliated and embarrassed. "If you ever embarrass me like that in front of *any*one again, I swear it'll be the last time," she found herself saying. "I didn't do or say anything to deserve being treated like that, and I won't take it again." She meant every single word.

Scott took her into his arms and just held her close for a bit, then pulled back and looked at her. "You're right," he said, nodding in agreement and, "you didn't do a thing to deserve what I said. I am so sorry. Will you forgive me?"

She looked long and hard, then sagged as much with relief as with a philosophical acknowledgment of who Scott was. "Don't I always?" she smiled wryly. He kissed her, then hugged her tight, eyes shut to the winks, eye-rolling and headshaking of his band.

"Then all is right with the world again," he said cheerfully.

SCOTT TOOK JENNA out to dinner that night, to Alfama, a little Portuguese bistro that had just opened a couple of towns over. It turned out to be everything anyone could hope for: the tapas were delicious, the restaurant itself atmospheric, dark and quiet. An elderly guitarist sat on a stool in the corner of the room, quietly picking his way through a seemingly bottomless repertoire of flamenco tunes.

Over a pair of tequila-free strawberry margaritas, Jenna brought up the subject that hadn't left her mind all afternoon. "I want to get pregnant. Right away," she stated unequivocally. "I'll stop touring the minute I do. I'll still want to perform with you guys whenever –"

"Whoa up a minute," Scott interrupted. "I know you've got this all planned, and look, I don't want to rain on your parade or anything. I know you're excited at the prospect, but we have to approach this sensibly."

Jenna's eyes narrowed and her hands went to her hips. This wasn't what she wanted to hear. "You whoa up, mister," she countered. "I'm as sensible as the next guy."

"I know that," he said, taking one of her hands from the hip it was angrily planted on and bringing it to his lips. "I just want to give this the absolute best shot we can. I take it, Julia's still saying this will be our only shot?" Jenna nodded reluctantly. "Then we have to be as careful as we possibly can be, babe. We have to plan this like a couple of generals planning D-Day."

Jenna sighed, then nodded. "You're right. We do."

"We're home for now, but Blacklace is gonna be on tour again later this summer," Scott said. "I don't want to take a chance on being away if something happens to you. I sat down with a calendar before we came out for dinner. Let's wait till summer to try. That way we'll be back long before you're due – plenty of time in case you're early again. Hell, waiting can only make things even better, medically speaking. I don't want you to go getting mad at me again – I'm just thinking it would be better if we give it a little more time. Do you hear what I'm saying?"

"I hear you. I – I'm…" Jenna wasn't entirely sure *what* she was or thought. The only thing she knew for sure was that the idea of waiting was exceptionally upsetting. "This day – well, it just hasn't turned out the way I'd hoped," she said, chagrinned. "I understand how you feel," she said slowly, working her thoughts through as she spoke, "and I know it does make sense to wait a little longer. You've got to promise me, though, that you won't come up with more reasons to put it off later on. If there are, I want to hear them now."

"None whatsoever," he said without hesitation.

THE FOLLOWING MORNING Jenna, Scott, Zach and Ellen were buckled in for an eight o'clock flight headed west. They would spend a total of twelve and a half hours in the sky, with an hour and a half layover in L.A., where Linda and Joe would be waiting to buy them lunch. They would spend the night in Honolulu, then catch a forty-minute island hopper the next morning to Kauai.

The ten days in Kauai were magical. The place they'd leased was spectacular, sited on a cliff overlooking Hanalei Bay. Practically every room of the huge plantation-style house sported a lanai of its own. It was hard to tell where the inside left off and the outside began.

It had been years since Jenna had last been in Hawaii; she'd forgotten its ability to astonish. She'd grown up under swaying palm trees, but that was where any comparison to California ended. The lush rain forest vegetation was natural, fed by the constant arrival of showers and storms riding the passing trade winds. No sprinkler system and army of gardeners could ever sustain the riot of plant life that called these islands home.

Even at the tender age of one, Zach seemed to be entirely awake to the beauty and amazing sights around him. Jenna and Scott had debated the value of such a trip for him, but were quickly glad they'd ignored their nagging doubts. Ellen had never been to Hawaii either, so Zach was introduced to it all through not only his parents' experienced eyes, but her newcomer's eyes as well.

Ten mornings started in the predawn light watching every sunrise; ten evenings ended watching the sunset, from a different viewpoint on the island. They visited volcanoes, they rode down into Waimea Canyon on horseback, and hiked through the Kalihiwai Valley to swim in the pools of Kalihiwai Falls. Zach covered miles on Scott, Jenna and Ellen's backs.

Scott and Jenna found time for themselves as well. On their last day there, Scott took her to a hidden beach he'd found out about and had been saving for a farewell swim. They had to hike a strenuous trail to reach it, but it was all he'd hoped for: a horseshoe of pure white sand at the foot of lava cliffs festooned with ferns and tangles of vines – and not another soul in sight.

Scott unloaded a backpack of scuba gear and towels. The two of them stripped out of their hiking attire down to their bathing suits, looked at each other – and kept on stripping.

BY THE MIDDLE OF May, Blacklace was putting plans together for another tour. It had been a productive period; the ten days in Hawaii, away from keyboards and studios, seemed to open up fresh veins of creativity for both Scott and Jenna.

Jenna's output was dark and brooding, however. The songs she found herself writing were about loss and fear and dissatisfaction and waiting, endless waiting – a perfect reflection of the holding pattern her life seemed to be in. She knew on a conscious level that her mood was affected by the fact that she would soon have to testify against Billy Malone. She didn't realize it was also very much affected by frustration over the fact that she could perhaps be pregnant by now, if Scott hadn't insisted they wait.

GOING THROUGH THE MAIL one day, Jenna found the envelope she knew was coming but dreaded opening regardless, a request from the District Attorney of Los Angeles County to discuss testifying at a Grand Jury hearing. Her eyes flew through the contents, hunting for a date. The appointment was scheduled for the week's end. She knew Scott was scheduled for a series of meetings and interviews in New York having to do with the release of their next CD and wouldn't be able to go with her, and was almost glad he couldn't. Somehow, facing this aspect of her problems on her own felt right. She was calm as she made reservations for Thursday, returning Monday and left a message with Adella telling her mother her plans. Then she called Matthew Caine.

Caine was halfway out the door of his office when the phone on his desk rang. He turned back with a grimace. "Caine," he said. Fifteen hundred miles away, Jenna could hear the grimace just fine.

"Matthew, it's Jenna Tenny."

"Jenna." The grimace vanished, replaced by a softer, more concerned tone. "You got the notice from the DA."

"Yeah. I'm coming out the day before."

"Scott gonna be with you?"

"No, he can't be. He's gotta be in New York."

"Want company?" Jenna thought about it for a moment before answering. "Yeah. Yeah, I would."

JENNA HAD ARRANGED for her mother to pick her and Zach up at LAX. As she scanned women's faces among the throng waiting just past the security checkpoint, her eye finally noticed Joe waving both hands over his head, one finger of each hand pointed skyward, like an aircraft handler signaling broadly to an incoming plane on the deck of a carrier. As soon as he caught her eye, the pointing fingers joined thumbs in a pair of A-OKs.

Making her way towards him, Jenna had to consciously suppress the image that suddenly filled her mind, of this benign, smiling, grey-haired man as a young man, administering a beating to his son. That was then, this is now, she reminded herself. If Scott can handle it, so can I. That's how things were in those days; that's probably how he'd been raised himself. My mother loves him; he's her husband. Again she was glad Scott wasn't along on this trip. She needed to face and overcome this obstacle for herself.

She'd run through this litany of thoughts several times before she reached him; for once, she was glad for the crowds. It had given her time to be able to give him a genuinely warm hug hello.

THE NEXT MORNING, Jenna waited for Caine at the front entrance of the huge building that housed the L.A. County Criminal Court and DA's offices. Traffic had been surprisingly light; she'd arrived early. Gazing up at the façade of hundreds upon hundreds of identical, deeply recessed windows, twenty stories worth she guessed, she pictured a deputy district attorney crouched behind each and every one of them. Then she started imagining a reporter or photographer, a TV anchor, entertainment show host or gossip columnist lurking behind every window. Then the face of Billy Malone filled, first in her mind's eye, then repeated like wallpaper, like a poster in every window above her.

"Mornin', Jenna." Matthew Caine's gruff greeting barged in on her morbid thoughts like a party crasher at a funeral. Turning, she was surprised to find the normally plain-clothed detective in uniform today. "Gotta dress for the big wigs," he said, accurately reading her mind. He cut quite a handsome figure in a uniform, Jenna found herself thinking. His take on non-descript plain clothes tended to the seedy. She smiled for a moment, then sighed.

"So what am I getting myself into today?" she asked him tersely. "Might as well know."

"Don't be nervous," he told her. "You'll be meeting with a deputy DA, Al Mandanowitz. He's okay. He'll brief you on the process and talk to you a bit about your testimony. Come on. Something tells me the sooner this is over, the happier you'll be."

"Got that right," Jenna agreed.

Taking her by the elbow, Caine escorted her into and through a vast lobby directly to a bank of elevators along the back wall. As the doors slid open on the next available car, they stepped in and he punched a button. Jenna watched the digital floor numbers rapidly rearranging themselves from one to two to three and on, until they finally came to a stop at seventeen.

Exiting the elevator, Caine bypassed the information desk and immediately headed for one of a number of sets of doors. "Mandanowitz, Jane," he called over his shoulder to the woman manning the desk.

"I'll let him know you're on your way, hon," the woman called after him. Suddenly Jenna was really glad she'd accepted Matthew's offer to accompany her.

Al Mandanowitz was a short pit bull of a man, with piercing black eyes, a compact bundle of energy one could easily picture in a court room prosecuting Mafia hit men. When they walked into his miniscule office, just as wide as one of those windows Jenna had been studying ten minutes earlier, he half rose and nodded in greeting, then gestured to Jenna to take a seat in front of his desk. The edge of the desktop was a wood-grained formica; no surface was visible through the jumble of files and paperwork that covered it.

Caine pushed a few folders aside and propped himself on the corner of a narrow credenza. "Mornin', Al," he said affably. "Jenna Tenny," he added with a nod in her direction. Mandanowitz scratched his ear, sizing her up.

"Pleased to meetcha," he said finally, then opened a file that sat ready for him on top of the heap. "Thanks for coming."

As if I had a choice, Jenna thought to herself.

"Okay," he said, leaning over the desk as he rifled through the file. "I don't know how much Matthew's explained to you, but because of the high-profile nature of the case, this landed in our division – Major Crimes. You being" – he looked up at her – "who you are and all." He pulled out a single sheet of paper, then settled back in his chair.

"Okay. We've had bureau investigators all over this thing. This Malone guy's so connected, it's almost impressive, for a kid so young. Turns out he wasn't just dealing drugs and stalking you. He was working for some mid-level crime figures, Scars and Puggy Sisman mostly."

"Oh, Christ, not them," Caine said, rolling his eyes. "The two most downwardly mobile guys Shakes and Carmen Milano ever made."

"His thing about Jenna was strictly personal. The rest just seals the deal. We can put him away for decades."

"Where is he?" Caine asked.

"Somewhere good and safe, don't worry," Mandanowitz assured him. "Of course he's trying his damnedest to sing, but he don't know nothing we don't know, which is frustratin' the hell out of him. Regardless, we consider him a target, so we've got him tucked away where the mob can't get at him."

"And my role?" Jenna finally asked, bracing herself for the answer.

"You're our – if you'll pardon the expression – star witness," Mandanowitz quipped. "You and your husband. But let me explain how this all works." Jenna nodded.

"Okay. The Grand Jury's job is decide if we have enough evidence to indict. It's a completely closed-door hearing. The Grand Jury, me, and a court reporter, that's it. Jurors are informed that it's a misdemeanor for any of them to disclose information as to what goes on in the court room. The entire proceedings remain secret if there's no indictment – except in this case, there's no way there won't be an indictment."

"So – no secret," Jenna said dismally.

"No, no secret. Once it goes to court, it all goes public."

"And the timetable?" Caine asked.

"We'll convene the Grand Jury late June. Once we have an indictment – and that should only take a few days, this'll get green-lighted, big time. The DA's up for re-election and he's pumping everyone to fast-track anything they've got that's high-profile. It'll go to trial by August first, latest."

JENNA DECIDED TO CUT the weekend short. She suddenly needed to be back home in Boston with Scott. She realized how hard it would be to make a weekend's worth of small talk with her mother and Joe, even to just have lunch with Kristin, with all this hanging over her.

Trying to couch the news as diplomatically as she could, it only took a sentence before Linda cut in. "Go. You belong at home with your husband," she said as if it had been her idea from the start. "You pack. I'll change your tickets."

For once, Jenna really appreciated her mother's innate ability to read minds and take charge. Seven hours later, she and a very sleepy Zach were in Scott's arms. By midnight, she was in bed. By two she'd woken up shaking from a terrifying nightmare – a nightmare every bit as vivid as any she'd had three years earlier, when the cold, appalling fact that she'd been abused and raped as a child – by Billy Malone's father – had first come to light.

Chapter 16

THE FOURTH OF JULY, 2003, came before they knew it. Everyone's schedule seemed to be jammed into overdrive, the best reason, Scott announced, that everyone walk away from their daily lives and get up to the lake for as much of the holiday weekend as they could possibly fit in.

Blacklace was finishing up a new album, and was in the final stages of preparing for another tour which would begin in October. Jenna had been back and forth to L.A., first to testify before the Grand Jury and then almost immediately for the trial itself. Mandanowitz had been right: the case had been fast-tracked by the DA for political reasons. While stuck on the West Coast, she used any down time she had to rehearse and record with her own band. During down time on the East Coast, she rehearsed and recorded with Blacklace. Whichever coast she found herself on, every night's sleep was punctuated by nightmares, replaying every aspect of the nightmares Billy Malone and his father has visited on her in real life. She was back to seeing her therapist, Melanie Campbell, weekly. If she couldn't be in Cambridge for an appointment, she closed a door and spent an hour on the telephone with Melanie. The week of her testimony in Malone's trial, she spoke with her therapist daily. Somehow, she got through it.

Scott had a running list of things to worry about longer than most people's daily "To Do" lists. His primary worry was Jenna and her nightmares.

Next, or maybe even top of Scott's list, if he really wanted to be honest with himself, was Jenna's desire to get pregnant again. He'd said 'summer.' Summer was here. He'd braced as Memorial Day loomed, but she hadn't said anything as that holiday came and went. He resumed his mental pacing as the Fourth of July weekend at the lake came on like a freight train.

By the night they got there, when Jenna did bring it up, he was ready. He cautiously suggested they wait until the Billy Malone case was put to rest, and she had agreed. Scott hoped she hadn't noticed his sigh of relief. But pregnancy, he knew, still simmered on the back burner. He had to admit the thought of Jenna going through another pregnancy flat-out terrified him.

Then there was the fact that he and the band had been arguing endlessly about the album they were working on. Albums always meant arguments, but nothing on the scale of these. On top of that, he'd been going head to head with Eddie Strang, his manager, and Big Bob O'Halligan, his tour manager, on a number of topics. Big Bob had been pushing Europe. "It's too long since you guys have been over there," he kept saying, and every time he brought it up, Scott kept reminding him that he had a toddler to consider. Big Bob acted like he didn't know what a toddler was.

Strang had a bee in his bonnet on the issue of accessibility – he wanted to see Scott more "touchy-feely" with his fans, as he put it with a leer.

"Sorry. I can't be more 'touchy-feely' anymore,'" Scott had countered. "It's not safe." Strang wasn't satisfied with his answer, but Scott refused to elaborate. They didn't need to know about that other major worry on his list: Ashley West. He'd started having his own nightmares – about her.

Another double-starred item on the list: Scott's throat had been bothering him, which made him exceptionally nervous. The last time he'd had throat problems, it had cost him a shitload of fear, a trip to the O.R. and several months of recuperation. After three anxious days, he gave in and took himself to the doctor. A thorough examination and some throat cultures revealed that it was nothing more than a virus, which cleared up completely after a round of antibiotics.

JENNA'S CELL RANG at eleven o'clock sharp on September twenty-ninth. "Matthew?" she answered, having glanced at the caller ID.

"Guilty. Kidnapping and assault with intent to commit murder. Concurrent terms of twenty-five to fifty years. He'll appeal."

"Let him," Jenna said. Suddenly, she felt as free as a zephyr breeze.

THE SMELL OF ROAST duck found its way to every corner of the house as Jenna set a cut crystal bowl of pink peonies on a small glass table by the window in the study. Adding a pair of crystal candlesticks with matching pink candles, she stood back to judge the effect. Too frou-frou, she decided. She swapped out the crystal candlesticks for a pair of wrought iron ones, changed the candles to black as well, and substituted a black porcelain bowl for the peonies. A pair of black linen placemats and matching napkins, their sleekest modern flatware, and a tall silver salt-and-pepper grinder finished her preparations. What she had in mind was a romantic dinner for two. Ellen had her orders: no interruptions. Jenna had plans for this evening.

Scott didn't get home till after seven; he'd spent most of the day in Boston on business, and then had gotten held up in traffic on the way home. He wasn't in the best of moods, Jenna noted. But, then again, what better motive for a romantic dinner, she reasoned – it'll get him out of his funk.

The two went up to the nursery to give Zach a goodnight kiss, then Jenna ushered Scott to the study. The candles were lit; a plate with greens and a pair of scallops in a Thai sauce were already waiting. "Uh, what's the occasion?" Scott asked blandly, though his radar was up and sirens wailing.

Jenna gave him a kiss. "No occasion. I just wanted to have a nice, quiet, romantic dinner with my husband."

They'd finished crème caramels and a pair of espressos when Jenna finally brought up the subject of pregnancy.

Scott looked up sharply. "I knew you had something planned besides just dinner," he said, his tone accusatory.

"I –"

"Why did you lie to me?" he asked, turning on her. "Just a nice quiet dinner? That's a crock, and you know it. You had an agenda right from the start. Whaddya think I am, anyway, fuckin' stupid or what?"

"Scott – what is wrong with you tonight?" Jenna asked, confounded, completely at a loss for words.

"You're what's wrong with me," Scott said without a moment's thought. "This was to seduce me, because you wanted to try for a pregnancy tonight. Right?"

"You know I want to get pregnant again," Jenna sputtered, but Scott wasn't listening now. He couldn't have stopped himself if he'd tried.

"That was your plan all along," he continued on blindly. "Woman, you just plain lied to me."

"You make it sound like I'm some kind of evil schemer," Jenna protested. "I did want to have a nice romantic dinner with you – we haven't done anything like this, just for the two of us, for ages. And so I didn't bring up the subject of pregnancy till afterwards – what's so wrong with that?"

Scott pushed back from the table and sat there, just shaking his head at her. "What's wrong with that?" he said, mimicking her. "You wanna know what's wrong with that, babe? What's wrong is that you planned it all along. Before dinner, after dinner – who gives a shit."

"Scott – stop this and *talk* to me," Jenna implored.

"Not now, no way," Scott said and stood up. "Subject closed. Drop it." He started out of the room.

Jenna was floored. Jumping to her feet, she followed close on his heels. "If you don't want to discuss it now, then when do you think you *will* be ready?" she demanded to know. "Tomorrow? Next week, next month? Never?"

"I said, drop it," Scott repeated, reached for the door handle, opened the door and started out into the hall.

Grabbing him by his shirt, Jenna pulled him back into the room. "You just wait one cotton-pickin' minute here, Scott. You talk about *me* having an agenda – what about you? You've avoided the subject every chance you could. Excuse after excuse, right from the day Julia told me we could try, all along, haven't you? Don't you dare question my intentions, when you've you had your own, a hell of a lot longer then me. As a matter of fact – why don't you just go straight to hell!"

Jenna stormed out of the room and headed for the staircase. Scott followed after her, slamming the door behind him. By the time he caught up with her, she had one hand on the handrail and a foot on the first step. "We're not finished with this yet," he said vehemently. "It wasn't me who said I didn't ever want to talk about it – you did. Don't you go telling *me* to go to hell. All you had to do was tell me why you really planned the dinner."

"Oh, sure," Jenna retorted. "I can just imagine your reaction to *that*."

"I know what my reaction would have been: I would have told you that I didn't want to discuss it tonight. I happen to have had a real fucked-up day and I'm not in a very good mood, in case you hadn't noticed. Damn it, Jenna, the last thing I want is to get into an argument with you. I'm tired. Let's just forget this whole thing. I promise, tomorrow night you and I will sit down and talk about getting pregnant. What do you say?"

Jenna sagged, then sat down on the staircase and looked up at him. "Scott," she said, stopped, thought for a moment what she really wanted to say, then continued, "I'm really tired of the fact that every time you have a bad day, you take it out on me. As far as talking tomorrow night," – again she hesitated before she spoke – "forget it. You'll just use tomorrow night to make up for tonight. If you can't talk about it because you *want* it as much as I do then, please, don't bother at all. Now if you'll excuse me, I'm going to bed."

Jenna got into bed, turned out the light and set to work trying to fall asleep. She doubted sleep would come easily tonight. A few minutes later, Scott came into the room, undressed in the dark and crawled in beside her. He tried to hold her, but she pushed him away. Upset, he turned away as well.

AFTER A RESTLESS night punctuated with new and different kinds of nightmare, Jenna opened her eyes at first light. Scott did too, and reached to hold her. Again she pushed him away.

"Scott, please leave me alone," she said firmly, then got out of bed, slipped into a robe and went to peek in on Zach, who was still sleeping peacefully. Standing in the door to the nursery, she sighed, then padded downstairs to put on a pot of coffee. A few minutes later, Scott came in.

"How long do you plan to be like this?" he asked.

She looked at him. "How long do I plan to be like this?" she repeated, incredulous. "I'm afraid I don't know right at the moment. I'm not sure how or what to feel." She turned away to pour some coffee and he came up behind her, turned her around and kissed her.

"Scott, I......" He stopped her with another kiss.

"Jenna, I'm sorry. What else do you want me to say?"

Jenna looked down, examining her thoughts, then looked back up at him, her gaze critical. "Saying I'm sorry just isn't good enough anymore," she said quietly. "You let me down once when we first talked about getting pregnant, but I agreed to wait like you suggested – even longer than you suggested. Now it sounds like you're just trying to find more excuses to back out of our agreement. You said some hurtful things last night. Now you think I should just jump back into bed with you because you say you're sorry. Please – let me go. Come talk to me when you figure out what it is you really want, what you *honestly* want."

Scott let her go and she walked out of the room. She went back upstairs, took a shower, dressed and left without saying more than a very quiet goodbye to him.

JENNA GOT INTO her car and drove into Boston on auto-pilot, unconsciously aware of the world around her, her mind in turmoil. She pulled up in front of the building where she'd lived when she first moved to Boston. Then she'd been living in her family's apartment; once it had belonged to her grandmother. Now it was hers. She'd held on to it after she'd married Scott, though it saw little use. Today she was glad she had.

Letting herself into the old familiar space felt like rushing into her grandmother's arms when she'd been a child. Her grandmother had always understood, known what to say, known what Jenna needed to hear. Today, Jenna had come there to listen to herself.

She turned the heat up, built a fire in the little fireplace, brewed herself an aromatic pot of tea and curled up on the couch under an afghan she had once watched her grandmother crochet. Slipping her fingers in and out of the holes in the open-weave design absentmindedly, she let her mind drift, examining the pieces of her life one by one, uninterrupted by anything but the crackling of the fire.

BY AFTERNOON, SHE felt ready to go home. She'd promised to get in some rehearsal time with the band before the day was over. Driving back, she felt at peace, with herself if not with Scott. She was clear on what she needed to say to him and what she needed to hear from him in return.

Her peace was short lived. Opening the outer door to the studio, she heard Scott yelling. She couldn't make out the words yet, but she could have written them down verbatim regardless. She knew the cadences of "fuck" and "goddam" and "what the *hell*."

Coming through the inner door, she wasted no time on small talk. "I hope this fight doesn't have anything to do with us, with our problems," she hissed at Scott, furious. "You get mad at me, you take it out on them. Every goddam time."

Already far beyond his limit, Scott lashed out at her. "Why don't you just get the fuck out of here. You couldn't be bothered talking to me this morning. Now you come waltzing in here and start right in on me. You have no idea what you've walked in on, so – just shut the fuck up."

The band looked at each other in disbelief.

"Fine," Jenna said between clenched teeth, "you want me to shut up and get out of here? You got it. I'll be taking Zach to my apartment. You want to see him, call me. Otherwise – go to hell." She started for the door.

"Jenna," Scott yelled, he tone suddenly panicky, "Jenna, please! You can't leave and take Zach from me too."

Tim looked to Jeremy, who could only shake his head and rolled his eyes. Tim nodded and got up from behind his drums. The rest of the band took their cue from them. Setting down instruments, they all quietly headed for the back door.

Jenna turned back to Scott. "You told me to get out, so that's what I'm doing. I'm taking Zach with me because he's my son. I love him. And he's the only child I'm ever going to have, since you obviously don't want me to have another one."

Jenna was almost out the door when Scott caught her arm and almost cried, "Baby Blue, I'm going to ask you once more: don't leave. Please, let's talk this out. I love you and I know you love me. We need to work this out."

"Let go of my arm," Jenna said coldly and he did. Hesitating, her hand on the doorknob, she stopped and turned back to him once more time. "I'm going over to the house and ask Ellen to take Zach for a walk. If you want, we can talk then."

JENNA WAS IN THE bedroom when Scott walked in.

"Sit down," he said, indicating the pair of chairs by the window. The view, a steely grey Atlantic under even greyer skies, did nothing for his mood. Jenna complied, but her expression was stark, cold, unforgiving, and she sat stiffly, arms folded, head held high. Scott sat down across from her, barely on the edge of his seat, leaning forward, his hands clasped under his chin as if in prayer. An ottoman occupied the no man's land between them.

Scott looked at her. She met his eyes for a moment, then looked away. He kept looking at her until he could hold her gaze, then started ticking off an inventory of the last couple of years' worth of disasters, pressures, woes and fears, first on his right hand, then on the left . When he ran out of fingers, he hauled off the cowboy boots he was wearing and socks beneath and continued on his toes.

"And then everything was going wrong this morning, rehearsing, every-thing," he said. "Nothin' was gelling. You walked in on like the nineteenth meltdown of that hour alone. And put me over the top." He stopped, dropped his head in his hands and heaved a weary sigh. Looking up at her, all he could do was close his eyes and shake his head. "How could I have ever said what I said to you?" he wondered aloud. "What was I thinking? I had no reason to say what I said. If I could take back those words, I would."

Jenna sat, still looking at him stonily, saying nothing. "You were right," he admitted. "I was taking out my frustrations on them." Then he changed gears. Sliding forward onto the ottoman, he reached for one of her wrists, toying the hand loose from her tightly crossed arms and taking it in his. She let him, but looked down at it like it belonged to someone else. When she raised her eyes to meet his again, her posture was still unyielding, her mood still implacable. Chagrined, Scott continued.

"Whether you believe me or not, I *do* want you to have another baby," he said quietly but earnestly. "We can talk about it right now – and all night and all day tomorrow too, if you want. I was really on edge last night. I just didn't want to talk about it then." Scott felt a stirring of Jenna's hand. After a moment, her hand squeezed his.

Looking her straight in the eye, he whispered, "I love you, babe," reached out and took her in his arms and just held her close to him. This time she didn't push him away.

"Honey," she finally said, "I know you're under enormous stress, but your lashing out at everyone is totally out of control. Some of the things you're saying are really hurtful – hateful. I can't speak for the rest of the people in your life, but I'm not sure how much more *I* can take."

Scott nodded reflectively. "No, you're right," he said. "When I'm calm like this, I know you're right. When I'm wacko, I can't think straight. I – I need to get myself back under control. I can. I have and I will. Hey," he went on, his mood brightening, "let's take a couple of days up at the lake after the shows this weekend. We can get to work on that baby you want."

"Whoa," Jenna said, bristling again. "Baby *I* want? What about baby *we* want, or have I been right all along: you really don't want another one?"

"No, no, no," Scott moaned. "Damn it, Jenna, why do you have to take everything I say so literally? That's not how I meant it and you know it. Are we going to start arguing all over again or can we please make up – and stay made up? I need to go finish up with the guys – and apologize to them. Then I want to take you over to Blue Skies for an early supper. And then we can get a head start on this baby *we* want." As he said "we," he pointed one pointer finger at her and the other at himself. Simultaneously.

HOLDING HANDS AT THEIR Table at Blue Skies, they were deep in conversation when a woman in a bright red, very short dress came weaving through the tables and brushed up against Scott as she passed, ostensibly on her way to the rest room. He only rolled his eyes at Jenna and continued what he was saying.

On her way back, the woman in red took the same route and again made bodily contact with him. This time she had to linger with her hip grazing Scott's arm to let a waiter with a full tray held high overhead make his way through in front of her. This time Jenna looked up. This time Jenna gasped. She knew the face. Once again, she was looking at the woman from the clipping. Here. At Blue Skies.

Chapter 17

※

BLACKLACE HIT THE ROAD again, just as foliage season was heating up. Trading the electric colors of autumn in New England for the pallid and predictable colors of the dessert southwest wasn't easy.

Then again, nothing about a Blacklace tour was easy, as anyone with a knowledge of the day-to-day realities of life on the road would readily tell anyone willing to listen. Traveling with an entourage of more than forty people meant that more than forty people had backlogs of great Blacklace stories to tell. Most of these tales were based on slivers of overheard exchanges or one-sided halves of phone or headset conversations, often through the din of rehearsals or shows, each from the unique perspective of a sound or lighting tech, a wardrobe girl, a security guard, a truck or bus driver. Words yelled in anger in public were always far easier to hear than apologies offered quietly in private. Most of their stories were either partially or entirely bogus. Many of them found their way into print or onto the airwaves. Cross words became ready grist for the rumor mill. This year, Blacklace was producing a bumper crop.

Jenna was turning into an emotional wreck and she knew it. She knew why, too. At the bottom of every seemingly unrelated screaming match was a frustration from which there was no escape: she wanted to get pregnant. She rarely said the word aloud – but it was on her mind, 24/7.

Jenna and Zach went on tour with Blacklace for a week, then she returned home with the baby; Scott flew home to them whenever he had more than a two-day layover anywhere. At first, Jenna couldn't wait for his arrival. His visits became escalating orgies of sex, each wilder than the last. Jenna went from acting like a hungry guppy, to a ravenous barracuda, to a school of sharks in a full-on feeding frenzy.

After he'd leave, she'd start monitoring her body in search of the elusive first signs of pregnancy. She wasted so many home pregnancy tests, she should have been buying them wholesale. She couldn't understand why she was having so much trouble simply getting pregnant; she'd never had a problem before.

Scott loved coming home to Zach – that part was easy – and he loved the sex, but he hated what now came with it. When they weren't making love or spending time together with Zach, they were fighting. Slamming doors, apologies and the sight of Jenna in tears were becoming commonplace, predictable. Homecoming was starting to create mixed emotions for him – the road was beginning to actually look good by comparison. So was the constant parade of women throwing themselves at him. He couldn't believe that they were beginning were look more inviting than his beautiful, talented, loving – but desperately needy – wife. Those around him weren't blind. Rumors began to multiply and thrive.

SCOTT HAD CAME HOME for a three-day break, which went a bit better than he'd expected. The day before he left again, he talked her into meeting him in Florida and doing at least one show together. They could use a few days alone together, he told her, and she agreed. They planned to meet at the end of the week, but she could only stay a few days. The album she and her band had been working on was set to be recorded; studio time had been booked in New York for them the following week. She would also be spending time with Laurel and Luka.

Jenna took an early flight into Miami and got to the house early enough to rest up before Scott pulled in from Orlando. One look, when he did arrive, told her he was in yet another lousy mood. "What's it now," she asked wearily.

"The sound system's off again," he muttered, "and everybody's driving me nuts. I don't want to talk about it. I just wanna fuck." Grabbing Jenna, he pulled her towards the nearest couch, but she stopped him.

"If you want to make love because you've missed me, fine. If you just want to fuck because you're pissed off and think it'll make you feel better, forget about it. We don't use each other that way, never have, never will."

Scott turned on her. "Well, fuckadoodledoo, Baby Blue. Let me get this straight. You can use me as a baby-making fuck machine and that's okay, eh? But if I have needs of my own, they're not? Huh. Now *that's* interesting."

Jenna stared at him. Then, shaking loose of his grip, she turned and left the room. Reaching the foyer, she saw her bag, her hat and her pocketbook sitting where she'd dropped them when she'd come in earlier. Putting on the hat, she shouldered her pocketbook, picked up her bag and stalked out the door.

SCOTT FOUND JENNA sitting at the beach, her bare toes dabbling in the incoming suds of the surf, an hour later. "Are you planning on staying here all day?" he asked, standing next to her, looking out to sea.

Jenna didn't answer him.

"Come on back to the house with me and we can start things over, the way they should have gone in the first place," he said quietly. He put his hand out for her to take but she continued to sit and ignore him.

Finally she looked up at him. Tears were streaming down her face. "If the fans didn't know I was singing tomorrow, I'd leave for home on the next available flight," she said. "I don't want to disappoint them so I'll stay, but I'm checking into a hotel until the show is over." Stunned, Scott sat down beside her and tried to put an arm around her. She instantly pushed him away.

"Nope. It's not going to work this time, Scott," she said. "You're not going to apologize, then make me want to give in to you. There's something very wrong between us. We need to figure it out or I'm afraid we're headed in dangerously different directions." She got up and started walking back to the house. Scott ran after her, begging her to stop.

"Going to a hotel isn't going to make things better. We need to talk this out," he insisted, catching her by the shoulder and stopping her in her tracks. "We can't if you're at a hotel."

She turned and looked at him. "Well, maybe you should have thought about that before you let yourself get out of control again, Scott," she said finally. Then she shook her head. "I – I just can't do this right now. I need to be away from you and think. I suggest you do the same. I'll see you over at Coral Sky."

JENNA GOT TO THE concert venue, an open-air amphitheatre, as late as possible. Anything to avoid getting into it again with Scott, she thought. She arrived in time for a pre-show backstage meeting with Jeremy and the rest of the guys, all of whom greeted Jenna with hugs, then fell back, deferring to Jeremy, as usual, to do the talking for them.

"Look, I – we just want to say that whatever the fuck's going on with you and Scott – well, we want you to know that it won't interfere with our friendship," he said, puzzling her. What had Scott been saying, she wondered. "If you need someone to talk to, don't to hesitate to call – me or any of us, for that matter." Everyone was nodding in agreement when Scott walked in the room and found Jenna standing there. One look at him and she burst into tears.

Scott sighed, took a deep breath, walked over to her and took her in his arms. He kissed her on the top of her head, and then on her lips. "Please come back to the house later," he whispered for her ears only.

"I want to," she said, not looking up at him, "but I just can't." She left the room.

Jeremy caught Scott by the arm before he could go after Jenna. "Look, give her some time, some space," he advised his friend. "Can't you see she's hurting? Get your shit together, man. Otherwise, you're going to fuck up the relationship completely."

Scott looked down at Jeremy's hand on his arm and shoved it off. "Thanks for the profound advice, Dr. Phil," he said acidly.

JENNA SAT WITH CARRIE and the other band wives before it was time for her to go on. Looking out from the wings, Scott could see Carrie holding her hand and talking to her, their heads bent to each other in that intimate way girlfriends talk to girlfriends. Jenna kept shaking her head, slowly and emphatically.

Finally, Jenna went backstage to await her cue. The house lights went black. When they came back up, she was standing at Scott's side, one hand in his, the other holding a mike to her lips.

She sang – but not for him. At every opportunity, Scott pulled her to him, sang to her, kissed her. She struggled to make it all look natural, as if everything was fine between them. Judging by the applause and cheering as she walked off the stage, she succeeded. She headed straight to the dressing room to get her things and left for the hotel before Scott could come stop her.

The next morning, she pulled the entertainment section out of the *Miami Herald* that had been delivered to her door with the breakfast she'd ordered and found a collage of photos from the concert splashed across the top of the first page. She was in three of the photos: one of Scott kissing her while she sang; one with him behind her, his arms wrapped around her, with one hand inching its way south of her waistline; one in which they were clearly singing in close harmony – she remembered that moment because of the words they were singing – "*Once we were two, but now we are one…*" They should know, she thought.

There were photos of the stage, the lightshow, the pyrotechnics, and one with Jeremy and Ryan, hair flying, backlit, both grinning as they riffed off each other. There were mob shots, and pictures of the band trying to get out of the place and into their car. In one, she saw the woman – "that woman," she'd come to think of her – pushing past Jeremy. In another, she was clearly interacting with Scott. It was impossible to say if hands were making contact with flesh, but it certainly looked like they might be.

Jenna was studying this photo intently when she heard a knock at the door. "Who is it?" she called. Her eyes rolled reflexively when she heard Scott's voice.

With a sigh, she got up to open the door to him. One look at her face ended any idea of trying to kiss her good morning. One look around the room made it clear she was packed and ready to leave. "Babe," he started, but she instantly cut him off.

"Don't," she said firmly. "Don't even start. We both need this time to think about what's going on with us and how we can fix it. I'll see you back home, after I'm done in New York and you're done in Atlanta."

"Are you sure this is how you want it?"

"Yes, I'm sure," Jenna said slowly, "but no, it's not what I want. I'd give anything if it could be different. I love you," she said as she kissed him on the cheek. "I really do." With that, she left for the airport.

JENNA'S WEEK IN New York, focusing on the album and spending time with Laurel, was productive. Laurel and Rick had insisted she stay with them rather than in a hotel, and she was glad she'd agreed to. It helped, not being alone and isolated with her troubles.

Laurel brought up Jenna's problems the first chance they had to sit quietly together. She'd been sensing that things weren't going well between Jenna and her father for some time, but felt optimistic for the two of them regardless.

"I know the man's crazy, but he's – he's different with you," Scott's younger daughter insisted. "He – how can I put this? – he *cares* what you think. He wants to get this right. I know he does." Jenna appreciated Laurel's candor, and found her optimism increasingly contagious the more time she spent with her.

On the flight back to Boston, Jenna felt calm for the first time in quite a while, she realized. She wanted to see Scott; she missed him. She wanted to work things out. So she was pleased to find him waiting for her at the airport, and ran into his arms without hesitation. She could honestly tell him how much she had missed him and hear what he had to say to her. He never let go of her until they got home, and then he only relinquished her to Zach's embrace.

When Zach went down for a nap, they did too.

"HATE TO WAKE YOU, babe, but we're meeting everyone at Blue Skies for dinner in half an hour," Scott whispered in Jenna's ear, gently bringing her back from a dreamless sleep. She smile, stretched, then rolled back into his arms.

"Gimme thirty seconds to wake up," she yawned, then kissed him. At thirty seconds, he broke it off. "Party pooper," she grumbled, then got up, slipped into some clean clothes and pulled a brush through her hair.

Dinner was a boisterous affair. A number of the wives and girlfriends hadn't seen each other for quite a while, busy as they were in their own worlds of motherhood and/or careers. And even though the band had been spending the past six weeks in each others' pockets on the road, they were all different people the minute they got back home. In many ways, they hadn't seen each other for quite a while, either. Even if this was merely a brief hiatus, time at home was precious to all of them.

Conversation eventually got around to the annual subject of plans for the holidays. "We doin' a holiday show in Boston this year, bro?" Jeremy yelled down the table to Scott. "We didn't last year." Scott threw the question out for discussion, though everyone knew that discussion was merely window dressing; Scott would do whatever he pleased. He just used the time that they spent considering all the pros and cons to make up his own mind.

"Yeah. Let's go back to doin' New Year's Eve," he said when the talk finally died down.

"I'll get Strang to work on it," Jeremy volunteered. Scott nodded.

"You and Jenna have anniversary plans yet?" Carrie asked Scott innocently. Jenna shot Scott a look, then started to answer for him.

"We haven't talked about it," she said. Her voice was neutral, but knowing the shaky state of their union, Carrie found herself wishing she hadn't brought the subject up.

But Scott reached over and took Jenna's hand. "I'm toying with an idea but hadn't mentioned it to Jenna yet. I wanted to look into some things first before I told her, but hell, this is as good time as any to bring it up. I'm thinking somewhere different this year, like maybe one of the Virgin Islands."

The fact that he'd given any thought to their anniversary, what with all the problems they'd been having, took Jenna by surprise. "Are you serious?" she said. "You were really looking into it? Or just thinking about it? When did you think of it?"

"What the hell is this, twenty questions?" Scott started to bristle, then stopped himself. "I've been thinking about it for the last few weeks, actually," he said, his manner defensive. "I just wasn't sure which island would be best. Touring doesn't exactly lend itself to travel planning, ya know." Jenna threw her hands up in supplication.

The rest of the evening came off smoothly. Everyone carefully stuck to neutral subjects.

"SO WHAT WAS WITH all the questions?" Scott said the minute they got in their car. "You made me look like a fool, all that 'are you really looking into it' shit. I said I was. Why isn't that enough for you? Did you think I was just making it up?"

"Cripes. I was just surprised is all," Jenna said, irritated. "Why does something that petty get you so angry? I'm sorry I said anything, all right?"

They both seethed silently the rest of the way home. When they got in the door, Jenna announced she was going to bed. "You do whatever the hell you want," she said by way of a goodnight.

She let her clothing lay where it fell, brushed her teeth, then climbed into bed in a complete funk and pulled herself into a tight ball, and was still in the same position when Scott joined her. He curled up around her, then laid a hand tentatively on her shoulder. She didn't react. After a few moments, the hand moved down her arm and again came to a rest. He gave her a little squeeze. She still didn't react. Emboldened, Scott let his hand start trailing across towards her breasts while, at the same time, he leaned over and pressed his lips to the back of her neck. Abruptly she pushed him away. Scott turned away from her in anger.

Eventually they both fell asleep but before long, Jenna started tossing and turning, then soon began to thrash about in the throes of another nightmare. She woke up in a cold sweat, screaming.

Scott stuffed a pillow behind him and sat up, took her shaking body into his arms and pulled the blanket up around her. Then he closed his eye and held her close, rocking her gently. It took quite a while, but she finally calmed. "Tell me about it," he whispered, but she didn't want to.

"Just hold me," she whispered fearfully. He kissed her forehead and pushed the hair back from her face.

"Try to go back to sleep," he said quietly. "Everything's going to be all right. You're right here with me." She finally fell asleep in his arms. He held her all night.

THE NEXT MORNING, he woke up early and carefully moved Jenna without waking her so he could get out of bed. Tucking the blankets back around her, he leaned down and kissed her on the forehead before going to take a shower.

In the kitchen he stood staring out the window, waiting for the coffee to brew. It had been almost four months since Billy Malone's trial had ended, but Jenna was still having of nightmares. He wondered if the stress of the nightmares was contributing to her inability to get pregnant. He'd been a real jerk with her last night, he thought; that probably didn't help the situation any, either. He thought about Jeremy's telling him he needed to get his shit together. How right he was.

Sitting down at the counter with a mug of coffee, he stared into the reflecting pool of steaming black liquid. It was time he did just that: get his shit together. He didn't want to lose Jenna. He knew he would if nothing changed.

"You still mad at me?" Jenna asked quietly, almost timidly, from the doorway.

"Hell no, babe, I'm not mad at you," Scott answered quickly. "Come here, baby. I thought you'd still be asleep after the night you had." He poured her some coffee and they sat down across from each other at the kitchen table.

"Feel like talking about the nightmare now?"

Jenna shook her head. "No," she said decisively. "I just want to forget about it – as if I could," she added with a bitter laugh.

"Are you gonna be okay when I leave again tomorrow?" he asked her.

"I'll be all right," she sighed.

"Honey, look – why don't you and Zach come with me, for a few days at least? Not Ellen, no motorhome – just the three of us. After last night, I'm gonna worry like hell about you otherwise."

"I can't tomorrow. I've got shelter business to take care of, and Zach's got a doctor's appointment the day after tomorrow." She glanced at a calendar over on the wall. "But we could meet you in D.C. on Wednesday – how about that?"

Scott looked at her tenderly, then took her hand and brought it up to his heart. "That's wonderful," he said and he meant it. "Tell ya what. Let's give Ellen the day off and just have it to ourselves, us and Zach." Jenna smiled. This Scott was so easy to love.

LATER IN THE DAY, Jenna returned from a longer than expected appointment on shelter business to find no one in the house. Scott's car was in the driveway. She looked over to the studio; the outer door was open.

Walking over, she could hear Scott and Zach before she reached the old barn. She found Scott sitting at the piano, Zach in his lap. "Yo, Mama!" Scott laughed when he saw her. "Men at work. We're making some serious music here." As if to emphasis his point, Zach raised his hands and brought them slamming down to play a crashing, random chord. "Music!" he bellowed. "Peeee-ano!"

"His vocabulary's growing by leaps and bounds," Jenna laughed.

"Whaddya think? Classical? Standards? Rock?" Scott played a few bars of each.

Jenna crossed over and sat down beside them. "Well, if he practices, he certainly could be a pianist like his daddy and his grampa, and play any kind he wants. For sure." The three of them stayed in the studio for a while, fooling around on all sorts of instruments, playing and singing.

After supper, Jenna suggested they take Zach for ice cream.

"I need to stop at Blue Skies to pick up the mail – forgot to last night," Scott said. "Let's go by there first. The ice cream adventure could get a little messy."

THEY ALL WENT IN when they got there. Zach was passed from waitress to waitress and enjoyed all the attention he got from them. "A chip off the ol' block," Jenna observed to Ann with a smile. "He was born a ladies' man, just like Scott. Enough of this and he's going to forget we'd promised him ice cream."

"We can get him ice cream," Ann said, and produced a dish in a matter of moments. While a couple of the waitresses took turns keeping Zach company, Scott and Jenna made the rounds, shaking hands and chatting with fans who'd come for dinner.

Finished with his ice cream, Zach came running over to find them. Scott picked him up, grabbed a napkin from a nearby empty table to tidy up his gooey face, then introduced him to the fans. "Man, he looks like you," one particularly pretty teenager cooed.

"That he does," Jenna agreed, after taking a step back and looking at the two men in her life as objectively as she could. Zach reached for the girl. "Looks like him, and behaves like him too."

"ZACH SURE DOES KNOW how to work a room," Scott observed with a chuckle as they got ready for bed later. "If I didn't know better, I'd say he's better at it than I am."

"Feeling a bit competitive, are we?" Jenna teased him.

"Proud," Scott admitted. "Just plain proud. You both make me so fuckin' proud."

Jenna pulled the low-cut, skin-tight black sweater she'd been wearing over her head, then reached over and unbuttoned his shirt, pulling him close in the process. As she got to the bottom button, he reached behind her, unfastened her bra and drew it off of her while she pulled his shirt open and slid her hands down his chest to the buttons of his jeans. "You packed, baby?" she asked huskily.

"Better believe it," he grinned lasciviously.

"I mean for real, suitcases, you know," she whispered into his ear. "Cuz, trust me, you're gonna be running late in the morning if you're not."

Chapter 18

✴

ANOTHER COUPLE OF WEEKS into this leg of the tour found Scott plummeting at warp speed into a black hole of desperation.

Jenna and Zach had spent several days with him in Washington as planned, which went well at first, then deteriorated, almost predictably now, back into conflict. By the time his wife and child headed home again, neither Jenna and Scott could say a civil goodbye. They were both beginning to use Zach as a buffer, and they knew they were, and both hated themselves for it.

As soon as Jenna was no longer the focus of his temper tantrums, Scott was right back at taking it all out on Blacklace personnel. If it wasn't flat merchandise sales, it was clumsy equipment wranglers. If it wasn't a truck pulling in late, it was the godawful food. Lighting was giving him fits. The sound was *never* right. Scott was everywhere, criticizing everything and everyone. No one was exempt. They all had no choice but to suck it up and carry on.

Chicago was the worst. Everything that could go wrong, did go wrong, in biblical proportions, to hear Scott tell it. "The mother of all clusterfucks," he summed it up when he made his perfunctory phone call to Jenna, late in the evening of the day of their arrival. Two of the thirteen trucks they were traveling with had been nailed in a twenty-seven-vehicle pileup on I-90 just south of Kankakee. Little in the trucks had been damaged, but it had taken half a day to offload some six tons of rigging and equipment into new trucks, and set-up couldn't start till the new trucks arrived. Forty roadies and over a hundred local hires milled around waiting, unable to do more than unload the trucks that had made it earlier, "and every last one of them on my nickel," Scott fumed to Jenna, "We've hit rock bottom here, if you'll pardon such a piss-poor pun," he said dolefully. He was quiet now; he'd been screaming at anyone and everyone all through the afternoon and evening. It had finally gotten so bad that Jeremy had intervened, fearing he'd strain his voice, he admitted. At Jeremy's insistence, he'd gone to an AA meeting earlier in the evening.

"Why does it take Jeremy to make you remember you have resources for dealing with all this stress?" Jenna challenged him.

"Hey, you're not the one out here," Scott snapped. "Just taking the time to get to AA means other things aren't getting done."

"You don't have to do everything yourself," Jenna pointed out patiently. "You don't have to oversee everything. You've got an army of really talented people who could probably do their jobs even better if you just let them."

Scott went silent for a moment, then blurted out, "Oh, fer crap's sake, Jenna. You run your life. I'll run mine."

He wasn't expecting the dial tone that followed this suggestion. He fumed for a few minutes, then called back. Ellen answered the phone. Jenna had gone out. She also mentioned that Jenna had had another screaming nightmare the night before.

TWENTY MINUTES LATER, Scott was sitting at the hotel bar, staring into a slim crystal shot glass filled to the brim with Southern Comfort. As a kid, SoCo had been his feel-good beverage of choice. It went so well with drugs, he mused. The color was so rich, so deep, so righteous. The scent brought back memories. He didn't reach for the glass. He only looked into it, like a fortuneteller with a client in no particular hurry.

"My goodness. Scotty boy! When did *you* start drinking again?" The husky voice of a woman at his elbow wormed its way into his consciousness. Slowly turning, he found himself looking directly into the smokey eyes of Ashley West, standing before him in all her scantily-clad, fleshy voluptuousness, a leather jacket and her long red hair slung casually over her shoulder.

"Well, well, and who do we have here?" he mumbled. Just when he thought the day couldn't get any worse. She dropped herself onto the empty barstool next to him.

"Buy a girl a drink?" Ashley suggested.

"You can have this one," Scott said, pushing it over until it sat before her.

"Never touch the stuff, myself," Ashley purred.

"Me either," he said, then covered his face with his hands and rubbed his eyes.

"Curious, buying a drink for no reason."

"I've done curiouser."

"That's for damn sure," she said agreeably. "Like that time –"

He cut her off. "Don't," he said simply.

"Where's the Missus?" Ashley asked offhandedly.

"Home. Where I wish I was," Scott said, and he meant it.

"Come on, tell Ashley all about it…"

HE HADN'T MEANT for a rundown of all his problems to lead to Ashley's ending up in his bed, but it did. "Just for old time's sake," she'd said invitingly, wriggling her shoulders and arching her back, the bulk of her assets on full display. "You deserve some good, old-fashioned, uncomplicated sex."

On some level, he had to agree. And he knew what her brand of good, old-fashioned, uncomplicated sex looked – and felt – like.

They made love voraciously, repeatedly, until first Ashley and then he finally fell asleep, well after two in the morning. Ashley hadn't needed to fake any orgasms. She did, however, fake slumber. Once she knew he was sleeping, she slid out of bed, grabbed her cell phone, went into the bathroom, closed the door and placed a call. "Yeah," she said. "Dead to the world." Hanging up, she went to the hotel room door, propped it open a hair, then got back into bed, arranging the sheets artfully to expose as much flesh as possible without waking Scott.

A few minutes later, the door opened. A man entered the room. Working in near-total darkness, he carefully, silently pulled a number of empty bottles out of a bag he'd brought with him and strewed them around the two bodies supposedly asleep in the bed. Then he pulled out a camera. Once he had all the pictures he wanted, he left the way he'd come. Then, and only then, did Ashley finally get to sleep.

JENNA WOKE FROM another nightmare about the same time the photographer exited Scott's hotel room. Laying awake, confused, frightened, she rebuked herself for baiting Scott as she had, for upsetting him, for hanging up on him. She longed for his arms.

Before sunrise, she'd made up her mind. A quiet phone call reserved her a seat on a private commuter jet leaving Boston at six-thirty. She could be at Scott's hotel by nine.

SCOTT WOKE FROM A salacious dream with a groan. Christ, I hate life on the road, was his first conscious thought. The next thing to enter his consciousness was the smell of strong perfume. His eyes flew open as he turned to find the obvious – and alarmingly close – source of the odor. Illumined by a slender band of light that had made its way through a narrow crack in the room-darkening curtains, he found a face, half covered in hair, laying inches from his. At the sight, the events of the previous evening came flooding back and he really groaned, this time loud enough to wake Ashley

"Oh, shit, what have I done," he cried. "What the fuck was I thinking? Oh, hell no – I can't have done this."

"Oh, hell yes – you did," Ashley said, smiling complacently. "And it was great," she added almost as an afterthought. "I bet you feel a lot better now."

"Better? Oh sure. I've cheated on my wife, the woman I love more than life itself. And that's supposed to make me feel better exactly how?"

"Oh, come on. What's a little fucking between friends?" Ashley said casually.

JENNA FOUND HERSELF feeling equal parts enterprising and pathetic as she ignored the do-not-disturb sign and slid the key card into the slot on Scott's door. Regardless of his mood, she couldn't wait to see the expression on his face. Tiptoeing into the room, she was halfway to the bed before she realized what she was both seeing and hearing.

"Get out. Get up, get dressed and get the fuck outta here," Scott was shouting. He had sat up and was just jumping, naked, from the bed when he saw Jenna and froze in his tracks, paralyzed. He could see the expression on her face plainly, and it killed him.

Moving towards her, he put his arms out beseechingly. "Jenna, Jenna, I'm sorry. Please let me explain. You gotta let me explain."

Jenna looked at Ashley, then at him, and burst into tears. Ashley, who had nonchalantly gotten up from the bed as well was also stark naked, and was smiling like the proverbial cat who'd swallowed the canary.

"You no good, fucking son of a bitch!" Jenna finally spewed out at Scott, when she could say anything at all. "I hate you, you bastard. Do you hear me? I hate you!" She turned and fled the room. Crying hysterically, she ran blindly down the hallway and had just come around a corner when she literally ran into Jeremy and Carrie, who were heading for the elevator.

"Jenna! Jenna, honey. What's the matter?" Carrie asked, stopping her by throwing her arms around her. "Slow down. Tell us what's the matter." Jenna was too hysterical to talk. Carrie could only hold her and rock her gently.

Scott appeared, now dressed. Ashley walked past him and on down the hall to the elevator without a backward glance. "Scott – what in the hell's going on here?" Carrie pressed him.

But Jeremy recognized Ashley; it didn't take much for him to put two and two together. "Oh, Christ. Do *not* tell me you did what I think you did, Tenny," he said, furious. "Well, you've really fucked it up this time, haven't you? Just when I thought you'd finally gotten your shit together. What the hell ever possessed you to go out and fuck an old girlfriend? When did Jenna become not enough for you?" He held up a hand to stop him when Scott tried to get a word in edgewise. "Don't say a word. I don't want to hear it, your excuses and your bullshit. I cannot fucking *believe* this, man."

Jeremy turned to Carrie. "Take Jenna to our room." Turning back to Scott, who was standing there holding his head, he said, "You I don't want to talk to. Asshole." Then he turned and stalked down the hall after Carrie and Jenna.

CARRIE SAT JENNA down on the sofa and tried to console her, but Jenna couldn't stop crying. "How could he do this to me?" she sobbed. "I know we've had our problems but, good God, why – this?"

"Honey," Jeremy said, taking her gently by the shoulders, "We're here for you. Every inch of the way."

"Why?" Jenna kept repeating, staggered. "What did I do to make him want somebody else?"

There was a knock at the door; Jeremy went to answer it. It was Scott, wanting to see Jenna. "Get the hell outta here," Jeremy told him pointblank, but Scott insisted, saying he wouldn't leave till he could see his wife. Over Jeremy's shoulder, he could see Carrie holding her. "Jenna, baby blue," he called to her, "please, let me try and explain."

Jenna lifted her head from Carrie's shoulder and looked him in the eyes. "Don't you ever call me that again," she said through clenched teeth. "I'm not your 'baby blue' anymore. I'm not your anything anymore. I'm going back home and getting Zach, then I'm leaving you – so you can get back to fucking your girlfriend. Now, get the hell out of here." Jeremy seconded the motion.

Carrie turned back to Jenna. "What are you gonna do," she asked compassionately.

Jenna sighed. "I'll move Zach and Ellen to my apartment," she said decisively, "until I can decide what to do. I – I don't want to take Zach away from his father. They love each other too much. I couldn't do that to either of them. All I know I have to leave, right now. Jeremy, would you mind booking me on the first flight out of this shithole?"

Jeremy was happy to.

WHEN HE WENT TO Scott's door, half an hour later, Jeremy took in the bottles, as well as a glass of clear liquid and a bottle sitting on the desk. He recognized the label as that of an ultra-cheap gin. "Oh, great. You fuck things up with Jenna, and now you're gonna fuck up everything else as well? Feeling sorry for yourself is what got you into this mess, Tenny. You know damn well it won't get you out. I have no idea what made you do what you did, but you sure as hell don't need to make things worse by starting to drink again."

"That's water. The bottle's empty. They all are," Scott said listlessly, indicating the several that still littered the bed. "Don't ask me where the fuck they came from. I haven't had a drop," he added, and heaved a huge sigh.

"Look, Scott," Jeremy said, shaking his head in disbelief, "you and me, we go back. We've been best friends for years. I may hate your guts right this minute, but I'm here to listen to your story. Tell me what happened."

"Your really want to know?' Jeremy nodded.

SCOTT TOLD JEREMY how Ashley'd been practically stalking him for the better part of a year. That he'd known her as a kid. That they'd grown up together, gone to school together, discovered drugs, sex and a hellova lot more together. "She was the school slut," he said blankly, "and I was the school stud. She was a walking sex ed class, and I majored in it. I grow up to be famous. I'm an easy target. That's the whole story."

What Scott didn't know was that even that wasn't half of the story.

ASHLEY WEST HAD been drinking in a Sunapee bar late one night a couple of summers back. Dave Schultz, another childhood friend and sexual science project, had been sitting a few barstools down from her. As the crowd thinned, they'd rediscovered each other.

Conversation lurched drunkenly from memories of moonlight trysts and wildly debauched parties on the lake to mutual friends, and "mutual fucks," as Ashley had put it rather crudely. Scott had been a mutual fuck. In fact, he, Dave and Ashley had spent more than a night or two exploring all the possibilities of mutual fucking in a king-size bed in a cabin David care-took for its absentee owners.

Ashley admitted to still "having a thing" for Scott, going to his shows when she could afford to. She'd made a career of waitressing, at different places around Sunapee in the summer, the rest of the year in Boston.

"Well, that sorry son of a bitch cost me a job," Dave said, polishing off a beer and pushing the glass toward the bartender for yet another refill.

"Yeah?" Ashley asked.

"Him and me, we got into a fight, or almost anyway, a couple years ago. I was workin' at Lake View Farm – you know, that joint that rents horses by the hour, halfway to George's Mill?" Ashley nodded; she knew the place. Any native did. "I insulted his woman."

"The famous Jenna?"

"Yeah, the famous Jenna. Jenna B. Tenny. Jenna Boobs Tenny. He got all manly. It almost turned into a knock-down. The owner later claimed he'd seen the whole thing and gave me my walkin' papers. Only, I know he wasn't even in the barn when it happened. Mr. Rock Star musta called and ratted me out."

"He acts all holier than thou when he sees me, that's for sure," Ashley grumbled in sympathy. "Like *his* shit don't smell."

"If ever anyone could use a comeuppance, it's our old pal Scott," Dave had said.

That was the beginning of the rest of the story. Dave had bankrolled Ashley's travels to catch every Blacklace show she could get to, often accompanying her himself. They knew their chance would come, if they were just persistent enough.

They finally hit paydirt in Chicago.

Chapter 19

❋

JENNA LOOKED AT HER watch as her cab turned to pull up their driveway, four and a half hours after she'd last laid eyes on Scott and '*her*' – that woman, the woman in the clipping, the woman she'd seen at shows, at the Grammys, at Blue Skies. The woman in whose arms Scott had spent the previous night – and who knew how many other nights.

The driver took her bag to the door, then turned back so she could pay him. He knew who his passenger was. A man who prided himself on having a good ear for body language, he had sensed immediately not to try making small talk. Jenna B. Tenny was clearly one distraught woman today; her body language screamed 'leave me alone.' Jenna recognized his sensitivity and rewarded it with a generous tip.

Letting herself in, she stepped into the foyer, set down her bag, squared her shoulders, lifted her chin and headed for the kitchen. "Ellen? Zach" she called, doing her best to hide any hint of the panic she felt.

"Out here," Ellen yelled from the back porch.

"Here," Zach echoed her.

Jenna followed their voices outside into the unusually warm October afternoon, where she found Zach in his sandbox wearing his Bob the Builder hard hat, humped over a bright yellow plastic backhoe, filling a dump truck with scoopfuls of sand. Ellen, not the type to sit by idly watching, was on her knees beside him, pushing sand around with a little bulldozer.

"Well, look at you two!" Jenna greeted them cheerfully. It was amazing how just the sight of Zach lifted her spirits.

Ellen's face registered first surprise, then confusion at the sight of her employer. Zach looked up the moment he heard her voice and yelled, "Mommy!" Then he jumped to his little feet and scuttled over to her. She pulled off his hard hat and wrapped him in a long hug. "Zachery Matthew Scott Tenny. How is my boy?"

"Wook, wook!" he babbled. "Digging a wake, Mommy! Wake Sun-pee!"

"Lake Sunapee?" she laughed. "Ah. You'll need a canoe!"

"An' oars?" Zach asked. Scott had brought him a book about boats the last time he was home.

"Paddles," Jenna corrected him.

"Paddles," Zach repeated, exaggerating the two syllables.

"You're back," Ellen said. "Your note this morning…?"

"I'm back. Can you come inside for a moment?" Jenna said. "We'll keep an eye on your man-made lake from the kitchen, Zach," she assured the youngster, who took his cue and got right back to work on his construction project. She put a kettle on to boil, then turned back to Ellen.

"I'm sorry I didn't let you know what was happening," Jenna began, looking back out at Zach to be sure they were out of his hearing. "Plans, uh, changed."

"Is everything okay," Ellen asked, immediately concerned.

"Well, yes – and no," Jenna said. "Scott and I are separating," she said quietly.

"*Separating?*" Ellen said, dumbfounded.

"For a while at least, Ellen. I – I don't know what's going to happen. I don't know if we can work through this. It's –" She stopped and took a long breath. "I – he –"

She stopped again. The kettle gave out the first hints of a whistle and she took the opportunity to turn back and take it off the heat. "That was quick," she said almost absentmindedly.

"I just fixed myself a cup ten minutes ago," Ellen said.

"Oh." She stared at the kettle, then remembered to reach for a mug and a teabag. She knew she was just buying time. "Ellen," she said, finally turning back to Zach's nanny, "I might as well tell you everything. My little surprise visit turned out to be one heck of a big surprise – for me. He was with another woman." Jenna blew out a long breath of air. She felt like she'd just bench-pressed a heavy set of barbells.

Ellen's mouth fell open. "Oh, no," she gasped. "No! How – how could he?"

"My sentiments precisely," Jenna said bitterly.

Jenna explained her short-term plans – moving Zach and herself to the Boston apartment – and asked Ellen if she would be willing to come along with them. Ellen's answer was an unqualified and immediate yes. "Thank you so much," Jenna said. "I can't tell you how much I appreciate your help."

"And support," Ellen volunteered. "One hundred percent. No question."

"Well," Jenna sighed, "I guess we have ourselves some packing to do."

JENNA STOOD STARING at the contents of her walk-in closet, unable to start the arduous task before her. Sinking to the floor, she reached into her back pocket for her cell phone, then hesitated. She needed to talk to her mother, maybe more than she ever had in her entire adult life.

But her mother was married to Scott's father – the problem she'd pushed from her mind, but had dreaded nonetheless, from the first moment it became clear that the two were being drawn magnetically to one another. She knew she'd have to tell them what was going on, but facing her own problems was almost more than she could do. She had no energy left to even contemplate the impact these problems would have on her mother and Joe. Like it or not, that would have to wait.

Just as she had when she'd walked in the door, she sat up, squared her shoulders, raised her chin, took a couple of deep breaths and gave herself a lecture. Jenna B, on your feet, she said to herself. You have work to do.

She decided she didn't have to move everything she owned, not that the apartment couldn't accommodate everything. Her grandmother had lived a lifetime in Boston's Back Bay in grand style; the apartment was a first-floor, eight-room floor-through with four bedrooms. Two of the bedrooms had private baths; two shared a bath. Ellen suggested that the shared-bath bed-rooms would make an ideal nursery and separate room for herself.

Though she'd always used the front bedroom, Jenna decided to take the bedroom at the back of the house for herself. It was the smaller of the two bedrooms with their own baths – the large front bedroom had been her grandmother's; its bath had a 1930s art deco grandeur to it. The back bedroom, on the other hand, had been designated the maid's room in those days, and had a tiny, utilitarian bath, but it was cozy and warm, and looked out over a sadly neglected pocket garden. Jenna had always loved the garden – it had been a showplace in her grandmother's day – and knew it would be her salvation through the hard times ahead. She would bring it back to life, maybe even turn it into a little lush jungle playground for Zach. The thought made her smile.

Jenna was suddenly glad for the big fourth bedroom. It facilitated the logistics of Scott being able to see and spend time with Zach. If Scott needed to stay, he could – at the opposite end of the apartment from her.

BY FIVE, BOTH ELLEN and Jenna's cars were packed to capacity. Ellen put Zach in his car seat while Jenna went back into the house and just stood there, looking around. She was still in a state of shock. Not eight hours had elapsed since she'd walked in on Scott and – that woman.

Three years of memories of her life in this house began to replay them-selves before her, like a slideshow of magical moments and wonderful times, and with them, tears finally forced their way past her steely resolve not to cry. Wandering back into the kitchen, which suddenly felt like somebody else's kitchen, not hers, as if it had *never* been hers, she grabbed a handful of tissues, put one to immediate use and stuffed the rest in her pocket. She knew she'd need them.

Glancing out into the mudroom, she saw Zach's sandbox construction equipment neatly parked beneath a bench and smiled through her tears. She picked up his favorite, the yellow backhoe.

Heading for the door, she pulled an envelope out of her pocket and set it on the hall table. It was a letter to Scott, simply telling him that she would send for the rest of her things.

Jenna closed the front door and went to her car. Opening the back door, she reached in, gave Zach a kiss and his backhoe, and closed the door.

Walking around the car to the driver's door felt like a defeat. With a sigh, she pulled out her keys and got in. Fumbling, she finally got the key into the ignition, started the car, sat for a moment composing herself, then turned around and said, "Okay, Zach-o, we're off to Boston."

"Boston!" Zach crowed.

Tears rolled silently down her cheeks the entire way there.

JENNA WAS STILL FIGHTING back tears as she unpacked Zach's clothes into a small dresser in what would now be called the nursery. "I wish my grandmother could have known Zach," she sad sadly. "I so wish I could have put him in her arms. She loved babies, more than anything. She was a wonderful woman."

Ellen stood looking about her as she emptied a bookshelf to accommodate the toys she'd brought along for Zach, who was currently running up and down the halls and generally making himself to home. Jenna had done a quick babyproofing when they had arrived and felt comfortable letting him have his run of the place for the moment.

"This is an amazing apartment," Ellen said. "It's so spacious. They don't make them like this anymore."

They don't make grandmothers like mine anymore, either, Jenna found herself thinking bitterly. They make grandmothers who go and marry their sons-in-law's fathers and complicate you life beyond all comprehension. She dreaded making that phone call.

THAT NIGHT, BLACKLACE put on their worst performance in years, as bad as any back in their drug-using years. The only difference was that they were all stone sober. Scott was a wreck. Everyone else in the band tried everything they could think of to cover for him, but it was hopeless from the moment the show started.

The band had come out and played one of their usual hot instrumental pieces to warm up the crowd. The stage went black for thirty seconds, time for Scott to come out from the wings and hit his mark. Jeremy knew they were in for the rollercoaster ride of their lives when the single spot came up on Scott – only to find him sitting on the floor of the stage, his head in his hands, his mike lying at his side. It probably looked dramatic from the audience, but it terrified Jeremy. Especially when the seconds ticked by and Scott didn't move a muscle.

Jeremy keyed his headset and whispered to Dan and Jeff. "What do we do?"

Dan answered. "You and me on either side of him, just get him on his feet?"

"Now," Jeremy came back, and the two strode over to the slumped-over form like a pair of cops teaming up to roust a drunk. Reaching down and taking him firmly by both elbows, they brought him upright. Jeremy steadied him as Dan picked up his mike and put it in his hand. "Sing," Jeremy hissed in Scott's ear. "It's what you do, remember?"

So Scott sang. Expressionless, mechanically, by rote. Fudging lyrics. Repeating entire verses instead of moving onto other verses. Standing rooted to that one spot the entire time, avoiding making eye contact with Jeremy or any of the others, or any of the audience at his feet. Somehow, he performed the entire set this way. Between songs, Jeremy tried talking to him through his headset, but got no response.

Dan finally keyed Jeremy on an open channel the rest of the band and head techs could hear. Before the show, Jeremy had filled them all in on what had happened between Scott and Jenna that morning, anticipating problems. They turned to him now. "You've gotta take charge, bro," Dan implored. "We'll take our cues from you. This is our show now – it's up to us. You've just been elected president."

Lighting quickly picked up on the fact that Scott wasn't planning on moving any time soon and switched from prerecorded light cues to seat-of-the-pants manual. They also canned some scheduled pyrotechnics. Where he was standing, the lead singer for the world-renowned Blacklace would have gone up in flames.

A huge venue full of fans quickly sensed that something was amiss. The band all took turns bantering with the audience between songs, but that could only go so far. Diehard fans cheered boisterously enough to overpower the catcalls, booing and hissing of a disgruntled minority that grew louder with each new song. It was clear that something was very wrong with Scott Tenny

But only one member of the audience knew just how wrong it was – and why. The slight smile that never left Ashley West's face all evening was only a suggestion of the inner thrill she felt witnessing the intensity of Scott Tenny's suffering.

JEREMY WAS ABLE TO drag Scott out for one encore. The minute it was over, he ran off the stage and hurried to his dressing room. Jeremy was right on his heels.

"Hey, what's the fuckin' rush?" he called after Scott's swiftly receding form. "Where are you off to in such a hurry?"

Scott turned and faced him. "I'm getting a private jet and flying home. I've got to see Jenna."

"I wondered what you were bustin' your butt thinkin' about out there," Jeremy said sarcastically. "Fuck, man, you can't go jerkin' your fans around like that. That was fuckin' unconscionable, Tenny!"

"Sometimes real life has a way of interfering with the dog and pony show," Scott said sullenly.

"Performing *is* our real life," Jeremy reminded him. "You owe a refund to every poor schmuck who wasted a week's paycheck on you tonight."

"I just want to get on a plane."

Jeremy snorted. "Well, I just want to wish you the best of luck on that. I can't imagine that she's anywhere ready to talk to you yet."

Jenna sent Ellen back to Scott's – already, she couldn't think of it as *their* house – for the night; the next morning, she'd be bringing a second carload of things they couldn't carry in the first load.

At first nervous about being alone, she was surprised to find that she actually welcomed the thought of a quiet night, just her and Zach. Tucking him in, she left a music box playing beside him. "Where's Daddy?" he asked her clearly. Jenna looked down at him and smiled sadly.

"Good question, Mr. Zachery. Good question…" She sang him a lullaby, then kissed him good night and quietly left the room. He'd had a long day. He was out like a light.

Wandering into the kitchen, Jenna fixed herself a cup of tea, then went out onto a narrow porch that ran the full width of the back of the building, and then down a half dozen steps into the old garden. A full moon filtered down through the now bare branches of the maple tree that had single-handedly shaded the small space in summer for more years than she could imagine. Maple leaves carpeted the ground. She added a pair of rakes, one full-sized, one Zach-sized, to her mental list of things she'd need.

With a sigh, she shivered, turned and went back inside. It was chilly in the late October night air. Taking her cup of tea, she went into her bedroom and got to work unpacking her own things. Stay busy, she told herself. She turned on the TV, but paid little attention to it. She wanted it on mainly for background noise, to break the stillness.

JENNA WAS SURPRISED to hear the eleven o'clock news come on; she hadn't realized it had gotten that late. Quickly folding the last of the sweaters that she'd piled on the bed, she cleared herself a spot, grabbed a pillow and sat back to watch, to get off her feet more than anything. She picked up her teacup and took the last few cold sips. She almost felt a need to look at problems far worse than her own, not that she really expected it to help in any way, and it didn't.

The last thing Jenna needed to see, early in the half hour, was her nemesis, Janice Long, the station's highest-ranking entertainment reporter. Jenna had experienced more than enough seemingly friendly interviews with the seemingly friendly woman to know that this reporter was a proverbial wolf in sheep's clothing. And Janice was clearly on to something big tonight. Her eyes were glittering with excitement. Jenna set her cup down and eased herself down to the end of the bed closest to the television set.

"Boston always wants to know what Boston's biggest hometown band is up to," the reporter said, turning the heat up under one of her favorite topics as footage of Blacklace's most recent Boston show came on behind her. "But fans in Boston are going to be as disappointed as fans in Chicago to hear how *poor* a performance Blacklace, and lead singer Scott Tenny in particular, turned in tonight."

The image on the screen was replaced by a montage of Scott. Scott sitting slumped over, hiding under his shaggy hair, on the stage. Scott being helped to his feet by Jeremy and Dan. Scott standing, dressed in funereal black leather and black silk head to foot, staring blankly out into the crowd. A close-up, Scott singing like someone had replaced his soul with the electronic circuitry of a robot.

"Performing at Chicago's United Center in front of a sold-out house of more than twenty-two thousand fans," Janice Long intoned, "Scott Tenny did little more than sleep-walk through the shortest performance by a major rock band in recent memory. The running time, for one set and only one encore, totaled all of fifty-seven minutes. Fans were dumbfounded. Rumors were that scalpers had gotten as much as a thousand dollars a ticket outside the venue earlier this evening."

The visual cut to Janice holding her microphone up to a long-haired man probably in his late forties, wearing a hot pink turtleneck, a black leather jacket and several heavy gold chains. "I paid $220 for a couple of pretty run-of-the-mill seats – $220 *each*," he said angrily. "Man, do I feel ripped off."

"And he's not the only one. I came all the way from Boston for this? This is Janice Long, live from Chicago. Back to you, Fred."

Jenna was thunderstruck.

THERE WAS NO GOING to sleep that night. Every time she closed her eyes, images of Scott played and replayed across a sixty-inch screen in her brain. His complete lack of professionalism aside, she was dismayed by how down-right bad he'd looked in the close-ups. She found herself wondering if he might have maybe accentuated the black circles beneath his eyes, he looked so sepulchral. It served him right for what he did, she thought, but there was no comfort in such thinking. It could do nothing to keep her from crying as she lay in the dark.

She was awake to hear the chimes of the nearby Arlington Street Church at midnight, one, two and three a.m. Almost as soon as she finally fell asleep, she found herself in the middle of a nightmare,

THE FIRST THING Scott saw upon entering his empty house was the envelope Jenna had left him. He knew to expect it, but that didn't soften the blow. Like an emotional uppercut to the jaw, it left him reeling. After reading the note a second time, he hurled a lamp at the wall and screamed at the top of his lungs. Then he got into his car and headed for Boston. He knew where she was. And he had a key.

Letting himself in, he peeked into the front bedroom and was surprised to find it empty. Assuming, correctly, that Ellen and Zach were in the connected bedrooms, he tiptoed quietly to the back bedroom. Before he could do any-thing, he heard a moan. Quickly silently, he opened the door and waited a moment for his eyes to adjust to the almost total absence of light. What he found was Jenna, sitting upright, trembling, crying, arms wrapped around knees drawn tightly against her chest, rocking herself. She was in a trance-like state, neither awake nor asleep. Though he had seen her do this many times, it was a sight he would never grow accustomed to.

Taking her in his arms, he moved to calm her as he always did. Jenna let him. "When is this going to stop?" she murmured. "I don't know how much more I can take."

"Honey," he whispered, knowing full well she that couldn't really hear him, "I wish I knew how to make it go away." After a while, Jenna finally calmed down and fell into a true sleep in Scott's arms. Settling her back under the covers without waking her, he lay down beside her and held her close.

IN THE MORNING Jenna awoke to find Scott's arms around her. It was all she could do to keep from screaming. The sight of him shook her to the core. "How – how could you?" she cried, waking him in the process, pushing herself away from him in disgust, as much with herself as with him. "Get out of here! I didn't think you could hurt me more than you have, but I was ever wrong."

"What? What the hell are you talking about?" Scott sputtered as he fought to come fully awake after only a few hours' sleep. Then it hit him; she thought they'd had sex. "Oh, for crissakes. That's great, Jenna. That's just great. Do you think I would actually let myself in, take advantage of the situation and make *love* to you without you knowledge? I didn't," he said vehemently. "I didn't and I wouldn't, and I can't believe you think I could."

"Yeah, well I never thought you'd cheat on me either, and look where that got me," she threw back at him.

"When I got here, you were in the middle of one of your nightmares. I couldn't very well leave you like that. I wanted to be here for you," he said, but even as he whispered the words, he knew how lame they sounded.

"I appreciate your 'being here for me,'" she said coldly, "but I have to learn to deal with it myself now. Just go. Leave me alone. If you want to see Zach, fine. Call me and we'll work it out. Otherwise I don't want to see you or hear from you, period. Now, please leave."

Scott rolled over and got up. He'd hadn't undressed, not had he gotten under the covers; he hit the floor ready to go. As he reached for the doorknob, he turned back to her. "Have you told our parents yet?"

Shaking her head, she fought the sudden urge to cry. "I started to, but I couldn't. I didn't know what to say. I take it you haven't talked with them either." It was a statement, not a question.

"No," he said, looking her in the eyes, "and I don't think I'm going to, either. *You* walked out on *me*. You tell them."

Infuriated, Jenna finally let her anger have free rein. "You son of a bitch!" she hissed quietly, still not wanting to waken Zach. "You go fuck an old girlfriend and get caught and that makes *me* the bad guy here? Now I suppose you're going to say there's no reason for me to walk out on you. Something tells me that, if it were the other way around, *you* sure as hell would. Fine. I'll tell them, but I can guarantee you're not gonna like my version of the story."

From down the hall, they both suddenly heard Zach start crying. It was easy to make out his tearful "Daddy, Daddy!"

"You better go see him while you're here," Jenna said grimly. Scott went down the hall, leaving Jenna to take a shower.

When she'd finished and dressed, she found them playing in the living room. "Say goodbye to Daddy," she told Zach. "He has to go now." Zach started to tear up, then seemed to think better of it and accept the fact. He went over, climbed into his father's lap and flung his arms around him.

"I'll call you," Scott said after he'd given Zach a kiss and a hug in return. "I know you don't believe it," he said over their son's head, "but I do love you. I'm not giving up on us."

LATER THAT DAY, Carrie called and invited herself over. "I don't want to talk about Scott, if that's what you're thinking," Jenna told her flatly before she'd agree.

"I just want to see how you're doing. Truly," Carrie said, her voice laced with genuine compassion. "My guess is you could use a friend to talk to right about now? You do still consider me your friend, I hope…"

"Of course I do," Jenna said wryly, "and, yes, I certainly do need someone to talk to. Come on over."

The two friends ended up talking for a couple of hours. Jenna shared her pain and confusion, and Carrie tried to help her brainstorm how to deal with Linda and Joe. Thanksgiving was only a few short weeks away; she and Scott would be expected in L.A., to celebrate both the holiday and their parent's second anniversary.

"What am I going to tell my mother – and his father? What is this going to do to *their* relationship? Oh, Carrie, how could he do this to us?"

Carrie was reduced to just shaking her head. "I don't have any answers for you, hon – but I think you should at least hear what he has to say."

"I knew you had an agenda when you came over," Jenna exclaimed, jumping to her feet angrily.

"Sit back down, girlfriend," Carrie said, unflustered, reaching up for one of Jenna's hands and tugging her back down to the couch. "You owe it to yourself – and to Zach – to at least say you gave him the chance to explain. I'm just saying this because I wouldn't want to see you regretting that you didn't, some day down the line."

Carrie left Jenna to ponder that thought. "Call me anytime," she said after hugging Jenna goodbye. "I love ya, babe. I only want to see you happy."

Chapter 20

THREE DAYS LATER, Jenna's phone rang. It was Scott. She stared at his name for two rings before she could make herself pick it up, but she couldn't make herself say anything, so Scott finally stepped in for her. "Hi," he said quietly. "Look, I'm just calling to see if it's okay with you if Zach comes down and stays with me for a couple or three days."

"Yes. That'd be okay," she said, her lips pursed with frustration at the image of an endless stream of phone calls of this nature this stretching for years into the future. "I know Zach would love it," she added.

"How about I come for him tomorrow around ten?"

"I have to be out. But Ellen's here. And you're gonna have to make your peace with her," Jenna pointed out, "so it's probably for the best."

"Yeah. I do. I will. Look, I think we should talk." Jenna sighed silently. She knew they needed to, but wasn't looking forward to it. The thought of it came loaded with visions of lawyers and judges and court orders – and pain. "Like maybe when I bring him back?"

"Okay," Jenna said coolly.

"Okay," Scott said. "We need to sit down and talk about telling your mom and my dad what's going on. I never should have said it was your job. I'm really sorry, Jenna. I don't know what the fuck I was thinking. I can be such an asshole."

"Right."

Scott went silent in tacit acceptance of her righteous anger. "How about I bring him back around seven on Friday? And then we can talk."

Jenna thought about it. Did she really want him here again, so soon? "I could come down there," she said quickly. " I forgot a number of things I really need."

"Anything I could bring tomorrow?"

"No," Jenna snapped. She was discovering that it was almost more painful for her to talk to the calm, conciliatory Scott than to the crazed, out-of-control version of this man who was still her husband.

JENNA PULLED UP to their house – *Scott*'s house, she quickly reminded herself – a little after three. The house was at its loveliest this time of day. The way the low, late afternoon sun glinted on the windowpanes and made the rambling old shingled house glow in its golden light took her breath away, as it always had. She loved this house that, for three years, she had made her home.

Climbing out of her car, she took a deep, bracing breath of sea air. When you lived here, you lost your ability to smell it, but after a week in Boston, it provided a bracing tonic for Jenna's soul. She stood looking beyond the house, across the lawn and out to sea, then turned and headed for the door.

Scott had been pacing the kitchen, agitated, waiting for her to arrive. He was across the kitchen in a few strides and yanking the door open the moment he heard the doorknob turn. Jenna stood, hesitated a moment, then stepped in.

Scott didn't give her time to think. "Let's go out on the porch," he suggested. "It's still warm enough. Coffee?" he said, pointing at an obviously recently-brewed pot. "Or tea? I've got water hot. Or iced tea? Juice?"

"Coffee," Jenna said. Scott pulled out a mug for her before she could make a move in that direction, filled it, put sugar in it the way she like it and set it on the counter in front of her. He had the door to the porch open before she'd picked it up, and held it for her like a doorman. "Ladies first," he said. Jenna couldn't help but reflect on the fact that this was the guy who was usually the first to barge through a door, irrespective of who he was with.

"Thank you," she said politely, just as her grandmother would have.

Looking around the vast wraparound porch at the myriad choices of places to settle, she immediately decided on an old straight-backed rocker with a matching footstool that sat before it. It fit her mood perfectly. Scott stood leaning against a column for a moment, then resumed his earlier pacing. He wasted no small talk getting to the subject.

"Look, Thanksgiving's in a couple of weeks. Everybody's gonna be there. Can't we pretend nothing's wrong till afterwards? I'd hate to spoil everything for them – our folks especially, it being their anniversary and all."

Jenna stared at him as his obviously prepared thoughts came out in a rush. Then she laughed harshly. "You hate to spoil everything? Maybe you should have thought of that before you slept with what's-her-name. How, may I ask, do you propose we pretend nothing is wrong when we sleep in separate bedrooms?"

"We don't sleep in separate bedrooms," Scott shrugged. He made it sound so simple.

"Uh, you're joking, right?" Jenna bristled. "Cuz if you're not, then I guess I better spell it out for you: we will *not* be sleeping together, not over Thanksgiving, not ever again. I guess this discussion's over," she said, getting back to her feet. "I'll just go get some more of my things together."

Jenna picked up her barely touched cup of coffee and headed indoors. Scott followed her. She was almost to the stairs when he asked, "Jenna, do you still love me?" She chose to ignore him, heading up instead. She was almost to the top when Scott, on the step below her, grabbed her by the arm and turned her to face him.

"Answer me, Jenna. Do you still love me?" His voice was in control, insistent. Compelling. Convincing.

Jenna stood there, suddenly blinking back tears.

"Why don't you answer me?" he persisted quietly. "Maybe because you know you *do* love me?"

Jenna didn't answer because she couldn't answer.

Scott kissed her on her chin, very gently. "Tell me right now that you don't love me," he whispered, just barely holding her, forcing nothing.

Jenna felt herself slipping into the deep end of the pool of his eyes, unable to save herself, no lifeguard in sight. "I can't tell you that," she whispered finally, "because I do still love you. I wish I didn't, but I do love you, so very much. Why else would this be so painful?"

Scott kissed her again, this time on the lips, just the slightest of kisses before he pulled back, his lips hovering a mere fraction of an inch from hers – and waited, drawing in his breath, drawing her with it. Until her lips came to his, of their own volition.

He carried her up the last few steps and into their bedroom – *his* bedroom, she tried to tell herself. And laid her down like a treasure on their bed – *his* bed, *his* bed, she wanted to scream – but didn't.

Instantly, he was beside her, touching her, their eyes locked, his wide with wonder, hers beseeching – for what, she didn't know. His lips joined his fingers, softly touching her, her neck, her cheeks, her ears, everywhere but on her lips, until she finally moaned and again brought hers to his.

Once she tried to say, "Scott, don't, please don't. We can't do this."

So he stopped, just as she asked him to. But he waited a moment, searching her eyes, then asked her, "Do you really want me to stop?" And waited for her answer. She finally had to say, "No," then let go, letting herself free-fall back into his kisses and his hands and the growing heat of his caresses.

BUT WITH CLIMAX came an unavoidable anticlimax, of confusion and bewilderment. A reflexive calm and contentment quickly gave way to reality, for Jenna anyway, as they lay together in each other's arms.

So Jenna was glad when an innocent, sleepy cry of "Daddy?" came from Zach's bedroom. She jumped up, gathered up her clothes that Scott has thrown in all directions and started pulling them back on.

Scott hadn't bothered undressing. With a few quick adjustments, he was heading out the door when Jenna, wriggling back into a pair of tight black jeans, said, "Don't think this changes anything."

He turned back and gave her a wicked grin. "Oh, yes it does," he said with a wink, then disappeared down the hall.

By the time she got to his room, Zach was sitting in Scott's lap having his shoelaces tied for him. The minute he saw Jenna, he crowed "Mommy! Mommy!" Squirming, he jumped down and ran over to her. She picked him up and spun him around, then held him close which made him giggle giddily.

Scott smiled to himself as he waved his wife and son off ten minutes later. "We didn't exactly get the Thanksgiving issue solved," he'd pointed out as he opened the door for her. She'd climbed in, retrieved her keys from behind the visor where she'd tucked them, then rolled down the window.

"I guess we'll have to just play it by ear," Jenna said noncommittally. "Guess we'll think of something."

As she pulled down the driveway, Zach turned in his seat and waved bye-bye to his daddy. Scott waved back, smiling broadly. Then Jenna put a hand out the window and gave him a small wave too. Scott hadn't realized it, but it was the sign he was waiting for. He knew it might take time – but he'd get her back.

SCOTT WASN'T SMILING when he opened a plain six-by-nine manila envelope an hour later. It bore no return address. What it did bear was a photo.

The photo was dark, but there was no denying what it detailed. It was a photo of himself and Ashley West, both lying on their backs, stark naked, limbs akimbo, hair wild, in bed, asleep. He counted: seven empty bottles lay strewn across the sheets. Sheets that covered one of Ashley's feet, and neither of Scott's.

With the photo was a typed note: "$10,000, first of every month. First payment, 12/1/03. And, buddy, don't even wonder if there's any such thing as a grace period."

With the note: a brochure detailing electronic deposit procedures for a bank account in Belize.

SCOTT AND THE BAND were in the studio rehearsing when the studio phone rang. They had just stopped for Scott and Jeff to work out a chord progression. A moment earlier they wouldn't have heard it ring at all.

Ryan was standing nearest; Scott nodded for him to answer it. Picking it up, he said a tentative, "Uh, yeah?" All eyes were on him until he followed that with an equally forthcoming, "Uh, okay." Rolling his eyes, he handed the phone over to Scott like a hand grenade. With the pin drawn. "It's Jenna. For you."

"Have you booked your flight to L.A. yet?" she asked, no greeting.

"Yeah. Seats for all three of us. I left a message on your voice mail."

"You sure it was mine?" she asked. "I never got it."

"Sure I'm sure," he said with irritation, but suddenly wondered if he *was* sure. "It was a recording. I mean a generic recording. You know, 'the party you have reached…' kinda shit –"

"Not mine," she cut him off.

"Well, I did. Flight 67. Eleven fifteen. Three seats, first class. Two together, one behind them. That way you and I can trade off with Zach. And sit together while he's napping," he added, his eyebrows wagging suggestively, strictly for the benefit of the eavesdroppers all around him.

"He'll nap with whoever's with him when he falls asleep," she said sharply, abruptly cutting off any snuggling-under-blankets fantasies he might have had. His remark irritated her; she knew he had an audience.

"Shit, if you want it that way, change 'em for seats at opposite ends of the friggin' cabin, for all I care." He slammed the phone down, and instantly turned on the band. "So what are *you* assholes lookin' at?"

"Knock it off," Jeremy said coldly. "Just knock it the fuck off. You hear any one of us say anything? Your problem with Jenna is your own damn fault, bro," the 'bro' dripping with acid-laced sarcasm. "Do *not* take it out on us. If you do –"

The phone rang again. Eyes locked on Jeremy's, Scott reached for it and held it to his ear. Saying nothing, just listening, his face gave them all a clear barometric reading on how the words he was hearing were affecting him, taking him from defensive, to wary, to neutral, to hopeful, to pleased, without ever uttering a word. "Okay. And, hey – thanks," was all he said, just before he hung up again.

"And…" Jeremy finally said, speaking for all of them.

"She called to apologize," Scott said offhandedly, but offered no more details.

"Oooo-kay," Jeremy said. "Then – back to work?"

"Back to work," Scott nodded. The rest of the afternoon went fine.

SCOTT HAD CALLED GEORGIE to drive them to the airport. Jenna and Zach were standing on the sidewalk waiting when they pulled up to the door of Jenna's apartment building. Both Scott and Georgie jumped out to help them with their luggage.

On the way out to the airport, while Zach made a playroom of the spacious twelve-seater limo, Jenna brought up the difficult subject of what they were going to tell their parents. "You know we can't put it off much longer," she said matter-of-factly. "What's your thinking?"

"I'm sorry," he said, shaking his head. "I haven't been able to come up with anything. And, frankly, I don't want to. I'm sorry Jenna, but you'll just have to wing it." Jenna looked at him in disbelief as his words sank in.

"So – we're back there again?" she said, her anger barely in check.

THOSE WERE THE LAST words either spoke directly to the other until they pulled up in front of Gramma Linda and Grampa Joe's house. All communication between them had been routed to – and through – Zach.

When it came to greeting their parents, Jenna had to draw on the little she'd learned in acting classes, back in the day when she'd attempted to fulfill her father's hopes and plans for her. Linda and Joe appeared on the front step the minute they heard Scott start beeping his horn halfway down the block, and greeted all three of them with ebullient hugs when they reached the door. A few moments later, Adella came running out to gather her precious Jenna, Scott and Zach into her arms as well. To any disinterested observer, there was no sign that anything was amiss between Jenna and Scott.

While Joe and Scott hustled the luggage into the house, half going up to Zach's bedroom, half to the bedroom that had been allotted to Jenna and Scott,

Linda gave Jenna – and now Zach – her customary maternal once-over, adjusting a collar here, rearranging a stray lock of hair there. Adella only beamed, and took Zach from Jenna's arms at the first possible moment. "Come to Auntie 'Della," she cooed to Zach. "Can you say 'Auntie Della'?"

"Tee Dewa," Zach grinned, proud of his verbal skills.

"Auntie," Adella coached him.

"Auntie," he said with no trouble.

"Della?"

"Dewa."

"Auntie Della?"

"Tee Dewa."

After several attempts, Adella finally gave up and accepted her new name. 'Tee Dewa' it would be, for years to come.

Scott came trotting back downstairs, wrapped an arm around Linda, planted a noisy kiss on her cheek, and gave Jenna a smirk and a wink.

Chapter 21

❋

THE FIRST HALF HOUR of the visit required constant vigilance on everyone's part to protect Zach. Racing about, he explored every accessible nook and cranny of Gramma Linda and Grampa Joe's house and grounds. This was his first fully mobile visit west. Fatigue fueled the pandemonium.

"That's my son's son," Joe observed, sweeping Zach up in his arms as he tore past him, heading pell-mell for a dip in the pool. "I'd recommend a pair of trunks and swimming lessons before you try that, young man," he laughed.

Adella caught Zach just as he was about to clamber into a corner cupboard full of fine china and glassware. "Two seconds later and the Wedgwood would have been missing some key pieces, Zach," Linda said, waving a finger sternly in his face, then softening her reprimand with a kiss.

No one, however, could get to him quickly enough to prevent him from falling down a step onto the lower patio. The ensuing tears were half due to pain, half to exhaustion. Jenna finally took charge and carried him upstairs for a nap, ignoring his cries of defiance all the way.

WHEN SHE CAME back down, she found Scott in the study. "Where are Mom and Dad?" Jenna asked.

"Here we are," Linda answered as the two of them came into the room. "Zach's all settled?"

"Asleep almost before I could get him into the crib," Jenna smiled.

Everyone sat down. Conversation flowed comfortably enough at first, but then started hitting snags, seemingly innocuous questions that would send Jenna looking to Scott for an answer or vice versa. After enough of these, Joe finally posed the question that had really been on his and Linda's minds all along. "So what was with the concert in Chicago?" he asked Scott. "The rags sure have had a field day with that one."

Scott tried to toss it off. "Win a few, lose a few – it was an off night. What can I say?"

"Which you decided to sit out? That was some kinda game plan?" Joe was determined to get a real answer out of his son. "What was that all about, when the lights came up? It was on Entertainment Tonight, the whole megillah, soup to nuts."

Jenna looked warily at Scott, who'd jumped up and gone over to the fireplace to look at a photo of Jenna and her brother Chris as youngsters. From across the room, she could feel Scott's blood pressure rising.

"I felt like crap," was all he was willing to say. "I was sick."

"Flu?" Linda asked.

"Something like that."

"So what happened to the old 'the show must go on,' son?" Joe asked unsympathetically; there was nothing sentimental about his use of the word 'son.'

Scott's eyes, still on Linda, swiveled to look at his father; his head did not. His father had rarely employed the term 'son' without sarcasm when Scott was a boy, and his use of it in that fashion had traditionally preceded outbursts of violence. The decades since he'd last heard Joe use the word that way evaporated, instantly plummeting him back into childhood scenarios of powerlessness and rage. The most primitive passions of fight and flight struggled for supremacy within him. Only the fact that he was in Linda's home inhibited him from physically attacking his father.

Jenna repressed the urge to intervene. She was through intervening in Scott's life. Let him make a fool of himself, she thought. He doesn't want to talk about it? Good luck. This was as good a way as any to bring up "the problem." She put her feet up on an ottoman, crossed her arms and sat back, almost pleased to have a front row seat to see how Scott was going to worm his way out of this one.

Scott turned to face his father square on, but made no move in his direction.

"And can it be true," Linda stepped in, "what I saw in the tabloids – that you're living apart?" she addressed this question to Jenna. So much for being able to play audience.

Jenna looked down, letting her hair fall to cover much of her face. She sighed, then shaking her hair back, looked firmly at Scott. Her eyes said it all: she made it perfectly clear that it was his job to explain.

"Okay. Okay. I'll tell you," Scott said, primarily addressing his father, but including Linda where Jenna was concerned.

He told them about everything, going back all the way to Zach's birth and the enormous stress that put him under. He told them about Jenna's miscarriage that followed, and Jenna's desperate desire to have another child. How Billy Malone's trial had plunged her back into nightmares and made her decide to wait on further attempts at getting pregnant until the living nightmare of Grand Jury testimony and the trial itself was over. He talked about their adjustments to life with Zach, to getting back out on the road touring and all the insanity that entailed. He hesitated, then looked his father in the eye and brought up his fears that he might one day turn violent with his own son. He left the rest of that thought unspoken, but Joe knew it all and looked away.

And then he told them about Ashley, about losing control, about going to a bar, about her showing up at the moment she did. "Who knows. I might have downed that shot and started a ten-day bender and who knows what all else. What did I do instead? I started World War III with my wife. I know it's no excuse, but I needed something or someone at that moment, desperately – and in she walked. I never went looking for anyone, and I never meant for anything to happen between us, but the next thing I knew I was in bed with her. The next morning Jenna came to surprise me. Great surprise. I've tried to explain it to her ever since, but this is actually the first time she's heard the whole story. What you saw, the show in Chicago – which was that night, the night of the morning Jenna walked in and found me in bed with this woman – was what was left of me after Jenna walked out. That's the whole thing."

Of course, it wasn't the whole thing; he didn't tell them about the blackmail. Only Scott knew about the blackmail, and that was how he intended to keep it. But it clearly was a relief for him to get this much off his chest.

"I'm sorry that it happened," he continued, now just addressing Jenna. "You don't know how sorry I am. I know how much I've hurt you. I'm hurting too – I never wanted this to happen, and now I don't know what to do to make it up to you."

Jenna sat silent, tears streaming down her face.

LINDA AND JOE sat silent for quite a while, too. Once again, it was Joe who got the conversation rolling again. In his plain-spoken way, he wasted no words cutting to the heart of the matter. "Well, son," he said – but this time he'd returned to the benign, nonjudgmental use of the word, "I guess I'd have to say you've got one big mess on your hands. What I'd like to know is, what are you planning on doing about it?"

Linda looked at Jenna, and had her say. "Jenna, you, I imagine, must be devastated. What are *you* going to do about it?"

Neither parent expressed anger. Scott was dumbfounded. He had just told them he had cheated on Jenna and they hadn't said a word about it. He would have expected his father to at least point out how thoroughly he'd screwed up again. And Linda should be furious for his cheating on her daughter.

But it was Jenna who gave voice to his confusion. "Wait a second here," she sputtered. "I don't get it. What's this 'what are you going to do about it' bullshit? Nobody's gonna give Scott holy hell for what *he* did?"

Linda looked at the two of them with genuine compassion. "Oh, don't worry, we're angry all right. We're angry that you haven't said word one to us about this whole situation. It's been how long – almost a month? As for what Scott did, you bet I'm mad, but it's not up to us to deal with it. We both love you – *both* of you – and we're here if you need our support, but you two need to deal with this together." Jenna and Scott looked at each, equally stunned.

"Just remember one thing, Jenna," Linda continued. "Your father cheated on me, and not only that, he even had another child. It took some time, but we were eventually able to get back together after all that – because we loved each other."

"And, Scott," Joe said quietly, soberly, "you didn't know about it, but I had an affair years back as well. It was the biggest mistake of my life, but your mother forgave me and we got back together. We know you're not us, and that everyone handles thing differently. But the bottom line is, if you truly love each other, and we know you do, then it's worth fighting for your marriage."

"I only have one question," Linda said, pragmatically. "Sleeping arrangements. You have Zach in one room and Chris is going to be in the other when he gets here. That just leaves the one room for the two of you."

"Hey, I'm all for it," Scott said. "No problem. It's a king-size. Plenty of room for the warring parties."

Jenna grimaced. "Fine," she said coolly, directing her answer specifically to Scott. "We'll share the same bed, but you better not lay one finger on me." She was relieved to have everything so completely out in the open. She was especially relieved to know she could talk to her mother about it all.

DINNER THAT EVENING was strained. Zach did his best to keep the conversational ball rolling, but it was hard work – these quiet adults weren't reacting to anything he said or did the way he'd come to expect. He ran through his entire bag of tricks but could barely get a rise from his audience. Some of them were real showstoppers, like his particular favorite, wearing spaghetti like a wig – that usually brought down the house. Tonight, nothing, just a quick and undignified clean-up.

Finally, they left him no choice: he stood up in his highchair and performed a perfect swan dive – onto the dinner table. *That* worked. Everyone was onto their feet and jabbering like crazy, just the way he loved it. Ten minutes later, Mommy was putting him to bed. Maybe he'd have to rethink that particular move.

JENNA AND SCOTT spent the evening apart. Scott made a couple of phone calls and decided to go out for a bit, but Jenna opted to stay home and spend time with her mother and Joe. She also decided to get to bed early.

Scott came in quietly. Jenna wasn't asleep yet. "Who were you with," she asked him as he undressed.

"Nobody you need to be jealous of," he answered lightly.

"No, really, who?" Jenna asked. "I'm not being jealous. I'm just being curious."

"Johnny Van Zant and Gary Rossington. I'd heard Johnny was in town. We're talking about maybe trying to have both our tours hook up for a few shows next summer. Blacklace/Skynard – it'd be a ballbuster. I told him I'd ask you if you'd like to get in on it. You and your band, not just singing with us. Actually, we got to thinking a couple more top acts and, hell, maybe we could make a festival out of it, somewhere where it could be huge, for a cause.

Lord knows the world'll never run out of causes. I could do with sharin' the pressure for a change."

He climbed into bed just as Jenna said, "Cool idea."

"Sure is. Something to look forward to. Big Bob'll hate it – it's a bloody logistical nightmare for him and his guys, but I know Strang won't take any arm-twisting."

"A good mix of acts. Any idea where?"

"We're thinking East Coast, them being from the south and us representing Yankee land. Call it the Mason Dixon something-the-fuck-or-other. And have it be just East Coast acts."

"Sure," Jenna said enthusiastically. "The Allman Brothers, of course. Hey, Dylan may be from Minnesota, but he's got plenty of New York credentials. Arlo Guthrie's Massachusetts."

"And born in Brooklyn. We could get Jerry Lee Lewis and Little Richard for southern roots. Too bad we can't have the Ramones."

"No, but you could have Phish."

"And a Boston ska band or two." Scott stopped, looked at her, then took her hand and started massaging it. "This is so much better than fighting." Jenna didn't say anything. "This is what we do best," he added, then brought her fingers to his lips, kissed them, then pressed them to his heart.

"Scott…" Jenna started, but his lips stopped her from saying anything further. While she couldn't protest, he pulled her close. Before long, there was no turning back. Once again Jenna couldn't control her physical desires. He slipped into her easily. "Try tellin' me you don't want this as much as I do," he chuckled quietly into her ear.

"I don't," she protested, but her body had to disagree. She clung to him hungrily even as her brain shouted, "Don't!" As she came, she cried, "Oh, God, don't let me love him so much."

In the aftermath, Scott held Jenna until she suddenly began sobbing and turned away from him. "I told you, sex doesn't change anything," she said when she could speak again.

"Christ," Scott said after several moments of gathering frustration. "Talk about mixed messages. What am I supposed to think?"

"Look," Jenna said patiently. "There's the intellectual conversation and there's the physical conversation. On the physical level, we speak the same language, fluently, unconsciously. But when it comes to *thinking* about what we're doing here, we might as well come from opposite ends of the universe."

Finally, she got up and went into the shower, leaving Scott lying in bed, thinking.

THANKSGIVING AND LINDA and Joe's anniversary were celebrated by a small gathering of the clan this year. Kristin was the first to arrive; Jenna announced she needed some serious sister time with Kris. With Linda's blessing, the two jumped back into Kristin's car and disappeared for a couple of hours.

Chris and Jim arrived together. Jim was batching it for the holiday; Sue was en route to Sacramento for a series of interviews for a top spot in Glenn Cattrell's campaign for the U.S. senate. She really wanted the job; it would be a hard-fought contest affording her terrific visibility. The fact that she'd be running the L.A. office, close to home, was just the icing on the cake.

Scott got up a game of patio touch football, himself, Zach and Joe on one team, Chris and Jim on the other. Joe ran interference for his flowerbeds as well as for his star quarterback, who played the entire game with Zach on his back. Zach quickly learned a few appropriate expressions of encouragement. Words like "Go, Daddy!" and "Get outta the way!" and "Kill 'em, Gwampa!" were soon rolling off his much-jostled tongue.

"So how are things?" Kristin asked Jenna as they pulled out the drive. Jenna took a deep breath, then told her just how things were. At one point Kristin had to pull over to the curb to simply stare at his sister. "How can you talk about all this and like keep your cool?" she asked in wonder. "I'd be facing like first degree murder charges by now."

"I – what can I say? It's – complicated," Jenna confessed. "I love him. I know I should have my head examined – I *am* having my head examined, and it really keeps us busy in my sessions, trying to sort out all my 'conflicted' thinking, as my therapist likes to call it. Just plain fucked up thinking, is what I call it. I just don't know if I could ever forgive what he did."

While Zach went for a walk with his "Gwampa" Joe, Chris, Jim and Scott were having basically the same conversation back home. Scott was overwhelmed and humbled by the nonjudgmental support his brothers-in-law had to offer.

Jenna and Scott sat across from each other at the Thanksgiving dinner table. Scott held her eyes as the family held hands around the table and Joe said grace. "Bless us, O Lord, and these Thy gifts which we are about to receive from Thy bounty. We thank you for bringing us all together today. We thank you for the hardships and difficulties you put in our paths, and for helping us to find our way through them and to hopefully grow in wisdom from the experience. Through Christ our Lord. Amen."

When they went to bed that night, Scott left Jenna alone as she had asked him.

THEIR PARTING THE NEXT day, after the long flight home, was amicable. Jenna encouraged him to call when he wanted to plan another visit with Zach. Otherwise, she had said little as they made their way into Boston from the airport.

When she got home and had put Zach down for his nap, she fixed herself a cup of tea, sat in front of a small fire and had a long, silent heart-to-heart with herself. By the time she went to bed she had made a serious decision. She had needed to be alone to make it.

Chapter 22

⁕

TWO WEEKS PASSED. Jenna and Scott fell into an uncomfortable routine. Scott would call, arrange to pick up Zach, bring him back, make a pass at Jenna and be consistently rebuffed. Her rejections grew a little bit firmer, a little bit angrier every time.

Jenna had booked extra sessions with her therapist and more than the usual number of lunches with her best friend. She needed help thinking her way through the realities of life with Scott. Cutting him slack has become almost an unconscious habit, to the point that she'd long since stopped questioning why she did it – and if she should.

Raising a child in the midst of this relationship put things in a new perspective. What kind of life lessons was Zach absorbing from growing up with all this? What kind of example was she setting for him? Was she accommodating Scott's idiosyncrasies or was she living a lie? Were his idiosyncrasies harmless or harmful? Heaven knew she had idiosyncrasies of her own. These were life questions, powerful and unavoidable, and it was time, she knew, to face them head on. She pondered them endlessly, with and without Melanie and Carrie's help.

She knew she had to make a decision. She knew the decision came down to her; Scott seemed capable of living with the status quo indefinitely. She could not.

SCOTT WAS FIXING himself and the rest of the band a late lunch when they all heard a knock at the back door. Ryan went to answer it, then reappeared in the kitchen. "It's someone to see you, Scott," he reported back.

"Somebody keep stirring for me," Scott said. Jeff stepped into the breech, taking up the wooden spatula without missing a beat. "Don't let that garlic burn."

Scott found a clean-cut, nondescript young man in a trim blue blazer and striped tie, standing at the door, looking over the property. He had a clipboard under his arm, Scott noted with annoyance. A petition, he guessed. A little too presentable for a save-the-earth type. Collecting signatures to get someone on the ballot? Bible salesman?

"Nice place," he said genially as he turned to Scott. "Are you Scott Tenny?" Clearly not a fan.

"I am."

"Could you sign here, please?" he asked, holding his clipboard up to Scott. Under the clip was simply an envelope and a receipt. So much for petitions. Scott scribbled his signature, then took the envelope. "Thanks. Have a nice day," the man said, turning to go. Then he turned back, almost as an afterthought. "You've been served."

Scott felt like he'd been slapped across the face. Hard. He'd heard the expression enough times. Now he knew why. He walked back into the kitchen like a sleepwalker.

"What is it?" Jeremy asked.

"I – I've 'been served.' Legal papers, I guess. I –" He stopped and looked down at the envelope in his hands. "What the –"

"Open it," Dan prompted him.

"You're among friends," Tim added. "What's a paternity suit among friends?" Scott found himself hoping that's all it was. Something told him otherwise.

Dropping his lank frame onto a stool at the counter, he discovered his hands were shaking as he went to open it. Dan pulled a knife from a wooden block on the counter and held it out to him. Jeremy grabbed a chop stick from a container of utensils and pushed it ahead of Dan's knife. "Use this. You're sure to take a finger off with that thing," he said.

Scott took the chopstick, slid it under the flap and ripped into the envelope. There was something satisfying about the sloppy edge the blunt instrument left in its wake. Reaching in, he pulled out a single sheet of paper. Silence reigned while he read it, though his eyes never got past the first sentence. Jenna has served him with divorce papers. "Motherfucker!" he exploded. "She can't be serious about this."

"What is it?" Jeremy dared to ask. "Who?"

"Jenna. Wants a divorce," Scott said, dazed. "I was just there a couple days ago. She never said a word. Hell, we made love at Thanksgiving."

He looked down again at the paper in his hand. It still said the same thing. Scott started shaking his head, then flung it across the room. "Well, I'm sure as hell not going to make this easy for her. She wants a divorce, she's gonna have herself one *very* long wait. Hell can freeze over –"

"Don't go doin' anything stupid," Jeremy interjected. "You've managed to fucked everything up good and proper up to this point. Don't go making matters any worse."

Scott started for door. "Hey, where are you going?" Jeremy called after him.

He stopped and turned back to Jeremy. "Don't worry, big brother. I'm not going to do anything stupid. Matter of fact – I'm gonna do just the opposite."

"For a change," Jeremy observed.

Outside, Scott pulled out his cell phone. Pacing the path between the house and the studio, he called Jenna. She answered on the third ring.

"Hey," he said noncommittally.

"Uh, hi," she said, equally coolly.

"Look, I just wanted to see if I can have Zach for the weekend."

"Uh, well...sure," Jenna said.

"Friday. Three okay?"

"Yeah...three's fine. Do you – would you like Ellen to come with you guys?"

"No. Give her the weekend off. She deserves it. Well, that's it really. See you Friday," he said casually. He flipped his phone closed and slipped it back into his pocket and smiled. He liked his plan.

Jenna sat looking at the dead phone in her hands, not knowing what to think.

SCOTT ARRIVED AT Jenna's ten minutes early Friday afternoon. Zach's things were ready by the door. Zach was just getting one more truck out of his toy box when the doorbell rang. "Daddy!" he yelled, grabbed out a black pickup truck and came racing down the hall and into Scott's open arms. Scott swung him up into the air and back down onto his feet with a grin.

"How are you, Zach-o?" he asked, dropping to his haunches to zip up his son's jacket. "You're gonna need this, little man. It's wicked cold outside." Turning to Jenna, he added, "I'll have him back by naptime Sunday. You have a good weekend, okay?"

He took Zach by one hand, opened the door, then picked up Zach's duffle with the other. "Get the door for me?" he asked over his shoulder with a wink, then he left.

Jenna stared after him, blinking, then went and closed the door. Then she dialed the phone, gave her name and asked for her lawyer. Chuck Lunt quickly came on the line. "What is it, Jenn?"

"Those papers were served on Scott, right?"

"Sure. Tuesday. They've been filed with the court. Why? What's the matter?"

"Nothing – I guess," Jenna said vaguely.

JENNA'S WEEKEND WITHOUT Zach vanished in all the last-minute details of the second annual – how she loved those two words! – fundraiser for South Shore First Step. The shelter, which had been operating at capacity almost every day this past year, was already suffering from growing pains. Word has spread rapidly through the area. Once a viable alternative had opened up, numerous women made the decision not to stay in abusive – in some cases dangerous – relationships. Jenna couldn't help but wince at the irony of her own situation. If only Scott didn't have a warm and loving side to him. But she knew it was precisely this kind of thinking that got so many women into serious trouble.

'If only…' She'd come to think of 'if only' the two most dangerous words in the English language.

Scott had been so proud of her, the night of the grand opening of the shelter, one year ago now. Jenna had to laugh – she had attended enough galas in her relatively short lifetime to last anyone a long lifetime, but that gala had been special beyond compare. That night wasn't just an event; it was an achievement, the fulfillment of a dream. It hadn't exorcised all her personal demons as she had to admit she'd hoped it might – if anything, it had served as an almost daily reminder of the traumas she had survived as a child. But if it prevented even one more such trauma from happening to another human being, then it gave meaning to her suffering.

This year's fundraiser was slated to be a scaled back version of last year's extravaganza, utilizing the ballroom of a local hotel and strictly local talent: a pair of hot Boston stand-up comedians, an urban/country fusion band from Quincy, and a truncated, mini-version of Blacklace: just Scott, Jeremy and Tim on the drums. Nevertheless, they'd had no trouble selling every seat in the ballroom, at the same price as the previous year. Jenna was terrified that Scott would blow before the event. But so far, he'd been nothing but a pussycat.

SCOTT BROUGHT ZACH back right on schedule and left his son with a warm and loving embrace, much to Zach's dismay, with still not one word to Jenna about the divorce. The best she could make of it, talking with Carrie a few minutes after Scott had left, was that maybe he was finally taking her seriously. Their marriage was over.

"Hey, hon," Carrie said, "he and Jeremy are having dinner at Blue Skies tonight. I know Jer plans to try and work him over, get him to talk about it. I'll let you know what I can get out of him when he gets home." Jeremy was as much in the dark regarding the divorce papers as anyone. He'd given Scott plenty of openings, but so far Scott hadn't said a word about any of it to anyone.

JEREMY WAS ALREADY there when Scott pulled into the parking lot outside Blue Skies. The lot was jammed. By now, Blacklace fans knew that Sunday night the odds went up for a Blacklace sighting.

A pair of really cute teenagers in matching pleated miniskirts and long, animated pigtails were hanging all over Jeremy when Scott walked in. The moment they saw him, they forgot about Jeremy; Scott became the focus of their giggling attentions. Scott gave them each a hug and an autograph and shooed them away.

"Fickle bitches," Jeremy groused as Scott sat down. "Man, these days you can't tell if they're just playin' dress-up or if they really are cheerleaders."

"Either way, they're jail bait, those two anyway," Scott chuckled. "Looked pretty yummy, though." He shook his head wistfully. "Ah, to be seventeen again."

"Don't go there," Jeremy said gravely.

"Nah," Scott dismissed the idea. "Wouldn't really want to anyway. Not unless I could take all this accumulated wisdom I've paid so dearly for with me."

"So, bro – um, like where you at, in the accumulated wisdom department, anyway?" Jeremy asked cautiously, but their conversation was immediately interrupted by the arrival of their waitress. They placed their order – a pair of lasagnas, a pair of Caesar salads, a pair of club sodas, then Jeremy immediately returned to his unanswered question.

Scott thought a moment before he spoke. "Man, if I knew last month what I know this month…" he said, intentionally vague.

Jeremy wasn't in the mood for vague. "Jenna served you with papers," he said plainly. "The topic is divorce. As in – divorce."

Much as Scott tried to dodge the topic, Jeremy held him to it. When it became plain that Jeremy wasn't going to let up until he was satisfied, Scott finally gave in and really addressed his thoughts, his emotions – and what he referred to several times as his 'cockeyed plan' to win Jenna back.

Neither noticed the man eating alone a couple of tables over. He wore what anyone would have assumed was a hearing aid, had anyone bothered to notice. It aided his hearing, all right, and it recorded it as well. It had a supersonic sound enhancer and he had calibrated the gizmo specifically to listen in on Scott and Jeremy's conversation. He'd paid practically two hundred bucks for the thing, off the Internet.

He'd followed Jeremy into the restaurant and had quietly slipped the maitre'd a twenty for "that nice table by the window."

THE PHONE RANG early the next morning, waking Jenna.

"Yeah?" she answered it after a few false fumbles.

"You seen the papers yet this morning, hon?" It was Carrie.

"No. I'm not up yet."

"Sorry. But you better take a look. Right away."

Jenna padded on to the kitchen in bathrobe and slippers. Ellen had already put on a pot of coffee and brought in the paper, which was sitting undisturbed on the kitchen counter. Jenna poured herself a cup of coffee, popped a bagel into the toaster, then sat down with the paper.

When she reached the entertainment section, she knew why Carrie had called. First she took in the picture of Scott and her singing together – the Boston Garden the preceding year, she thought. Then she took in the headline: "Boston's Cinderella Couple Headed for Divorce." Her eyes glued to the headline, she reached for the phone. Carrie picked up on the first ring.

"Where the hell did this come from?" Jenna wailed. "Oh, my God, I don't believe this. Has Scott seen it yet?"

"Oh, yeah," Carrie told her. "He called here over an hour ago. He was raging. Somebody obviously leaked it to the press. I asked him if he was going to call you but he said no. He – he said he figured you wouldn't care, since you're the one who filed for the divorce in the first place."

"I – I – where would he get that idea?" Jenna sputtered. "I may have filed for it, sure, but I value my privacy every bit as much as he does his. This is ungodly! I – I really can't talk. This is – just too damned much." She hung up the phone and cried, as much because she'd had to hear about it from Carrie rather than Scott.

JENNA WAS JUST GLAD that all of the meetings for the benefit were already over. Mortified, she had no desire to face people. What still needed attention could be handled on the phone.

The people she did have to call were respectful; nobody brought up the story, though she knew they'd all seen and/or heard either the original itself or any of the avalanche of spin-offs that ended up in other papers and on radio and television. You'd have to be a hermit in the Himalayas not to have come across it; no one involved on the benefit committee was a hermit in the Himalayas.

JENNA SPENT LONGER than usual dressing for the benefit. She fussed with her hair until she finally just said, "Screw it," and glued it in place with hairspray. Her gown, which had looked like a glowing sea green print when she'd tried it on, looked like camouflage under the lights in her bathroom. It made her look green, she thought with a groan, squinting at herself as she reached for the blusher.

Jenna had never felt so alone as when she walked into the lavishly decorated hall where the event was taking place, though people immediately started coming up to her, drawing her into noticeably over-animated conversation. It helped, but she couldn't stop herself from keeping half a lookout for Scott. She knew he and the rest of the band were there mingling as well. She still hadn't run into him when it was time for her to get up and make her speech.

Jenna waited at the foot of the podium as speaker after speak sung her praises. "It would be easy for Jenna Tenny to simply lend her name – and her fame – to this ambitious enterprise, and let it go at that," said the president of the board. "Many celebrities do. Please don't misunderstand. I am not belittling their contributions or intentions – they play a tremendously valuable role just bringing attention to many worthy causes. But Jenna B. Tenny, whose brain child we are here to celebrate and support tonight, has stayed involved, from the inception, through the realization of her dream, and beyond. I do not exaggerate when I say that Jenna Tenny is a star among stars. Jenna Tenny!"

Jenna climbed the three steps to the podium and took her place behind the microphone as the entire room rose to its feet and applauded her. Smiling broadly, she waited them out until she could finally speak.

As she spoke, from the heart and without notes, she found herself scanning the crowd, looking for Scott in spite of herself. When she suddenly spotted him, their eyes locked and she lost her train of thought momentarily. It took all the will power and presence of mind she could muster for her to tear her gaze away from him and finish her remarks.

After the speeches were over, Jenna found herself drawn to the part of the room where she'd last seen Scott. She kept telling herself she wasn't trying to find him – but she was, and she knew it. She started to assume he'd left to get ready to perform when a voice behind her, speaking intimately into her ear, startled her. "Looking for me?" She turned to find Scott standing before her.

A lie came to her lips – but the truth, or at least a fairly reasonable facsimile of the truth, came out. "I – I just wanted to thank you for being here, that's all."

He smiled at her, then took her hand. "It's my pleasure. You've done good work for the shelter." Looking deep into her eyes, he brought her hand to his lips, took his time kissing it, then turned around and walked away.

THE EVENT MADE the Boston papers the following morning, with far more about Jenna and Scott than about the shelter and the benefit that had brought them together for an evening. Someone had shot several pictures of them. The *Herald* had run four of them, including one of Scott kissing her hand. The caption under that picture shot read, "Is Scott Tenny back to playing Prince Charming?"

Jenna smiled – and found herself wishing she was sharing the article and pictures with him.

Chapter 23

※

JENNA WAS STILL SMILING when the phone rang, and she was still looking at the picture as she answered it. It was her mother, which only served to deepen her smile.

"About Christmas." No hello, how are you. Linda was in her all-business mode this morning. Jenna's smile started to slide. "What's this I hear now? You're having it at Scott's? What's wrong with Boston?"

"Guest rooms, Mom. Remember?"

"And I have to hear this from Joe? I mean, whatever happened to keeping me in the loop? I *am* your mother."

"Oh, I know *that*," Jenna said. (Except when you're not, her inner twelve-year-old had to remind her. Shut up, Jenna told her sharply.) "I'm sorry, Mom. It's been crazy. Last night was the benefit." Silence. "Which went really well. We raised close to a hundred thousand dollars." Silence. "For the shelter." This time Jenna waited out her mother's silence.

"Well, that's very nice. That's great, dear," Linda finally begrudged her daughter. "You got my social conscience."

Mom, why does it always have to be about you? Jenna's inner adult sighed. Getting through Christmas was going to be tough enough.

PULLING IN JUST BEFORE dark, Jenna and Zach were the last to arrive at Scott's. She practically had to park on the street. Everyone was there – all of Blacklace and its extended family, Scott's daughters and their families. Scott's sister and her husband had arrived in one car; his nephew and niece had both driven up from Connecticut in their own cars, "In case either of us needs to make a quick getaway," David had explained to Scott when he got there.

"When did you get so smart?" Scott laughed.

"Takin' notes," David grinned. The two were just exchanging a high-five when Annie came into the room.

"Well, there you are, David. What on earth took you so long?" she asked her son suspiciously. "And why you had to come in your own car is beyond me. All that gas. It doesn't grow on trees, you know." David rolled his eyes for Scott's benefit only. Annie would have had plenty more to say on the subject had Jenna and Zach not chosen that moment to make their entrance.

Jenna set Zach on his feet and he burst into the living room like a greyhound released from the starting gate. Jenna, on the other hand, hung back at the door, feeling awkward and self-conscious.

Scott hurried over to her, in the role of gracious host, not wronged husband, to her surprise – and relief. Helping her out of her coat, he threw it over his arm and encouraged her to go into the living room while he hung it up.

By the time he returned, she'd been welcomed by all and was sitting cross-legged in a chair by the fire, with Luka and Zach in her lap and Aiden and Travis hanging over her. At sixteen and fifteen respectively, the two Sons of Blacklace, as they'd taken to calling themselves, were getting used to their clumsy, lanky teenage bodies as gracefully as any teenagers could. The official ranks of the Sons of Blacklace would swell to include Luka and Zach before Christmas was over.

"Oh, I need to get our presents from the car," Jenna announced, starting to dislodge Zach and Luka.

"Stay where you are," Scott said. "I'll get them." She tossed him the keys, which he caught single-handedly.

"Hey, you should be playing for the Sox," Aiden said.

"Left-handed," Scott said, holding them up for all to see. "Not bad for a righty."

Jeremy followed him as he went out to the driveway, which turned out to be a good thing; there were more presents than one person could carry.

"You okay?" Jeremy asked Scott as he loaded him up.

"I'm okay," Scott said.

"How are you guys gonna get through this?"

"Beats me. I tried talkin' to her about it last night," Scott said. "All she'd say was she'd be fine. We'll just have to wait and see. As for me, don't worry – I *will* be fine. It may not be as bad as you think. Really."

Jeremy shot him a look. Scott was clearly up to something. He also knew it was pointless to ask.

MISSY CAME OVER and asked Jenna if she and Laurel could talk to her alone.

"Sure, hon," Jenna said. "Let's go into the study." The three of them did.

Laurel was clearly the designated spokesperson for the two sisters. "Jenna," she said, a bit uncomfortably at first, "we just want to let you know that no matter what happens between you and Dad, we both plan to stay in contact with you. After all, Zach's our brother. But more than that – we both love you."

Jenna was moved to tears, tears she'd told herself were not going to happen to spoil anyone's holiday. Laurel hugged her warmly and the tears finally flowed.

"I can't believe Dad was such an ass, what he did," she whispered in Jenna's ear. Missy wrapped her arms around both her sister and Jenna and hugged them both hard. Jenna welcomed their warmth and love, but had to pull away.

"You two are incredible," she said, trying to choke back her tears. "I really appreciate your love and support but I – I just can't talk about it now. I don't want to break down in front of everyone."

"We understand," Laurel said, squeezing her hand. "We just needed to tell you."

Jenna smiled at her bleakly. "I love you both," she whispered.

Laurel and Missy returned to the living room while Jenna pulled herself back together. She finally felt able to join them and had just walked back in as Scott entered from the kitchen and announced that dinner was ready. Turning, he took Jenna's hand without any fanfare, as if it were the most natural thing in the world, and launched into a brief prayer. "Bless, oh Lord, this food to thy use, and make us ever mindful of the wants and needs of others. Amen."

Releasing her hand with only a small squeeze and a quick smile, he started herding everyone towards the kitchen. Jenna hung back, finding herself once again fighting tears. Oh, how she loved this Scott. Every good and normal thing he did was like an exquisitely sharp scalpel slipping easily into the most tender, indefensible part of her heart.

Scott came over to her again. "Go eat," he said. "I'll take care of seeing that Zach does." She turned away from him, but not before he saw her tears, caught her and turned her back to him. Shaking his head, his expression one of genuine sadness and regret, for her, for himself, for both of them, he gently kissed her on the cheek. Just as quickly, he released her and caught Zach as he raced by, picked him up and carried him off to the kitchen. Jenna's hand touched the phantom imprint of his lips on her cheek.

After dinner, Laurel and Rick began what they knew was going to be the difficult process of getting Luka to go to bed. "I wanna stay up till Santa comes!" he screamed. Then he ran over to Zach, whose energy was running down quickly. "Do you know who Santa is?" he asked his uncle, his eyes wide with excitement.

"Santa!" Zach said, waking back up with Luka's enthusiasm.

"Presents!" Luka summed it all up, his arms flying in the air like a victorious boxer.

"Pwesents!" Zach agreed, and the two high-fived with all the cool of a pair of frat boys. They brought the house down.

Just before midnight, everyone who was still awake gathered around the tree to sing "Silent Night." Jenna stood to the back of the gathering, by herself. Scott turned and found her, then quietly stepped back beside her and put his arm around her as they sang, and she leaned her head against his chest reflexively, without thinking.

When they finished the song, Scott kissed her, then whispered, "I love you. Happy Anniversary." She turned, buried her head in his chest, crying silently. Scott felt warm tears soak through his shirt.

The plan was for Jenna to bunk with Zach, who was sound asleep when she finally came in; there would be no need to tiptoe. As she undressed, she heard a quiet knock on the door. Without waiting for an invitation, Scott stepped into the room to find her naked to the waist. She quickly grabbed her shirt to cover herself.

"What are you doing in here?" she whispered angrily.

Scott came over to her, took the shirt out of her hand and stood looking at it, not her. "You don't need to cover up in front of me," he said quietly but forcefully. "You know and I know that this isn't how either one of us hoped our anniversary would turn out. Jenna, we need to talk. Come with me, into our bedroom."

He reached a hand out to her but Jenna didn't take it. "Jenna, please, just come with me," he pressed her, handing her the shirt, which she slipped into, buttoning several buttons. "I promise if you want to come back I won't try and stop you. I don't want to wake Zach." She relented, but still didn't take his hand.

Walking into their bedroom, her mouth fell open. The room was aglow with candles and red roses. At first, she couldn't say anything. Then she stammered, "What – why – why did you do this?" she turned to him. "What are you trying to prove?" she said, but not in anger. She was genuinely astonished.

"I did it because I love you. I did it because it's our anniversary." He took her in his arms. "I'm trying to show you that I still love you. I'm hoping – counting on the fact – that we still love each other. We owe it to ourselves, and our son, to try to work things out between us."

Holding her at arms length, he looked into her eyes, searching for some sign to fuel his slim supply of hope. "Jenna, I know you love me," he insisted, his tone earnest, beseeching. "As you know, I haven't said a word about your filing for divorce." He let go of her and dropped to the edge of the bed, holding his head in his hands. "Don't get me wrong," he said, looking up at her. "It's not because I didn't want to come over and shove those fuckin' papers down your throat. I did it to show you that I'd do *anything* to make you happy. If you think a divorce is going to do that, then fine. Tell me so and I'll let you walk out of here right now without saying another word. It's completely up to you."

Jenna stood looking at him, then looked down and closed her eyes. Then she opened them and started for the door. Then she stopped.

She turned around, "I can't, I can't do it. I can't walk out," she said.

QUITE A WHILE LATER, as they lay in each other's arms catching their breath, Scott turned to her. Tracing a finger down her profile backlit by a December moon, he whispered, "Jenna, do you have any regrets?"

She turned to him. "Just one," she said. "There's something I forgot."

"What?"

She didn't answer. Instead, sliding sinuously down his naked body, she let her lips show him what she'd neglected.

"Does that answer your question?" she asked him finally, when he had come yet again. Scott wrapped an arm and both legs around her as they both fell asleep, as if he feared that she might not be there when he woke in the morning otherwise.

CHRISTMAS DAY BROUGHT with it a dark sky ready to deliver the first snow of the season. Scott and Jenna woke almost simultaneously, so extraordinary it seemed to be waking up together again. They immediately moved into a mutual kiss, both needing to reassure themselves that the night before hadn't been a dream.

Scott pulled back, looked at her and smiled. "What a Christmas present, you in our bed," he said quietly. "Last night meant more to me than you'll ever know. I just hope it meant as much you."

Jenna nodded sleepily. "It did. I love you, Scott," she whispered. He took her hands in his.

"Jenna, I want you back," he said fervently. "I want to wake up with you like this every morning for the rest of my life. I know you're still hurt and angry with me, as well you should be. I deserve it. But I'm asking you to stop this divorce business. Will you go to counseling with me? Are you willing to give our marriage another chance? Will you do that with me?"

Jenna leaned into him and gave him another kiss. "Yes," she said solemnly. "I want to give us another chance. I will go to counseling with you. But there's one condition: I can't move back here. I'm not ready for that yet. If you can accept that, then let's make an appointment tomorrow."

Scott hugged her tight, then found her lips with his. "Oh, babe, thank you, thank you," he said, happier than she could remember seeing him in a long, long time. "I promise I'll never let you down again. Can we go tell everyone?"

Jenna smiled at him as he still lay in bed. "Sure. What are you waiting for? We can't tell them if you don't get up." He was out of bed like a jackrabbit.

EVERYONE WAS UP when Jenna and Scott appeared in the living room, hand in hand. Linda was the only one who didn't look surprised. She knew Jenna hadn't slept in Zach's room. She'd heard her grandson as she was waking up and hadn't understood why Jenna hadn't gotten up with him.

Approaching his room, Linda saw that Zach's door was open. Peeking in to find Zach with one leg over the bars of his crib and a devious grin on his face, it was immediately obvious that Jenna hadn't slept there. Her motherly radar had been keenly attuned to the chemistry between Scott and Jenna the night before. She was ready to bet serious money on just where her daughter had passed the night.

Scott didn't give anyone a moment to ask questions or make snide remarks. "I have an announcement," he said, clearing his throat like someone attempting an impersonation of a radio announcer. He delighted in the puzzled looks on so many of the faces before him. "Jenna and I have a Christmas present for all of you," he continued. "We're going to give our marriage a second chance. She's agreed to go to counseling with me."

Reactions all over the room ran the gamut from cheers and praise to groans and catcalls. "Poor Jenna," Dan cried, his voice carrying easily over the rest. "Can you imagine being in joint therapy with Scott Tenny!" Everyone jumped up to offer hugs and pats on the back.

"It's going to be a great holiday after all," declared Joe. "Thank the Lord! I feel like we've just survived a visit from an extra ghost from A Christmas Carol – the ghost of Marriages Past. God bless us every one!"

SCOTT, TRAVIS AND AIDEN gave Zach and Luka all the help they needed opening their gifts. Jenna and the rest sat back and enjoyed the chaos. Watching Scott with the kids was pure pleasure, Jenna mused.

When the kids had finished opening presents, the adults passed theirs around. Many of them were funny – inside jokes or jokes everyone could get. Dan's gift for everyone in the band, for example, was industrial-strength ear plugs in a glowing neon rainbow of colors, in boxes of 144 pairs each, in plain brown wrapping with caution tape for ribbon.

Scott waited until everyone was finished before taking an elegantly wrapped little package down from the mantle and presenting it to Jenna, taking her entirely by surprise. Tears sprang up as she sat with it in her lap for a moment. Gulping them back, she smiled up at him. "I – I don't –"

"It doesn't matter," he said. "Agreeing to give our marriage a second chance is Christmas present enough for me. Go ahead. Open it."

Gently, she pulled on one end of the satin ribbon, which slid apart effortlessly. Reaching under, she freed the tape and the wrapping on the gift fell open. Pushing it aside, she found a black velvet box inside. Her mouth dropped when she opened the cover. Inside was a magnificent sapphire and diamond necklace, set in fourteen-carat gold. She gasped. She knew this necklace. They'd seen it one day window shopping during their trip to Hawaii.

"Hawaii!" she exclaimed. "Scott, this is so much like –"

"Nope, it *is* the one you saw. I got it while you and Zach were napping one day," he said with the satisfied grin of the giver who's just presented someone he loves with a guaranteed perfect gift. "I'd planned on giving it to you on your birthday, but we were arguing so much, I didn't, and I'm really glad I didn't. It means so much more now. Merry Christmas – and Happy Anniversary, babe."

Scott helped her put it on. Jenna went to a mirror to see what it looked like on her. It was positively stunning – even with flannel pajamas.

CHRISTMAS DAY COULDN'T have been more perfect. Fat, heavy snowflakes started falling as everyone enjoyed a brunch of made-to-order omelets. Scott had laid out an extensive array of fillings, and had thrown his refrigerator open to scavengers who really wanted to get creative. When all the votes were cast, the award for Most Creative Omelet on a Christmas Day went to Tim

Knowleston's "Italian/Asian Fusion" concoction, a pastiche of pastrami, Italian hot peppers and provolone, a fiery oriental plum sauce "adding insult to injury," as he kept telling anyone willing to listen. The drummer's eyes were watering and his face went beet red, but he managed to eat it all, smacking his burning lips like he was actually enjoying every bite.

By the time everyone had eaten, there was sufficient snow on the ground to lure them outside to play, and they played as only adults can when they've got four kids available for inspiration. Luka took on the role of director and cheerleader, ordering everyone about, assigning tasks, and generally keeping morale high. Aiden and Travis humored him, but had their own agendas as well. They were both deadly accurate in their snowball delivery.

OVER A LATE AFTERNOON Christmas dinner, conversation turned, as it so often did, to the next spate of touring and the upcoming New Year's Eve Boston show. Jenna and her management team had decided to only schedule some random appearances until spring; she didn't want to head south as that would take her so far from home, and she didn't want to have to worry about battling northern weather. "Come spring, I'll decide about another full-on tour," she told them. "As for New Year's Eve, I'll be there, but I'm not going to sing." Scott, visibly disappointed, said nothing. Given the obviously fragile state of their relationship, nobody pressed her.

Blacklace had a fairly demanding southern tour lined out, ending up in Los Angeles in late February for the Grammys, as usual; Jenna and Scott had been asked to be presenters again this year. Jenna sat thinking as Jeremy ticked off from memory the cities they'd be playing: Atlanta, Baton Rouge, Memphis, then Montgomery, Alabama, and Jackson, Mississippi, Oklahoma City, Amarillo, Albuquerque, Phoenix, San Diego, home for a quick breather, and then L.A. As she listened, Jenna decided on the spot that she, Zach and Ellen would join them for a couple of weeks, mid-tour.

Throughout the day, when his hands weren't otherwise engaged, Scott and Jenna held hands. And as they went to bed that night, he took her by the hand and led her to their bedroom. At the door, he pressed her fingers to his lips. "If you're not ready to move back home yet," he said, "I better take advantage of what time I've got. I know you usually get pregnant at Sunapee, but maybe we could make ourselves a Christmas miracle baby here, tonight."

The thought melted the last bit of fear that remained in Jenna's heart.

Chapter 24

A NEW YEAR'S EVE blizzard didn't stop a single Blacklace fan from attending the Blacklace blow-out at the Garden. New Year's Eve, 2003, was the kind of night that tribulations would be measured against for years to come.

Security guards let Jenna in through a rear entrance shortly before the show was scheduled to start. She went directly to the dressing room, glad to see the halls were tightly patrolled and free of reporters. There she found Scott, ready and pacing, dressed in a loose, ripped sleeveless black t-shirt, his tattoos bared, and a pair of skin-tight zebra-striped lowriders.

"I was beginning to think you weren't coming," he said as he embraced her. "I was gettin' worried, babe." He pulled back and devoured her with appreciative, hungry eyes. "Man, you are so beautiful tonight," he marveled and they kissed.

Jenna was an eyeful. Her mode of dress, every time he'd seen her since they'd separated, had been entirely appropriate for a convent. Tonight, plenty of skin was showing under the floor-skimming black leather coat she'd promptly unbuttoned as soon as she'd gotten inside the building. Scott's eyes roamed freely, bounding like a mountain goat from curves to cleavage and back again.

"Like what you see, mister?" she said, posing for him with a wink, her smile calibrated for seduction. She ran a finger playfully over a tattoo, a pair of wings that spanned his delts.

"I had visions of you in a seventy-car pile-up," Scott said.

"Between here and the Back Bay?" She laughed." We didn't even get on the Storrow. We stayed on surface streets all the way. I came late on purpose, hon. I'm sorry – I should have told you. I'm just so sick of the press."

"Tell me about it," Scott said through gritted teeth.

"They're everywhere, like cockroaches," Jenna said as she reached behind him and quickly sorted through a selection of long scarves on a hook that held a dozen or more. Pulling out a couple, she slung them around his neck, one a red-and-black print, one yellow. Frowning, she swapped the yellow one out for a really long shiny silver one, then nodded at the effect. "I swear I wouldn't be surprised to open my closet and find a reporter with a mike in there," she continued. "And another one in the bed waiting impatiently for me to get finished with the closet one. And three or four photographers and guys with mini-cams under the bed."

Jenna tried to make light of the problem, but it was clear she was exhausted with the effort of maintaining some semblance of privacy. Ever since the divorce headlines, she'd been hounded like never before. Once the press had discovered where she was living, the streets of Boston were no longer hers to walk. A dozen of the heartiest had set up camp in an alley across the street from the entrance to the apartment house, looking like a band of hopelessly stranded arctic explorers.

They arrived at the crack of dawn and milled around till they saw the last light go out in Jenna's windows, stomping their feet in an attempt to ward off frostbite. All independent operators, they came well provisioned; taking a lunch break, much less refilling an empty thermos of coffee, was out of the question. They all sprang to attention at the slightest movement at the front door of the building, poised to stampede across the street en mass if there was the slightest possibility of getting a scoop. Another half-dozen of the paparazzi had similarly staked out the back entrance of the building.

Jenna walked out into the melee only once, she told Scott, but fortunately had a car waiting for her; she was able to make a relatively quick getaway. "However," she said with a grin, "the punk teeny-bopper breezing out of my building sporting a different hair color every day hardly warrants a raised eyebrow any more. As long as they don't see though that old disguise, I'll have room to navigate."

"That's my girl," Scott chuckled. He knew about her escapade a couple of years earlier, her use of her old punk props to try to entrap him in inappropriate behavior. When he'd found out about it, he'd considered it a compliment. He was also eternally grateful that he had passed the test that night – as he hadn't with Ashley West, he thought. His lips pursed as his smile faded. Jenna had no trouble following his thoughts as they trudged across his face.

"Hey, don't go there," she whispered and kissed him again. "But let me tell you how Ellen handled the problem," she said, returning to her rant in the hopes of preventing him going into a funk. Her delivery was animated. "So they like tried to swarm Zach and her when she went to take him to the park that first day. She hid Zach behind her and then made a basically one-sentence speech that required zero amplification: 'If any one of you thinks that this child is fair game, you just better have yourself a *very* good lawyer.' Then she just told them to get out of her way. And they did. From then on, whenever she came out, whoever spotted her first simply passed the word back that it was 'just the bitch nanny.' I was proud of her. She handled herself like a pro."

"This too shall pass, my pretty," Scott said. "Now, m'dam – may I escort you to the ol' ladies' section? The show is about to begin." Scott gallantly offered an arm. Taking it, Jenna gave it a squeeze. She had started the evening in a giddy, mischievous mood. She felt like the punker girl without the wig, on holiday, out for a good time, without a care in the world. This New Year's Eve she was going to have fun.

Turnout was one hundred percent for the "ol' ladies section" this year –
in fact it was over one hundred percent. Tim's wife Paula, Dan's girlfriend Jill
and Jeff's wife Denise were all in attendance. Of the three seats below them,
the aisle seat was empty, presumably saved for Jenna, then there was Carrie,
and then beyond her a women Jenna didn't recognize. Had she not been
looking at her like she was about to be introduced, Jenna would have automatically assumed she was part of the next group over. Jenna smiled at the
delicate, exotic, dark-haired beauty as Carrie said with suspiciously exaggerated good manners, "Jenna, Arlona Patel. Arlona, this is Jenna Tenny," as
Jenna reached across Carrie to shake hands. Arlona is Ryan's new girlfriend,"
Carrie added dryly.

"Well, uh, hi," Jenna greeted the newcomer, struggling to keep her smile
in place as she abruptly ended the handshake with Kristin's replacement in
Ryan's life. Taking the empty seat on the aisle side of Carrie, she gave Carrie
a hug and an air kiss, whispering, "Oh, my!"

Carrie gave her a hug, a kiss and a whisper in response. "I give it a month,
tops," she said. "She's not built for this life."

Jenna reached up behind her to squeeze hands with Jill, who acknowledged Arlona's intrusion into their tight little circle with a sarcastic wink.
Denise's eyes rolled. Paula made a grimace and shook her head solemnly.
Kristin had been easily accepted into their circle for two reasons: one, of
course, was that she was Jenna's half sister; the other was that Ryan had just
joined the band when he and Kristin hooked up.

At that moment, Jenna knew that if she and Scott had split, the rest of the
"ol' ladies" would close ranks against any interloper on her behalf as well. She
suddenly felt an enormous warmth for these four women – the "Blacklace
Women's Auxiliary and Marching Band," as Dan had once dubbed them –
whose trust she too had once had to earn.

Jenna sat back, savoring both the feeling of camaraderie and the heightened excitement of the crowd as time for the show drew close. But gazing up
into the rafters and the close to twenty thousand fans ready to rock, she felt a
twinge of the kind of innate disappointment performers always feel when they
find themselves sitting in an audience. Just like innkeepers staying at a
four-star hotel, or hairdressers having their hair done, or chefs dining out, no
matter how hard they try, they can never quite separate themselves from the
mechanics of the performance, any more than the innkeeper could keep from
critiquing the service, the hairdresser her friend's cutting techniques, the chef
another chef's cuisine. Jenna had long since accepted it as just a fact of stage
life.

On the other hand, no matter how closely related she was to the person
about to go on, she enjoyed the fact that she didn't have to experience the
nerves, the butterflies, the anguish that she and everyone she knew went
through as the stage manager went through the final count-down to lights out.
That aspect of performance she never missed.

She was just thinking that very thought when the house went out and the stentorian voice of the house announcer cut through the inky blackness, "Ladies and gentlemen, Blacklace!"

AS ALWAYS, THE BAND opened with their usual three brief instrumental pieces. As always, each performer took a solo, another of the band introducing him by name to the audience. As always each was cheered loudly by his particular fans, raucously in Jeremy's case. As always, the excitement grew.

Just for fun, the band feigned starting in on a fourth instrumental number, but the audience wasn't having any of that. Shouts of "Scott! Scott!" and "Tenny! Tenny! Tenny!" started springing up spontaneously here and there around the hall, until they coalesced into a universal chanting of "Tenny! Tenny! Tenny!" that drowned out the band.

At which point Scott came ambling in with a look on his face like, "Oh, holy crap, I'm late!" The crowd ate it up, whistling and shouting themselves hoarse while he made the rounds, pretending to greet each of the band members as if for the first time tonight, chagrined at his error. Finally, he made his way to the lone mike stand front and center, grabbed it by the throat and began putting it to his own signature brand of use. The house went wild.

Within three songs, career-long fans had thought they'd pretty much seen everything in Scott Tenny's playbook – he'd been dancing far up in the rigging; he'd practically split his britches doing leaps into full-out splits; he'd sung his heart out at one hundred ten percent. And that was just for starters.

Every time he got near the end of the stage closest to where Jenna was sitting, he went into virtual paroxysms of musical mania. It was perfectly clear to the audience what was going on from the first moment he did it. Jenna was back, and tonight was for her, and Boston plainly loved him for it. The legions of female fans who risked life and limb to get as close to the action as possible, jammed up against the stage for two hours straight, even forgave him for paying them virtually no notice. Tonight even they couldn't begrudge Jenna his undivided attentions.

The only problem of the evening was the fact that everyone in the audience *knew* Jenna was there – multiple video monitors guaranteed that no matter where you were sitting, you were going to get a close-up view of the action, both on the stage and in the stands. A huge roar went up every time her image flashed across the giant screens. Early on, calls of "Jenna!" started ringing out along with song requests.

As Blacklace finally launched into the first of the encores, it immediately became clear that no one planned on leaving until they'd heard her sing. When she didn't appear at the start of the second encore, a howl of outrage rose to the rooftops; the band couldn't be heard over the furious din. Scott finally threw up his hands, then put them together prayerfully and bowed to the audience, as if to say, "Your every wish is my command. Let me see what I can do about it."

Hastening down to Jenna's end of the stage, where the cameras were already on her, ready to project her response to every corner of the Garden, Scott threw himself to his knees and begged with all the melodrama of Al Jolson singing "Mammy."

Jenna knew she had no choice. She grinned, waved across every monitor to all their fans, jumped up and quickly made her way backstage. Scott had run off into the wings to meet her, keying his headset to tell Jeremy to pass the word: they'd sing "To Be Loved by You," followed by "I'm Ready to Go." He just prayed Jenna'd agree.

Pulling her close the moment she was within reach, he hugged her and gave her the lineup simultaneously. Looking like she questioned his choices, Scott held a finger up to silence her. "It's what they want – you know that. And it's what the guys are gonna play, so I'd suggest you go along with me on this one, okay?"

Abashed, Jenna apologized. "Sorry. I know this is no time to argue. Just this once, anyway." She kissed him, combed her fingertips through her hair and giving it a couple of good hard shakes. A few quick pinches to her cheeks, then she took Scott's impatient hand and the two high-tailed it out onto the stage. The minute Scott grabbed the mike, the crowd fell silent. "Is this what you want, Boston?" he growled, pointing to Jenna with his thumb. "You got it! Jenna B. Tenny, everybody!!"

Jenna hadn't taken her usual focused care deciding the perfect outfit to wear. Her somewhat goofy mood had translated itself into a clingy red baby doll mini-dress over a pair of multi-colored polka dot tights and thigh-high purple boots. Placing her two hands over Scott's on the mike, she listened, rapt, as he sang her the opening line of "To Be Loved by You."

> *She sobers. She chills. She inspires. She thrills.*
> *What a woman.*

Bringing her lips closer to the mike, Jenna smiled to herself before she sang her version of the next line. Transposing it to the feminine added an almost comic irony that they were both still way to close to the facts to find funny, though the audience certainly did.

> *Since I met him it's all been uphill.*
> *I'm his woman.*

But she knew as she sang the words that, no question, she *was* his woman.

When it was all over and they were headed for the dressing rooms, Scott with an arm around Jenna and a look on his face that suggested he might just never let her go again, he realized that for the first time in recent memory, he had no idea if Ashley West had been in the crowd. He'd completely forgotten to look for her. If she'd been in the house tonight, he didn't know and he could have cared less.

"Let's go welcome in the New Year, babe" he said. "And I know where I want to take you. Shelley's."

Jenna's smile turned into an ear-to-ear grin. "Absolutely! Our first date!" she gasped. "Perfect."

"You're all invited," Scott said over his shoulder to the rest of the band. "My treat."

"We're there," Jeremy yelled for everyone.

They made it to Shelley's in time for the midnight countdown. The well-known hangout for musicians was jammed. Precisely at the stroke of twelve, Scott took Jenna in his arms. "Happy New Year, baby," he yelled over the din. "I love you." There was just enough room to arch her backwards into a classic Hollywood kiss.

When their lips parted, she smiled blissfully. "And I do love you, Scott Tenny," she told him, then turned the tables and made *him* the recipient of her own Hollywood kiss.

SCOTT HADN'T WANTED to drive that night. Instead he'd had Georgie bring him in by limo, which was waiting for them outside Shelley's when they decided to call it a night an hour later. Georgie jumped out and opened the door when he saw them coming out the door.

Jenna stepped in first. Scott slid in right beside her, then pressed the button for the intercom. "We'll take Jenna home first, Georgie," he said and started to give him the address.

"No, not tonight, Georgie," Jenna interrupted him. "We'll be going – home." Then she lifted Scott's hand off the intercom button.

"You're coming to the house?" Scott said, mystified, barely daring to hope. "What about Zach?" Jenna kissed him.

"Zach's asleep. Ellen's there with him. I'll leave her a message. Scott, I want to be with you tonight."

Scott looked at her. "Babe," was all he could say, then he pulled her to him and wrapped her in his arms, filling them with the feel of her, filling his lungs with the scent of her, overcome by the reality of how close he'd come to losing this woman. "Oh, God, how –"

Jenna didn't let him finish the sentence.

"UNZIP ME?" SHE asked Scott. They had been standing just inside the front door, kissing, their bodies pressing closer and closer yet, their two tormented souls melding back into one.

"Your servant," Scott murmured as he reached around her and drew the zipper down her back in maddening slow motion. Her little dress slithered to the floor.

"Unhook me?"

"If you insist." He unhooked her bra, then slid it off her, tossed it across the foyer and feasted his eyes on her. "Happy fuckin' New Year," he groaned in abject admiration.

Jenna put her hands on her butt and threw her shoulders back, making the most of a terrific pair of assets. The house was chilly; her nipples were especially prominent. "Some goose bumps, huh?" she laughed, looking down on them.

"Your boots, my love?" he asked, dropping to his knees before her to unzip each one of them. His hands ran from the ankle of one leg up the long expanse of supple leather, up her calf, over her knee, up her thigh to the top – and beyond. "Oops," he said. "Got a little lost there. Sorry." But, of course, he wasn't. Again he slowly drew the zipper down, then peeled back the leather and removed it from her leg. He had the same "problem" finding his way to the top of the zipper of the second. He unzipped it even slower.

Once he'd freed her from both boots, he slid his hands from her toes exasperatingly slowly up to her waist, grasped her tights and brought them down, all in one expert movement.

"My, you're good at that," Jenna sighed as she put a hand on his head for balance and stepped out of the tights with his help. As soon as she was out, the tights went flying in the same general direction as the bra.

"Sorry. I'm all thumbs," he apologized as his thumbs took liberties with the strings of her thong undies. "Oh, yum. Black. My favorite color." He planted a kiss square on the tiny black lace inset.

"Mine too," Jenna whispered, her voice beginning to quaver. She bent over and kissed him on the top of his head, just as he hooked his thumbs in the strings of her undies and started them on the long slide down her spectacular legs.

Then he gathered her naked, trembling form into his arms and headed up the stairs.

EVEN THOUGH THEY SLEPT in till long past noon the next day, neither got anywhere near a proper eight hours' sleep. Their lovemaking had been alternately nostalgic and inventive, creativity sparking further inspiration, each seemingly determined to outdo the other in the physical, sensual reassertion of their love.

Finally Jenna rolled over and faced the clock. "Oh, dear God, it's two o'clock! I've gotta get up. Would you take me into town to the apartment? I promised Ellen she could have the day off."

Hopping into a pair of jeans, Jenna grabbed her cell phone and called Ellen to apologize for being so late. Ellen was unperturbed. Nevertheless, Jenna told her to take that night and the following day as well.

Ellen drew a long, audible breath before answering. "Hon," she finally said to Jenna, "I want to tell you that whatever makes you happy makes Zach happy, and whatever makes Zach happy makes me happy." That was the closest she'd ever come to making a personal comment on the rift between her employers.

"Ellen – thank you. Thank you so much." The warmth in Jenna's voice reassured her that she hadn't overstepped any boundaries.

AS THEY HEADED OUT the door, Scott turned back to her. "I – I'd like to spend some time with Zach today. If that's all right," Scott hurried to add.

Jenna had to laugh. "And with me too, I hope," she said, her look of feigned concern amusing combined as it was with a particularly provocative pose.

"Oh, hell yes, and with you, too," Scott assured her. "That's exactly how I'd like to spend this first day of this new year. With the two people I love more than life itself." He was hoping he could look at this day as nothing less than the critical first day of the rest of their lives – together.

Chapter 25

❋

THE MONTH OF JANUARY went by quickly. Even with Blacklace on tour, Scott made it back to Boston weekly for their counseling sessions. One week, when the weather looked too threatening, he paid the extremely high price of canceling a show to fly in a day early. Nothing, he told Jenna, was going to stand in the way of this. A priority had to be a priority. The band understood. Management did not. Scott assured management he could care less.

Their counselor, Max Moses, was a gentle-looking, scraggily-bearded man with a maddeningly calm demeanor, who had an uncanny way of exposing foolish behavior for what it was. The more either Scott or Jenna would rationalize their actions, the quieter he'd get. When he went totally silent, they were left with nothing to do but face their separate realities. It worked every time. Silence led to insight. Insight led understanding. Understanding led to breakthroughs. Week by arduous week, they tackled subject after subject, picking apart reflexive, toxic patterns of behavior. Week by week, they came to know each other better. Week after week, they left Max's office encouraged.

Until the week they finally got into the issue of infidelity, the elephant that had been accompanying them faithfully to each session, parking its wrinkled carcass in the corner of the office, dropping heavily to the carpet with a sigh, stretching its front legs out and taking itself a contented snooze, snoring softly amidst the office greenery. It knew its lazy days were numbered.

Scott was the one to bring it up.

"I blame myself," Jenna jumped in, practically before he could finish his sentence. "It was all my fault. I put so much pressure on him. I drove him to drink."

"No, you didn't. I mean, I didn't drink – yeah, I was face-to-face with it in a bar, and that led us to everything else and got us where we are now. But, no, it was *my* fault," Scott said. "I have no one to blame but myself. This was just the kind of situation sponsors were invented for."

Lumbering to its feet, the elephant snorted in protest. He'd come to enjoy his visits to Dr. Moses. As it shambled out of the office, it almost tripped over the other bit of undiscussed baggage Scott always brought along, unbeknownst to Jenna – a big, bulging bag full of blackmail. He'd been posting monthly checks, ten thousand dollars at a clip, to a post office box in Burbank for four months now.

JENNA'S DAYS WERE full to overflowing. Between writing, working with her band and playing a good number of one-night engagements, in venues large and small, the musical side of her life was feeling gratifying and rewarding. She particularly enjoyed playing in the smaller houses. She booked into the Palladium in Worcester twice in January and early February to try out new material. An audience of two thousand was her idea of intimate.

The shelter kept her equally busy. Money from the fall fundraiser had gone directly into architectural renderings to take before the planning board. Jenna wanted to see South Shore First Step grow.

A routine developed. Each week when Scott flew in for counseling, he'd take Zach for a special day of father-son fun. Jenna would put those days to personal use, unless Scott invited her to join them.

Whatever the outcome of their marital problems, they both wanted Zach to suffer as little disruption as possible. Given the come-and-go realities of both his parents' lives, coupled with the stability of knowing Ellen was there for him every day, Zach was developing a flexible, take-life-as-it-comes resiliency. Under his accepting façade, however, Jenna knew there was a normal boy with normal needs. At the same time, she maintained a constant vigilance against projecting any of her own childhood insecurities onto her innocent child.

Parenthood, she had come to realize, was hard work, no matter how much help she had. She often found herself comparing the parental state with life under the big top – the days when she felt like a juggler, a tightrope walker, an acrobat, a clown and a lion tamer all rolled into one. Some days it felt like she was being shot from a cannon.

The bottom line was perfectly clear to her, however: Zach must know he had two parents in his life who loved him unconditionally.

SINCE NEW YEAR'S DAY, through all Scott's comings and goings, Jenna and he had slept in separate beds in separate bedrooms in separate domiciles. It had been one the first items Jenna had brought up in counseling. She hadn't wanted each parting to be a negotiation, a seduction, a question mark. Sex had always been easy between the two of them, too easy perhaps, often substituting as an escape from other more difficult aspects of their relationship. They both agreed, and had stuck to their agreement, that they wouldn't complicate the current situation with sex. I t was complicated enough as it was.

"So you'll be staying with us, right?" Linda asked. Jenna had called her to finalize plans for their upcoming trip to L.A. for this year's Grammy awards.

"We'll be staying with you," Jenna said. "But same drill as last time: separate bedrooms."

"Separate bedrooms. Uh, right," Linda said, making no attempt to veil her skepticism.

Jenna chose to ignore her mother's remark. "Ellen will be with us, so she'll bunk with Zach," she went on. "I'll use the blue room."

"No," her mother said, "Chris will be using the blue room. He's sublet his condo, he's traveling so much. But he really wanted to be here when you came out. Sorry, sweetie – he made his reservation first." Linda didn't sound remotely sorry. She sounded like her usual conniving self, Jenna thought, grinding her teeth in silent frustration.

"Think you two can coexist in one bedroom for three days?" Linda finally said, sounding quite pleased with this arrangement.

"You know the three days isn't the problem. It's the three *nights*. In one bed."

"So much for marital bliss," her mother snorted. "I'll rent a cot."

SCOTT HAD HIS OWN ideas too. Dropping Zach back home to Jenna a few days after she'd spoken with Linda, he sat down so they could firm up plans for L.A. He'd decided to stay at the hotel with the rest of the band the night they got there, he told her.

As they started talking, Zach appeared at Scott's side, begging for a pony ride, his latest favorite pastime. Reaching down, Scott scooped the toddler up with a grin and settled him on his knees, giving him his hands to use for reins. As soon as Zach gave him the sign, his knees were off and galloping and he got back to his conversation with Jenna.

"We've booked rehearsal space at some ungodly hour the next morning," he explained, his voice bouncing in time with his son. "We figgered we could use the down-time in L.A. to finish up that new song we've been working on for so long. We're so close, it's drivin' us all – *nuts*." On the word 'nuts,' he dropped his knees and let Zach go into a controlled slide down his legs, ending up sitting on the floor on his bum, giggling happily. In an instant, he was back for more. "I'll go out to the house with you and Zach, then go back over to the hotel," Scott continued.

"The Fig?" Jenna asked. Scott nodded.

Jenna gulped. Though she'd never stayed there, she knew the Hotel Figueroa. Somehow, the thought of Scott on his own in the lavish, Moorish decadence of the 1928 landmark hotel, just down the block from the Staples Center where the Grammys were held, instantly filled her with misgivings.

Jenna, goddammit, you be an adult about this, she stopped and lectured herself sternly. Why should you worry about him staying in a hotel in downtown L.A. any more than in downtown Peoria or downtown Philadelphia, which was where he and the band were headed the next day.

"That's silly, Scott. The hotel's on the way. We'll just stop there and drop you off, then continue on to Mom's. Actually, we could have Randy pick us up at the airport, you know." Randy had been her family's chauffeur as long as Jenna could remember. "We'll drop you off, then on to Beverly Hills, no problem." Jenna was rather proud of herself.

When Scott left, Jenna took Zach to a window at the front of the apartment to wave goodbye. As soon as Scott came out the front door of the building, Jenna threw open the window and Zach yelled, "Daddy! Bye-bye, Daddy!"

Scott turned around and blew Zach a kiss. "Bye, Zach-o. You take good care of Mommy, hear?"

"I will!" Zach called back.

Scott's final kiss and wave were for Jenna.

Jenna closed the window and sat down. Zach came running to her and buried his head in her lap. Absentmindedly, she stroked his long blond curls as she bent down to kiss him. Already, his baby white-blond hair was beginning to darken, just as hers had as a child. She'd been born with hair even lighter than his. By five, her hair was as dark as it was today.

SCOTT HAD NO REASON to expect to see Jenna's car sitting in his driveway when he got back home five days later. He had no idea what to expect when he stepped into the mudroom and then into the kitchen. What he found was Jenna stretched out in the kitchen window seat with a cup of coffee on the table and Zach in her lap, reading him a book. When he saw his father come through the door, Zach jumped down and ran across the room. Wrapping himself around one of Scott's legs, he looked up grinning and yelled, "Daddy's home!" at the top of his tiny lungs.

Jenna smiled up at him.

"What a sight for sore eyes," Scott said softly. "What's the occasion?"

"None. I just knew you'd like it."

"I'm afraid 'like it' doesn't quite cover the range of emotions I'm feeling right now, lady," Scott chuckled. "Any more than 'what a pleasant surprise to come home to' would say it. The two most important people in the world waiting for me – man, it doesn't get any better. I could get used to this, you know."

He turned away, suddenly concerned that he might have overstepped, that Jenna might take umbrage at his words. Then he turned back to her. Better to face his fear head-on, he decided. "Hey, sorry. I don't mean to pressure you," he said.

"Hey, it didn't feel like pressure," Jenna reassured him, getting up, still smiling. She came over to him and gave him a warm hug. "We missed you too."

Scott felt like dancing. Instead, he poured himself a cup of coffee and came to the table to sit with her while Zach went out to the mudroom and ransacked a toy box out there. As he filled her in on the last several days of touring, Jenna couldn't help but notice the positive nature of his remarks. Usually Scott's version of a week on the road was little more than a detailed complaint list.

As Jenna got ready to leave, she turned to Scott who was busy refilling a tote bag of toys Zach had brought with him. "Tomorrow night, if you wanted, you could stay at my place. It'd save time the next morning, and be one less stop the limo driver would have to make."

Mystified, Scott hesitated before answering. "The guest room," Jenna answered his unspoken question.

He smiled. "Okay. Heck, sure. Anything to be with you guys. To be with *you*," he said, even more honestly, and looked her in the eye as he said it.

THE FOLLOWING NIGHT, Scott arrived after dinner. Jenna was just about to give Zach his bath; Ellen had the night off.

"Are you packed," he asked Jenna as he picked Zach up and gave him a hug.

"Started…three hours ago," Jenna admitted.

"You go finish your packing," he told her. "I'll give this gent his bath. We're good at that, aren't we, Zach."

"Hey, I really appreciate it," she said.

"And then I'll read him a bedtime story," Scott continued. "If he's really good, maybe *two* bedtime stories!"

"Two?" Zach said. Holding up two fingers, he studied them studiously. "No. Five!" he suddenly announced, beaming as he held up all five fingers victoriously. Closing them back down into a fist, he counted them out one at a time. "One. Two. Thwee. Four. Five! Five bedtime storwees!"

"Where did you learn that, Zach?!" Jenna cried in astonishment.

"He learned that at the Scott Tenny Correctional Facility for Wayward Boys," Scott grinned, proud as could be of his handiwork.

JENNA TUCKED ZACH in and both she and Scott sat on either side of him, taking turns reading his bedtime stories. Zach lay there totally content, one arm up under his head on the pillow, his "bwankie," the black crocheted blanket that had been a baby gift from Tom and Sally up at Tiny's coffee shop at the lake, tucked securely under his other arm. His free hand laid on top of the covers, two, three, four fingers splayed to keep count. When the fifth and final story had been read, they kissed him goodnight, turned off the light and tiptoed down the hall to the living room.

Jenna flopped across a couch. It had been a long day. Scott dropped himself into an overstuffed chintz armchair, pulled his shoes off and put his feet up on its matching ottoman.

"Can you believe Zach's almost two?" he said, shaking his head.

"Two years," Jenna said, holding up two fingers with a crooked grin. "Wow."

"Are you planning a party?"

"Not really. It's too much for everyone to come out here. Maybe we can celebrate it early with his California relatives while we're out there, and then just you and I could do something special with him for his actual birthday. He really doesn't understand what birthdays are all about yet anyway. Is that all right with you? I don't want you thinking you don't have a say in the matter."

"Thanks," Scott said, and he meant it. "I think doing something, just the three of us, is a great idea. Think he's old enough for Disneyland yet?"

"We can look into it. Florida'd be a great idea, regardless."

"But I'll bet the folks will want to come out anyway, either here or Florida."

"It'd be fun to have them down there. They've never seen the place." Jenna smiled at the thought.

"Great idea," Scott said. Stretching, he stood up. "However, it's getting late and we all have to be up early in the morning. I'm hittin' the sack." Scott came over, kissed Jenna on the top of her head and disappeared down the hall without another word.

Jenna stayed up a little while longer, staring out the window at the night lights of Boston. Contented.

Finally she roused herself. She checked in on Zach, then passed the room where Scott was sleeping. Stopping at his door, she hesitated, sighed, then continued down the hall to her room. It was tempting, but Jenna chose not to give in to temptation. She went to bed alone.

Chapter 26

IN AN EXPANSIVE MOOD, Scott booked a jet for the entire band and entourage to make the trip to L.A. for this year's Grammys. The luxurious charter, a Gulfstream G550, provided a five-hour coast-to-coast party in the sky and a playroom for Zach that required some improvisation with suitcase netting from the cargo hold to contain him within safe bounds.

Jenna and Scott staked out one end of a long couch for themselves and Zach's paraphernalia. Zach was in a mood where Ellen wouldn't do – he only wanted his parents' attentions. Scott noticed the effort it was taking Jenna to rise to the occasion every time Zach ran back to her. Clearly, she was fighting fatigue.

"You didn't get much sleep last night," he said casually.

"And how would you know that?" Jenna challenged him.

"Don't worry – I wasn't prowling around spying on you, if that's what you think," he said. "You never sleep well the night before we come out here. You've either been too excited because of some special occasion, or you've been upset about something. Tell me I'm wrong."

Jenna had to laugh. "You're right. And this time, I guess it's both. Dealing with my mother is never a walk in the park. Dealing with my mother when she's got an agenda all lined out for you and me feels like walking into a human-size Have-a-Heart trap, with your eyes wide open."

"Honey, you'll be fine. We'll be fine. We can handle your mother – even your mother on a mission. All I know is, you're a zombie, and the coffee you've been downing hasn't begun to make a dent. You need a nap. I'll keep the ZachMan preoccupied and out of your hair."

Jenna nodded appreciatively. Grabbing pillow and a throw, she curled up and fell asleep in a matter of moments. The next time Zach came barreling over to check in with her, he stopped short at the sight.

Scott held a finger to his lips. Zach mimicked him, backing away from Jenna on tiptoe, giving her wide berth and approaching Scott's lap from the opposite direction. "Good boy!" Scott whispered to him as his son settled in. Reaching over, Zach grabbed for his blankie, pulled it over him and popped a thumb in his mouth. "Sweepie too, Daddy," he told his father.

"You know what, Zach-o?" Scott said. "You two aren't the only ones." Pretty soon, all three of them were dreaming away at thirty-five thousand feet.

ELLEN CAME OVER and woke Scott and Jenna as the plane began its approach. Zach had woken earlier and extricated himself from Scott's lap without disturbing his father. "That's incredible," Scott said. "The kid's a veritable Houdini! I should have woken up."

"Don't feel bad. I wasn't the only one who didn't get a great night's sleep last night, if I guess correctly," Jenna observed.

"Maybe not," Scott admitted.

"As in, maybe you're a little nervous too?"

"As in, maybe I was last night. Not today. Today's a whole 'nuther matter." He smiled. "Today it's like, bring her on. And my dad too. Just let them try to interfere with our lives and our marriage. This is our problem, not theirs."

"I wish I could be so optimistic. I wonder if this wasn't her plan all along," Jenna mused. "To pose herself as the 'common enemy,' so to speak. Face it, nothing brings two people together faster than having to team up to defend themselves against an external threat."

"You make her sound so Machiavellian."

"She is. She's a manipulator from way back. She was famous for playing Chris and me against Jim, or Jim and Chris against me, or all of us against our father, whatever happened to serve her purposes at any given moment."

"We'll deal with it," Scott reassured her.

"That's easy for you to say. You're staying at the Fig," Jenna said with envy. She found herself wishing she was too.

JOE AND KRISTIN were standing in the doorway when Jenna, Zach and Ellen arrived. Zach jumped out of the limo the moment Randy opened the door for him and ran straight up the walkway and into his grandparents open arms, yelling "Gwampa, Gwampa!" as he came.

Joe caught Zach up and swung him into the air. "I swear, boy, you're even bigger than you were at Christmas," he declared to Zach, "and that's only a couple of months ago now. Give your Auntie Kris a hug, too."

Zach looked at Kristin suspiciously, then hid his eyes in Joe's shoulder. "You don't have to be shy," Joe teased him. "You remember your Auntie Kristin. Say 'hi, Auntie Kristin.'"

"Hi, Auntie Kwistin," Zach managed, then squirmed away from having to give her the expected hug. Kristin was crestfallen at the snub.

"Don't worry," Joe told her. "He'll remember who you are before you know it." Turning to Jenna, he threw a spare arm around her and have her half a hug. "You're looking well, too, m'dear," he said. 'Come on in."

Kristin caught Jenna's hand as she started to go into the house and gave it a squeeze. "Hey, big sis." The two hugged, Kristin whispering, "Lots to tell you," as they did. As they separated, she gave Jenna a wink. Jenna took a second look at her; something seemed different, but she didn't have time to ponder what it might be. Linda was coming down the stairs just as they all stepped inside.

"Sweetie!" she exclaimed as Kristin stepped aside to allow her to sweep Jenna up in her most motherly of hugs. "You're here. Finally!"

"We're actually a few minutes ahead of schedule," Jenna started to say, but Linda was already pursuing Zach as he ran out to see Adella in the kitchen. He was in Adella's arms before Linda could catch up with him. Adella, ever the diplomat, gave him a squeeze, then passed him right over to his grandmother.

"Zachery Matthew Scott Tenny!" Linda cried, running a hand through Zach's blond locks. "How is my number one and only blood grandson?" Zach impetuously buried his head in the crook of Linda's neck and hugged her enthusiastically. "Oh, how I have missed you!" Linda said, hugging and tickling him till he giggled.

ZACH STAYED DOWNSTAIRS with Linda and Joe while Kristin helped carry bags and get Jenna and Ellen settled in. Jenna grimaced when she walked into the guestroom to find no cot in the corner. "Somebody tell me why hope springs eternal," she murmured.

"What?" Kristin asked.

"Oh, nothing. I mean, I knew not to expect miracles…"

"From…?"

"Mom. You know, the old tell 'em what they want to hear department."

Kristin dropped in a chair and pulled her feet up under her. "I've heard her version of how things are going between you and Scott. Something tells me I need to hear your version."

"We're making progress. But I'm sticking to my guns. I'm trying to keep distance between us – physical distance – while we work through our problems. For us, kiss and make up is too easy." With a sigh, she turned and looked at the ornately carved antique headboard, a family heirloom adapted for use with a king-size bed.

"Is that why he's not here tonight?"

"Sorta. Except that he gets credit for tonight, not me. They've scheduled an early work session for tomorrow morning."

"So that's one night where it's not an issue."

"Except that he's staying at the Hotel Figueroa. You ever been in that place?" Kristin shook her head no. "It's some crack-head set designer's idea of a bordello in Morocco. It just reeks of late-night rendezvous and illicit sex. Oh, God, listen to me. I sound like some suburban housewife worried about her husband having an affair with his secretary. Can you tell I'm having issues with trust?"

"I'll say," Kristin chuckled sardonically.

"You didn't walk in on what I walked in on. The sight of him – *them* – is like forever seared in my memory. You haven't lived until –" Jenna stopped short, realizing the insensitivity of what she was saying in front of a sister who was still nursing boyfriend-induced pain of her own. "Hey, enough about me," she said in a far softer tone as she sat down on the edge of the bed. "Tell me how you're doing."

A smile broke out across Kristin's face. "Great!" she beamed, then laughed out loud at Jenna's reaction of amazement. "I'm sorry, Jenn, but you've been dealing with such heavy shit, it just didn't feel right, crowing about this wonderful person I'd met and everything."

Jenna put her hands on her hips and shook her head in disapproval. "What wonderful person you met?" she asked. "You, my little sister, dare keep me, your big sister, outta the loop? Because I'm dealing with 'heavy shit'? That's like just plain *bogus*."

"Well, you know, I wasn't sure it was gonna go anywhere. But it is. Or at least it sure seems to be."

"Tell me about him. It is a him, right?" she asked, settling back on the pillows for some real sister talk.

"It sure is. His name's Doug. Doug Patterson. That's his acting name. His real name's Doug McClure, but no way he wanted everyone asking him if he was Doug McClure's son, or thinking he was getting roles because he was Doug McClure's son. So he came up with this cool last name, Patterson. If you know Latin, the 'Patter' part could be interpreted as father. Father-son."

"So, *is* he Doug McClure's son?"

"Nope. He's Harry McClure's son. Harry McClure the accountant from Des Moines. And, just in case you're wondering, Harry had a lotta brothers, but none of them were named Doug. He was named for his mother's brother. They could have cared less about actors. It never crossed their minds. It crossed Doug's, though. He sometimes wonders if it's why he got into acting. Anyway, I sort of knew him from the Actors Studio. He's a great actor. We met trying out for roles in a David Mamet film. We both got really good parts in it!"

"Kris!" Jenna said. "That's fabulous! What's it called?"

"Right now they're just calling it *Project X*. They're still working on a title, apparently. It's sorta sci-fi, about a bunch of sleezeballs, set way the future. In the story, we're an item. We're in rehearsals. Mamet's really big on rehearsal. He treats movies like filmed stageplays. And rehearses them like they're stageplays. That's how he gets those incredibly long, uncut takes – everyone has to *really* know their lines. And man, the dialog never quits. It's a great experience, getting to work with him. And really great working with Doug. Since, like I said, we're an item in the script. Let's just say, all those kisses in rehearsal led to kisses off the set…"

Jenna laughed. "You're blushing!" she exclaimed.

"I can't wait for you to meet him," Kristin said, ignoring Jenna's comment. "I'm bringing him tomorrow night."

"Excellent," Jenna said. She knew it was petty, high school behavior, but she couldn't wait for Ryan to see Kristin's new boyfriend. Suddenly she found herself really looking forward to the after party.

Joe found endless reasons to carp about the fact that Scott hadn't joined them for supper. Every subject that came up gave him yet another opportunity to sound off on the subject. Jenna'd had it when a simple comment to her mother – "Is Claude still cutting your hair? It looks different somehow." – elicited a harrumph from Joe, followed by, "What isn't different? Even my son's comings and goings are different. He's a part of this family. At least, I coulda sworn he was. At least, last time I heard he was..."

In the silence that followed, Jenna cleared her throat. "Joe," she finally said, firmly but choosing her words with careful precision, "Scott's very much a part of this family, but he also is very much a part of Blacklace. Not to make excuses for him, but he – and they – take their work very seriously. It's what put them where they are today. It's one of the things I most admire about him and all the rest of them. They have a work ethic that can only be termed Yankee." That seemed to do the trick. If Joe had further gripes where his son was concerned, he kept them to himself for the rest of the meal.

After supper was over, Linda sent Joe, Kristin and Zach on a quick walk around the block. Ellen was assigned to child-proofing the den into a playroom for Zach, while mother and daughter did the dishes. Jenna sighed inwardly as Linda gave everyone their marching orders. It was like having a control freak for a director on a movie set. She knew what came next: cross-examination by one of the country's hottest forensic attorneys. As soon as the kitchen was theirs, Linda started in.

"Sooo…" she said, drawing out her opening syllable, "how exactly *are* things between you and the guy with the great Yankee work ethic?" She certainly didn't waste any time getting to the point, Jenna thought with irritation.

"Coming along," she answered noncommittally, reaching for a towel to dry her mother's gold-rimmed glassware. Two could play at this game.

"Coming along, eh? Slowly? Rapidly? Glacially, it seems to me."

"Coming along at the pace at which it all needs to come along. Some things can't be rushed." Can't be rushed in order to please you, my impatient mother, Jenna mused.

"You have a child to consider," Linda said sharply. Jenna swallowed hard. Her mother had always known how to find her weakest point.

"I know, Mom," she said with a sigh. "I've been consulting a child therapist on the best way to handle things from Zach's perspective, since this all started. I didn't want to wing it." At the mention of a child therapist, Linda turned and stared at her daughter. Jenna knew her mother's weak points, too.

Yes, Mom, I consulted a child therapist – which is more than you ever did, Jenna thought bitterly. It would be so easy to say those words aloud and send this conversation reeling off onto an entirely different trajectory altogether, but Jenna had no intention of letting that happen. In that respect, she was *not* her mother's daughter.

Instead, she said, "Zach's rolling with it all. We have a routine going, a routine he can count on. It's clear he's not happy when Scott leaves, but he knows his daddy'll be back. It's no different than if his father was a truck driver who had to be away from home for long stretches of time, you know."

"A truck driver," Linda said disdainfully. "A truck driver, indeed."

"Mom, you know what I mean. Someone whose work takes him away. A pilot – is that better?"

"You don't have to get hostile with me, young lady," Linda said most predictably.

"Look, Mom, I travel too. And when I get back to touring again, he'll deal with that too. He's the first thing I think about, not the last, believe me."

Linda went quiet for a moment, then turned to Jenna. "I'm sorry, honey, I can be such a bitch." Jenna couldn't believe her ears. "It's practically a reflex. I really need to stop. Forgive me?" She opened her arms. Jenna moved into them without hesitation.

"Somebody pinch me," she said. To her further amazement, her mother laughed.

BEFORE JOE, ZACH AND Kristin returned, they'd had a real heart-to-heart, starting with Jenna's feeling that she was in large part to blame for Scott's transgression. "I've given Scott so much to worry about," she said. "I never realized how much it affected him. I know what happened to me wasn't my fault, but I never stopped to think about the toll its taken on him emotionally. Sure, there were other issues but I was his biggest one. Towards the end it just got to be too much for him." Linda, for the first time Jenna could remember, just listened. Taking advantage of the moment, she hurried on.

"The trial, my nightmares again, all the usual problems with the band – and me wanting to get pregnant again, so badly. I feel like I literally drove him to drink – whether he took that drink or not. He keeps telling me I didn't, of course. But the fact is, he tried to handle way too many things on his own. When everything started going wrong, it left him feeling helpless. Instead of turning to his sponsor or someone when he got overwhelmed like that, he turned to the bottle. Then turned to her. In a funny way, I almost feel like it was a good thing, his old girlfriend coming along when she did. God knows what else worse might have happened. What other trouble he might have gotten himself into. He could have gotten himself killed."

Jenna realized as she said the words, words she'd never said, that they were true. The enormity of the thought made her need to sit down. She perched herself on a stool, put her elbows on the counter and dropped her head in her hands. Linda seemed prepared to continue listening, so Jenna let herself keep talking.

"I realize now that we were both to blame. Forgive and forget…? I know I can forgive him. I love him that much. What I don't know is if I'll ever forget. Will I doubt him every time he goes away? Will I wonder if he'll turn to some other woman when we have a fight and he takes off? Mom, what made you decide to finally go back to Daddy?"

Linda shook her head, smiled and took her daughter's hand. "The same things that will bring you back to Scott. Love and your son. That's right," she said in response to a dubious look from her daughter. "Don't get me wrong, sweetie. I had the same questions as you do. I'm not saying it was easy, either. Hell, the first few times your father was away, I was a crazy woman. After time, though, I can honestly say that even those thoughts passed. Your father and I loved each other, and we had three beautiful children who we both loved. With both those thing in mind, I chose to give our marriage another chance – and it paid off."

"Even with what you learned, after he died?"

Linda stopped and let her thoughts hop-scotch back almost twenty-five years. "Yes, even with that. Jenna, the love you and Scott share is so much more than what your father and I had. I know that if we could do it, you and Scott can find your way back to each other as well."

Jenna and Linda had just moved into a heart-felt embrace when Zach came bursting through the door. "Mommy!" he cried. Not letting go of her mother, Jenna reached down, scooped him up and brought him into their hug.

"Hey, room for me in there?" Joe asked, joustling his way in.

"Me, too," Kristin said feigning a pout. "Group hug!"

When the hug fest finally dissolved into giggles, Joe took the stool next to Jenna.

"I heard what you were saying as we came in," he said. "I've gotta add my two cents, if you don't mind. You know I cheated on Scott's mother, a very long time ago. I wasn't perfect by any means – I could be a real bastard when I wanted to be. You know I use to hit Scott when he was younger." Joe's gaze drilled into his daughter-in-law's eyes. Jenna tried to remain unreadable, but Joe wasn't buying it.

"Don't look at me like you don't know," he said, a bit quieter. "Scott told me about that day he almost hit Zach, how it brought back memories for him. The one that haunts him the most is about what caused me to cheat on his mom." Joe looked away. Jenna could only imagine what it was costing him to bare his soul in this fashion.

"I got really angry at him one day, for all the drinking and the drugs. The cops had come to the house. Again. It was hardly the first time he'd gotten caught. They planned on hauling him down to the station, but as a favor to me, they brought him home. Some favor. I promised them I'd handle it. I handled it all right. I practically beat the living shit of him. If Lydia hadn't stopped me, I don't know what I would have done." Joe stopped, pained by the memories he'd decided he had to get off his chest.

"She and I ended up in a terrible fight, as you can imagine," he finally forced himself to continue. "I ended up walking out and headed to a bar. Familiar story, isn't it? Well, I didn't have an old girlfriend but I did have several drinks. I met someone and you can picture the rest." His demeanor turned grim. He scratched his head, as if he almost still couldn't believe what he had done so long ago.

"Lydia found out a few weeks later and threw me out of the house. It took us six months to get back together. Looking back now, I was damn lucky she forgave me. Not only had I cheated on her but I beat my son. I wasn't very proud of myself then and I sure don't feel very proud as I'm telling you about it now. I guess the point I'm trying to make is, my son didn't beat his son, then go get stinking drunk and screw someone he didn't even know. He's a better man than I was."

Joe took Jenna's hand. "I know he hurt you terribly but, Jenna, if you truly love him – as I know you do, I know you can forgive him." Jenna reached over and hugged her father-in-law.

"Scott never shared any of that with me," she said, sitting back. "He told me you hit him from time to time. He never used the word 'beat,' though. No wonder he freaked out so badly the night he almost hit Zach. Joe – thanks. You've given me a lot to think about."

Jenna hugged him again, then excused herself and took Zach upstairs. Letting him play for a few moments before getting ready for bed, she sat watching him grab up a couple of toys and go off into his private world of his own imagination. How simple – and how complex – life is for a child, she thought.

Her mind went back over all that Linda and Joe had just told her. She knew her parents' story, and she could understand how her mother could have forgiven her father. How Lydia could have forgiven Joe, especially for what he had done to Scott, she really couldn't understand. She wished Scott were with her right now. She had so many questions.

AFTER SHE GOT ZACH tucked in for the night, she tried to call Scott but he didn't answer. As the prompt played, her mind reeled through possible messages she could leave him, what she wanted to say. Taking a breath as the tone beeped, she settled for a quiet, "Hi, honey. I love you."

It was late, but when she came back downstairs, Linda encouraged Jenna to go visit Jim and Sue. "They told me they wanted you to come over tonight," she insisted. "They're both leaving town tomorrow. Zach has Ellen if he wakes up."

"I'll go too," Kristin decided. "I'll drive." That settled it.

It was only a ten-minute drive to Jim and Sue's house which was, if possible, even less homey than the house their mother now owned had looked when she'd taken possession. When he and Sue had owned it, it had the utilitarian look of off-campus housing for grad students. By comparison, their new place looked like a flop house.

"Hey, guys! 'Scuse the mess," Jim said as he greeted them at the door. "We both have seven a.m. flights to catch in the morning." Sue and Jenna exchanged a warm, sisterly hug. Sue accepted Kristin just as openly.

Ten minutes' conversation got everyone pretty much caught up with each other. Once satisfied, Jim got to the point. "Look, Jenn – it's late and we've gotta hit the sack. But I have to weigh in on your thing with Scott." Jenna smiled wryly at her brother's customarily blunt approach. Tact had never had any place in their relationship over the years.

"Shoot," she said. "Everyone else has."

"Look, I'm not gonna say that what he did was right. But he regrets it and is willing to do whatever it takes to get you back. You know yourself – he loves you, more than anything else. Guys like that don't grow on trees. I just know what he went through – and what he put *me* through – to get to the bottom of what happened to you when you were a kid. *That* was love. Whatever you decide, I'll support you, but I think you'd be a fool not to go back to him."

ON THEIR WAY HOME, Jenna asked Kristin her opinion. "You're the only one who hasn't told me what to do. Surely you have something to add.

"Well, okay, since you asked" Kristin said. "I've been there for a lot of things you two have gone through. I gotta tell you, Jenn, Scott went through hell when you lost the baby. And then the way you almost died during Zach's birth. And that's like just for starters. I know he can be difficult – well, okay, a flat-out bastard – sometimes, but he does love you. You two have been able to forgive each other for so much. Hopefully this will be the hardest thing you'll ever have to forgive him for. I don't know, sis, who am I to say? But – if you love each other so much, isn't it worth forgiving him one more time?"

WHEN THEY GOT BACK to the house, Joe and Linda had retired, but a message was taped on Jenna's bedroom door. Scott had called and wanted her to call him back.

Climbing into bed, she opened her cell phone and dialed him. He answered on the first ring, just as she was pulling the covers up over her. "Babe," he said, his voice as tender as a caress.

Suddenly, Jenna was overcome by a luxurious, comforting warmth. Fleeting as it was, the feeling hit her like a hot wind coming off the desert in the wake of a bone-chilling rainstorm. Stretching, she purred into the phone, "Hi, hon. I miss you. I – I want you. Might as well admit it. This bed's damned empty without you. Not that –"

"Whoa. Stop, babe. Just let me treasure the moment you find yourself wanting me. You don't have to explain yourself or regret what you said. You don't have to rewind and lay down a new track. Honey, I want you too."

They talked for a long time, about their plans for the following day, about what the band had in mind, about what they needed to get accomplished. They would meet at the Staples Center for a noontime rehearsal, then go to lunch, just the two of them, before returning to the house.

As they finally said goodnight Jenna knew she had to make a decision about their relationship, soon.

Chapter 27

※

JENNA NEVER FELL Asleep till close to four, replaying all the family input she'd gotten the day and evening before. She woke to a combination of Kristin's voice in her ear and the sound of Zach demanding her attentions from down the hall.

"Wake up, sleepy head," said Kristin. "You said you had to be out of here by eleven."

"No! I want my mommy!" came Zach's wail from his room.

Jenna bolted out of bed, shrugged into a robe and went to placate her son, but the minute he saw her, his cries switched to, "No! Daddy! I want my daddy!"

"Man, you really know how to make a mommy feel special," Jenna said as she reached down to give her son a good morning hug. "I love you, Zach." But Zach would have none of it. One by one, he heaved his toys to the farthest corners of the room, muttering a seemingly endless list of complaints.

"There's no pleasing young Master Tenny this morning," Ellen said, rolling her eyes. "He woke up like this."

He was still complaining when Jenna came back an hour later to tell him she had to go to rehearsal, setting him off wailing in earnest. "No! Don't go! I want my daddy! Now!" 'Now' had become his favorite word of late.

"I'll have your daddy with me when I come back," she promised him. Zach gave her a look that clearly said, "You darned well better."

"Really, I will," she cajoled him. "And tomorrow we'll go for a hike in the hills. Promise."

Zach still looked dubious as she kissed him goodbye.

JENNA WAS PULLING around the side of the Staples Center, headed for the performers' entrance, when she passed a woman standing on the corner, at a considerable distance from the fans, bleachers and red carpet leading into the front entrance. The woman had the look of a hooker out trolling for business.

Suddenly she realized she was looking at Ashley West, a *lot* of Ashley West, barely covered by a tiny halter top and probably the lowest-cut, shortest denim miniskirt on record. Oh, great, she thought. This is all I need. She's probably watching for Scott. Averting her head, she slid by the woman without making eye contact. She doubted she'd gone unnoticed, however.

She was relieved to find that Scott was already inside, and had been for over half an hour. She didn't bother asking if Ashley had seen him; she knew the band had arrived by limo, protected from recognition by tinted windows. She really didn't care if he'd seen Ashley, she realize, simultaneously recognizing that her level of trust must be improving.

Rehearsal for Jenna and Scott, when it was finally their turn, only required a quick run-through of their presentation lines. As they waited, he proposed an early lunch at a little café nearby that Dan had discovered the night before. Half an hour later, Jenna at the wheel, they pulled out of the performer's lot and headed the opposite direction from the corner where she could still see Ashley at her post.

The café was everything Dan had said it was: the décor was idiosyncratic and fun, the food outstanding. Zach was the main topic of conversation. Jenna was growing concerned with his angry outbursts.

"Maybe he's just a little precocious," Scott suggested. "The terrible twos are just around the corner."

"Maybe he's more affected by our comings and goings than I like to think he is," Jenna fretted. "He's clear on the fact that Ellen isn't Mommy or Daddy."

"Lots of kids grow up without seeing Mommy or Daddy every day of their formative years, for an endless list of reasons."

"Zach isn't 'lots of kids.' Zach's our son. I only want what's best for him. I've made a decision. I know part of this is 'mommy hormones' talking, but I've put a lot of thought into it. I'm putting my career on hold. Zach deserves it, and if I can get pregnant again, that's even more reason to." Jenna stopped to gauge Scott's reaction. When he started nodding, she went on. "I know it's the right thing to do right now. The world will still be there when I'm ready to go back. Plenty of artists have."

Scott reached across the table and took her hand. "Zach's one lucky child," he said quietly. "And hopefully, I'm one lucky man."

AS THEY PULLED UP the street to Linda and Joe's, Zach was out playing in the yard, attempting to do somersaults with Ellen's assistance. Before he saw them, Jenna pulled over to the curb to watch. Zach clearly didn't want Ellen's help, but without it he could only manage to put his hands to the ground, tuck his head and collapse into a roll to one side or the other. Regardless, he seemed determined to master this new skill on his own. The results were reminiscent of some of Charlie Chaplin's best work.

"If I only had a camera," Scott lamented, then jumped out of the car. The minute Zach heard the door behind him, he wheeled, saw Scott and barreled into him, yelling "Daddy! Daddy! Daddy!" at the top of his tiny lungs. Scott caught him up by the hands and spun him around like an amusement fair airplane ride until both of them collapsed in a laughing heap on the grass.

Linda, Joe and Adella formed an audience at the door, attracted by the boisterous commotion. Linda was the first out the door. Scott picked himself up, dusted himself off, then accepted the warm hug she had for him. Joe joined them and gave his son a pat on the back as they all made their way inside.

Within moments, Adella was fussing over them on the patio, pressing iced teas into every hand. Zach pasted himself to Scott's side, wrapping one arm around his father's leg, guzzling from a sippy cup of fresh-squeezed orange juice with the other. "We're gonna have to start calling you Velcro, little man," he teased the youngster.

They had barely gotten into conversation when Adella reappeared at the door. "Phone call for you, Meester Scott," she announced. Scott excused himself and went in to take it.

While he was gone, Joe asked Jenna how the rehearsal had gone. "Oh, it was fine," she assured him breezily. "You know they've got us presenting together this year." The looks on both Linda and Joe's faces suggested they didn't. Jenna had to laugh.

"It seems that you guys aren't the only ones trying to get us back together. We're presenting the award for Song of the Year. Together. They claim that 'somebody' got the bright idea to make it a double feature, have the winners from the past two years make this year's presentation. I'm sure it's *just* sheer coincidence that it *just* happened to be us," she said with a wry smile

As Scott returned from the kitchen, Jenna looked at her watch. "Oh, goodness, I can't believe the time. We have to get a move on. We're due back there at 5:15 latest." Jumping up, she headed for the door. "You visit," she told Scott. "It takes me longer to get ready than it does you."

SCOTT HAD CHANGED BY the time she came back down and had been waiting for her, pacing the living room. He was dressed in black leather head to toe, over a barely buttoned purple silk shirt. Jenna found him momentarily stationary, primping in the mirror over the mantelpiece, running his hands through his long, wild hair in an effort to make it look even wilder than usual. A docile Zach sat with Linda and Joe on the couch amidst a scattering of picture books, a thumb in his mouth, the other hand fiddling absentmindedly with his own wild long hair. Linda was performing a particularly dramatic reading of *Where the Wild Things Are*. She had Zach's undivided attention, at least until his mother reappeared.

"Wow!" Scott and Zach said in perfect unison. Jenna was resplendent in a shimmering, sequined blue satin gown by Guilio Casare, with a strapless, form-fitting bodice that flared just above the knees into a skirt that swept the floor behind her.

"Mommy's a bwew mermaid!" Zach exclaimed, jumping to his feet. "A real bwew mermaid!"

"She's a real stunner is what she is," Scott said quietly, and then saw that she was wearing the sapphire and diamond necklace he had given her for Christmas.

Even Joe stood with his mouth gaping open at the sight of his daughter-in-law.

Linda looked from father to son and back again. "If you two are going to drool over my daughter, I better outfit you with bibs. Scott, aren't you going to say something to your wife? And you, husband of mine," she added, slipping an arm into his, "isn't she absolutely gorgeous? Your son's a complete idiot if he doesn't find a way to hang on to her."

Scott walked over to Jenna, took her by the hand and gently pulled her close. Then, much to the delight of both parents, they kissed. Zach came running over and wiggled his way in between them. "Me too! I wanna mermaid kiss!"

A FEW MINUTES LATER, they were in the limo, headed for downtown. Zach had let her go only after extracting from her the promise that she'd still "be a bwew mermaid" when he woke up in the morning. "For you, Zachery Matthew Scott Tenny, I'll be a blue mermaid any time you want me to be!" she promised, hugging him goodnight and blowing him a kiss as she climbed into the car, before settling in for the slog through rush hour L.A. traffic.

Smoothing her dress beneath her, she turned to Scott to find he had whipped out his cell phone and had placed a call. Holding it to his ear, he held a finger up to her. After a brief pause, his call was answered.

"Matthew," he said, his voice spiked with urgency, "this is Scott Tenny. Jenna and I need your help." Another pause. "Can you meet us at the Staples Center, back entrance?" Pause. "We're into really some deep shit here." Pause. "Okay, Matthew. Excellent. Twenty minutes. Hey – thanks, man."

As Scott clicked his phone shut, Jenna could only stare at him, dumbfounded. She knew only one Matthew who Scott might speak to in that tone of voice. Matthew Caine, L.A.P.D.

"Scott?"

"Honey, we gotta talk."

BY THE TIME RANDY had pulled the limo down into the maw of the back entrance to the huge Staples arena, Jenna was reeling. As they had crossed Wilshire, Scott had told her that he was being blackmailed. Sitting through two light cycles at the corner of Pico and South La Cienega gave him plenty of time to explain, and plenty of time for her to grasp, the Ashley West/Dave Schultz connection. Before they'd reached the 110 Freeway, she was trying to wrap her mind around the latest development, the phone call Scott had received back at the house. Dave Schultz was upping the ante.

Ten thousand dollars a month, he'd informed Scott, was chump change for a guy as rich as the lead singer for Blacklace. "I need to know I can count on you keeping me in the style to which I'm rapidly becoming accustomed," Schultz had said mockingly. Then his voice had turned as sharp and as dangerous as a freshly minted razor blade. "Shit happens, Tenny. You could

go broke, you know. You've certainly done it before. You could die…"
Schultz let the thought hang in the air.

"So…" Scott said finally, wanting to know where this was headed.

"So…I want a lump sum payout," Schultz informed him. "A *big* lump
sum payout."

Scott waited him out in seething silence.

"Five million dollars, to be deposited in that Belize bank account."

"Yeah, right," Scott had responded sarcastically.

"Dead right," Schultz had snapped back at him. "As in if you don't, your
woman – whether she's your woman these days or not – is dead. Right?"

Before Scott could begin to process this information, Schultz had added,
almost as an afterthought, "Oh, yeah, and Tenny, I'll be there tonight. And just
so you know I'm serious, I plan on giving you a little demo of just how
vulnerable the bitch is."

THEY SAW MATTHEW CAINE standing at the entrance to the elevator just as
he'd promised Scott he would be. Scott had Randy pull up directly in front of
him, and the detective quickly climbed in. Dispensing with greetings, Scott
tersely brought Caine up to speed.

"Holy…" he responded when Scott got the part about what would happen
if he didn't pay up, and Schultz's plans for a "demo." He looked over at Jenna.
"Are you okay?"

"Not really," Jenna had to admit.

"No way I'm gonna give in to that sorry son of a bitch," Scott said
through clenched teeth. "But what do we do? I'm afraid to even walk in there."

"Give me a minute and I'll get the cavalry up to speed and in place, for
starters," Caine said succinctly, pulling a phone from his pocket and taking a
few steps away. He made three calls in rapid succession, then turned back to
them. "Okay, security's all over it. But we have a problem."

Scott rolled his eyes. "You bet your sweet patootie we got a problem. Tell
me somethin' I don't know."

"We can't arrest them simply for showing up. They could be sitting in the
front row of the stands along the red carpet and we couldn't make an arrest.
Security's going to be all over you, all evening, and they'll grab them if they
try to actually do anything, but beyond that, our hands are tied. I have a
suspicion it's gonna be a waste of my precious breath, but I'd like to suggest
that you two fine people go home. Go out for dinner. Go back to Boston."

Scott grabbed his temples and groaned. "But they're back in Boston,
Matthew. They're everywhere we go. There's no end to this."

Even though he'd touched on it as they drove over, Jenna finally understood the truly enormous pressure Scott had been bearing up under, alone, for
so long. The stress of it was legible in the corded, bulging blood vessels
pulsating up the side of his neck. She put a hand on his arm. She doubted he
could feel it.

"There could be," she said quietly. "There could be an end to this."

Both men looked at her.

"I can draw them out, apparently."

"Over my dead body," Scott said vehemently. "This is my problem, not yours. No way am I going to let you get in harm's way, tonight or any night."

"That's easy to say, Scott," Caine interjected. "It's a hellova hard promise to keep."

"Nor is it any longer only your problem," Jenna pointed out. "We're in this together, babe, whether we like it or not. Without me, there's no blackmail."

"Don't be so sure of that," Scott said through clenched teeth. "There's Zach, too. I've never felt so vulnerable."

"Which is why we have to end it here." Jenna's voice was quiet and firm. Scott looked at her with amazement.

"How can you be so cool about this?"

"Maybe because I love you?" she whispered.

Chapter 28

✺

RANDY PULLED THE LIMO back around to the main entrance of the Staple Center and joined the lumbering queue of luxury vehicles disgorging luminaries of the music world, their entourages and escorts.

As Scott finally stepped out onto the pavement and turned back to for Jenna, Caine, sitting back in the shadows, couldn't help saying, "Be careful," then shook his head. After all these years, after all the mayhem the veteran detective had seen in his day, he couldn't believe he was still capable of uttering such fatuous words.

Scott took Jenna's hand and helped her out into the glare and frenzy of the media circus that annually took up residence for the event. It didn't matter how many times one walked the red carpet, it always came as a fresh shock to the system. Predators bristling with microphones lunged at each new arrival, trying to scoop the competition for the most quotable line of the night.

Most stars welcomed the turmoil of attention as evidence of their celebrity in the music world. Tonight, Jenna and Scott only found it all upsetting and distracting. Their eyes were everywhere but on those of their would-be interviewers. As Jenna's gaze raked the crowds, she spotted Jeremy and Carrie ahead of them and quickly pointed them out to Scott.

"Safety in numbers," Scott whispered to her and put a protective arm around her as they pushed their way through to catch up with them. Before they could reach them, however, they hit a roadblock, a phalanx of reporters standing shoulder to shoulder. Jenna sighed and turned her attention to the closest, a reed of a man with a seasoned, hard face and a shock of white hair tied back in a ponytail.

"Brad Caswell, Jenna," he said in that way that said they had once been introduced at a cocktail party and that she should remember him. "Jenna, is the fact that you're here with your husband – with his arm around you, in fact – proof positive that the two of you have reconciled?!" The reporter couched the question with a smug air of amazement. Jenna's mouth fell open, and she could only blink in genuine amazement at the man's barefaced offensiveness. Her reaction didn't seem to alter Brad Caswell's equanimity a bit.

"Scott and I are here as presenters. The fact that we're here together for the occasion means just that, that we are here together for the occasion. Nothing more and nothing less," she spat out angrily.

"But –"

"But nothing. That's all I have to say on that subject," she said clearly. "If you want to ask me something about music, feel free." Apparently he didn't. Seeing Beyoncé working the reporters as she came up behind Jenna, he abandoned this clearly uncooperative subject for easier prey.

THE ENTIRE BLACKLACE contingent was given a block of front and second row seats. The more exposed they were, the easier it would be to protect them, Caine had explained as he and house security had coordinated plans on the fly.

As Jenna glanced about the huge hall, she couldn't help noticing security seemingly everywhere, patrolling the stage, the wings, the doors, the balconies. It started to look like just about everyone there was on Security's payroll.

Everyone but Schultz and Ashley, and who knew where they were at this moment, Jenna thought with a palpable shiver of fear.

THE EVENING PROCEEDED as normally as awards shows ever do. Billy Crystal was emceeing and clearly had his marching orders to bring the show in on schedule. He had his work cut out for him.

A constant stream of presenters gave out awards for the most special of the ever-expanding list of categories that multiplied with every year and every new addition to the art form. Some presenters attempted to take advantage of their moment for a bit of impromptu riffing. For this contingency, the musical director had his orders – a little goosing from the brass section quickly got them back on script. Presentations were broken up by the bands and soloists whose work had been nominated for Best Album of the Year. Blacklace's entry this year, *Forever New*, was up against stiff competition.

As Blacklace prepared to be ushered backstage to perform, Scott leaned over and gave Jenna a small kiss. "This whole thing'll be over before you know it," he whispered. "I love you, babe." He didn't whisper so quietly that Carrie, who was sitting next to Jenna, couldn't hear the sentiment. It made her smile.

Once the band had departed, she reached over and whispered, "Maybe there *is* hope for you two lunatics," into Jenna's ear.

Jenna hadn't planned on telling Carrie what was going on, but suddenly she needed to, very badly. Quietly, she filled her in on the threat, the heightened security, her worst fears. Once some guards had been pointed out to her, Carrie started realizing she was seeing plainclothes security in every corner as Jenna continued to quietly elaborate.

"You probably shouldn't even be sitting with me," Jenna said miserably, when she'd finished.

Carrie straightened up in her seat, turned and looked Jenna in the eye. "What are friends for?" she asked her rhetorically, then reached over and took Jenna's hand in hers. "You'll be okay. We'll all be okay."

The words were barely out of her mouth when the lights came up on Blacklace. The band performed, brilliantly, while Jenna held her breath. Carrie never let go of her hand.

Jenna's breath released in a flood of relief as the audience exploded in appreciation. If Grammys were awarded based on applause meters, *Forever New* was a lock to win.

BEFORE THE CLAPPING had had time to die down, an usher approached Jenna to bring her backstage. Giving Carrie a little hug, she rose and went with the man. Even trusting him wasn't easy, though she had been introduced to him earlier in the day. Her eyes sought out and met the eyes of several security guards along her route. Each seemed to have a tiny, reassuring nod for her.

Overwhelmed, she realized she had never felt so protected – and so alone – in her life. By the time she and the usher had reached the wings, they had a pair of security guards at their elbows. The usher smiled at Scott and excused himself.

Scott was just finishing up wiping the sweat from his brow and receiving the final attentions of a makeup girl with a huge powder puff when Jenna arrived. Sliding her arm through his, she felt like she was slipping on a Kevlar vest. And just as if she were donning a heavy bulletproof vest, she felt as someone wearing such a vest must feel: still terribly exposed in all the extremities.

As if he could read her mind, Scott reached over with his free hand and gave her a gentle squeeze. "We're okay," he said, then repeated himself. Jenna knew she had never felt less okay.

"And now, to present this year's award for Song of the Year, please welcome the winners for Song of the Year for the past two years, Jenna and Scott Tenny," they heard resonate over the loudspeakers.

"You're on," the stage manager whispered gratuitously.

Scott and Jenna looked at each other, suddenly feeling like the only two human beings on the face of the earth. No, make that four, instantly went through Jenna's mind. Somewhere out there…

Jenna reached up, touched Scott's cheek and kissed him. Then they headed for the podium.

YOU HAD TO GIVE Dave Schultz credit for allowing U2 their due. Scott and Jenna had made their way through the less than inspired banter that the writers for the Grammys seemed to think passed for humor, lightheartedness, humility and sincerity, and had gotten to the opening of the envelope. The award had been announced, and Bono had accepted for U2 via satellite feed from Dublin. Jenna and Scott had stood watching the screen along with the rest of the audience, then waited patiently for their cue to turn and exit the stage as applause took over.

Finally, one of the stage ushers reached for Jenna's elbow to indicate that she and Scott could now leave. But before Jenna could take the first step, the air about her was suddenly filled with a snowstorm of feathers, cascading down from high in the rigging above her.

As Jenna started flailing at the incomprehensible, invasive whiteness around her, no one in the audience had any doubt that this was not a rehearsed moment. Clearly, Jenna and those around her were terrified. Security was on the spot instantly, and Scott and she were hustled headlong off the stage.

Billy Crystal, as host for the evening, took a deep breath, thought fast and headed for the podium. "Well, we all know Bono's a saint, but he really needs to do something about the ways those wings of his molt," he riffed, toeing the pile of feathers where Jenna had just been standing. "Really."

THOROUGHLY RATTLED, JENNA ended up shaking in the arms of Matthew Caine. "We've got an army headed up there. They'll get him," he assured her. "He's history. It isn't exactly assault with a deadly weapon, but it'll have to do. We'll have him where we want him before Cinderella's clock strikes twelve. He won't get out of the building without a full police escort."

"But you will," Scott said decisively to Jenna. "Matthew, can you take her to our folks' house? I want her out of here. Schultz has made his point."

"Done," Caine said.

Jenna had never taken kindly to being spoken of in the third person, but tonight she was too shaken to object.

"You go with Matthew. I'll be home as soon as we're done," he told her, then gave her kiss. Pulling back, he removed a feather from her hair and slipped it in his pocket. "One day we'll laugh about this, promise," he told her.

Within the half hour, long before Scott and the rest of Blacklace had returned to the podium to receive the award for Best Album, Caine was escorting Jenna up to her mother's door.

"You get yourself a good night's sleep. We'll get the son of a bitch," he was still saying as she reached for the knocker. "He won't get out of the building."

BUT SCHULTZ DID GET out of the building. Both the L.A.P.D. and house security combed every inch of the Staples Center, most areas twice, some three times, but no trace of either Schultz or Ashley West was found.

The only thing out of the ordinary to turn up was a large, plastic bin secured by bungee cords onto the rigging. It's hinged lid had apparently been tripped by remote control. A few white feathers still clung to the lip of the empty container.

After conferring with Grammy officials, two things quickly became clear. Whoever timed the release had been present during rehearsal and had precise knowledge of where Jenna would be standing during Bono's acceptance speech (that U2 were the winners and that he would accept via satellite had been a tightly held secret). And whoever timed the release had been in the building, or at the very least had a pair of eyes inside the building, at the time of the release. Broadcast time-delay meant it could not have been accomplished by monitoring an off-site television.

Caine added his own third observation. "Whoever timed the release knows his stuff."

Chapter 29

✳

JOE OPENED THE DOOR to Jenna. Before he could even give her half a hug, Linda came running, crying, "Will somebody tell me what in the hell that was all about! Never in my life…" She stopped at the sight of her badly shaken daughter.

"That — that wasn't a prank, was it," she said, her mouth falling open. "Baby! What in God's name…"

"Mom, Joe, come sit down. I'll explain everything — as best I can, anyway. We don't know everything. But, no, it wasn't a prank. It was damned serious. Wait. Let me get changed," she said, looking down and pulling yet another feather off the blue sequined gown. "I'll be right back down."

A few minutes later, Jenna was curled up in a corner of the couch in silk lounging pajamas and a cozy velour bathrobe, sipping a cup of hot tea and unburdening herself of the whole sordid mess. To her surprise, she found she was able to explain it all calmly and dispassionately.

Jenna found herself wishing that she didn't have to involve her mother at all, that she could gloss over the facts, make light of the situation, but she knew she that would be tempting fate — her mother had a sixth sense for the truth and zero tolerance for lies. At the same time, she had to admit it felt good to share this new, particularly cumbersome load of trouble with two seasoned veterans of the public arena.

After the initial shock had worn off, Linda appeared to take Jenna's news very much in stride. By the time Scott returned, his mother-in-law was examining the pros and cons of calling a press conference. "Why not take the bull by the horns?" she was asking her husband and daughter.

Entering the living room, Scott jumped in on the tail end of the conversation. "Personally, I'd want to know what breed we're talkin' about before *I'd* go taking any bulls by any horns. So what breed *are* we talkin'?"

"Longhorned media," Joe said dryly, and gave him a two-sentence distillation of Linda's ideas on the subject.

Scott thought about it for a moment. Looking at Jenna, he said, "This isn't for us to decide. This is something we have to tackle with both of our publicists and managers — tomorrow. Not to mention security. And the police.

Matthew plans on being here at nine. The last thing he said before I left tonight was that just going back to Boston wasn't going to solve this problem."

Jenna grimaced at the thought, but nodded her agreement, then smiled and held a hand out to him.

"Come sit," she said, nodding at the cushion beside her. He did and she took his hand. "I've told Mom and Pop the whole thing, the blackmail, everything."

Scott looked down at his hand in hers, then looked up at all of them. "Does life get any screwier than this?" he asked rhetorically.

Linda never let anybody get away with rhetorical questions. "Yes, it actually can. Apparently there are no limits on how screwy life can get. I should know," she added sardonically as she reached over and gave Joe's hand a quick squeeze.

As they all sat rehashing how the bizarre evening had unfolded, Jenna brought Scott's fingertips to her lips. Without even being aware of it, she had come to a decision. Tonight, she would welcome her husband back into her bed.

ADJUSTING TO THE COOL touch of the sheets on her naked skin, she marveled at how solid Scott felt in her arms. She buried her head in his shoulder, then finally burst into tears for the first time tonight, and cried herself out. Wrapping her in his arms and peppering her with kisses and caresses, Scott smoothed the wrinkles from her worried forehead with his fingers, his lips and his words.

As one by one she consciously let go of pain and panic, anxiety and apprehension, dread and fear, she felt each emotion's departure leave behind it a void, and each void found the others and they grew, expanding, ballooning into a single great void of stillness and silence, a sea of tranquility. Then, suddenly, without forewarning, a tsunami of passion rushed in to fill the void.

AFTERWARDS, JENNA DRIFTED directly into a deep sleep. Scott discovered he couldn't. His gaze, when he finally gave up and opened his eyes, quickly roamed out the window and into the half-light of a Beverly Hills night. It was never perfectly dark in Los Angeles, no matter how far up into the hills you got; there was far too much ambient light, even on those nights when the sky was cloud-covered or moonless.

The night had grown cool, damp and windy. Scott could make out silhouettes of palm trees swaying with hypnotic grace against the perpetual dusk. The smell of acacia filled the room. The thrum of tree frogs masked the persistent sounds of the living city spread at the canyon's foot.

Scott felt himself being seduced by the beauty beyond the window. Throwing an arm over his eyes, he groaned inwardly. Then he brought himself back to the moment and to the woman whose lithe, trusting body had fallen asleep entangled with his. The woman whose final words to him tonight had been, "If our mothers could forgive their husbands, then I can too..."

Sliding his arm back around her, he felt her warmth draw him in. He brushed the crook of her neck with his lips, nibbled the lobe of her ear, then whispered, "Thank God there are no more secrets."

THE FRONT PAGE OF the entertainment section of the following morning's *Los Angeles Times* was spread out on the kitchen table for them to see when they finally came down for breakfast. "Grammy Prank Has Music World Guessing" read the headline. "Practical Joker Had to Have Inside Info," was the subhead.

Speculation ran the gamut. Some suspected Scott of cooking up some grandiose if misguided special effect to 'win Jenna back.' Rose petals might have made a better impression, the reporter suggested helpfully, noting Jenna's obvious distress at the 'feather incident.' Others opined that perhaps it was the handiwork of a disaffected or misguided member of Blacklace itself – Dan, the perennial joker, or maybe Jeremy, who the writer had thought looked particularly peeved while they played, were singled out for individual mention.

"Jeremy wasn't peeved," Jenna said, shaking her head in never-ending amazement at the media's creativity when it came to inventing facts and motivations. "Carrie said his shoulder had been giving him hell the past couple of days. He's getting it looked at today."

Joe came in from running errands, a copy of *Variety* under his arm. "You won't believe what *they* had to say," he chortled. "The headline's something like 'Tenny Trying to Refeather Nest?' Wait'll the weeklies get to work on you guys. You're gonna want to make reservations for a six-month trip to Tahiti."

"I don't give a damn what they say," Scott said vehemently. "We're going to go ahead and live our lives. We can't run away and we can't barricade ourselves up in some medieval French fortress somewhere. They'll surface again, and the cops will be waiting for them when they do. Wherever it is. We just have to be wicked careful in the meantime." And with that, the doorbell rang.

Adella brought Matthew Caine back to the kitchen and automatically poured him a cup of coffee while he greeted everyone. As he was sitting down, Jenna disappeared for a moment, then came back in carrying a squirming Zach. Settling him on her hip, she brought him over and sat on the stool next to Caine.

"Zach, say hi to your Uncle Matthew," she suggested.

Zach managed a shy "hi."

"Would ya look at this!" Caine crowed. "This kid's almost ready to try out for them New England Patriots. He was just a pipsqueak the last time I saw him."

"Show Uncle Matthew your muscle," Jenna prompted him and the youngster made a tiny fist, bent his elbow and, grinning, held his arm up for all to see.

"Stwong!" he declared. Caine gave the little muscle an appreciative squeeze.

"Man, you sure are, kid," he said, ruffling Zach's hair playfully. "I'm not gonna get in any fights with you!"

THE REST OF THE day was spent in conference with a shifting cast of characters. Adella made pot after pot of coffee, and Caine stayed throughout.

While he was having breakfast, Scott took a call from Eddie Strang, who told him he'd been on the phone to Stan Havlik before the last feather had hit the stage the night before. "He's already got a release out. We just got in on the red eye. Where are you?"

"Our parents' place." He gave Strang the address, which he heard Strang repeat to the driver.

"He says we'll be there in ten," he told Scott. "Big Bob and Pete will meet us there later. Pete's at the Staples Center, comparing notes with their security guys."

Jenna's people were all in L.A. anyway. Her phone had rung just as she was crawling into bed the night before. "Just tell me, please – what the *fuck* was that stunt about?" came the unmistakable voice of her manager. Brian had been in the audience. Jenna assured him wearily that it was no stunt, and filled him as briefly as she could on Schultz and Ashley West. "You're at your mother's?" Jenna told him she was. "I'll be there at ten."

Brian arrived promptly at ten, Bella trying to keep up with his hurried pace, talking her head off at him. Frank Kalkorian, Jenna's road manager, and another man she didn't recognize brought up the rear. After perfunctory greetings, Brian introduced the newcomer as Jim Almer. "I've hired him as a consultant on security," he explained.

"You can call me Jimbo," Almer said as he reached over to shake first Jenna's, then Caine's hands.

"This guy's a legend – a *legend* – in L.A. security circles," Bella brayed, nodding her blessing.

Members of both bands dropped in, joined in the discussions and drifted back out as they saw fit. Jenna's band was the least impacted since she wasn't currently on tour. They mainly came by in a show of solidarity. For Blacklace it was another matter. They'd be going back out on the road in a few days.

BY THE TIME THEY'D said their goodbyes and wearily climbed onto an airplane headed east, Jenna and Scott were more than ready to see the last of L.A. for a while. And when they finally climbed back off that airplane five hours later, after midnight Boston time, they felt nothing but exhausted relief. Jenna, carrying a snoring Zach, climbed into the limo that was waiting for them while Scott and Georgie loaded luggage into the trunk.

As they started to pull out of the airport, Scott keyed the intercom. "Jenna's first, Georgie," he said and started to draw his hand back. Jenna stopped him. Looking him straight in the eye while she kept the pressure on the key, she spoke into the intercom herself.

"No stop in Boston, Georgie. There's only one stop we'll need to make from now on. Take us home, Georgie." Jenna took hold of Scott's hand and squeezed it tight.

"Is – this like last time? Or does this mean you're really coming back – for keeps? Not just for tonight?" Scott hardly dared believe what he thought he was hearing.

"Not just for tonight. You're stuck with me from now on," Jenna said, then smiled at him. Then she reached over and kissed him.

Scott pulled back and looked her in the eye. "Why?" he asked simply.

"I'll explain everything when we get home."

Behind the wheel, Georgie smiled broadly. "Yes, ma'am!" he responded with pleasure.

AS THEY CURLED UP in bed, in their home, in their bedroom, Jenna whispered to Scott about all the conversations she'd had with her family, including the ones with his father.

"He even told me about the beatings," she told him.

"You're kidding."

"I was surprised he told me too," she admitted. "He even told me he knew why you freaked out when Zach hit me that day, because of all the times he hit or beat you. At least you and he have mended fences since then. The point is that, after listening to everyone's top ten reasons why I should stay with you, I've thought about it long and hard. I finally decided that if my mother and your mother – especially *your* mother – could forgive their husbands, I should be able to forgive mine. I love you too much not to."

Scott kissed her, a long, slow kiss. When it had finally run its course, Jenna continued. "That moment – before those fuckin' feathers – when you had your arm around me during Bono's acceptance speech, I made my decision. I knew I didn't want to be away from you any longer. And then, of course, all hell broke loose."

"It didn't change your mind, thank God."

"No way. Interrupted my train of thought something fierce. But by the time the mayhem had died down, I decided to wait – till we were back home, back here, back in our own bed, to tell you."

The kiss that followed could have qualified for a place in the Guinness book of records, had there been witnesses with stop watches to substantiate the fact.

JENNA WOKE THE following morning to find that both Scott and Zach had gone missing, as had Scott's car. A note on the kitchen counter explained all: the two men of the household had gone into Boston to get Zach's and her things and bring them home from her apartment. The word 'home' was underlined. Jenna smiled.

Carrying a cup of coffee and the morning paper back upstairs with her, she gave herself permission to crawl back under the covers and luxuriate.

Not until she was comfortably situated and had taken her first sip of coffee did she turn her attention to the paper, starting automatically with the entertainment section. Above the fold were two photos of them, one just at the moment the feathers flew, the other as Scott helped Jenna into their limo in Boston. The first caption read, "Is Boston's Cinderella Couple Under Siege?" The second, "Non-Stop from the Airport: Are They a Couple Again?"

The article rehashed the fiasco at the Grammys, then went on to quote an anonymous tipster who had witnessed three Tennys climb into a limo at Logan Airport late last night, and who had followed the limo directly to Scott Tenny's door. No stop in Boston.

"God, what passes for news these days," Jenna groaned out loud. Reaching for the phone, she dialed California, then settled back against the pillows.

Linda answered. "Hi, Ma," Jenna said. "Um, there's something you guys might want to know. God forbid you should read about it in the papers before you hear it from me."

"Yesssss?" Linda drew the affirmative out into a question.

"I want to make it official. Scott and I are back together. No more apartment. We're home, for keeps."

"Oh, baby girl, that is wonderful! That is *so* wonderful! Adella, go tell Joe they're back together!" she told her housekeeper, then returned to Jenna. "Oh, I am just so happy for the two of you, sweetie. You made the right decision – but I don't have to tell you that. Go be with your husband; we'll talk later."

SCOTT AND ZACH CAME tromping up the stair just as Jenna hung up the phone and jumped out of bed to see what she could do to help. "Oh my goodness. Look at all this!" she exclaimed, beaming. Scott was carrying an armload of clothing. Zach was patiently dragging a huge canvas bag full of stuffed animals and toys up one stair at a time.

"I couldn't believe you guys went into the city to get stuff this morning! You're not in much of a hurry to have us back, are you!"

Scott pulled her to him and kissed her, Zach protesting that he wanted a kiss too. Scooping him up, the three hugged and danced around the hallway and back into Jenna and Scott's room, laughing and shouting and singing at the tops of their lungs until they all collapsed in a heap on the unmade bed, sending sections of the paper flying. Jenna went scrambling and retrieved the section with their pictures.

"Check this out," she giggled. Scott rolled onto his back and scanned the front page.

"They're gonna be all over us now. They probably figure it was a publicity stunt or something," Scott surmised. "Ya know actually, in terms of publicity, Schultz really did do us a hellova favor. I mean, Boston's gonna use our picture whatever, but I'll bet we're on the front page of entertainment sections all over the country this morning."

"Yeah. Remind me to send him a thank you note," Jenna said sarcastically.

"Maybe we should put Boston out of its misery. Rent some billboards on 93 and put up an announcement. 'Yes, people, we *are* back together.' Maybe with a really hot shot of the two of us. And of course some feathers."

"You're in an unusually chipper mood this morning," Jenna smiled at him quizzically. "Any particular reason?"

"Well, let's see. Maybe because the most gorgeous, sexiest dame I've ever laid – I mean, laid eyes on – told me she loved me and wanted to be mine for the rest of time? That kinda made my day," he grinned.

"Gee, what a coincidence. The handsomest, sexiest guy *I've* ever met told me pretty much the same thing. I guess we're both doing okay in the luck department."

"It's a good thing for you that Zach's up," Scott said, wrapping her up in arms and legs in a full-body hug. "Otherwise you might never get out of this bed all day."

Jenna slid free of his arms, reached for a pillow and bopped him over the head with it as best she could, given that she had virtually no room to maneuver. Scott grabbed the pillow out of her hands and hid it behind him as he set to work tickling her. Giggling, Jenna scrambled to free herself from his assault, which only encouraged him to tickle her all the more. Every tickle was spiced with a kiss.

Suddenly he connected with Jenna's most vulnerably ticklish spot. "No fair!" she cried, her voice rising into a giggling shriek. "Lemme go!" She twisted violently, trying to wrench herself free of his firm grip.

They were laughing so hard, they couldn't hear Zach's little voice calling out for them to stop. Suddenly, Zach had climbed on top of them, trying to pull them apart, pounding on Scott and screaming, "Mommy, Mommy!"

"Oh my God, Scott, he thinks you're hurting me. Stop. Zachy, Zachy, it's okay, it's okay," she crooned pulling the youngster to her and holding him tight. "Daddy was just playing. Really. Just playing. "Mommy and daddy were just playing."

"I wasn't hurting your mommy, Zach. You know how I tickle you? That's what I was doing with Mommy."

Zach looked dubious for a moment, then fell upon Scott, tickling him for all he was worth. Scott pulled him into a bear hug, and Jenna let out a big sigh. Zach rolled into an upright sitting position, settled back against Scott's chest, heaved a sigh of his own and popped a thumb in his mouth.

"And peace returns to the valley," Jenna smiled. "And if you ask me, I think somebody might be ready for a nap right about now." Jenna gathered him up, took him to his room and kissed him as he climbed into bed. "You're such a good little Zachy," she whispered as she tucked him in.

"Bwankie?" Zach whispered. She found it on the floor and slipped it under his arm where he liked to keep it. "Vark?" Looking around, she found his favorite plush aardvark and tucked it under the covers with him.

"Vark," Zach whispered, and started fingering the soft fur as his eyes fluttered, fighting sleep. She pressed her lips to his forehead.

"I love you, little Zach," she whispered.

"Wuv you, Mommy," Zach whispered in return.

RETURNING TO THE bedroom, Jenna found Scott lying on the bed staring at the ceiling. "Are you okay?" she asked.

"Yeah. I'm all right. Sorry. I – I just feel bad that the poor little guy had to be traumatized by thinking I was hurting you. I can only imagine what it's gotta be like for kids who actually do see their mothers really being beaten up by their fathers."

Jenna lay down beside him and pulled him close. "It's got to be just horrible for them. I see how it affects them in the shelter. They just cling to their mothers. It's so sad."

Scott rolled over to face her. "That will never happen with us," he stated fiercely. "You know that, don't you?"

Jenna sat up and looked at him, searching deep into his soul. "Of course I know that," she said, equally vehemently. She leaned over him and kissed him as he reached up and drew her down to him.

"We only have two days before I have to leave," Scott pointed out, kissing her.

"We best make the most of our time together, babe," Jenna agreed. "Naptime for Mommy and Daddy."

NAPTIME – THOUGH IT looked a lot more like adult play time – was cut short by a phone call. Pausing to catch their breath and wait out the answering machine, they both heard a deep, menacing, monotone male voice come slicing between them. "Tenny. I know you're there. Better not start playing coy with me. Pick up the phone." Scott groaned and then did, with great reluctance.

"Yeah," he said bitterly.

"Scottie boy. How *are* you," the harsh voice gushed like some long-lost friend. "Saw ya make it home last night. Sure hope I didn't upset the Missus too bad. I was –"

"Whaddya want, Schultz," Scott cut in.

"You know what I want. Five mil, transferred. Except to a different account I'm gonna give you. In fact, the info's in the mail – you'll get it today. No fancy footwork. No drops for cops to blow. Thanks to the wonders of on-line banking, you can handle this with a laptop, curled up in the privacy of your very own bed, under the covers, where I imagine you two are right now…" He let the thought hang in the air.

Scott clenched his teeth, the rage of a cornered animal increasing with each passing moment.

"Where I imagine…"

"You just shut the fuck up, Schultz. You can go fuck yourself every which way to Sunday."

"The way you fuck her, Tenny?" Schultz jumped in. "Which way are you fuckin' her right now?"

Scott sat bolt upright and heaved the cordless phone across the room. It bounced off a chair and skidded across the floor till it hit a wall with a thud. Schultz's harsh laughter filled the room. Then he yelled, loud enough for both Scott and Jenna to hear him quite clearly.

"You're leavin' town in a couple days, Tenny. Maybe I'll stop by and try out some of those ways on the Missus…" The line went dead.

THE NEXT FEW HOURS were spent coordinating phone calls from Matthew Caine, the Boston PD, the FBI and Blacklace security. Early in the afternoon, Jenna went down to the street to retrieve the mail. Sure enough, in the midst of the usual stack of bills, circulars, magazines and advertising was a single small, plain white envelope, with no return address. It was postmarked Boston.

Inside was a slip of paper with a web address, codes, the amount, which hadn't changed, and one new piece of information: a deadline. The deposit was to be made no later than the end of business two days hence, Greenwich Mean Time. It was probably no coincidence that two days hence, Blacklace was scheduled to take to the road again.

Discovering Dave Schultz's whereabouts was critical. Photos of both Schultz and Ashley West were widely circulated. Security ringed the house. Traces were put on Scott's phones, both in the house and in the studio, but Schultz seemed prepared for that. Their next communication from him came again through the mail, this time in the form of a crudely hand-made post card. Glued to the picture side was a very clear photo of Scott and Ashley. On the business side of the post card, in a feminine scrawl: "Oh, do I miss you, baby! Can't wait to see you again. XXOO."

JENNA, SCOTT, ZACH and Ellen spent much of their time in the studio, which began to take on all the qualities of a bunker in wartime. Ellen stocked the fridge with some of Zach's staples and hauled over a laundry basket full of his toys, and Jenna brought over an electric blanket which made for cozy napping on the couch. Somehow the studio, tucked far to the back of the property, felt safer than the more exposed house. Scott and Jenna knew they were only kidding themselves, but that didn't stop them from finding comfort where they could.

Ellen was included in all discussions. The entire situation had been laid out for her – Scott made no effort to gloss over either his misbehavior or the seriousness of their predicament. No one was underestimating Schultz's ability to strike in unexpected ways. She was asked if she would like to take a vacation for the duration, or if she'd prefer to find new employment – they would certainly understand. She'd hear nothing of it.

TWO DAYS LATER, Jenna kissed Scott goodbye. Neither wanted the kiss to end. "Be careful," they whispered to each other, more than once.

"Ten days," Scott whispered.

"We'll meet you in Tampa," Jenna assured him. "I'll sing with you there." She smiled as brave a smile as she'd ever attempted. "And then we'll all go down to Coral Gables and celebrate Zach's birthday."

"Zachy birfday!" Zach burbled, wrapped around Scott's leg. Scott came down to Zach's level.

"You're gonna have one blow-out of a world-class birthday party, little man," he promised his son. "How many kids get a to have a world-class band play Happy Birthday for them?!"

No deposit of any dreamed-of five million dollars had made it through the ether and into an empty numbered Swiss bank account opened recently with the code name 'IRA.' No name appeared on any statements issued for this account. Only a few officials of the bank, those on a 'need to know' basis, had ever laid eyes on the name David M. Schultz.

Chapter 30

SCHULTZ DRAINED HIS THIRD little Thermos-cap cup of coffee with a grimace. He didn't care what the ads said. A mild hint of plastic, with aftertastes of crank case oil, he thought to himself sarcastically. Blindfolded, he could pick out coffee that had spent six hours in a Thermos any day.

Sitting low in his beat-up Suzuki Sidekick, parked inconspicuously in the driveway of an empty summer home three blocks from the Tenny house, Schultz finally saw what he'd been waiting for since just before dawn: Scott's limo gliding by at the residential neighborhood's strict speed limit of twenty miles per hour. He couldn't see Scott, but he could see Georgie Del Guercio at the wheel just fine. A big burly black man, Georgie was easily recognized at this speed by his fastidiously trimmed little goatee.

Punching in a few keys on his laptop, Schultz quickly verified that his Swiss account remained every bit as empty as the day he opened it. "Big mistake, Scottie boy," he whispered almost wistfully with a two-fingered wave at the retreating limo. "Bye-bye, Tenny." Reaching for the keys, he started the car.

JENNA SAT STARING into the bottom of her almost empty mug of coffee. Reaching for the phone, she dialed. Looking up at the clock, she knew it was early in L.A. Regardless, Matthew Caine answered his phone on the first ring. "Yeah? Caine."

"Matthew. It's Jenna."

"Jenna. Are you okay? Talk to me."

"Yeah, I'm okay. Scott just left, for the next ten days. I'm supposed to meet him in Tampa on the thirteenth."

"And…"

"And I'm here, alone – well, not alone – with Ellen and Zach – in this big house, ringed by security, with a body guard who's at my side if I so much as step foot out the door to go pick a flower, with a chopper passing by every so often, for crying out loud. I can't live like this."

"Today was the deadline. I take it Scott didn't make Schultz's day."

"God, no," Jenna said. "No way is he cooperating. Now that I know everything, now that I can weigh in on the decision-making here – well, I don't mean to second-guess how Scott's handled Schultz up to now, but things have gotta be different from here on out."

"As in…"

"As in I'm in this thing too. And I'm not just going to sit here and wait for Schultz to do something. I can't. I'm just not made that way. Matthew —"

"What? Ask."

"Can you come east? Something's going to happen," Jenna hurried on, "and my sense is that it's going to happen quickly. I just have this feeling. I can't sit around here picking out tunes on the piano while Schultz is getting ready to make his move."

"I'm on the next plane. I'll call you when I land."

The phone rang at two-thirty. Caine didn't bother with greetings. "Look, I've set up a meeting with the Boston PD. They're gonna pick me up at Logan and bring me into town. And they're gonna come get you and bring you down-town. You'll get a call from them, any minute now. No police cars, nothing obvious. You got a wig you can put on, make yourself less recognizable?"

Jenna laughed. "Don't worry. I'm a pro at that."

"I want you to assume you're being watched."

"Okay," Jenna said, chilled by his tone of voice. "I'll be careful, and I'll see you in Boston. Mathew?"

"Yeah?"

"Thanks."

"Thanks for calling me," Caine countered. "I'd hate to think of you taking this thing into your own hands. My goal is to keep them pickin' out tunes on the piano."

"WE CAN ASSUME SCHULTZ is capable of pulling off something pretty sophis-ticated. He's not going to just try for a grab 'n run," Caine told the half dozen Boston police sitting around the table. "He's thought this thing through. And he's got a Plan B."

"And C and D, is my guess," said a man who'd been introduced to Jenna as Capt. Spillman, and who seemed to be in charge of the meeting. "And I don't think a donation to the Policemen's Benevolent Society is one of his plans. I've been talking to the guys in New Hampshire. Schultz has a record a mile long."

"Ms. West, too," said a small, bald, muscular man wearing a black t-shirt and black jeans who introduced himself as Martin Maxley. "Max for short," he added. "What a piece of work that one is."

"Yeah," Spillman continued, "and we see her as the weak link here."

"No question she knows her stuff, but she makes mistakes, and she makes herself so damned visible," Max added. "Dumb. Dumb, dumb, dumb."

"Yeah, dumb but dangerous," Caine offered. "She's proven that."

"She's been hanging around Newbury Street a lot," a good-looking plain-clothes woman detective named Sadie Larson volunteered. "Our guess is that she's looking for you, Jenna."

"I'm down there a lot," Jenna admitted. "Whenever I get an itch to go shopping for clothes, that's where I head."

"Any particular favorites?" Spillman asked.

"Let me guess," Sadie interrupted, and started ticking names off on her fingers. "Patty T's. Thalonoki. Stragus. Walla. Barnes. Liliboy. Deuces Are Wild."

Jenna shook her head in amazement. "How do you know that?"

"She ignores every other shop on the street. Just haunts those," said Sadie matter-of-factly. "They know her by name in all of them now. She's really cultivated them, bought stuff at all of them. I wouldn't mind being on that broad's expense account."

"This is good," Caine said, thinking out loud.

"Are you thinking what I'm thinking?" Jenna said. "That I can draw her out?"

"Yep. If we can get our hands on Ashley West, we can get our hands on Schultz."

"HEY, WHERE YA BEEN?" Jenna asked drowsily, coming awake as the phone rang. She glanced over at the clock. It was 1:30 in the morning.

"Sorry to call so frickin' late, babe. Everybody's here. They all send their love and so wish you were here. We've all been out gettin' caught up with each other. Oh, man, babe, I miss you something fierce."

Blacklace was in Montreal for three days, taking part in a mini-festival with Kiss, Pearl Jam, Limp Bizkit, Henry Rollins, Dropkick Murphy and Nine Inch Nails. "The competition is electric, to say the least – everybody's trying to outdo everybody else. The audience is gettin' their money's worth, that's for damned sure. How are you, honey? Things okay there?"

"Quiet as a church sanctuary, my love. It's sorta eerie. I mean, I know they're all out there, but you don't hear or see a thing, unless you know exactly where to look. They're good. Zach hasn't noticed anything out of the ordinary. Except, of course, that you're not here."

"Eight days till Tampa."

"And counting…" Jenna said seductively.

"Oh, do I ever have plans for you in Tampa, Baby Blue," Scott whispered huskily.

SCHULTZ HAD PLANS for Jenna too, but they sure didn't involve Tampa. Get his hands on her and he'd have all the leverage he needed. The kid would do too, but he apparently never left that fortress of a house. Jenna and the kid would be optimal, but Schultz never planned for optimal. Do-able would do just fine.

He was orchestrating his plan from the relative safety of Lake Sunapee. Sunapee in the winter fell off the face of the map, except for a few dozen year-rounders and some die-hard ice-fishermen, weekend snowmobilers and the wing nuts who just had to get drunk and drive around on the ice, but a mild winter had taken care of most of that. There hadn't been a long enough stretch of deep cold to freeze the lake to a point of safety so far this year. Not that that stopped everything. He'd help fish a truck out of the lake just two days earlier, not from any good Samaritan motivation. He just wanted to be seen up there, in case an alibi was needed.

Schultz had played caretaker, then inherited, a wreck of an old camp, in the low-rent district across the road from the shoreline. It had a great lake view, for the six leafless months of the year. He'd put some work into the place, insulating it primarily. From the outside, it was still nothing to look at. He liked it like that.

Tossing another log into the old cast-iron stove, he threw himself across a battered sofa and picked up the phone. Waiting impatiently for Ashley to answer, he studied the ceiling and the state of some of the weaker beams that held it up. The previous year he'd been thinking about putting some work into them. Not this year. When he had Scott's – *his* five million in the bank, he'd torch the place. He'd already picked out the house of his dreams. On another lake. In another state. And he hadn't told Ashley about it, either.

Just before he thought he'd be getting her voice mail, Ashley picked up, sounding like she'd been woken from a deep, hung-over sleep. Her "yeah" dragged out across the miles between them.

"What are you doing at the apartment?" Schultz barked.

"Gotta sleep sometime, you bastard," Ashley managed.

"Not when you're after the kinda money we're after," Schultz said. "Get the fuck back on the street. The bitch has to show up sooner or later."

"Okay, okay. Hell, it's –" There was a pause while she attempted to read the clock by her bedside. "Christ, it's only nine-thirty. I've never seen her come shopping before eleven. Never. Fuck."

"The way you sound, you'll be lucky to be out there by eleven yourself. Get up, for cryin' out loud. I'm heading south right now."

Climbing into his SUV, he sighed. This stakeout business was getting old. The daily two-hour drive was beginning to feel like what guys in suits did – commuting. That was where the comparison with guys in suits ended, however. For months, he'd been cultivating a very convincing street bum appearance. His looks today bore virtually no likeness to the most recent mug shots he knew must be circulating widely since his Grammy stunt. He felt secure behind a thin but scroungy beard, under far scroungier long hair he'd been growing for quite a while anyway. A trip to the dumpster behind a local thrift shop scored him a ragged wool coat, a filthy knit cap and a pair of sneakers with holes in them. A pair of jeans he only hung onto for the dirtiest of dirty work and he was dressed for another day at "work."

JENNA HAD TAKEN AN INSTANT liking to Sadie Larson. A tall, slim, confident dirty blond in her mid-thirties, Sadie normally played down her good looks for street work. She looked like a runway model when she and Jenna met at eleven o'clock sharp at a nondescript corner coffee shop on Hereford Street, a couple of blocks off Newbury. Jenna had arrived first, wearing a black, short-haired wig, but had disappeared into the restroom and removed it, shaking out her thick, full head of naturally wavy brunette locks like she was about to go on stage. The two women, sitting in a booth in back away from the windows, turned the heads of the few late-morning patrons sitting at the counter. They also put a grin on the face of Matthew Caine when he approached their table a few minutes later.

"One of the rare perks of this crazy-ass job," he said, sliding in next to Jenna.

As soon as Caine arrived, Sadie got right to the point. "Okay. I've met with the owners of all the boutiques. We're all on the same page. They all know exactly who we're talking about. I flashed a picture and every single one of them ID'd her without hesitation. By name."

"She'd be pretty hard to miss," Jenna agreed.

"We wait till she sees us and follows us in. I want it to be Deuces. The set-up lends itself. The owner –" She stopped to check her notes. "Ms. Ellison's willing to leave a tray of bracelets on top of the counter. I've got the one she pulled out. There will be an obvious gap. All I have to do is get it into Ashley's bag. Shouldn't be hard."

"If." Jenna stopped. "If she follows us in. The big if. She knows I'd recognize her."

"If she doesn't, then we go to Plan B – you stay inside and I go back out and plant it on her in the street, where she'll be waiting for you to come back out. Either way, we get her."

"And I work the sidewalk," said Caine. "Neither of them knows me. I promise you, Schultz'll be out there. With any luck, we get us a two-fer."

JENNA AND SADIE APPROACHED Deuces Are Wild from opposite directions. Jenna went directly in without hesitation. Sadie paused to look in the window, checking out the sampling of the shop's unique vintage offerings, looking undecided. She appeared to glance down at her watch, as if she were short on time, but kept her eyes glued on the shop window which provided her with a good mirror on the street. To buy further time, she reached into her pocket for a cell phone and pretended to make a call. As she went into an animated one-sided conversation, she wrapped an arm around herself, the phone pressed to her ear, and casually turned to look up and down Newbury Street. Ashley was standing on the corner, looking like she was waiting impatiently for someone to meet her. We're all actresses, Sadie thought to herself.

Caine was sitting on a bench across the street in front of a bistro, looking like he too was waiting for someone, checking his watch constantly and with obvious irritation. Sadie gave him a quick nod toward the corner where Ashley stood, then turned back to the shop window as she feigned finishing her conversation. As she slid her phone back into her pocket, she wrapped her fingers around the antique garnet and diamond bracelet that was also in the same pocket, then with a sigh of regret, moved away form the shop and on down the street towards Ashley.

Caine's eyes had been sweeping the street relentlessly for the past fifteen minutes, looking for anyone who seemed suspicious. He would have preferred a nasty winter streetscape, where a lurker would have stuck out like a sore thumb. Unfortunately, the day was mild and pre-lunch pedestrians were plentiful. He dismissed a bum going through a trash can halfway down the block beyond Ashley as sadly nothing out of the ordinary.

Inside, Jenna thanked the owner for her cooperation, and set to shopping as if nothing were out of the ordinary.

Chapter 31

✸

CAINE WAS GROWING ANXIOUS. The fact that Ashley lingered on the corner could only mean that Jenna was meant to be followed when she came back out.

As Sadie started across the intersection, she dove deep into her voluminous, long-strapped pocketbook as if hunting for something. Reaching the opposite corner and supposedly distracted, she feigned a collision with Ashley who was firmly planted against a non-yielding light post. As they came into physical contact, Sadie adroitly let her long-strapped bag tangle momentarily with the big, open tote that hung from Ashley's shoulder. Slipping the garnet bracelet into Ashley's bag was hardly a challenge.

Some of the contents of Sadie's bag had gone flying in the collision. Quickly retrieving them, she babbled a profuse apology, then went on her way. She too failed to notice the bum loitering in the middle of the block, who had a sudden suspicion he shouldn't be letting Sadie simply walk away.

Stepping directly in her path but averting his gaze with the humility of his supposed straights, the "bum" put a hand out to Sadie and mumbled something that could have been "coffee?" or "carfare?" – Sadie wasn't sure. She paused, fumbled in her coat pocket, produced a dollar bill and pressed it in the poor man's hand.

"Hey, thanks," the bum said, now looking directly at her. There was genuine appreciation in his voice. And something like surprise. "Uh, God bless you."

The "uh" stayed with Sadie as she continued on down the street. Why, she couldn't say.

JENNA STAYED IN THE shop for ten minutes, then came out with a small shopping bag and started down the block, headed the opposite direction from Ashley. Ashley made her move, pausing a few moments, then going through a pantomime of giving up on waiting any longer and starting across the intersection.

Sadie, who had continued down the block, then quickly circled back three blocks before regaining Newbury Street, found Jenna walking towards her just where they'd planned. Ashley, maintaining a half-block gap between herself and Jenna, failed to notice Sadie approaching her beyond Jenna. Schultz did. Schultz wasn't missing anything.

When Jenna had started down Newbury Street, Caine rose and started tracking Jenna's progress from the opposite side of the street. Schultz immediately got the connection. Chuckling quietly to himself, he crossed over mid-block and shuffled along, following Caine. He knew where this was headed. Shaking his head, he ducked into a doorway to watch Sadie's sting play out.

The moment Sadie stepped out from behind Jenna and confronted Ashley, flashing her Boston PD badge, he quietly turned, shambled away, headed around the corner and vanished from sight.

Caine, still watching from across the street, saw Ashley in her confusion and fear turn and look back up the street from where she'd come. There was no one in sight. It was clear that she thought there should be.

Sadie took control of the situation with speed and efficiently while Jenna, who never turned to make eye contact with Ashley, quickly crossed the street. She was shaking when she joined Caine.

"You have the right to remain silent. Anything you say can and will be used…" Reciting Ashley her rights, Sadie ignored the woman' protestations of innocence, cuffed her and led her three paces over to the unmarked squad car she'd left there for the purpose. Stuffing Ashley none too gently into the back seat and belting her in since the car had no divider between front and back, she came around to the driver's side only to find a parking ticket under the windshield wiper. Grabbing it with a hopeless shake of the head, she tossed it across the seat as she slid in. "Fuckin' meter maids. Don't they teach them anything any more?" she said.

"Fuckin' cops. Don't they teach *you* anything any more," Ashley retorted hotly from the back seat. "You can't just pick me up for standing on a fuckin' street corner."

"I sure can, Ms. West."

Sadie's use of Ashley's name threw her. She decided to take the "remain silent" part of her rights seriously for the balance of her ride downtown.

"WE HAVE AN AFFIDAVIT from the owner of the shop that a bracelet worth twenty-two hundred dollars went missing yesterday. The said owner, who knows you, tells us you were in her shop yesterday. Said bracelet was found in your bag today. You, Ms. West, are not in what is typically referred to as a position of power here." Sadie was thoroughly enjoying herself.

"You put it there, you bitch," Ashley groaned for the nineteenth time, "and you damn well know it.

Just then, orchestrated for full effect, Martin Maxley stepped into the interrogation room. The room wasn't particularly small, and Max was, but his beefy, perpetually aggravated presence instantly filled every square inch of it. All but the store-bought color drained out of Ashley's face.

Max pulled up a chair close to Ashley's left, then locked eyes with her and let the tension mount. "Little lady," he finally said, flatly, like a third-rate actor reciting poorly rehearsed lines from a bad play, "you're basically fucked. However, we gotta deal for you."

By this time, Ashley had been through three and a half hours of non-stop questioning by Sadie and two other female interrogators, mostly about her connection with "one David M. Schultz," as well as a barrage of questions about her connections with both Jenna and Scott Tenny.

Ashley found herself ready to listen. She was tired. She was scared. She'd been growing wary of "one David M. Schultz" for some time now. She was beginning to see herself as taking the fall for a guy she seriously doubted could care less.

"ASHLEY HAD NOTHING on her to force Jenna to go with her," Sadie said as they started sifting back through the facts for the third time.

"No, somebody else was gonna do the grab," Caine said. "Ashley's job was just to relay information to whoever that was. I doubt it was Schultz himself. Though I'd be equally surprised if he'd want to bring anyone else into his plans."

"Schultz is going to make try after try at getting his hands on either you or Zach," Sadie addressed Jenna soberly. "He'll keep trying till he succeeds. And every time he tries, the situation grows more dangerous."

"Bottom line, we need to flush him out before he *can* succeed," Jenna said quietly. "We need Ashley to take us to him. But I don't see her doing that. And I'm not sure he'd fall for it. Ten to one, he knows you guys have her. He'll never trust her again."

Caine sat back in his chair and looked over at the singer-songwriter, sultry even at this time of day in the mundane beige and steel grey environs of a city police station. He gave her a grin of admiration. "You know, you'd be good at this, Jenna. You think like a cop." Running his hand through his hair, he pondered his take on the facts. "Now, I know you want to see this all wrapped up before your hubby gets to Tampa, but Jenna, I'm just not sure it can work that way. I'm thinking that we need to bring Scott back into this."

Jenna crossed her arms, dropped her head and closed her eyes in thought. She so wanted to deliver Scott from the burden he alone had been bearing for so long. She also knew she was way out of her league here. But after a moment's deliberation, she looked back up at him.

"We can try to get to Schultz through Ashley again – keep workin' Plan A. But I'm thinking we'll end up needing to let Schultz get me – Plan B," Jenna countered.

"Since Scott's not here, I do have to enter his Plan C into the discussion, at least," Caine said tersely. "You know, the one where we keep you safe."

After some hard negotiation, a compromise was reached.

ASHLEY WAS TURNED LOOSE after accepting a deal with the Boston PD. She'd go back to Schultz as if nothing had happened. If he knew she'd been picked up, she was to tell him it was for loitering, that they had picked her up for streetwalking.

She wore a wire – actually a wireless wire, a bit of micro-technology stitched into a black satin scrunchie, one of many she normally used to half-tame her wild long hair. A location device had been slipped into the lining of her bag without her knowledge. She didn't need to know that; she took it for granted that they'd be watching her every move, one way or another. One false step, she'd been told, and the deal was off. She'd be facing serious jail time.

She told them where she'd be going, where she knew she'd find Schultz, but she was tailed anyway. He was, as she had told them, holed up in a weekly rental in East Boston. A team of surveillance people monitored her from a bagel delivery truck parked across the street.

Sergeant Tony Borodsky was monitoring the headphones. A recording device would immortalize Schultz and Ashley's words; Borodsky's job was to alert the plainclothes equivalent of a SWAT team to storm the building if anything should go awry.

Borodsky heard Ashley walk up four flights of stairs. The building, hardly more than a flop house, had an elevator, but an "out-of-service" sign had hung across its doors since it had failed a city inspection three years earlier. The team of detectives already knew this; they'd put a junior member of the team to work pulling all the records on the address the minute Ashley gave it to them.

Borodsky heard Ashley give a couple of short raps on a door. When no one answered, she knocked again, louder this time. Finally, he heard the door open.

"So what took you so long?" he heard Ashley ask. Irritation came through the ether loud and clear.

"I was in the can," came Schultz's gravelly smoker's voice. Turning to a computer beside him, Borodsky did a quick match with an archived print of Schultz's voice, taken from a police interview two years earlier in Sunapee. Schultz's seemingly harmless five words provided him with a positive ID. "But I'm the one who should be askin' the questions. What took *you* so long?" Schultz countered. "I was expectin' you hours ago. They picked you up, didn't they." It wasn't question."

"Yeah, the dumb cops – they got it all wrong," Ashley said, trying to make light of it. "Had me pegged for a streetwalker. Hurt my feelin's somethin' fierce."

"Yeah, sure. So like you got feelin's now. That's a good one." They'd moved into the apartment. Borodsky heard the door shut behind them.

"Now *you*'re hurtin' my feelin's," Ashley complained, then clearly moved in for a kiss. From the sounds of it, it had to be a humdinger. Unconsciously, Borodsky squirmed in his seat. Consciously, he rolled his eyes.

"So, you miss me?" Ashley asked, seductively.

Schultz grunted in the affirmative.

"So, you plan on tellin' me what's goin' on?"

Schultz grunted in the negative.

"Well, how in the hell am I supposed to help you if you won't tell me what the fuck's happenin', Dave?" Her words were harsh but her tone was little-girl wheedling.

"You tried to help. Look where that got me. I'm still where I was. With bubkiss in the bank."

"I? What happened to we?"

"I, we – what the fuck's the difference? Your plan was worthless. Worse than worthless. It got you picked up."

"They don't have anything on me."

"They better not have. I don't need problems for partners. You gettin' picked up was a problem."

"I told you. They questioned me. They turned me loose. They coulda apologized – that woulda been nice. But who gives a shit. I was in there less'en an hour."

"Congratulations."

"So you gotta have a Plan B."

"I'm workin' on one."

"So tell me about it."

"You're only on a need-to-know basis."

"I know that. And I need to know."

"Look, stop. Let's get somethin' clear here. *I* decide what you need to know. And what I'm workin' on is nothin' you need to know. Now, com'ere."

Borodsky heard the creaking of ancient bedsprings. A lot of creaking.

"Hey, easy, Schultzy!" came Ashley's voice. "You don't need to rip it offa me. I can take it off, you know."

"It's more fun to rip it off," Schultz crooned.

"Oh, pu-leeze," Borodsky moaned to himself, rolling his eyes again.

"What am I supposed to wear home?" Ashley asked him coyly.

"Maybe I don't want you to go home," Schultz countered.

"Oh, cripes, not the hair. Don't throw that. I don't want to lose it." There was a brief pause.

"Nope. Not on your wrist," Schultz announced. "I want you necked. One hundred percent stark-staring necked."

"What about my tattoos? I suppose you want me to take *them* –"
Suddenly the sound of Ashley's voice went muffled. Borodsky could barely make out the end of the sentence. "– off too?" Something had happened to Ashley's schrunchie.

Concentrating on the muffled sounds he was still getting, Borodsky decided the schrunchie had to be floating around in the bed, and at the moment, someone seemed to be lying on it. Occasionally, reception suddenly came in loud and clear, enlightening fragments like "– too damned good!"

only to be followed by "Oh, but how about –" and the voices would submerge once again. Borodsky started feeling seasick.

"Hey!" suddenly came through particularly clearly. Borodsky sat up straight.

"Wow! Oh, how fashionable, and *such* a perfect fit!" came Ashley's giggles. "I wanna see what *that* feels like." Some pronounced squeals of the bedsprings. "Oooo, baby, oooo, that feels soooooo cool, honey. More, more," she begged. "I love what that feels like when you slam into me, all cool and satiny like that. What should we call it? A phallic schrunchie?"

"Ya can't call it a phallic schrunchie," protested Schultz, his voice strained.

"How about a cock muff? A satin gasket?"

"I don't care what the fuck," Schultz groaned again.

"All I know is, I think we've invented a brand new sex toy! We figure out how to market this and, baby, you can forget whatever you're getting' from Scott Tenny. We'll be multi-mega-gillionaires!"

Borodsky couldn't wait to write up his report. This was definitely a first in the annals of police surveillance.

AN HOUR LATER, a determined Ashley was back to trying to pump Schultz for information. After all, she had a job to do, and she knew her job performance would affect both her immediate and longer-term future. Her determination, as she kept doggedly introducing and reintroducing the subject of Jenna, became first, annoying, and then finally, obvious to Schultz. Subtlety was not Ashley's sixth sense.

Borodsky found himself cringing when he heard her say, "Aw, com'on, you *gotta* tell me, Schultzy. You just *gotta*." You'd have to be psychologically tone-deaf to miss the desperation in the woman's voice.

And you'd have to be psychologically tone-deaf to miss the growing distrust in Schultz's voice. His point-blank, "You're too damned fuckin' nosy, bitch" should have told Ashley to give it up for now. She didn't.

"You didn't call me' too nosy' when I was getting you what you needed to try and get your hands on her the first time. But now I'm 'too damned fuckin' nosy.' It's not *my* fault it didn't work the first time, Mr. High-and-Mighty. Let me in on your new plan and I'll help you. Maybe you'll have half a chance of making this one work."

A sudden loud noise caused Borodsky to flinch. Then reception went fuzzy again. "Fuckin' broad," he was able to make out. "You're wearin' a wire, bitch. I don't know where the damn thing is, but I know you're wired."

A few more muffled noises gave Borodsky the distinct impression that someone – and that would most probably be Schultz – was beating Ashley senseless. He never heard her voice again.

Chapter 32

✳

SCHULTZ WAS NEVER observed leaving the building, but had to be assumed he had after Borodsky reported a full thirty minutes of total silence on his monitors. A search of the building brought to light the fact that the commercial kitchen on its first floor, which served a modest coffee shop, connected with a slightly more upscale eatery next door; a passageway between the two had been installed when both properties came under common ownership several years earlier.

When his picture was shown around, an eagle-eyed hostess of the next door establishment recognized him as "the odd guy" who had exited maybe an hour earlier. He'd caught in the revolving door of her memory only because she'd realized at the time that she hadn't been aware of his ever having entered the premises. He'd mumbled some remark as he left, something to the effect of, "I guess the bitch stood me up." The hostess had been offended by his foul language, she told the policeman as she fingered a cross hanging from a chain around her neck. She would have been more offended by what he had done.

Ashley was found clubbed to death in the small room on the fourth floor that had been rented to one David M. Schultz.

Jenna stood next to Caine, looking down on the battered body with a mixture of disgust and pity. No one should have to die so brutally, she thought. But she couldn't control the voice inside her that kept taunting, "But she was begging for it."

BACK AT HEADQUARTERS, body language told the story: everyone sat slumped around the table, doodling or toying with pencils, scratching their heads, looking to the ceiling and closing their eyes, desperate to visualize a way to flush Schultz out of hiding. Only Jenna sat upright, quietly thinking her way through what she was both capable of and willing to do. When nobody had anything else to offer, she finally spoke.

"You all know and I know that it's gotta be me," she said simply, then looked around the table at everyone individually. When she got to Caine, he crossed his arms, regarded her as objectively as he could, but ended up shaking his head. "No, Jenna. It can't be you. It's just too damned risky. When he got on top of his grief, Scott would come and kill me personally."

"Let me worry about Scott. Your worry is to get this guy off the streets. He's dangerous. He's killed Ashley. He could kill again."

"Precisely my point," Caine sighed. "I rest my case."

"I can do this," Jenna insisted. "I *have* to do this. Look at everything Scott's done for me. I have to do this for him. This is our lives I'm talking about. We can't go on living like this."

"Would you at least talk it over with him?" Caine asked her for the third time today, with no illusions that she'd change her mind.

"Matthew, I told you – no." She stood and started pacing as she talked. She'd always thought best on her feet. All eyes followed her as she strode back and forth before the chaos of a whiteboard that hadn't been cleaned in months, a football coach's nightmare of overlapping plays for a crime-laden city.

"Okay. My latest thought is – how about staging a publicity stunt? Something that'll make the evening news and the morning papers." She looked around the room. A few heads were nodding, though none were what you'd call enthusiastic. Still, Jenna sensed enough support to keep going.

"How about something to do with the shelter? How about…how about somebody shows up at the shelter and threatens a resident. And I'm there, and somehow I disarm the situation. That'd make the news…" Her voice trailed off. She let the thought penetrate before taking another informal polling of responses.

"We'd have to empty the place out, have cops in there as the residents," Sadie said quickly.

"We take everyone out on outings all the time. That's nothing unusual. It'd be easy," Jenna said.

"Easy," Caine echoed, tossing his pen down on the table in exasper. "Easy like catching Jessee James…or the clap."

"TENNY, YOU'RE GONNA really wish you'd paid me off at five mil," came the unmistakable voice of Dave Schultz when Scott flipped open his phone that night. "I've about had it with you, old buddy. I've decided I hafta add in a little for all the pain and suff'rin' I've had to take here, what with you and your fuckin' delays. Delays cost, Tenny. Now it's ten mil or nothin'. Don't get me wrong, though, Tenny. I'm willin' to work for my ten mil. I can do a lot of damage for ten mil."

End of conversation.

SCOTT STARED AT his phone for a moment, then dialed Jenna who answered before it could ring twice. "Hi, honey," she whispered. "Gotta keep it down. I just got Zach to sleep," she explained.

"Where's Ellen?" Scott asked.

"I gave her the night off. She went downtown to have dinner with a friend. She'll be home soon."

"You're being careful, right?"

"Of course I'm being careful. Why? You sound –"

"I'm just concerned. I just don't see Schultz givin' up and goin' away."

"No, um, neither do I," Jenna said carefully. "Has – something happened?"

"Um." Now it was Scott's turn to decide how much he wanted to tell her. "Okay, well, yes. He called again. He's upped the ante."

"Do me a favor," Jenna cut in. She really didn't want to know how much Schultz was talking about now. "Call Matthew. He's in Boston, coordinating with the Boston PD. He needs to know."

"I will, babe. You just be super careful, all right?"

"Of course I'll will," Jenna said, closing her eyes as she told what she only considered a partial lie. She'd be as careful as she could be as she put herself in harm's way.

SCOTT CALLED MATTHEW early the next morning. Caine wandered out into the hallway to take the call. This one, he knew, was going to be tricky.

Scott brought Caine up to speed on Schultz's latest demands. Caine had to bring Scott up to speed on the sobering reality of Ashley's murder. The fact that Schultz was capable of murder cast a pall over the rest of the conversation. Caine struggled with his conscience, but in the end told Scott nothing about Jenna's determination to play an active role in bringing Schultz out into the open.

THE NEXT MORNING, as she kissed Zach goodbye, Jenna told Ellen she'd be at the shelter for much of the day. There was nothing unusual in this; she often was. "I'll be back by three, latest," she told her. But rather than have her bodyguard drive her the three miles to the shelter, she had him take her into Boston to police headquarters.

Like any good stage production, the cast of today's fabrication had to rehearse how the scene at the shelter would come down, first at headquarters, then at the shelter itself. They arrived at South Shore First Step just minutes after a bus full of happy residents headed to Salem for the day, first to visit the town's famous Witch Museum, and then to spend the afternoon at the Peabody Museum's art center for kids and families. They wouldn't be back till well after dark.

Eleven cop actors and Jenna would be involved inside; a real SWAT team would play itself outside. Information from a call to 911 would quickly reach both the local police department and the local media which routinely monitored police communications. Once word got out that Jenna was involved, regional media would swarm to the bait.

The plan came off without a hitch. By one o'clock that afternoon, the streets surrounding the shelter were a sea of mobile broadcast trucks, antennas and satellite dishes and the story was being flashed around the world. Jenna Bradford Tenny was square in the middle of a hostage situation.

The story that they'd prepared for public consumption was that an aggrieved ex-boyfriend had discovered his girlfriend's whereabouts and had come looking for her. When staff had made it clear to him that he could not see her, he'd pulled a gun. Jenna had supposedly been there for a board meeting, and was talking to the man in an effort to prevent a debacle. After a dramatic hour and a half, she and the ex-boyfriend came out of the building together, he with his hands in the air. Jenna gingerly handed his gun over to the closest uniformed policeman. The media ate it up.

At an impromptu news conference, she told the press that the situation had been defused, that no one had come to any harm, and that they had been gratified by both the promptness of the police response and the restraint the police had demonstrated throughout a difficult afternoon. "It's reassuring to know that we can count on help when we need it. I think this also serves as fair warning to anyone who might consider trying anything similar in the future. From the moment it was clear what the gentleman's intent was, our front desk staff, who had been well prepared for such situations, went into lockdown mode. None of our residents were in any danger at any time."

The media had cleared out long before those residents returned from their day's jaunt. The adults, as well as the entire shelter staff, were assembled and Jenna came back to explain the entire situation to them herself. Women who had survived their own share of personal drama and danger, they were more than willing to help Jenna cope with hers. Jenna's secret couldn't be safer with them, they assured her.

The press returned the next morning, as expected, to interview staff and any residents willing to talk to them, who were ready and quite willing to do their part to keep up the pretense.

SARAH ROEMER HAD been working the desk since the shelter had opened. She understood that this whole ruse had been a desperate attempt to lure a man to her front desk, and she had no doubt that she was looking at him now.

The man who stood before her wanted to look rich, but he clearly hadn't had time to cover the finer points. His grey pin-stripe suit was no doubt expensive, but no proper men's clothier would have ever allowed him to take it home until the sleeves had been lengthened an inch. And when he turned to look at a dog that had just come loping through the door, Sarah could see that the jacket was extremely tight across the man's muscular back, to the point of constricting his movement. The fit was clearly a compromise. Every other detail screamed new. His squeaky shoes, his fresh-from-the-barber haircut, his perfectly tied tie and matching handkerchief, poufing out of his pocket *just so*, his obviously expensive watch. He neglected, however, to think about his hands, which were a dead giveaway. Sarah tried not to stare at the dirt under his ragged fingernails.

"Come here, Bozo," she called out gently to the old golden retriever as she opened her desk drawer and pulled out a dog biscuit, as much to calm her own nerves in the presence of this obvious fraud of a man as anything. Bozo had been a fixture at the shelter since the day it had opened. Everyone agreed that he did more for morale for many of the residents than the entire staff of trained social workers put together.

Tail wagging, Bozo came trotting over to claim his the treat, then went around and sniffed at the stranger at the desk, to see if he might have something for him as well. When the man ignored him, he went on about his business and Sarah looked up. "Don't mind Bozo," she said. "Good morning. Can I help you?"

"Good morning," the man said, then cleared his throat and repeated his greeting nervously before settling into what he'd supposedly come to say. "Good morning. I – I was deeply moved by what I saw on the news last night. I would very much like to make a donation to your shelter."

"How very kind of you," Sarah said, fearful that *her* nervousness showed.

"I'd like to make – a very large donation," the man continued blandly.

"Of course – of course, sir," Sarah responded. Great – could you think of anything lamer? she chastised herself. "I'd be happy to have the director come out and see you."

"I'd appreciate that," he said smoothly. Sarah keyed the intercom.

"Isabelle, there's a gentleman here to see you," she said. "He'd – like to make a donation," she added. She wanted Isabelle to be on her toes. Nobody had ever come to the front desk to make a donation.

"I'll be right out," Isabelle answered. "Uh, thank you very much, Sarah." Isabelle had never thanked Sarah, or anyone else at the shelter, for anything. It was just her way, she had told everyone the day she started, and everyone had grown used to it and had learned to take no offense. Sarah knew this profession of thanks could only be a return signal.

ISABELLE APPROACHED THE MAN at the desk briskly, with a hand extended before her. "Hello," she said. "I'm Isabelle Young, the executive director. How may I help you?" She ushered the man to a pair of chintz-covered chairs in an alcove with windows that looked out on the street.

Schultz introduced himself as Alan Sullivan, talked a bit about a sister who had suffered years of spousal abuse in silence until she'd finally found the courage to seek the same kind of shelter First Steps provided for the women of his adopted home town. He was prepared to make a sizeable donation in honor of her courage, he said.

"Would you be interested in sponsoring a particular project, Mr. Sullivan? We have a number of initiatives on the planning boards just waiting for benefactors like yourself to adopt them. In fact, any of them can be looked at as naming opportunities. Bearing your name, or your sister's name perhaps?"

"For personal reasons, I'd prefer to keep anything I do anonymous," the man said modestly, a hand moving unconsciously to his tie.

"Of course, Mr. Sullivan," Isabelle demurred. "May I take the liberty of sending you information about some of the shelter's more pressing needs?"

"Actually, I'd prefer to simply write you a check, for you to spend as you and your board see fit. You know far better than I ever could the needs of this organization."

Schultz reached into his breast pocket for a checkbook he'd found on a Boston bus years before. He'd kept at the back of a drawer ever since, sure that some day he'd find the ideal use for Alan Sullivan's checks and Back Bay address.

Reaching into another pocket, he produced a gold Montblanc pen with a small smile, as if it was a given that Isabelle also knew just how much this fine writing instrument had set him back, though in fact, he'd merely stolen it, just that morning, while the salesman had been putting cuff links back in the case. Isabelle returned his small smile with an equally small one of her own.

Balancing the checkbook on the impeccably ironed crease of a brand new trouser leg, Schultz took his time writing out a check for two hundred fifty thousand dollars, blew softly across the wet ink, tore it carefully out of the checkbook, waved it a few times to finish the drying process, then handed it over to Isabelle, who tried to act like this kind of thing happened every day.

"Your generosity is overwhelming, Mr. Sullivan," she was able to say quite genuinely as she took in the figures. "Is there *no* way we can acknowledge your largesse?"

Schultz feigned giving the idea consideration, then said, as if the thought had just popped into his head, "Well, now that you mention it – this is going to sound so childish, but is there any chance I could actually meet Jenna Tenny? I have always been a fan. It would mean such a great deal…"

Isabelle feigned surprise as she reached into her pocket for a phone.

JENNA AGREED TO MEET "Mr. Sullivan" the following morning at eleven, then called Matthew, to overcome for the nineteenth time his objections and to work out the details for her protection her during the meeting at the shelter. Another all-day outing would be planned for the residents.

By the next morning all the particulars had been worked out. Caine and the Boston PD arrived at the house before ten. Technicians wired her and outfitted her with a homing device. The house would be used as command central.

Ellen had taken Zach over to Carrie's house for the day. Carrie was only too happy to help in this small way. It had been hard for Jenna to ask her friend the evening before – it meant explaining everything. In the telling, Jenna realized how it had become almost second nature to keep much of her problems from Carrie. She hated asking Carrie to join her in keeping secrets from Scott.

Jenna had fought tears as she kissed Zach goodbye for the day. She'd given him an extra-big hug, which he returned in kind with a giggle of delight. "You have fun today, little Zach-o," she whispered in his ear, her voice breaking as the reality of what she was doing hit home. She was confronting a man who had killed someone who stood in his way just three days earlier.

"You have fun, Mommy-o," he responded light-heartedly, then automatically raised a hand to her for a high-five. She smiled and kissed the hand he held up instead.

AS SARAH AND ISABELLE checked off names by the door of the bus, one resident lingered. "Is there gonna be another show-down here today?" she asked jokingly.

"Heavens, no!" Isabelle assured her. "Whatever put such an idea in your head?"

"No press trying to interview us when we get back tonight?"

"Sorry." Isabelle smiled. "Have yourselves a great day. We'll hold down the fort. I doubt anything more exiting than a linen delivery's going to happen here today."

Isabelle, it turned out, was right.

Chapter 33

ALREADY IN HER COAT and hat, Jenna stood alone before the kitchen window and looked out across the snow-covered lawn and the bare wind-blown branches of winter, across the cold sliver of the Atlantic Ocean off in the distance, gathering her thoughts before she turned to gather her things. It was time.

Caine came up behind her. "A proverbial penny for your thoughts, Mrs. Tenny," he said quietly.

Jenna turned to him. "I'm focusing. It's what I do." There was nothing flip to her reply. "Finding my center. Before I go on. Do you know what I mean, Matthew?" she asked him, looking him straight in the eye. He held her gaze.

"Yes. It's what all good cops do. The ones who come back."

"I've been performing all my life," Jenna ruminated, "but this may be the most important performance I've ever had to give."

"Only difference, the reviews won't be in the morning paper – they'll be in each shift's daily briefing" Matthew observed, smiling almost imperceptibly. "You pull this off, you'll get three standing ovations tomorrow, trust me. Everyone who knows about it is rooting for you."

"Thanks, Matthew," Jenna said, and gave him an impulsive kiss on the cheek. "That helps. Really. I mean that."

Matthew's hand was still touching his cheek when she stepped out the back door and into the cold.

JENNA'S LITTLE MIATA had been brought out of the garage, turned around and was waiting for her in the driveway. Coming around to the passenger side, she started to get into the car, then hesitate. "Uh, wait a sec –" she started to say, but then realized she did recognize the driver who, anticipating her concern, had already pulled out his badge.

"Pendergast, Sergeant Raymond J., Boston PD," the man said crisply. "I came in at the end of the meeting yesterday."

"Right. I'm sorry, Sergeant Pendergast. All you plainclothes –"

"I know, I know, we all look alike," Pendergast groused. "That's why they hire us in the first place. Central casting goes out looking for the most anonymous Joes and Janes they can find, give us some training and put us out in the field. No pretty uniforms, no recognition, at least of the good kind, no 'Thank you, Officer, sir,' no ma'm, not for the likes of me."

"And you don't mind a bit, I take it," Jenna grinned in response to his sarcastic delivery.

"Nope. Never wanted to be in a uniform. Applied for plainclothes right out of the academy. Fits me to a tee," said Pendergast, fingering a hole in his black tee-shirt as they reached the bottom of the driveway and stopped to let a car go by before pulling out onto the street.

"Hey, any chance, when all this is over, that maybe I could drive myself back home for a change?" Jenna asked. "I'm just plain tired of being chauffeured everywhere."

"You got yourself a deal. You get this guy to incriminate himself good and proper, you drive yourself back home."

Heading down the street, he'd only gone a few blocks when a black panel truck ran a stop sign as it came flying out of a side street, careened past him, then suddenly came to a screeching halt in front of him, skidding sideways and blocking the narrow street as it did.

Two men in ski masks, one tall, one short, stepped out of the truck simultaneously, both holding guns. The short one's was trained on the driver. The other's was pointed straight at Jenna. While Pendergast kept his eyes glued on the gun of the man approaching him, the other reached Jenna's door, pulled it open, leaned in and fired across her, killing Pendergast. Then, taking a firm grasp on the collar of her coat, he dragged her out of the car and out onto the pavement.

Sprawled at his feet, Jenna could only struggle for breath as the second man reached down and caught her up by the arm, hauled her across the few feet separating the two vehicles, opened the back door and threw her in. By this time, the other man had climbed back in behind the wheel. As he hit the gas, his partner jumped in after Jenna, slamming the door shut in his wake.

"Elapsed time, forty-four seconds," the driver announced, his lips sneering through the oval mouth of his ski mask which Jenna could see in the rear view mirror.

"Who the –" was the first and last thing Jenna got to say before her mouth was duct-taped shut for the duration of the ride.

Flailing, she was quickly pinioned by the man in the back with her, the short one, who pulled her hat off and flung it up to the front of the truck. The driver must have been expecting it – he reached up, caught it as it came, rolled down his window and tossed it out, all in one smooth move.

Then piece by piece, her coat, her sweater, her scarf (and the wire), the skirt she was wearing, her underwear (and the homing device), her hose, her boots, all were removed from her and tossed to the driver, one piece at a time. He pitched them out the window, one piece at a time, leaving a widely spaced, erotic Hansel-and-Gretel type trail, no clue closer than a quarter mile from the last. Cold air whipped in through the open window, defeating what scant hot air the old truck's heater could still put out, but the driver had no intention of closing it until his work was finished.

Struggle as Jenna might, the man holding her was far stronger than she was. As soon as he'd stripped her of everything that had to come off by way of her arms, her hands were duct-taped behind her back. When she was completely naked, her ankles were taped too. The man kneeled over her, leering at the sight of her. Then he reached for a blanket and tossed it over her. As the fight had drained out of her, she had started shivering.

Jenna curled up into a tight ball, wriggling to get some of the blanket between herself and the cold bare steel of the floor. Then she closed her eyes. Tight.

THE OFFICER MONITORING Jenna's wire and tracking transponder looked up from his computer screen. "All I'm getting is the sound of passing vehicles and the tracker's gone stationary, sir," he reported to his superior. "Either they're taking the world's longest pit-stop, or..." He left drawing conclusions to the brass.

AFTER A WHILE, Jenna reopened her eyes and glanced about her without moving. Letting her eyes adjust to the dark light of the interior of the truck, Jenna saw the man who had stripped her sitting across from her, leaning back against the opposite wall. He had a gun in his hand, trained on her. She had no idea what kind of gun it was, but she knew that thing on the delivery end of it was a silencer. For several moments, she couldn't take her eyes off it. When she could, she raised her eyes to those of the man holding it. He was no longer wearing his ski mask. She didn't know him from Adam. "Leo," he said, his unblinking eyes locked on hers.

Leo, who was proud of the fact that his legal name, Leonidas Thanos Diakos, appeared in no police records, in this country, anyway, was a guy Schultz could call on. He'd leant Leo a hand, more than once, and Leo was always ready to return the favor. Leo was a no-nonsense heavyweight. When he set out to get something done, it got done and it stayed done. Not like that dumb broad, Ashley West. Ashley'd had her uses, but her skills had been strictly amateur hour.

Leo's job, for the moment, was to keep Jenna immobilized and quiet.

Slowly, Jenna swiveled her eyes to the rear view mirror. The driver too had abandoned his ski mask. She found herself looking at a section of what was unmistakably the face of David Schultz. Schultz's eyes met hers.

"So, ya wanna talk about a donation, lady," Schultz asked brazenly. Then he was momentarily overcome by some of the least humorous laughter Jenna had ever heard.

SCHULTZ CONTINUED TO LAUGH periodically, but not a word was spoken for the next hour or more – Jenna had lost track of the time completely. She kept her eyes glued to the view through the front windshield, not allowing her eyes to return to the sight of Leo and his gun. With a silent groan, she watched the "Welcome to New Hampshire – Live Free or Die" sign fly by. The truck barely slowed as it went through the E-Z Pass lane at the Hampton toll. Schultz bore to left where the interstate offered two choices. Three lanes to the right continued north into Maine. Jenna knew that the two lanes to the left carried traffic into New Hampshire's lake country.

Things could be worse, Jenna thought to herself. It was pretty clear where they were headed. And Leo had left her alone.

ONCE THEY WERE OFF the major interstates, Schultz pulled off onto the shoulder, stopped the car, turned off the ignition, and turned to the back of the truck.

"Get the tape off her mouth," he ordered Leo. Leo ripped it off roughly. Jenna suppressed a scream but couldn't keep tears from welling up in her eyes. "Need a little information," Schultz told her. "Tenny's cell phone. The number."

Jenna squeezed her eyes shut.

"Yeah, bitch," he persisted, "gimme the number – if you ever want to see your family again." She turned her eyes to look Schultz full in the face.

"Five-oh-eight, four-seven-oh," she said, her voice quaking as she delivered over each syllable, "two-two-three-nine."

When Schultz got the prompt to leave a message, he turned back to Leo and nodded, Leo's sign to duct-tape Jenna's mouth shut again.

"Hit star sixty-nine, you fuckin' son of a bitch, if you ever want to see your wife alive again," he screamed into the phone when the message finished, then closed the phone and dropped it in his pocket. Then he programmed Scott's number into several more cell phones he had in a tool bag sitting on the passenger's seat. He didn't intend to use any one of them more than once. When he finished that chore, he pulled back out on the highway.

SCOTT GOT OUT of the shower to find Schultz's message.

He and the band had just landed in Toronto for two nights for a pair of sold-out gigs. The call came barely ten minutes after Scott had checked into his room. Before he followed Schultz's directions, he used the house phone to put a call into Caine.

"Matthew. Scott. I just had a call from Schultz. He claims he's got Jenna. What in the *fuck's* going on?" Caine, who was camped out in Sadie's office, sat straight up in his corner chair.

"Talk to me."

"He just called and left a message. He says he's got Jenna. I'm supposed to star-sixty-nine him. I'm calling you on another phone."

"Call him back," Matthew said tersely. "Leave this line open while you talk to him. Don't commit to anything."

Scott's fingers shook as he found the star button, followed most reluctantly by the six and the nine. Schultz answered on the first ring.

"I've got your wife, Tenny boy, and you don't," he taunted Scott. "Drop whatever the fuck you're doing, go find a fuckin' bank and transfer the ten million, you fool. You know the account number. Ta for now. Oh – Scott? You've got an hour."

The next sound Scott heard was a dial tone. The conversation was over before it had begun. He'd never had a chance to say a word.

Furious, he hit star-six-nine again. "Lemme talk to Jenna," he growled when Schultz finally answered it.

"Sure," Schultz said laconically. "Why not." Pulling over again, he turned around to Leo. "He wants to hear his wife beg," he said, handing the phone back to him. Jenna gritted her teeth as Leo reached for the fresh piece of duct tape, yanked this one off, then held the phone to her ear.

"Honey," she whispered.

"Jenna, baby, tell me you're okay, hon," Scott said, every word freighted with desperation.

"I am. So far."

"Where –" he started to ask. She thought fast.

"Where babies come from," she answered enigmatically. "I think so, anyway. You know, where –"

"Sorry, lady, this one don't come with no thousand-minute plan," Leo quipped as he pulled the phone away from her and handed it back to Schultz.

"One hour," Schultz reminded Scott. "And don't bother trying to get me on this phone again." Schultz tossed the phone out the window and into the passing lane of New Hampshire State Highway 16. Scott heard it hit the pavement.

The phone received glancing blows from a few cars before an eighteen-wheeler completely pulverized it thirty seconds later.

SCOTT CLOSED AND pocketed his cell phone and sat thinking about what Jenna had said until he realized he was hearing Caine's tiny voice attempting to yell at him from the open line in his other hand. Holding that phone up to his ear, he pulled it away quickly, screaming, "Okay, okay, I hear you," then returned it to his ear midway through Caine's apology which he cut short.

"Okay. Fuck the sorries. I want answers, Caine," Scott said angrily. "How the hell did this happen? How the hell did he get her?"

Caine gave him a fast run-down of the bald facts, ending with what he knew sounded like a pretty lame excuse. "You know your wife better than I do, Scott. You know she's gonna do what she decides she's gonna do."

Scott was quiet for a moment before he finally said, "I know, Matthew. It's not your fault. So what do I do? He's given me a hour to make the transfer. What are my options here?"

Caine considered Scott's options. It was a damnably short list. "Pay it," he said.

SCOTT HURRIED INTO A bank across the street from his hotel to arrange the transfer. As he waited for the bank officer to verify all the details, he turned over Jenna's words. "Where babies come from. I think so, anyway," he repeated to himself twice, then jumped to his feet as he suddenly understood what she'd been trying to tell him. Excusing himself, he quickly stepped outside and phoned Caine again.

"She's in Sunapee," he told him.

"Where's that?"

"It's where he's from. It's where I have a lake house." It's where Jenna gets pregnant, he thought to himself.

"Where the hell is it?"

"Two hours and a bit northwest of Boston."

"He only got his hands on her less than an hour ago."

"Then, trust me, that's where they're headed."

SCHULTZ TOOK JENNA up highways she recognized, then off onto a rat's nest of back roads she didn't know at all, most booby-trapped with winter potholes. Finally they jounced up the driveway of a ramshackle cabin that sat far back and above a lake and pulled in behind an equally decrepit barn. Cutting the engine, Schultz turned to face her. His eyes were ice cold and granite hard.

At that moment, fear caught Jenna with the full force of a pack of starving wolves. As Leo yanked her and the blanket out the back of the truck, her eyes stayed locked on Schultz's, until Schultz turned to get out of the truck. As Leo scooped her up, threw her over his shoulder and hauled her to the house, she finally started to cry. She didn't want to cry. She was furious with herself that she was crying, but the fact was that she had absolutely no control over her tears.

Schultz had the door open before Leo, grunting, got her up the back steps. With one last heave, he made it through the door and dumped her unceremoniously in the middle of the kitchen floor. Half-covered, Jenna lay where she fell, stunned.

"Basement?" Leo asked, looking to Schultz for direction.

"Upstairs. I'll be up in a minute."

By the time Schultz joined them, Leo had dropped Jenna and her blanket on the bare mattress of a single bed in a tiny bedroom. All she could do was squirm under the blanket till enough of it covered her for modesty's sake, then turn her face to a wall of peeling, faded wallpaper. "Not feeling particularly sociable, are we," Leo said blandly. "You and I could get to be good friends, ya know." Jenna didn't move.

She stopped breathing altogether when she heard Schultz come pounding up the stairs and enter the room. Coming over to the side of the bed, he reached down, took her by the shoulder and pushed her onto her back, then seized her by the chin and forced her to look at him. He studied her for a moment, relishing the power he held over her, until a hideous smile broke over his features. "Oh boy, are we gonna have us a good time tonight, baby," he promised her.

Leo grimaced. Schultz noticed. "Don't *you* bother gettin' any big ideas, buddy," he warned his hired thug. "Downstairs," he ordered him with a nod of his head towards the door. Leo got the message. Schultz, right on his heels, turned back at the door and gave Jenna another ugly smirk before he closed the door behind him. She heard a key turn in the lock from the outside.

JENNA ROLLED BACK to face the wall and closed her eyes again. Never had she felt so alone in her life. If only this were a nightmare. But she couldn't remember every having nightmares that included smells, smells like mold or the overpowering, putrid stench of decay, like this one did. Tears began to well up in her eyes once again. This time she succeeded in fighting them back.

Rolling back over, she swung her feet to the ground, letting the blanket slide completely off of her. Her eyes flew around the room, desperate to find some way to free herself from her duck-tape bonds. A solution, inefficient as she knew it would be, presented itself in the form of the cheap, rusted bed frame that held the mattress she'd been lying on. Hooking her feet around one exposed end of the frame, she started carefully drawing the duct tape back and forth across it. Her legs cramped with the effort, but as the tape began to fray, she redoubled her efforts. Finally, it gave.

Reversing her position on the bed, lying on her back, Jenna was just able to reach down to the corner of the bed frame with her taped wrists. The pressure it put on her back, arms and neck quickly grew almost unbearable, but she steeled herself to the task, willing herself into an almost Zen-like trance, until eventually that tape too unraveled to the point that, with what little strength she still had left, she was able to tear through the last of its reinforcing filaments. Her hands were free.

Gently, she removed the tape from her mouth for the third time today.

Chapter 34

✸

JENNA ROLLED OVER and jumped up from the bed. Grabbing the blanket from the floor, she wrapped herself in it, then quickly set to work assessing her situation. Through the window, encrusted as it was with years of filth, through the blessedly bare-branched vegetation, she could see water in the distance – and a glimpse of a lighthouse. Sunapee had three. Other New Hampshire lakes had lighthouses, too, she knew, but the odds were good that this was Sunapee. She was also pleased to see that there was a barely sloping shed roof just beneath the window.

The room that she was in had only the bed she'd been thrown on, a chair, the one window and two doors. One of these, she knew, led to the hallway. Opening the other, she found a closet crammed full with tattered, dirty men's clothes. The floor was knee- deep in old shoes and work boots. A nail on the closet door held numerous sets of suspenders. She pulled out an armload of flannel shirts and heavy pants.

Heading with them over to the bed, she noticed the edge of a small trunk under the bed frame. Kneeling down, she dragged it out and opened it. Inside was a jumble of stuff. Tipping it all out, Jenna decided these were the kinds of things you'd expect to find in an old man's dresser: long- and short-sleeved tee-shirts, ragged undershirts, vintage underpants, well-worn long underwear, socks full of holes, some darned, many not. In the middle of it all: a single, incongruous red and black striped silk tie, in perfect condition.

Feverishly, Jenna grabbed at the pile, picking up an item and slipping it on, then another and another, topping it all with a frayed red cotton union suit. Then she started layering the flannel shirts and a couple of pairs of the pants. The first pair, so worn that it was almost impossible to tell they had been made of corduroy, she belted with a stiff leather belt that still inhabited the loops.

The original owner hadn't been a large man, thank goodness, but he'd been tall. She turned up the cuffs, then wriggled into a second pair, these flannel-lined jeans. Grabbing a pair of suspenders off the closet door, she attached them in back, brought them over her shoulders, clamped them onto the waistband in front and adjusted them for her height.

Pulling out three pairs of socks, she sat down on the edge of the bed and hurriedly pulled the smallest of them on, followed by a second and a third pair. Going back to the closet, she saw one ragged old Bean boot laying on its side. Searching frantically through the pile of other footwear, she located its mate and took them back to the bed. Even with three pairs of socks, the boots were too big. She layered more socks in the bottom and stuffed a pair in the toes and tried again. Laced tightly, she knew they'd at least stay put and keep her feet relatively dry. The rubber bottoms were intact, if frustratingly short. The leather uppers had seen better days; they were sure to leak. The snow on the ground looked deep from the window.

Two things she hadn't found – gloves or a hat. She layered more socks to double for mittens. A couple of big bandanas would at least serve to cover her ears.

Jenna unlocked the single window, then tried to raise the lower sash. As she feared, it had warped shut years ago. Struggling as quietly as she could, she shoved it back and forth in its tracks until it finally worked loose and opened sufficiently that she and her many layers could make their way through.

Exiting feet first, she lay out flat on her back and wriggled like an inch worm through the snow silently down toward the edge. She hadn't been able to pay much attention to the layout of the house, but she had a feeling she was on the roof of the kitchen and, ten-to-one, Schultz and Leo were sitting at the kitchen table. Assuming it was, she moved as carefully as she could, determined not to dislodge any snow that might give her away if one or both happened to be looking out a window.

When she'd finally made it to the edge, she gingerly got to her knees to consider what her next move should be. Crawling to the corners, she laid out flat on her stomach to peek over each edge. One end of the add-on had no windows and at that end, the drop appeared to be only about five feet. Hopefully, the snow would act as a cushion. It looked fluffy, soft and yielding, but Jenna knew how deceptive snow could be; a thin dusting of newly fallen snow could disguise a layer of hard, bone-breaking ice just beneath it.

Turning around, she got herself in position to jump feet first, then sat there dangling her legs a moment, looking about her in all directions, planning her course away from the house. She could see neither barn nor driveway from where she was, but given the slope of the landscape and the glimpse of lake, she assumed that if she made her way to her left, she'd have to come upon a road before long. Whether this was Sunapee or not, all these old summer resort lakes had roads ringing them.

Holding her breath like she was jumping into cold water, Jenna dropped the five feet to the winter surface. She was in luck. The snow was soft, deep and forgiving. She landed almost silently, sprawling in an awkward heap a few feet from the side of the house. She was free.

JENNA BLESSED THE snow she fell into, but it wasn't long before she was cursing it. Sinking up to her knees and feeling about as agile as a runaway snowman, it took double effort to lift each foot free of the snow's frozen embrace. She quickly discovered that unless she added a twist to the normal lifting movement, she'd be bootless when her leg reappeared.

She struggled for several minutes before daring to take a look back at the house. Expecting it to be well behind her by now, she moaned aloud when she saw how little ground she'd covered. Gritting her teeth, she turned away again and redoubled her efforts. With concentration, she began to find a rhythm to her actions. Her speed picked up, if only a bit, but she knew that every bit count. She had to reach a road before Schultz discovered she was gone.

After another five minutes or so, she had to stop to catch her breath. Looking back, panting, she was glad to see that the house was in fact quite a distance behind her now, much of it obscured by a line of boulders dropped along this ridge by a glacier passing this way centuries earlier. Jenna took a moment to consciously study the roof line and crumbling rock chimney of the old place, in the hopes that she would be leading the police to it before long.

Looking ahead of her again, Jenna was alarmed to see how quickly the afternoon was disappearing in the west. In spite of the cold, she was warm from all the effort it had taken to get this far. Just stopping for a few moments quickly reminded her though just how cold it actually was. She pushed forward. Her reward: ten minutes later she finally stumbled out of the woods and onto a plowed road.

She had no idea which way to go on the road. She was fairly certain that to head to her left would take her back down the road Schultz had used to approach the house. She remembered thinking how empty that road had been. She moved off to her right instead.

Picking up the pace to a jog-trot, she hurried to make up for all the time lost in the woods. On the few occasions when she heard a vehicle approaching, she jumped back off the road, throwing herself down behind boulders or nestling into bushes. She knew any one of these could be Schultz in his truck, out to reclaim his prize catch. Watching carefully from her hiding spot, she was relieved each time someone passed. So far, so good – no Schultz.

Each time she stopped like this, she quickly became aware of how wet her feet were getting and how quickly the cold could overtake her.

BACK AT THE HOUSE, Schultz brought up his account information for the Banque Fortis Canton Vaud in Lausanne. He'd chosen his Swiss bank at random from hundreds accessible via the internet, drawn as much as anything by the picture of the building, a Baroque wedding cake of marble and granite which spoke, most discretely, of old European money – bundles and bundles of old European money. The picture came up every time he accessed the account, and he'd become quite fond of the old hulk. Maybe some day he'd visit it, he thought.

Three million of the ten had actually been deposited. He'd have preferred it come in as one lump payment, but hey, even he knew getting your hands on ten million dollars would be a job for anyone, even Scott Tenny. "Well, holy sh–" he started to exclaim, then realized the last thing he needed was for Leo to have any idea what the stakes were in this one. He put a quick lid on his excitement.

"So?" Leo said, looking up from a tattered paperback he'd picked up in the living room, an old who-done-it judging by the cover. Leo was a voracious reader. Half an hour and he was already almost a quarter of the way through the book. "Ya win the lottery or what?"

"I should wish. Naw, a horse I bet on this morning came through – paid forty-to-one. Coulda had more ones on it, but what the fuck. A winner's a winner, right?"

"I'll drink to that," said Leo, taking a swig from the beer at his elbow. Draining the can dry, Leo tossed it across the room into an empty grocery bag sitting on the floor, reached for another from the six-pack sitting on the table, then returned his attention to his book.

Reaching for one of the phones in the bag he'd brought in, Schultz hit the speed-dial for Scott's number. Scott answered immediately. "Yeah?"

"You're seven short."

"I'm workin' on it. You'll have the rest of it shortly, you sorry son of a –"

"You got –" Schultz looked at his watch. "You got thirty-nine minutes to finish the job. Clock's tickin'…" He snapped the phone shut and, just like Leo, tossed the phone across the room and into the empty grocery bag.

"I'm in a good mood," Schultz said, closing his laptop. "Think I'll pay me a little social call upstairs."

"Forty-to-one says you get just as lucky up there," Leo said.

"Luck ain't got nothin' to do with what's upstairs," Schultz said.

"No, s'pose not," Leo said, "not when you're the guy wit' the gun."

Leo resigned himself to having to listen to Schultz get it on with the beauty in the back bedroom. The last thing he expected to hear was something immediately hitting the wall and Schultz screaming "Bloody fuck!" over and over at the top of his lungs.

Leo was on his feet by the time Schultz came pounding back down the stairs. "The goddamned bitch is gone," he hissed as he grabbed his coat, shrugging into it as he headed out the back door. By the time he got to his truck, Leo was right behind him.

Schultz drove back the way he'd come, then doubled back and continued on beyond his place for several miles, then fanned out onto back roads in both directions. Finally, he pulled up at the end of a dead end road. "No telling where the bitch headed, once she made it to the fuckin' road," he cursed, slamming the steering wheel in complete frustration. "Goddam son of a –"

"It's gettin' dark," Leo observed.

"Of course it's gettin' dark," Schultz said sarcastically. "What, you expect it to get light at five o'clock in the middle of winter?"

"Hey, I was just makin' conversation. I was also gonna point out that the wind's pickin' up, or don't you want to hear that neither?"

"Aren't you the observant one. Amaze me again, dick wad."

"Well, actually, I was just gonna say that you better find her quick, 'cuz I can't imagine she's dressed to spend the night in the woods, not wit' the wind and all."

"Man, get this guy an honorary Daniel Boone cap. You're a regular mountain man, aren't you, Diakos. Maybe you'd like to get out there on a pair of snowshoes and try trackin' her. Let the bitch fall in a hole and freeze her fabulous ass to death. I could care."

"But aren't you tryin' to ransom this bitch?"

"He talked to her. She was alive then. That's all that matters. He'll come through. Hey, I can't guarantee the broad's safety if she's dumb enough to take off on her own. Not *my* problem."

THE COMING NIGHT terrified Jenna, but moving under the cover of darkness might be easier, she reasoned in a half-hearted attempt to quell her fears. When night did fall, however, she discovered one unexpected advantage that did come with it: sound travels differently at night, off the frozen expanse of the lake. Even over the rising wind, she could identify the source of any noise that came her way far better than she had been able to up until then. She reached a cross-road, listened carefully, then let her ears choose the road to the right for her.

It wasn't long before she finally started to see lights. She headed for the closest one, moving as quickly as she dared in the darkness. A full moon hung low in the night sky, but it was forced to share its sky with a fleet of rowdy, disorderly clouds tonight. Driven before the wind that chilled her down here on the icy ground, they teased Jenna like an irritating uncle does a child, hiding the moon, letting it show in its full glory for mere seconds, then hiding it again.

She was almost within shouting distance of a tiny light when she saw a much brighter light go on over a porch, outlining the front of a modest little house. She made straight for the light and finally found herself on a shoveled path between the house and a much larger barn nearby. After all her struggles, it felt like she'd just come onto a major highway.

Shuffling quickly now, she almost fell over her clumsy feet trampling up the three steps to the door. Pulling off her "mittens," she knocked on the outer storm door and wondered if the feeble sound could be heard within. The little house had neither doorbell or knocker.

She had nothing to worry about. The old man and his even older wife heard the noise coming up the steps just fine. The woman came to the door and opened it cautiously.

"Yes?" she said, immediately suspicious of the strangely dressed creature standing gawking at her from under the porch light. She would have been hard-pressed to tell if what she was looking at was male or female, until Jenna pulled off the bandana she was wearing and shook her hair loose. "Oh, my goodness! Come in, dear, come in," the old lady said immediately once that question was settled.

"Can you tell me where I am?" Jenna asked. "Can I use a phone?"

"I'M IN SUNAPEE, on the opposite side of the lake from our place. Some very kind people have let me use their phone," Jenna told Caine, smiling up at the old man. "I asked them if they knew Schultz. They said only by reputation. But it can't be far from here." The woman came back from the kitchen with a steaming mug of tea for Jenna, who beamed at her in appreciation. Taking turns wrapping each hand around the mug to warm them, she held onto the phone with the other.

"I'll have someone from the local police up there come get you," he said. "What's the number there?" Jenna gave it to him. "Good. They'll call you and get the particulars. I'm heading up there right now."

"Okay," Jenna said.

"Thank God you're all right," Caine said. He paused. He hated what he had to tell her. "Scott knows that Schultz got you," he said quietly.

"Shit" was Jenna's one-word response.

"And he's paid the ransom." She closed her eyes and shook her head. "And he figured out where you are. Ten to one he's on his way here."

"Well, the worst is over, at least," Jenna said after a pause, almost in a whisper.

"Yeah, but you still be careful, hear? Don't go with anyone unless you know for sure they're legit."

"I won't. Matthew?"

"Yeah?"

"Thanks. It may not have quite worked to plan, but it's working. They'll get him now."

"I hope you're right. I hope he hasn't cleared out."

"Me too."

"See you as soon as I can get there."

Jenna cut the connection, then dialed Scott. He sounded rushed and angry when he answered with a brusque, "Yeah? Now what?"

"Honey, it's me."

"Jenna? Babe? Oh, my God, thank you, thank you, thank you! Where – where are you, Jenn?"

"I got away from him. I'm a few miles away, I think. Do you know a Mr. and Mrs. Swenson, from across the lake? They say they know your dad."

"Alfred Swenson," the old man offered.

"Alfred Swenson," Jenna repeated.

"Absolutely," Scott exclaimed. "Alfred and Anna. Tell them hi for me. Hell, I'll tell them hello myself. I'm at Logan. I just got off a plane. Caine was sending a car for me. I'll have them bring me up there. Nah, hell, I'll get a small plane to take me up there. There's an airport in New London. I can be up there before he can. I'll find you, babe."

THE SUNAPEE POLICE called the Swensons' within minutes, and the chief of police and an officer were at the door in less than fifteen. By the time they'd arrived, Anna had put Jenna into some dry, warm clothes that fit her reasonably well, and smelled far better than what she'd arrived in.

"If he's still in Sunapee, he's gonna have a heck of a hard time leaving," the police chief assured them. "We've got cops from all the surrounding towns helping set up roadblocks; the FBI are getting in on it too. There aren't all that many roads in and out of this area, especially this time of year. Unless he's a skimobiler, of course – let's hope he ain't one of them Ski-Doo types. Anyway, we'd like to put you in a cruiser and see if you can't maybe spot the house for us."

"Sure," Jenna agreed. "Anything to see this guy behind bars."

Chapter 35

THE SUNAPEE CHIEF of Police introduced himself to Jenna as Fred Webber –
he pronounced it "Webbah." The officer with him, he told her, was Ted Gray.
"The other officer on duty's a Gray too, Ted's cousin Ned. He's out in the
cruiser."

"Fred, Ted and – Ned? Right?" Jenna said.

"Yeah," Fred replied in a manner clearly intended to close the subject.
"Okay, let's get rolling."

"Hang on a minute," Anna Swenson objected, hurried to a closet and
returned with an old plaid flannel hat with fur-lined ear flaps and a long grey
scarf. Jenna pulled the hat on while Anna wrapped the scarf around her neck,
then stood back smiling at her handiwork. "You stay warm, child," she said
kindly.

Ted Gray smirked. "Just hope Geno McNally hasn't gotten wind of the
fact that you're up here," he laughed. "He's our local Jimmy Olsen – the
paparazzi to you, Ms. Tenny."

"Okay, okay," Webber said. "This ain't meant to be no fashion show.
Let's roll."

Lumbering back out into the snow, Jenna was struck immediately by how
much easier it was for her to get around in Anna's calf-high rubber boots,
which fit her far better than those she'd started that afternoon out in.

Fred and Ted got in the back seat of the cruiser. Climbing into the
passenger seat, Fred introduced her to Ned. "Okay, let's start by headin' down
toward Blodgett Landing. You were back from the lake, and up above it, and
in a remote area. My guess it it's gotta be something back off 103 down
thattaway."

Judging by the terse shorthand that passed for conversation for the next
quarter hour, the three men clearly knew the roads they criss-crossed intimately. Jenna kept her eyes glued to the passing landscape as they mumbled back
and forth to each other. "Top of Page there's a cabin," Ted suggested as he
turned off the main road onto a windy one that climbed quickly to the top of a
ridge, then rode it, rising and falling with its crest, for a mile or more before
he turned back off it and headed down again.

"Yeah, but she says she saw a lighthouse," Ted pointed out. "You wouldn't see Burkehaven from Page. King Hill maybe, or along that ridge on Stoney Brook."

"But that's practically the suburbs these days, what with all that new building goin' on up along there." Ned wasn't buying that theory.

"Still a couple old places above it," Webber volunteered, then went back to thinking.

"But there's no way she coulda missed those new houses coming down from his place if it was above there," Ned protested.

"Right. Had to be south of there," Ted was of the same opinion as his cousin.

"I'm thinking above Stoney Brook before you get to Baker," Webber said.

"I was too," Ned agreed. "A number of places way back off the road up that way."

SCHULTZ GAVE UP LOOKING for Jenna and headed back to his place. Pulling his truck back up the driveway, he executed a three-point turn in the two-foot-deep snow, ready to make his getaway, then threw it into park and told Leo to wait for him. Hurrying inside, he went straight to his laptop. Opening it again, he sat down at the kitchen table to wait for the Internet to connect him to the bank in Switzerland.

In his impatience, the damned thing seemed to be moving at the speed of cold molasses. Finally, a prompt for a user name and password and he was in. He hit 'account balance.'

Even though he was expecting it, the sight of $10,000,000 US took his breath away. It was all there. He found himself gulping for air, then slammed his fist down on the table, jumped up and did a kidnapper's equivalent of a slap-happy touchdown dance. Then he slammed the laptop shut.

Grabbing up what he needed, he gave the place one last quick look around and headed for the door. Forget torching it. He was part of the moneyed class now; time to start thinking like a rich guy. The next person to see it would be a realtor. Regardless, he didn't bother locking the door behind him.

AS THE POLICE CRUISER pulled around a heavily wooded bend and started up an open hill of birch, Jenna's breath caught. The clouds had just separated again; moonlight briefly floodlit the winter landscape. Through the birch, she could see the unmistakable roofline of the house she'd escaped, the roofline she'd memorized in the midst of her panicked flight. "That's it!" she gasped. "That's his place. I know it."

Ned slowed and peered up towards where she was pointing. "The Gaston place," Ted said. "Nobody lives there that I know of. Old Man Gaston died – what was it? – three years ago?"

Ned nodded. "Went to the kids, wherever the hell they are."

"Had a caretaker," Webber said. "Could have been Schultz for all we know."

"What did Gaston look like," Jenna asked.

"Tall, gawky old guy, Yankee through and through. Tough old bird."

"No excess baggage?"

"Nope."

"Those were his clothes I was wearing," Jenna said quietly.

The cruiser came to the foot of the driveway. Multiple sets of fresh tracks indicated that a four-wheel drive vehicle had made more than one trip up and down it recently.

"Think they're up there now?" Ted said quietly, as if Schultz could hear.

Ned had just finished saying, "Could be," when a pair of headlights snapped on above them.

"Seems they are," said Webber dryly. "Block the driveway," he directed Ned, who pulled forward a few more feet, then put the car in park but left the engine running. Quietly, all three opened their doors. Ned and Ted stepped out. "You stay here," Webber directed Jenna before he too exited the car. "Stay down."

The moon vanished behind the clouds.

STARTING TO EASE the truck down the driveway, it was only a matter of yards before Schultz saw the three cops pulling their guns. "Holy shit," he whispered. Leo, who'd been stuffing his gloves in his pockets in anticipation of a warm ride back to civilization, looked up.

"Oh, fuck, who the bejesus called them."

",Goddammit to hell! She musta made it to somebody's house. Here. Take this." Schultz fished around under his seat, pulling out a Glock 35 and a couple of extra magazines of ammo. "Circle down behind them. I'll keep 'em busy. You get fifteen shots to the clip. Use them wisely." Leo opened his door quietly and slipped out into the darkness.

Schultz pulled a Beretta from his pocket and opened up on the cops below him with three bursts of gunfire. He was pleased to see that one bullet caught one cop in the calf, dropping him to the ground just beside the cop car. The door closest to him opened – that must be Jenna inside, he though – and the downed officer dragged himself inside the car. Leo saw it too, as he made his way down through the trees.

Webber took his time trying to get a fix on Schultz. The truck's headlights blinded him to what was going on beyond them. Schultz could be anywhere. And there was the other guy, this Leo Jenna had told them about. Most likely, he was up there in the dark with Schultz as well.

For a brief moment, the moon came out again. Webber could just make out Schultz's form behind the truck door. No sign of the other guy. Webber got off a couple of rounds, then dove back behind the car to avoid Schultz's instantaneous response. He had just hit the ground when Leo came up from behind him and put a single bullet in his brain.

Ted, whose gun had also been trained on the truck, spun on his heels at the sound of gunfire behind him but could see nothing. Leo had ducked low behind the car. Several rounds from Schultz forced Ted to return his attention to the truck up the hill.

Leo quietly made his way around the dead cop and on around the car, avoiding the side where the door had so recently opened. Within a few seconds, he had Ted in his sights. One second later, Ted Gray lay dead at his feet. Then he turned his attention to the occupants of the car.

Yanking open the driver's side door, he found himself face to face with Jenna, and with Ned's service revolver which was shaking in her hands. The amount of time it took her to get up the courage to squeeze off a shot gave him more than enough time to jump out of harm's way, then reach back in and grab her before she could figure out what to do next.

"Hey, this ain't no game for amateurs, lady," he cackled as he dragged her out of the car. Once he had a good hold on her, he turned back to the open door and put a bullet through the back of Ned Gray's head as well.

Then he forcibly escorted Jenna back up the driveway, one beefy arm restraining her movements like a boa constrictor, the other holding the Glock to her head.

Schultz came slogging halfway down the driveway to meet them. In the harsh glare of the headlights, he studied Leo's prize. Then he spat and turned on Leo.

"*This*," he said, indicating Jenna with his head, "we don't need, asshole. She's just one fuck hell of a complication. Do her." And he turned and headed back to the truck.

Leo's mind moving in slow-motion was quicker than most people's in high gear. Never relaxing his grip, his eyes locked on Jenna's, he performed a quick needs-and-resources assessment and came to the conclusion that Jenna alive could very well be worth something to *him.* Clearly she'd been worth something to Schultz. Hell, anything worth ransoming once most probably would be worth ransoming twice.

He turned the gun, which had been so recently pressed to Jenna's temple, on Schultz. Schultz never made it to his truck.

Propelling Jenna back up to the house, Leo pushed her in the door ahead of him and was happy to see that Schultz had left the duct tape where he remembered last seeing in. It's shiny surface stood out in the midst of all the ancient, dust-covered clutter on the kitchen counter.

Reaching for it, he quickly had Jenna gagged and bound again, then pushed her down onto a chair. Looking around, he spotted the duffle of cell phones Schultz had so conveniently pre-programmed for him. Oh, this was just too damned easy! Grabbing one out, he hit the speed dial.

THE SMALL TURBO-PROP Scott had chartered to make the trip up to New London was in its descent when Scott's cell phone vibrated in his pocket. He answered it with a wary "Yeah?"

"Yeah," Leo answered casually. "I gotta message for you. Schultz was pleased as punch when you got your shit together and transferred it to him. Now you're gonna go and find some more shit – and transfer it to me."

Silence. Finally, Scott said, "Who's this?"

"Another pal of Schultz's, just like you. You know the drill. Any friend of Schultzie's is a friend of mine. Schultz has – had – such a wide circle of friends. I guess I oughta let you know. He's dead."

"Good Christ."

"My condolences."

Scott said nothing.

"Hey, I'm sorry I had to break it to you like that, Tenny. I know you two were close. He told me all about it. And there's the fact that you two had something in common, right? Something real special. This broad I find myself stuck with. I sure wouldn't mind getting the bitch offa my hands. She's been nothin' but trouble since Schultz dragged me into this thing. And of course now I'm not gonna get paid, not by him anyway. By *you* – this is what I was hopin' we could discuss, ya know, mano à mano, as friends of the dearly departed."

While Leo gloated on, Scott pushed himself back in his seat, clenching his fists as he looked up at the ceiling and closed his eyes, trying to rein in the turmoil of utter helplessness that was swelling within him. He knew there was no time for rage. He needed his wits about him.

"So – what do you propose – friend?" he asked the voice on the other end of the line, who snorted at the tsunami of sarcasm that came through with Tenny's final word.

"Now, that's the spirit. 'Friend.' I like that. Come to think of it, now that Schultz is gone, I'm feelin' sorta friendless. Guess I'm gonna have to make it on my own in the world now. Feel like contributin' to the Leo Diakos fund, in memory of ol' Dave Schultz, ya know, like in lieu of flowers?"

"Not really."

"Well then, how about contributin' to the Leo Diakos fund or come pick up your wife's dead body?

Chapter 36

✸

LEO HAD NO IDEA how much Schultz had been demanding of this big-time rock star; he imagined it was the kind of money that allows one to vanish off the face of the earth. Leo's mind had always operated on a more modest scale, which was why he'd always be an employee and never a boss. His needs were few, his friends many. He liked his life. He had no desire to disappear. He quickly improvised a ransom demand of his own.

Scott had to stifle the urge to say, "That's all?" when he'd heard Leo's terms.

Leo Diakos wanted a one-time payment of half a million dollars, and was willing to give Scott twenty-four hours to come up with it in cash. "You meet me where I tell you, you give me the bagful of cash, I give you your wife. Clean and simple."

"Clean, maybe," Scott said, stalling for time. "Simple, no. I'm in Canada. I'd have to arrange for the money and then – where would you want to do this, anyway?"

"Boston. Piece'a cake for a big shot like you," Leo assured him. "Guys like you say the word, and shit happens. You make it happen, you get your wife back in one piece. I really don't want her on my conscience." Then he laughed, or at least what passed for the laugh of psychopath, considering his utter lack of a conscience. "Schultz told me to kill her. I killed him instead."

After a pregnant pause, Leo added, "Please. Do not make me kill her. Man, *that* would be a hellova waste."

SCOTT WAS ON THE PHONE with Caine before the plane landed. "Now what the fuck do I do?" he asked wearily.

"I just got off the phone with the Sunapee police. They've lost communication with their guys." Caine hesitated. "Jenna'd gone out with them to see if she could spot the place. It – doesn't sound good."

"Doesn't sound good!" Scott exploded. "Now some gun-for-hire lowlife's got Jenna and all you can say is it doesn't sound good?! Shit, Matthew. You gotta do better than that!"

"They know the general location where they were looking. They've got resources they're calling on. I should be there in less than ten minutes now. I'll call New London PD and have them pick you up."

Scott cut the conversation short, pocketed his phone, then dropped his face in his hands and rubbed his eyes. He wanted off this nightmare rollercoaster ride. He was overcome by an image of his family each laying on a float, bobbing gently on the surface of the pool in Florida, caressed by warm breezes. In his imagination, he held Jenna's hand in one of his and Zach's in the other.

LEO KNEW HE HAD some housekeeping to do, though the last place he wanted to be was back out in the cold and the snow and the dark. Leo was a city guy. He lived where there were people to shovel well-lit sidewalks, for crying out loud. Bundling back up, he steeled himself for the first slap in the face of the bitter, wind-driven cold.

He'd only been inside for ten minutes but even in that short amount of time, he'd warmed up just enough that the contrast between inside and out was worse than ever. With a groan, he pushed out the back door and down the back steps and started trudging down the driveway again. It had just begun to snow.

The door to Schultz's truck still stood open and the key was still in the ignition. Leo climbed in and slammed the door behind him. Starting up the engine, he revved it a couple of times, then following his progress in the side rearview mirror, reversed the truck back up the driveway and around behind that sorry excuse for a barn. Then he climbed out and headed down to the bottom of the driveway.

Wrestling Ted Gray's two hundred pounds into the cop car warmed him back up, at least. Shoving Ned Gray aside, he got in, started the car, backed it up, then pulled it straight up the driveway. Pausing beside Schultz's body, he threw the cruiser in park with a sigh, got out and hauled another couple hundred pounds of dead meat into the back seat. It never failed to amaze him how, with a little exercise, you could be sweating bullets in the middle of a freakin' blizzard. Okay, this didn't quite qualify as a blizzard – it was just spitting snow so far – but for story-telling purposes, he'd make it a full-on blizzard, he decided, as he pulled the cop car out of sight behind the barn as well.

FBI AGENT HENRY KROUSE was waiting for Scott when he hurried down the steps of the little Beech King Air C90 he'd leased. From the door of the plane to the door of the waiting black Durango was at most fifteen feet.

"Jump in," Krouse yelled over the rising wind. "We're meeting up with Caine about five miles from here. We have a fix on the house."

"Great," Scott said grimly, settling in for yet another ride at this middle-of-the-night amusement park hallucination.

"Like your music," Krouse said after a few moments of silence broken only by the steady hum of the SUV's tires eating up the snowy roads.

"Thanks."

"It's gotta be a hell of a life – concerts, recording, all the screaming fans."

"I guess." Scott's mind was anywhere but on his musical career. "It's a living." Then he grimaced. "Sorry. I'm a little preoccupied."

"Course you are. Sorry." Krouse went silent again. "You guys have a kid…"

"Yeah. And he's not growing up without his mother," Scott said harshly.

The SUV raced through the darkness. It was snowing harder now.

SEVERAL VEHICLES HAD CONVERGED at the intersection of Stoney Brook and King Hill, and a dozen men huddled at the rear of a surveillance truck. Its rear doors open, light and a modicum of heat spilled out over them as they conferred, sizing up the situation as they understood it and hashing out potential scenarios.

Caine looked up as Scott jumped out of the Durango and came hurrying over. "Scott, you're here. Oh, man. I am so sorry," he said, putting one hand out for a shake and reaching for Scott's shoulder with the other.

"It's not your fault, brother," Scott said, taking the proffered hand but also giving Caine a one-armed hug. "But wait till I get my hands on that woman of mine. Is she ever in for a piece of my mind."

"Well, we've got some good minds at work on it here. They're creative. They'll come up with something workable. We're getting her out of the there, whatever it takes."

"Amen to that. What can I do?"

"Be patient."

"Oh, sure."

"Okay, listen up, everyone," said a small, dark-skinned man in plain clothes.

"Andrew Gaillard," Caine told Scott quietly. "Ranking FBI, out of Concord."

"We're going to lure Diakos out of the house. Hooper here is going to just walk up to the door on snowshoes looking for Schultz to get some help." A heavily-bearded, pony-tailed old cop from Newbury, dressed like the plainest of oldtimers around these parts, had volunteered to be the bait.

"He'll wait till the rest of us are in place. With night scopes, once Hooper has him at the door, or gets him to at least stick his head out a window, whatever, it shouldn't be a problem picking him off."

TEN MINUTES LATER Hooper, wearing a pair of traditional long-tail snowshoes, came loping up across the snow to the front door of the old Gaston place. Light from a kitchen window at the back of the structure illuminated the falling snow. "Schultz! Hey, Schultz!" Hooper yelled as he came. "It's me, George Hoopah. Need your help, man! Schultz!" Silence.

By now, Hooper had maneuvered his way sideways up the three steps to the front door. Banging on it, he resumed his cry. "Schultz! Wake up, David. I need your help! The missus fell and broke her leg. I need you to call for an ambulance for me."

To the left and right of the door were sidelights, the kind domestic householders quite often obscure with either opaque glass or a sheer curtain, but neither Schultz, nor Gaston before him, had ever been accused of domesticity. Through the left-hand sidelight, Hooper could clearly see a form silhouetted against the light coming from the kitchen. Whispering into a mike affixed to the cuff of his mitten, he said, "Subject is on the move."

A voice in his earpiece came back immediately. "We still show one heat source stationary in the kitchen. That's gotta be Jenna. And, check that, another on the move."

Hooper set to hollering again, each word separate and distinct. "Schultz, for pity's sake, wake up! It's me, Hoopah. The wife's broke her leg. I need you to make a call for me. Schultz, help me out here, for cryin' out loud!" Then he banged on the door like he was trying to break it down with his fists. "Wake up, you old fool. You've probably gone and drunk yourself into oblivion again," he threw in for good measure. "Dagnabbit, Schultz, I know you're home. Wake up!"

The silhouette disappeared from the hallway. "What's he doing?" Hooper whispered into his mike.

"Moving to your right. Going up a staircase. Bang on the door again."

Hooper resumed his pounding.

"Subject's moving into an upstairs front room. Uh-oh. Subject in kitchen's moving. Slowly. On the floor. Everyone got that?"

Hooper confirmed, then pounded some more. "David Schultz, for God's sakes, will you *please* wake up!"

"He's turned. He's coming back downstairs," said the voice monitoring the heat sensors.

"Where's Jenna?" came another voice.

"Still in the kitchen, about halfway to the hallway to the front of the house. She's just stopped moving. She hears him coming back down. He's down. He's – he's not moving. He's probably at the bottom of the stairs. Repeat, neither subject's moving."

Hooper knew he had to get – and keep – Diakos's attention. Yanking off both of his snowshoes, he used one to reach across and bang on the nearest full window, which he did several times, again yelling for Schultz. Then, taking the snowshoe by its tail and using it like the world's clumsiest baseball bat, he reached back and gave it all he had. The nose of the snowshoe sent shards of shattered glass flying through the night.

"Hey, what the fuck are you doing?" Diakos yelled from the hallway. "Schultz ain't here. I'm a friend of his. He told me I could use the place. He didn't say I'd have to worry about being broken in on. Said the place was nice and quiet, for crissakes."

"Hey, man, sorry to scare you. I'm a neighbah of David's. My wife broke her leg. I don't have a phone. I just need someone to call an ambulance for me. Can you please help me out here?"

"Talk to me," Hooper whispered into his mike.

"Jenna's staying put."

"Good."

"And so's he."

"Not good. I gotta get him somewhere useful." With that, Hooper yelled again, "Hey, just come to the door and let me talk to you. I know you city-folk are paranoid when you get out here in the boonies. Nothin' to worry about. I'm not no talkin' grizzly bear, ya know."

"Just a talkin' pig," came sarcastic whispering over Hooper's earpiece.

Diakos passed the broken window, taking a good look at Hooper, then continued on to the door. Hooper held his breath as he heard the door being unlocked. Diakos opened it, a crack.

Not enough of a crack. Hooper put on his most persuasive tone. "Hey, man, can you help me here? Schultz never bothahed with a land line, but he always had one of them portable phones on him. Any chance you do?"

"What's your name?" Leo asked nervously.

"George Hoopah. Live half a mile from heah, as the crow flies. Had a feud with ol' Gaston, but me and Schultz are buddies. Tip one back together every so often. An' I can count on him not to tell the missus. True friend. An' what's *your* name?"

"Leo. Leo Diakos."

"From Manchester?"

"From Boston."

"Got family in Manchester? Jason Diakos? Alex Diakos? Father and son." Pretending his nose was running, Hooper wiped it down his jacket sleeve. Into his mike, he whispered, "She still down?"

"Yep," answered the voice on the headphones.

"Nope," answered Diakos.

"Well, can you help me out here? I gotta get an ambulance for the wife."

"Okay." George Hooper stepped back as Leo Diakos opened the door.

Chapter 37

✳

THREE BULLETS DROPPED Leo Diakos before he could even begin to wonder why this George Hooper would back off as he came out the door. One came from the Remington 700 of Bill Truslow, a New London police office hiding behind a woodpile to the right side of the door.

A second came from a police sniper rifle in the hands of FBI agent Donald Welch, who'd taken up position behind a clump of prickly holly to the left and below Truslow's position. As the tense moments ticked on, he had time to regret his choice of cover.

The third came from the sidearm of Matthew Caine, who'd positioned himself behind the hulk of one of those rusted old junkers that seemed to be required ornamentation for any proper Yankee cabin. He didn't need any fancy night scopes to do his bit to put an end to Jenna and Scott Tenny's woes. The light from the house was more than enough to illuminate his target. This one was personal.

An FBI agent had to forcibly restrain Scott from entering the house until it had been determined that it was safe to enter, then took him straight to Jenna whose hands and feet were in the process of being freed.

The moment she could, she scrambled awkwardly to her feet and threw her numb arms around him. Scott wrapped his arms around her and held her as still as she could ever remember having been held. In the midst of the chaos, the two stood unmoving, finding their way back to a most private world of their own, letting their hearts seek out and rejoin with the other's beat, finding their inner harmonies in silence. Finally, Jenna raised her lips to his and they kissed.

They knew their privacy couldn't last long, and it didn't. Within moments, they were surrounded by FBI. Regardless, they never let go of one another the rest of the night.

THEY SPENT THE NEXT few hours being debriefed by every law enforcement organization with even the smallest stake in the case, from the FBI to the Sullivan County Sheriff's Department. It only took Matthew Caine ten minutes to take their deposition for the LAPD – he knew the case inside-out, cold.

It took Jenna and Scott almost as long to find the words to express their profound appreciation for his help and his support, for the role he'd come to play in their family. Caine, a modest man, tried to wave it all off.

He didn't know what to do with Jenna's finally farewell however, as she hugged him before he climbed into the Sunapee cruiser that was waiting to take him to the airport. "You're my guardian angel, Matthew," she'd whispered in his ear.

Offering her an ironic smile as he pulled back from her, he mumbled, "No, lady, I'm just one lucky cop." With a wink, he was gone.

IN THE HALF LIGHT that precedes sunrise, Scott unlocked the front door of the lake house and let Jenna and himself in. They were both struck immediately with the interior cold, a special mid-winter cold that smelled of century-old pine and century-old fires. The house was maintained for the winter at the bare minimum temperature it took to keep the pipes from freezing. It wasn't so cold that they could see their breath, but it was cold enough that neither wanted to take off a stitch of clothing. "I'll meet you in the bedroom," he told her as he finally relinquished her hand and headed for the attic, stopping only to turn up the thermostat. He returned triumphant with a old electric blanket

"Okay, pull back the sheets, babe," he said. As soon as she did, he threw the blanket over the bed like a fisherman casting his net, quickly pulled the top sheet, quilt and blanket back over it, then hurried around to the other side to plug it in.

"We'll have her toasty in two minutes," he promised his exhausted wife, "and I, my love, will keep you toasty until then." Grabbing a quilt off a nearby rack, he wrapped her in it, then wrapped his arms around her and the quilt and held her close in an animated squeeze. And then they kissed, an unhurried kiss that grew the way sputtering, bone-dry kindling can start a roaring blaze.

When they couldn't stand a moment longer, Scott reached behind him, pulled the covers back, drew them into the bed and the covers quickly back over them. Then, and only then, did they start removing the clothing from each other, shivering whenever a bare arm had to emerge into the cold to toss a sweater, a shirt, a pair of jeans – nothing was said, but it was clear that both had decided that nothing would remain under the covers but the two of them and the delicious warmth generated by both themselves and the electric blanket. Finally, skin to skin, breath to breath, sigh to sigh, moan to moan, they found and clung to one another.

"I wish I could unzip you and climb right inside of you," Jenna whispered. "And I inside of you, and then be able to zip a casing closed around the two of us – the three of us," he added hastily. "Zach too."

Jenna reveled in the thought, but then started to giggle. "Not until he's potty trained," she whispered, her last cogent thought as she completely gave herself over to animal passion born of the most profound fears – fears of never seeing Scott again, never seeing Zach again, never being together again, the blackest fears she'd ever experienced in a life that already knew far too much about fear.

She'd felt like she was drowning in frigid fear, but one by one, she let go of each terror, tossing it from her like the clothing that had dropped to the floor about the bed, like slabs of lead ballast she'd been carrying in her pockets. She felt herself grow lighter and warmer; she felt a buoyancy carry her back to the surface. Finally she was able to feel Scott's arms and hands and lips and loins as he swept her before him to the shores of forgetfulness, where she eventually lay gasping in pulsating pleasure, in gratitude and exhaustion.

THEY WOKE HOURS LATER to find the house warm and toasty – and wrapped in a snowstorm of near-blizzard proportions. Phone reception was practically nonexistent, but they were able to get a few calls through, the most important to Ellen, who had heard hours earlier from Matthew that they were all right and had already spread the word. Hanging up, Jenna grinned at Scott. "The outside world's fine, and we're snowed in. Does life get any better than this?"

"Strang's gonna have an off-the-charts shit-fit," Scott laughed, "but the band's gonna love it – it's clearly gonna be a couple more days before I can get back up there." He came up behind Jenna who was bundled in a heavy fleece robe, gazing out the window at the swirling whiteness. Wrapping her in his arms, he whispered in her ear, "If this isn't the classic recipe for another baby, I do *not* know what is."

BUT IT TURNED OUT it wasn't. The day before Jenna, Ellen and Zach were scheduled to finally fly down to Tampa to reunite with Scott and the band, Jenna had an appointment with Julia Williams, her gynecologist.

Carrie joined her for lunch first, to get caught up. They hadn't had time to really visit since the Grammy awards. Carrie knew the whole story behind the blackmail and abduction – the whole world knew that story. What she wanted to know was the whole story behind the reconciliation. She'd also promised to accompany Jenna to her appointment, for moral support.

"The bottom line is – I love him and I know he loves me," Jenna confided in Carrie over steaming bowls of egg drop soup. "We let things get out of control and consequently things fell apart. We'll never make that mistake again."

"And it's not just the stress of what you two have been through?" Carrie pressed. "You're sure this is for real?"

"I couldn't be more sure, hon," Jenna answered without hesitation. "I know we still have plenty of work to do but, bottom line – I know we're going to be okay."

Carrie reached across the table for Jenna's hand and squeezed it. "I couldn't be happier for you, Jenn. I couldn't be happier for both of you. I know you'll work everything out. Just remember we're both here, for both of you."

Jenna reached over and gave Carrie a hug. "You are so wonderful, my friend," she said with tears standing in her eyes.

DR. WILLIAMS SAT DOWN to talk with Jenna before her examination. "I've never had any problem getting pregnant before, as you well know," Jenna said, holding her hands up in dismay. "It's been several months. I just don't understand what could be wrong. You told me the last time I was fine, but there has to be *something* wrong."

"I hear your frustration, Jenna," Julia said sympathetically. "Let me do an exam, and I'll order some tests. We'll get to the bottom of what's going on, I promise you."

After her exam, Jenna once again faced Julia across her desk. "I'm beginning to suspect that it might be a blockage of the fallopian tubes, Jenna," Julia said, reaching for a visual aid to help in her explanation. "I want to order a hysterosalpingogram."

"A – what?" Jenna asked.

"It's basically an X-ray test that examines the inside of the uterus, the fallopian tubes, and surrounding area," Julia explained. "A contrast is injected through a catheter that's inserted through the vagina and the cervix into the uterus. Because the uterus and the fallopian tubes are connected, the contrast material then flows into the fallopian tubes." Julia indicated the path the contrast would be taking, using her pen as a pointer. "As it's passing through the uterus and fallopian tubes, continuous X-rays are being taken. The test can reveal a number of possible problems – injuries or abnormalities that may be preventing you from getting pregnant. We can do the procedure right here, and you will know the results immediately."

"Okay," Jenna said, nodding thoughtfully as she worked to take it all in. "With all the trauma you've been through, it's quite possible there's a blockage. I can schedule it for next week if you like. You will need someone to come with you to drive you home. You will probably have some pain and cramping afterwards."

"We're on our way down to Florida tomorrow," Jenna told her, "but the following week would be fine." Scott would be home for a couple of days and could come in with her. Jenna went ahead and scheduled the appointment. She would tell Scott when she talked with him later in the day, she told herself, and it was the first thing Jenna brought up when Scott called.

"I hope you're not angry with me for scheduling it before checking with you," she told him. "I'm just so anxious to get it done, and I so want you there with me."

"Good grief, honey, I'm not mad," Scott chuckled. "I'm really glad you planned it for when I can be there. You know I want to be with you, babe.

Now, can I ask you something I've sort of already planned for *you*?" His words came out in a guilty rush.

"Uh, yeah…" Jenna said warily.

"The band – no, *I* would really like you to sing with us in Tampa. We – well, we've got a whole play list worked out. I mean, we could change it if you don't want to, but –"

"Hey, fair's fair. I made plans for you. Yes, I'll sing."

"Babe. Thank you. I mean it," Scott said with an equal mix of genuine appreciation and relief.

"We're all ready for Florida," Jenna said, now ready to change the subject.

"Oh, God, I can't wait to see you – and pick up where we left off. As a matter of fact, I remember *exactly* what we were doing when we left off," Scott said suggestively. From the background noise, he wasn't alone. Jenna had long been aware of his penchant for what she liked to think of as cell phone exhibitionism.

"And I believe I do too. So what exactly do *you* recall?" Jenna teased.

"Hmmm…it seems to me to have involved whipped cream, did it not?"

"My, you have a good memory. I remember cherries, too, maraschino cherries, a fairly large, fairly full bottle of maraschino cherries."

"But I doubt you remember the chocolate syrup, my pet," Scott said softly.

"And what chocolate syrup would that be, my little chickadee?"

"That would be the chocolate syrup I made a mental note to pick up next chance I got."

"And…have you?" Jenna asked coyly.

"At the risk of sounding like a sixth-grader, that's for me to know and for you to find out," Scott said in his best rendition of a sixth-grade voice. "See you tomorrow, babe."

As he hung up, Jenna found herself literally licking her lips in anticipation of their reunion.

AS SHE EMERGED from the twin shadows of blackmail and marital discord, Jenna had experienced a surge of creative energy the likes of which reminded her of a much earlier incarnation of herself. Out in the studio, she felt like a teenager who'd been turned loose with all the tools of the trade and nobody looking over her shoulder.

Hour after hour, when Zach was napping or after his bedtime, she found herself at the keyboard or on a guitar, trying out ideas, playing with lyrics that vied for her attention like a roomful of unruly children. Laying down tracks, she improvised and embellished from what felt like a bottomless well of inspiration.

Calling Brian in L.A., Jenna told him to let her band know that she'd need them back east soon after she returned from Florida. She'd firm up the dates after she'd had what she'd started referring to as her 'hysterical X-ray."

Packing for the week in Florida, Jenna decided to bring a keyboard along with her, sensing that her runaway creativity could only be enhanced by being with Scott in the verdant, steamy air of the tropics. Digging through a pile of instrument cases amidst other extraneous equipment, she finally found the case for the smaller of the two studio Yamahas. She'd have preferred the bigger one, but Ryan had it on the road for this trip.

She dismantled the keyboard and stowed each component in its proper spot, then started digging through the stacks of notebooks and sheaves of loose composition paper that littered shelves at one end of the studio, looking for old material it might be fun to revisit. Vacations were good for that.

She smiled at the obvious difference between the haphazard approach to organization of most musicians – Scott tended to scrawl a date on the front of a notebook when he started using it. She was more apt to scrawl where she was on the front of hers. She was looking for her notes from when she'd first arrived in Boston. Making a stack of any said 'Boston,' she sat down and skimmed through them to find the earliest. She wanted to revisit who she was when she'd come east, four years and a couple of lifetimes ago.

As she was returning the rest of the notebooks to the shelves, she noticed one on Scott's handwriting dated 2/28/02. Her mind went whirling back to that tempestuous time, when she was pregnant with Zach, when a polyp on Scott's vocal chord had rendered him silenced for months, when he'd spent so much time composing. Picking up the notebook, she hummed lines of melodies, some of which he'd developed, some of which had obviously stayed buried in these pages. And she read lyrics. Some, likewise, had gone on to be performed and recorded. Some were fully realized but never used. Some were mere fragments, cursory ideas, random jottings.

One page brought tears to her eyes. It held only two and a half lines. "I wish for you, my son, a life so unlike mine. I wish for you, my son, a life as fine as mine. I wish for you, my son…" She tucked his notebook in the case along with hers.

JENNA AND ZACH WERE literally the first off the plane in Tampa, and Scott was the first in line waiting at security to grab them both up in his arms as they led the pack surging through the gates.

Zach was deliriously happy to see his daddy. Once he got Scott's hand in his, he was determined he wasn't letting go of it, even when he was reluctantly strapped into the car seat in the limo that awaited them outside the terminal.

His face lit right back up, however, when Scott came around to the other side of the vehicle, climbed in and slid across the seat to sit next to him. With Zach on his left and Jenna on his right, Scott couldn't stop grinning with contentment or shaking his head in pleased amazement of how good life could sometimes be. Ellen, who was sitting across from them, snapped pictures of the happy family all the way to the waterfront hotel Scott had checked into the day before.

JENNA FOUND HERSELF typically nervous as she waited to make her entrance at the outdoor Ford Ampitheatre at the Florida Fairgrounds. Over twenty thousand tickets had been sold, and the excitement had been mounting through the beginning of the show as the audience tried to guess when Jenna would make her appearance. A surprise banner advertising that she would also be performing greeted attendees as they arrived.

Half a dozen songs into the show, the lights went black and she simply appeared at Scott's side, mike in hand, ready to sing. Just as she started to raise the mike to her lips, Scott leaned to her ear. "I've got the syrup," he whispered. Jenna gave him a dirty look, lowered the mike to regain her composure, then finally launched into a searing solo version of an early Blacklace hit, with only Tim on the drums as an odd and haunting backup. Scott joined her on her next song. One hot duet followed the next for the rest of the set. During the second half of the show, the entire band joined in for what one reviewer the next day claimed was simply one of *the* hottest nights ever in the history of rock 'n roll.

The night was certainly one of the most electric Jenna could remember in her entire career. Unable to come down off the euphoria, she, Scott and the rest of the band went out on the town after the show, shocking numerous club-goers at small venues where they gracefully refused to take a bit of the limelight from whoever had the stage, thoroughly enjoying listening to new talents.

It was after three when they finally tiptoed into their room back to the hotel. Jenna had to stifle her laughter when she saw the jar of chocolate syrup and a single rose sitting on the dresser waiting for her. Neither she nor Scott fell asleep till well after dawn.

Chapter 38

❋

ZACH BURST THROUGH their door several hours later, waking them up. "Daddy! Mommy!" he screamed as he launched himself across the room and tried to make a flying leap up onto their bed. He almost made it.

Scott rolled over, reached down and got a good hold on the squirming child. "Elevator going up," he said as he brought a giggling Zach up the rest of the way and deposited him snugly between his parents.

"I kept him outdoors as long as I could," Ellen called in apology from the hall, "but he knew you were up here and he finally had a very public meltdown."

"Hey, that's okay, hon," Jenna called to her. "We've had more than enough sleep. We can all catch naps later."

"Zachy birfday! Zachy birfday!" Zach cried, jumping to his feet.

Scott pulled him back down and gave him a bear hug. "It sure is, little guy. We better get up. Everyone's gonna be here before we've even had our breakfast. Did you have your breakfast?"

Zach nodded solemnly, then broke out in a grin. "Fwench toast! Yum!"

By the time they were dressed, Laurel, Missy and Luka had arrived, having taken an early flight down from New York. Luka, almost five now, came dashing through the door looking for his Uncle Zach. The two hugged like brothers reunited after years of separation while Scott wrapped his arms around Laurel and Missy, planted big kisses on them, and pronounced for the benefit of anyone within hearing distance that he was just about the luckiest guy in the world.

Everyone jumped into bathing suits and headed down to the pool for some Florida sun. Even Scott, after several days in the south, was still New England lily white.

The pool was surprisingly quiet for such a beautiful day. "Everyone's out shopping or down at the beach, a waiter told them when he brought them drinks. "Come back at four – that's crush time here."

They had no intentions of making an appearance at four, but when the rest of Blacklace showed up at two, it was decided that, considering how much privacy they were enjoying, there was no reason not to just go ahead and celebrate Zach's birthday poolside. Zach, with Luka supervising, opened each of his presents, took the time to really see what it was, pulling each piece free of its packaging and blowing kisses and thanks to whoever had given it to him.

The only present that stopped him in his tracks was a snow saucer from the guys in the band. Luka had been preinstructed not to let on what it was. Puzzled, Zach sat in front of it and rocked it on the poolside cement, got up and picked it up, turned it over, righted it again and still couldn't figure out what it was for. Finally, he looked up at Scott. "Daddy?" he said, baffled.

Laughing, Scott jumped up, picked Zach up and deposited him square in the middle of the saucer. "Now, imagine it's snowing. And you're at the top of a hill. And I give you a little push. What do you think would happen, Zachy?"

Zach considered. Then he got it. Looking up at everyone with a huge grin, he said, "Swoosh!"

"You got it! My son the genius!" Scott said with paternal pride.

THE NEXT DAY, the band went north for a much-needed break and the rest of them hopped a plane to Miami to spend the remainder of the week at Coral Gables. The big house rang with laughter from morning till night. Laurel and Missy took one of the guest rooms together and giggled late into the night every night, enjoying sister time they never had as children. Zach and Luka were inseparable. Luka even reverted to taking naps, just to be with Zach.

Jenna set one room up as a music room. With its giant curved window and its floor-to-ceiling view of palm trees and the warm Atlantic, it was a room custom made for creativity. Inspired, Missy ran down to a local music shop and brought back a second-hand guitar for herself and a couple of used African drums and a little wooden-slatted marimba for the kids to have fun with. Before long, everyone was spending more time in the music room than in the pool.

Jenna was up early one morning composing on the keyboard when Scott slipped in silently, not wanting to disturb her. She turned, smiling, when the smell of coffee reached her nose. "That's beautiful," he said, referring to the tune she was working up. "It's new."

"Yeah," she said, accepting the steaming mug he offered her. "I don't know what's got into me, but I'm writing like crazy."

He sat down next to her, put an arm around her, pushed her hair back from her neck and kissed her there. "I know what's gotten into you. Normality. Life's back on track. Or at least what passes for normal for folks like us."

She smiled and nodded. Then she set down her coffee and went fishing through the notebooks in the bottom of the keyboard case. Pulling out the one in Scott's handwriting, she turned to the song he'd started for Zach and handed it to him without a word. He looked at it, surprised. He dropped his head in thought, then turned to look Jenna full in the eyes.

"Want to help me finish it? Let's finish it – together. It's – important."

"Yes," Jenna said without hesitation, smiling. "I agree."

THE WEEK EVAPORATED in a warm haze of child-oriented pleasure. Zach and Luka were the motors that kept everything churning from early morning till bedtime. Later evening was adult time, special time with Laurel and Missy, and what felt like a cornucopia of private time for Jenna and Scott. No moment was taken for granted.

But before they knew it, Jenna and Scott were back in Boston, and back sitting across the desk from Julia Williams in her office as she went into greater detail about the X-ray procedure that Jenna would be undergoing. "Unfortunately, there is discomfort involved, and intrauterine anesthesia has proven of little therapeutic value," she told them frankly. "The complete procedure should take about fifteen minutes."

Jenna gulped. "I'll be okay," she assured herself, her gynecologist and her husband, then excused herself to go change. Julia suggest Scott wait in her office so he wouldn't be bothered in the waiting room. He accepted her offer gratefully.

Julia was right; the procedure was extremely uncomfortable. At each step, she checked with Jenna, who nodded she was all right. Her body language said otherwise, as she cringed, closed down on cramps and clutched the table in response to pain that sliced right through her. At one point, she thought she was going to pass out, but finally the worst was over.

Julia retrieved Scott from her office and had him come with her to look at the results, while Jenna recovered. She was still in a great deal of discomfort when they came to share the results with her. Julia ordered medication for the pain, then explained her findings to Jenna.

"Well, I hate it when I'm right. With all the trauma, your tubes are definitely blocked with scar tissue. One tube is completely blocked, the other about three quarters. I'm afraid that's what caused the worst of your pain during the procedure, Jenna. The good news," she said to both of them, "is that I'm pretty sure, with surgery, I can repair the damage. It will require a couple of days of hospitalization. You just say the word and we'll schedule everything." She left Scott and Jenna to confer in privacy.

Scott took Jenna's hand, overwhelmed at her suffering. "Oh, babe, I wish this were easier. I wish I could do it for you."

"Don't worry about me. It's over," Jenna said, though her body was nowhere near ready to relax yet.

"I'd like you to wait till I'm back from the next few weeks' shows," Scott said. "I know you want to get it over with – I would – but I'd feel so much better if I could be here with you. We'll be finished touring till the fall and I can really be there for you."

Jenna brought his hand to her lips. "I'll wait. I want you here, too."

"I'll go find Julia and get it scheduled." Leaning down, he gave her a tender kiss.

JENNA WENT TO BED when she got home and Scott spent most of the day with Zach. He was concerned about leaving again in the morning if she was still in pain, but it turned out that she was able to get up later in the afternoon. Scott made dinner for the three of them.

When Scott left the room, Zach came over and started to climb into his mother's lap but understood when Jenna told him he couldn't for a little while, that mommy's tummy hurt. From that moment on, he was solicitude itself, trying to find ways to ease her discomfort. She winced as she laughed when he brought her a stuffed zebra he always kept in his bed. "Zebwa makes me feel better when I feel bad," he assured her. "Hold Zebwa, like this." He demonstrated tucking Zebra under his chin. As he did, his thumb went into his mouth and one hand started searching for his blankie, reflexively.

Jenna took Zebra, snuggled up next to Zach, tucked the animal under her chin like he did and smiled down at him. Sleepy, his thumb was still in his mouth. She put her thumb in hers and gave him a wink, which set the two-year-old off in such a fit of giggles that Scott had to come from the kitchen to see what was going on. "Hold that pose," he laughed, grabbing for a camera from the coffee table.

AFTER DINNER, ZACH went to bed, Jenna took more pain medication and she and Scott sat together and talked while she waited for it to take effect. Before long, she admitted she was fighting sleep. "Don't fight it," Scott whispered, picked her up, carried her upstairs and tucked her in.

Jenna felt considerably better in the morning, to Scott's relief. "You keep taking it easy, though," he cautioned her. "Let Ellen do the heavy lifting."

Jenna promised she would, then kissed him goodbye through the open window of an airport limo. An hour later he and the rest of the band were boarding a charter for New Orleans. That afternoon Jenna was on the phone to Brian. "Get me my band," she demanded, "or I'm gonna loose my tiny mind." Two days later, her band was setting up out in the studio, ready to get to work on a selection of the songs that had been pouring out of her in such a steady flow.

Her goal: an album of new material – *before* she went in for surgery. And she did. Four days before Scott was due home, she and the band went down to New York to record.

She stayed with Laurel while she was there. In the middle of all the hard work, they were able to find a little quiet time together. Jenna told Laurel about her pending surgery. Laurel reached over and gave her a hug.

"I do hope it goes well," she said prayerfully.

Jenna nodded. "Me too, hon. I want to have another baby so badly. I so hope this works." Jenna hesitated, then went on to ask a question that she'd wondered about for quite some time. "Not to be nosy, but do you and Rick ever think about having another?"

"We want to wait a bit longer. Our lives are so chaotic as it is. Luka's survived it okay, but I'd rather bring another child into something a little bit more stable, settled. If that's even possible in this day and age." She smiled, took Jenna's hand and kissed it. "I wish you luck with the surgery. I hope *you* get pregnant really soon."

"I HOPE THIS IS A total success and we get you pregnant *really* soon," Scott whispered as Jenna's pre-surgical anesthesia started to take effect. Then he started humming the song in her ear that he and she had spent an hour working on the night before.

He'd gotten home early that morning. They'd had a full day together with Zach, and had taken him out for an early dinner with them to Blue Skies. When Ellen took him upstairs, Scott took Jenna's hand and said, "Hey, babe, let's go work on that song for Zach. Except that I've been thinking we should make it for Zach and for Zach's someday brother or sister." He didn't have to ask Jenna twice.

By the time they came back in from the studio, well after midnight, they'd worked out a tune they both loved, half lullaby, half rock 'n roll, and had made some progress on lyrics. But they'd spent the better part of their time on the couch. "For inspiration," they both agreed.

AND SO ONCE AGAIN, Scott found himself settling in to wait while Jenna underwent surgery and Carrie and Jeremy had once again come along with him for support. He'd been told he could expect the surgery to take about two hours.

They'd all run out of idle conversation as the clock started into its third hour. Worried, Scott was up and pacing. Finally he could contain himself no longer. "What the hell's taking so damn long?"

Just then, to his relief, Jeremy saw Dr. Williams approaching them. Clearly, she'd heard Scott's outburst.

Motioning to Scott, she took him aside. "I'm sorry that took so long, Scott," she said, then went on quickly. "Jenna had a lot more scar tissue then I'd expected. I was only able to clear out one of her tubes. The other is completely blocked. There was just no chance of a successful result. She's going to be in a lot more pain then I'd initially expected because of the extensive work that had to be done. I'll definitely have to keep her a couple of days to get it under control." Scott nodded. "I'll go back and check on her now. You won't be able to see her for few hours. Why don't you go get yourself some coffee."

"I will," Scott said. "Thank you, Julia. Give her my love."

TAKING THE DOCTOR'S advice, Scott, Carrie and Jeremy went down to the hospital cafeteria. "I'm just thankful she's all right," he told them as he sat stirring his cup absentmindedly. "I know it'll be that much harder for her to get pregnant with only the one tube…" He let the thought trail off.

"At least she has a chance," said Carrie. "It means so much to her to have another baby."

Scott agreed. "I don't know what she'd do if the surgery wasn't at least a partial success. And I don't know what I'd do without friends like you to hold me together through these things. God, there have been so many of them."

"We know, bro," said Jeremy, reaching over and squeezing Scott's shoulder.

"We know. She's worth it."

WHEN HE WAS FINALLY able to see her, Jenna was in extreme pain and practically in tears. She'd never anticipated pain like this. Dr. Williams came in and talked with both of them, reviewing her findings. "As I told Scott," she told Jenna, "there was a lot more scarring then I expected. That's why you have so much pain."

"But – the outcome?" Jenna asked wearily. "Can I – ?"

"It will be harder for you to get pregnant but it won't be impossible. We can talk about it further when you're feeling better. I'm going to have them give you something that will let you sleep for several hours. You two visit until it takes effect." She smiled at them encouragingly. "You've both been though a lot today."

"Yeah," Jenna winced. "But thanks. Really. I'll be in better shape to thank you when that painkiller kicks in." She waved a little goodbye to Julia as she left, then tried to settle back into a more comfortable position. Within a minute, a nurse appeared to introduce a heavy sedative into her IV line.

Scott pulled up a chair and dropped his head on Jenna's pillow. She turned to brush the hair out of his eyes. "Poor Scott. What I put you through."

"No 'poor Scott,' you crazy woman," he protested. "Neither of us are poor here. We both just want the best for you, and for us. I so hope this works for you. You've given so much of yourself to make this work."

"I'm just going to hold onto my belief that it will," Jenna said fiercely, then she smiled. "I have a feeling she's going to put us back on her sex-starvation diet again."

"I'd be shocked if she didn't."

"Maybe without the sex we can get Zach's – song – finished." She'd barely gotten the sentence out of her mouth when she fell asleep. Scott kissed each closed eyelid, kissed her on the lips, then got up with a sigh and went home.

JENNA WAS BACK on her feet in a few days and back to feeling pretty much normal in a week. Just as they'd expected, Julia insisted that they refrain from sex at least until Jenna had come back in for a three-week check. A couple of days before her appointment with Julia, her new album, *Home Alone*, debuted at number three on the charts. The following week it would be number one.

Blacklace, with a couple of weeks of R&R under their belts, were ready to get back to work in the studio. They'd talked about getting a new album out by summer. Nobody would admit it, but Jenna's success with hers was making them all feel a little competitive.

Dan summed it up for all of them. "We better do at *least* as well as the lady of the house, or there'll be no livin' with the man of the house."

JENNA'S CHECK-UP went well. Julia was pleased with what she saw, and gave them the green light on resuming sex. "But I don't want you getting upset or frustrated if you don't get pregnant right away," she admonished them. "Remember, it could take a while. If it nothing happens within six months, we'll all sit down and look at other options."

Jenna and Scott left her office with only one thing on their mind – going home and making love.

Chapter 39

⁂

LIFE SETTLED BACK DOWN to something like a routine. So when Jenna came home late one afternoon from a shelter board meeting and found that Scott wasn't at home as expected, she was surprised. She went looking for Ellen to see if she could shed any light on his whereabouts.

"All I know is that he got a phone call, around one, and then left," Ellen told her. "He didn't leave any message for you."

"And Zach?"

"He's down for his nap," Ellen reported.

Puzzled, Jenna shrugged, pulled on a coat and headed out to the studio. She was halfway down the path to the old barn when Scott pulled up the driveway.

She headed back to greet him, staying to the shoveled path. Much of the winter's snow had finally started to melt, leaving the back lawn a swampy mire. Without boots, cutting across it was not an option.

When she got to the car, Scott rolled down his window rather than get out.

"Hi, hon," she said and reached in to give him a kiss. She started to pull back, but he reached up, took a hank of hair in his hand and gently drew her lips back to his, continuing where they'd just left off.

Finally, they parted. "Hi to you, beautiful," he smiled.

"Where you been?"

"In town. Strang called a meeting. I need to talk with you about it. How about an early supper at Blue Skies – we can talk there."

Jenna ran in, let Ellen know what was happening, took a quick look at herself in the mud-room mirror, gave her hair a fluff, then ran back out to the car.

OTHER THAN A half dozen drinkers who'd come early for happy hour, Blue Skies was practically empty when they arrived. Scott poked his head in the kitchen, then he and Jenna took a table in a small function room where they wouldn't be interrupted. As soon as they were settled and had ordered a light meal, Scott got right to the point.

"Strang's just booked a show for us here in Boston the first week of May."

"Wow. That's pretty last minute," Jenna said, surprised.

"Tell me about it," Scott nodded. "We've all agreed we want to at least do something different, not just a rerun of what we've been doing for the last six months. It's really gotten old. Which means designing and throwing a new show together in three weeks flat."

Scott paused and reached for Jenna's hand. "I know we haven't really sat down and talked about you coming back and singing with us yet," he said, "so don't get the feeling that I'm just taking it for granted after Tampa, but I'd really love it if you would sing with us for this show. Everyone wants you to be a part of it, the band, the organizers, everyone. But I told them I'd have to speak with you first. Like I say, I'm not taking this for granted. It's totally up to you."

They were sitting face to face at a small table. Jenna got up and brought her chair around so that it was next to Scott's, then sat down again at his side. Reaching over, she touched his face, then kissed him. "Now that's what I call communication. You did that beautifully," she said, and kissed him again. "And because you did, you know what? I'm gonna do better than that. I'm willing to make a commitment that I'll join you for some of the fall tour, as well. There's only one condition."

Scott interrupted her with a kiss. Then he asked her, "What's the condition?"

"That we keep working on getting me pregnant."

He took her hand and laughed as he looked into her eyes. "That, my love, is a condition I can live with. Let's eat dinner, then go home for dessert."

THEY GOT HOME, checked in on Zach, then went right to their bedroom. Scott shut the door quietly behind them, then turned and took Jenna into his arms. As they melted into a prolonged kiss, he pulled her turtleneck out of her jeans, slid his hands up under it and unhooked her bra, pushing it aside. His hands explored her upper body unimpeded as her eyes closed and a small moan escaped her. In one fluid motion, he drew both the turtleneck and bra up and off of her and let them fall to the floor.

Jenna stood before him and set to work slowly unbuttoning the buttons of his shirt, punctuating her efforts with a kiss between each one. When she was finally done, she pulled it off and let it also fall to the floor.

Scott kissed her forehead, then trailed his lips down her cheek, down one side of her neck, lingering as he crossed her throat, then up the other side and across to her mouth, then kept his lips pressed to hers as he lowered her to the bed.

They lay there alternating between a brushing of lips, murmured thoughts and profoundly deep French kisses as he fondled her breasts and she slowly unbuckled his belt and unbuttoned his jeans.

"We've come so close to loosing one another," he whispered.

"So many times," she sighed.

He began to suck one of her nipples while continuing to fondle the other breast.

"Oh God, it's like it's for the first time," Jenna said softly, shuddering.

He moved to her other nipple. She freed him from his jeans.

"Me too," he whispered, directly in her ear, then followed his words with his tongue. Then he voiced a thought that had been growing within him for weeks. "In some ways, I think we're better since you came back to me."

"Maybe it's realizing what we almost lost," Jenna said.

"Or that we're still working out things?" he said, reaching up to run his fingers through her hair, almost in wonder.

Jenna rolled to her side to face him. "You mean, like we're on our best behavior?" She took his hand and kissed each of his fingertips individually, then put his hand up against her cheek.

Scott thought about that possibility, then laughed. "Nah. As anyone'll tell you, I couldn't do that if I tried. I don't know what it is, but I do know I don't want it to stop."

"I feel the same way," Jenna said quietly. "I wish I had the answer too, but – I almost feel like I don't need an answer. I just know I don't want it to stop either."

SCOTT'S STEP HAD A noticeable spring to it when he stopped by Jeremy's studio the next morning. Jeremy was perched on a stool, guitar in hand, penciling notations on an arrangement on a music stand in front of him. "You're lookin' chipper enough, bro," he said as he ran through what he'd just changed, nodding at how it now sounded.

"Jenna's agreed to sing with us for the Boston event," Scott announced. "And – drum roll, please – she's agreed to tour with us again too."

Jeremy could hear the jubilation in Scott's voice. "Excellent!" He played through a line of melody as Scott dropped on a couch and stretched out full-length. "I do hope you know how damned lucky you are, my friend," Jeremy said, looking down on him while he continued to play. "And I hope the hell you keep it that way and don't go screwing your life – and Jenna's life – up again."

"I have no intention of screwing anything up again, my brother. I never thought I'd be saying this but everything is just – better with us. We've both changed. She feels it too. Even sex – excuse me, *making love* – with her is better then ever. I can't put it into words, but no *way* I'm ever screwing up again. I'm *never* traveling *that* road again."

Jeremy grinned over at Scott. "You know something? I think you've finally found yourself," Jeremy said, shaking his head in genuine amazement. "I didn't think I'd ever see it happen but I sure am damn glad it has. We've both come a long way since we were kids – we all have. There were times I wasn't sure either one of us would ever make the next day, never mind come this far. We have a lot to be thankful for and I think our women are a big reason that we do."

Scott could only nod and answer with a hearty "Amen brother, amen."

FOR THE NEXT TWO weeks, while Big Bob O'Halligan burned the midnight oil with the stage, sound and lighting engineers, Blacklace put together a fresh set list for the show. They rehearsed single-mindedly, by themselves and with Jenna. Scott and Jenna chose the songs they would sing together. Though they were happy to have her do more, Jenna decided to only perform one song from her new album.

No one could help but notice how smoothly rehearsals were going. For the first time in living memory, conflicts led, not to World War III, but to discussion, negotiation and resolution. In asides, no one in the band trusted it to last – they just decided to enjoy it while it lasted, and took advantage of this strange sea change to air a number of old grievances that had seemed far too petty at the time to bother raising Scott's ire over. The band exploited what Dan started referring to as first "the Christmas-in-May truce" and then "the longest Christmas truce in history – to get a lot off their collective chests.

A week before the show, things were in such good shape that Scott decided that he, Jenna and Zach should steal a few days to run up to Sunapee. He knew he hadn't been able to give Zach as much of his time as he'd have preferred through the period of heavy rehearsal. Three days in the woods would go a long way to ease his guilty conscience.

He discussed it with Jenna over lunch and she agreed. She stood watching from the door when Scott went into the living room, grabbed Zach up, swung him around in the air a few times, then pulled him close and said, "Hey, little guy, want to go to the lake?"

"The wake, the wake! Swimming! Canoes! Yaks!" Zach was instantly deliriously happy.

"Canoes and kayaks, for sure, Zacho, but I'm not so sure you're gonna want to go swimming," Scott said. "The lake's still pretty cold this time of year, my man. You need to pack your backpack – we're leaving in an hour!"

Zack instantly struggled to get down, and went running off to find his nanny. "Ellen! Ellen!" he yelled at the top of his tiny lungs. "We're going to the wake! We have to pack!"

Jenna came over and gave Scott a kiss. "And I'll go pack our backpacks, lover," she smiled.

"Forget the nightgown," he grinned back at her. "We're goin' to the lake. 'The place where babies come from.' God, I'll never be able to think of it as anything but that again. Maybe this time, if we work *really* hard, the lake will help make *us* another baby."

THEY WERE ON the road in forty-five minutes and got up to the lake in time to have supper at Tiny's. Zach, who'd been asleep in his car seat when they pulled in, cried when they woke him, then started reaching reflexively around him for the blanket that never left his sight. "Bwankie, bwankie," he sniveled. Scott found his blanket, wrapped it around Zach against the cold night air, and unbuckled his seatbelt.

"Do you want to meet the lady who made you your blankie?" he asked
Zach looked puzzled. "Make my bwankie?"

"Yep. Come on inside and I'll introduce you. You met her a while back, but you were probably way too little to remember."

Tom was at the door saying goodnight to some locals as they came in. "Well, look what the cats of spring drug in this time!" he said, clapping a beefy arm around Scott, then giving Jenna a gentler hug. "And – wait a second – you're not telling me this is the little spud ya brought in last time you were heah, are ya?"

By this time Sally had come hustling from the kitchen. Totally ignoring Scott and Jenna, she made a beeline for Zach, who returned her hug like they were the oldest of friends.

"Zach," Scott said formally, "you remember your Aunt Sally. She's the lady I was telling you about who made your blankie for you."

"Great Aunt Sally," Sally laughed, "or maybe it's great-great. Would ya look at this little fellah. And the blankie's holdin' up just fine."

"He's yet to leave home without it," Jenna assured her, giving her a hug. "My guess is he'll still be carrying it the day he walks down the aisle. Every aisle – graduation from kindergarten, eighth grade, high school, college, when he gets married, you name it." Sally beamed.

"Well, come in, come in. If ya haven't had your dinnah, ya must be hungrier than a bear comin' outta hibernation. Tom, you go get Mr. Zachary Tenny here the best highchair in the house." She ushered them to a table where she could still visit with them from behind the counter.

Tom produced a chair for Zach and helped Scott maneuver him into it. "Now, you all sit down and I'll get you menus."

"Do you have your lasagna on the menu tonight?" Scott asked.

"Does the sun shine on the Fourth of July at Sunapee?" Sally countered.

"How about lasagna for all of us, okay?" he said, looking to Jenna.

"Sounds great. And some side salads. That's be perfect."
Sally called the order back to the kitchen, then came back to marvel over Zach some more. "Considering the scare he gave you all when he was born, he's certainly growing up into quite a fine-lookin' young man," she told Jenna. She reached down and pinched Zach's plump little cheek, causing Zach to pull back in disapproval. "Sorry – just can't help myself. That a cheek that's just beggin' to be pinched. Where does the time go? It seems like only yesterday I was making that blanket for him."

Tom came over to the table and leaned over Scott while the women were talking.

"Well, seems you almost went and screwed things up for yourself good and propah, I heard," he said quietly.

Scott could only shake his head. "Yep. Scott Tenny fucked up again."

"Well, it looks like you've been able to work it out. She's a good woman, Scott. Don't let her go again."

"She and Zach are my life, and I aim to keep it that way," Scott assured him. "That's insider information you can bank on."

"Like the sound of that," Tom said, with a wink, then went back to the kitchen. In a few minutes, he reappeared with their meals.

THEY WERE FINISHED with dinner when Tom appeared at the table with a giant brownie decorated with a single lit candle in the middle of it. "It's never too late to celebrate a birthday – or *anything* you just might want to be celebra-tin'," he said, smiling broadly at all three of them. "Think you can blow that out, young man?" he asked Zach.

"I can bwow," Zach assured him seriously, and squared himself in his seat to demonstrate his expertise in this particular skill. Taking a deep breath, he leaned as close to the flame as he dared and gave a little puff. The flame flickered and vanished, and Zach's arms went flying up in victory.

"You sure can," Sally laughed. "Here are three forks. Go to it, kids!"

They shared the brownie, then gathered themselves and got ready to leave. "Got to get this little guy to bed," Scott said. Amidst the hugs, Sally slipped Jenna a small pastry box.

"More brownies for the weekend," she smiled. "We'll see you in July, Zach," she said, giving him a peck on his pinched cheek, "and make sure you bring your mommy and daddy back with you."

JENNA, SCOTT AND ZACH stayed in Sunapee for three days. One day started with a flurry of snow and ended up with a misty rainbow at sunset. The next day was crystal clear and the thermometer broke fifty. The third day provided nothing but ice-cold pouring rain. And they loved all three days equally.

After breakfast on the snowy morning, they all donned boots and went tramping through the woods. They were canoeing when the rainbow appeared. The clear day was spent introducing Zach to all of Scott's favorite childhood haunts. Some Jenna had already seen, but most were new to her too. Towards the end of the morning, he brought them to a fort he and some friends had built in the woods far up the lake when he was eight or nine.

Fort Boot Camp, as they'd called it, was still very much intact. No ramshackle affair, this little citadel was built of good-sized boulders rolled into place as walls. Several feet of interior dirt had been dug out to allow for headroom, and old lumber and branches had been laid across part of the top to form a roof. Zach's eyes grew round when he saw it, and when it became clear that a team of Clydesdales wasn't going to be able to drag him away, Jenna drove home, fixed a picnic lunch and brought it back for all to enjoy sitting cross-legged on an old blanket on the packed dirt floor. She had also returned with her camera.

"Wunch in Daddy's fort!" Zach kept crowing, as Jenna snapped picture after picture of her two men. Then Scott took over so he'd have pictures of her too. And since it was a simple point-and-shoot, even Zach gave it a try. Out of countless flashes, he managed to get four that actually included both Jenna and Scott's heads.

And the rainy day was spent quietly in front of a roaring fire. Zach was more than happy to play with toys he'd chosen to bring, as well as an old set of blocks that Jenna had found up in the attic one of the first times she'd ever been up here and had tucked away again without showing them to anyone, almost superstitiously, until the day she would have a child of her own old enough not to chew on them.

Busy building his own fort, Zach was content to play by himself, humming a tune of his own imagining, while Jenna and Scott sat on the couch, quietly working on the lyrics of what they'd tentatively titled "Child of Mine, Child of Thine." At this point they had separate verses on separate pages which they kept handing back and forth for major changes and minor tweaks. Each change brought exaggerated reactions, everything from approval to disbelief to total disdain, from the other. Everyone was having fun.

AND EACH NIGHT AFTER Zach went to bed, Scott and Jenna would lie in front of the fire, wrapped a quilt, talking and making love, by turns. Their love was passionate and comical, by turns. Their talk was sentimental and practical, by turns.

They talked about their first time here together and Jenna's first impressions. They talked about having the July Fourth get-together again this year. They talked about the fall tour and what shows Jenna thought she might want to sing. She told Scott she'd been thinking she might like to do some of her own shows with her band as well through the fall, and asked him what he thought.

Scott encouraged her to – but then whispered in her ear a reminder: "Just don't loose sight of the fact that you may very well be pregnant by then, my sweet." At the thought of which they made love yet again.

THE LAST MORNING DAWNED bright, windy and cold. Before they left for home, Scott took Jenna and Zach for a last walk, through the woods and back along the lake. They ended up sitting on the end of the dock, arms around each other for warmth and for Zach's protection, boots dangling down to within inches, in Scott's case, of the surface. It was a beautiful day and the lake, rough with whitecaps, looked more like a miniature ocean from this point of view.

Zach was enthralled with the wildness of it all, and with a pair of hawks that seemed to be hunting together, wheeling through the brilliant sky. "They're getting lunch for their little Zachs back at the nest," Scott told him.

"I want wunch too," Zach announced.

"Okay, one last stop at Tiny's and then we hit the road."

Everything was reloaded into the car and Zach was strapped into his seat.

As Jenna came around to take her place in the passenger seat, she looked back up as one of the hawks circled almost directly overhead, and whispered a quiet prayer to the heavens that she might at this very moment once again be pregnant.

THE MORNING AFTER they got home, Jenna started a telephoning campaign. Every chance she could, when Scott was out of the house, she made phone calls, leaving messages with Missy and Laurel, Annie, Joe and her mother, hoping she could get them all to put in surprise appearances at the show on Friday night and maybe stay for the weekend. She knew it would mean a great deal to Scott to have them in the audience. What she didn't know was that Scott had had a duplicate brainstorm and was leaving practically identical messages with her family as well.

One by one, she got calls back from those she'd invited. To her surprise, Annie was the first to respond, and to her amazement, told her that the entire Fitzgerald family would be there. Missy called for both herself and Laurel; the New York contingent would all be coming too. The only regrets came from Joe and her mother.

"I'm really sorry we can't get there," Joe told Jenna, "seeing's how your mother's got us just about to leave for two weeks in Hawaii. Get them hula dancers ready. Waikiki, here we come!" Linda, who was sitting next to Joe as he talked to Jenna, gave him a poke in the ribs for the hula comment, and gave Scott her own version of the same excuse five minutes later. Then the two got up and danced a foxtrot to Frank Sinatra singing "You Make Me Feel So Young" on the stereo.

"By the way, Mrs. Tenny," Joe said, looking down at his wife with a grin, "I'd dance a foxtrot with you over dancing the hula with ten dozen girls in grass skirts any day of the week."

"I should think so, Mr. Tenny," Linda said dryly.

Chapter 40

✺

ON FRIDAY NIGHT, Scott insisted that Jenna have her own dressing room and arranged that her stylist, Yumi Tagomi, fly out specially from L.A. He wanted to utterly spoil her.

However, when he told her she'd have her own dressing room, she seemed miffed. They had occasionally shared a dressing room, and for tonight it seemed particularly apt. She started to protest.

He held up his hands to stop her before she could even get going. "Don't ask questions, not tonight of all nights," he said, teasingly. "Indulge me. Tonight I just think you should have your own."

As he walked her past his dressing room down the hall to hers, he found himself feeling badly because he could see his surprise had actually upset her. When they got to the door he opened it for her and stood back so she could enter.

"Oh my God. I don't believe you!" Jenna cried once she saw what he had done. The room was filled with red and white roses. "They're from all of us," Scott told her. "It's Blacklace's official welcome back."

"This is why you wanted me to have my own room. I thought –" Scott kissed her before she could finish the sentence.

"I know what you were thinking, and I'm sorry. Does this make up for it?" And Yumi popped out from behind a screen in the corner of the room. Jenna made her way through all the roses to hug her. Then she turned back to Scott.

"Oh, baby, it more than makes up for it."

With a wave from Scott, the rest of the band piled in, wives and all, all with words of affection and warmth. Jenna could only shake her head in delight and amazement.

Dan cleared his throat, then launched into what had clearly been planned as an official speech. "Jenna B. Tenny, first and foremost, we all want you to know that they could have lit half of Boston with the energy we all expended worrying about you in the last couple of months – every one of us thanks God that everything's turned out the way it has. There aren't words…" Murmurs of agreement went around the little room.

"But even more, we want you to know that we practically blew down the Hancock Tower when we all simultaneously gave a breath of relief – when you came back to Scott. This has been a real edge-of-your-seats kinda year, for those of us in the wings, so to speak. We just wanted you to know how happy your return has made all of us."

Overcome with emotion, Jenna took the tissue that Yumi held out to her, then made her way around to everyone, expressing her love and appreciation as best she could. "I don't know how I can thank you, thank you all, for your love, support and friendship," she told them all. "It means so much to me. These roses – they're so beautiful and I appreciate it so much, but – I have a question." She'd stopped crying and almost started to laugh now. "What on earth am I going to do with them after the show?" Her laughter started everyone else laughing.

"Don't you worry, babe," Scott said, giving her a big hug. "I've already arranged to have them sent to the house. Now put yourself in Yumi's capable hands and relax. It's my gift to you." On cue, Jeremy reached behind him and adjusted the dimmer on the overhead light as Yumi pulled back the screen to reveal her massage table, all set up and ready. Jenna couldn't help but burst into tears again.

"You guys!" she cried.

FIVE MINUTES BEFORE showtime, Jenna went to Scott's dressing room. "And I have something I need to show you before the show starts," she told him. She took his hand and started tugging him towards the door.

"Wait a second. I'm not finished," he tried to complain. "I'm not ready."

"Oh, be quiet and just come with me," she said. "You look fabulous, dahlink. You don't need to do another thing with yourself. Besides what I have to show you is more important. You're not going to believe who's here." As they approached the seating area for family, he thought he knew already who'd be sitting there and wondered how Jenna had found out.

Both, smug in their secret knowledge, found themselves dumbfounded. Scott raised a dazed hand to wave at Laurel, Rick and Luka, Missy and Alex, Annie, Mark, David and Nancy – and Linda and his father. Jenna's hands flew to her mouth when, in turn, she found herself realizing that she was seeing Jim and Sue, Chris, Kristin and her now steady boyfriend Doug – and Joe and her mother. They barely had time to absorb the prank they'd played on each other before it was time to run backstage.

THE SHOW BEGAN, Jenna hanging back in the wings until it was time for her to go onstage. Scott was in top form, which had Jenna beaming. When he and the group had finished their fourth song, one of their new ones, she waited until the racket died down before she ran out onto the stage.

The crowd cheered louder than she had ever heard. It was humbling. She handed her mike to Scott, held her hands to her mouth shaking her head, then blew kisses to every corner of the Boston Garden. "Boston, I love you!" she said when the noise died down enough that she could be heard.

Before the audience could break into pandemonium again, she and Scott jumped straight into "The Hard Way," skipping any giveaway lead in.

> *Workin' hard, playin' hard, lovin' hard –*
> *Livin' life the hard way*
> *Work by day, love by night –*
> *Livin' life the hard way...*

After the two lines, Scott held his mike out to the audience and the whole thing exploded into a 19,500-person sing-along. The song had been a Black-lace hit since 1993.

When it was over and the audience had calmed back down, Scott started one of his familiar chats with the crowd. "Is she something or what?"

"Yeah!" came roaring back.

"Am I the luckiest guy on planet Earth?"

"Yeeeaaahhh!"

"Are we gonna so keep tonight's show G-rated 'cuz our families are in the audience?"

"Noooooo!" resounded up through the rigging.

"Well, it's not gonna exceed R – okay, Mom? Okay, Dad?"

Everyone laughed.

"I hope you'll all take this song to heart. We do."

On cue, Tim started a galvanizing beat with the drums. Dan and Jeremy brought their hands up over their heads to get the audience clapping. The band came in, one instrument at a time. Clearly, this was the lead-in to "The Harley Guy Thing."

But at the last possible moment, the band changed both tempo and into a minor key. Jenna and Scott each took a deep breath and went into a brand new song, a slow, sexy love song that they sang as a duet start to finish, neither taking a solo. The house hung on to every word. Their bodies moved in unison as they sang.

> *Life's mistakes, they cost ya.*
> *I almost lost ya.*
> *No way that's ever happenin' again.*
> *I've never known such fear.*
> *I hold and need you near.*
> *That's never happenin' again. Amen.*
>
> *I see you with new eyes.*
> *Just hellos, no more goodbyes.*
> *No way that's ever happenin' again.*
> *We'll fall asleep in each others sight,*
> *Dreaming fearless through the night.*
> *What happened's never happenin' again. Amen.*

The bridge was a searing falsetto, a wail of pain:

> *How could it happen to us, of all people?*
> *How could it ever have happened to two such happy people?*
> *How could it have happened to us?*

And they finished with a repeat of the second verse, but this time it was rendered in an upbeat, major key. They'd worried ahead of time that the song was too slow, that the audience wouldn't come along with them where they needed to go with it, but they agreed that this was the only way to sing this song. As it turned out, they need never had worried.

For the last song of the night, the last of a truly unusual five encores, Scott sang the opening lines of "Inappropriate Behavior," another great old favorite. Halfway into the first verse, Jenna wrapped herself around Scott and started weaving "I'm Ready to Go" into the lyrics. One by one, the backup musicians exited the stage with a wave, until it was just Jenna and Scott singing the last verse a capella. They sang the last few words with their lips millimeters from each others, kissed when the song was over, and left the stage clinging to each other. It took a full ten minutes for the house to finally accept that the concert was over.

"OH, BABY, YOU WERE incredible tonight," Scott had to practically shout in her ear as they made their way backstage.

"No, *you* were," Jenna said. "I was *nothing* compared to you."

"Oh, man, are we gonna have the fight of the century when we finally get some privacy tonight," Scott assured her. They shook hands and hugged friends and strangers alike as they struggled through a crowd of reporters and cameramen to get to their dressing rooms.

"You really think so?" Jenna yelled back at him.

"Oh, yeah. I mean, if you don't know how amazing you were…"

"No, I mean it, honey, you were *phenomenal*," Jenna insisted over the din.

"Well, I don't know about on stage, but how about we go home and you let me show you how else I can be phenomenal?" he shouted as directly as he could into her ear. Jenna shook her head at him.

"We already know that. However, before anything, don't forget – we seem to have a houseful of relatives to entertain, my darling."

EVERYBODY WENT BACK to the house. Stepping in the door, they found themselves adrift in the sea of roses that had been magically transplanted to Boston's South Shore. Between family, band and entourage, easily seventy people strained the spaciousness of their home, which seemed to swell to accommodate more and more as they arrived. The party lasted till four in the morning.

When Scott and Jenna finally faced each other across the expanse of their king size bed, they both just had to laugh. "I guess I'll have to postpone demonstrating how truly phenomenal I can be until tomorrow," Scott admitted.

"Thank God," Jenna laughed. "I would have been asleep before you'd even gotten warmed up." True to her word, she was asleep before he could even turn out the lights.

BUT IT WAS, IN FACT, the weekend itself that turned out to be truly phenomenal. Jenna and Scott's joy and inner peace was contagious. Missy and Laurel were particularly elated to see how deeply happy their father had become since Jenna had taken him back, and Kristin was ecstatic to see Jenna so indisputably, profoundly content. They'd all had glimpses of how well things were going, but the full weekend confirmed their hopes and prayers. Even Annie managed to keep from making any disparaging remarks about what her brother had done to Jenna.

Sunday afternoon finally came, though, and everyone in turn prepared to depart. Never in the memory of those present had a parting been so sincerely warm – or prolonged. Every hug was heartfelt. Every separation required numerous words. Everyone had so much to say to everyone else as they made ready to go.

But, finally, it was just the three of them. Zach looked up at his parents quizzically. "Just us now?" he asked, and Jenna reached down and brought him up into her arms for a hug.

"Just us," she said and gave him a kiss on the noggin.

"It's quiet," he observed.

Scott took him from Jenna's arms. "Only unless we want to make a lot of noise of our own," he laughed. And then he set Zach down and yelled at the top of his lungs, his hands cups around his mouth, "It's so quiet in here!" Echoes bounced off the two-story ceiling.

Which started Zach mimicking him and yelling, "It's so quiet in here!" His voice didn't carry quite far enough to raise echoes.

Scott produced another echo, and Zach tried again and again. Finally he asked Scott, "Daddy, who's the other Daddy?"

Scott taught him the word 'echo.'

WHEN ZACH FINALLY ran down, they tucked him in for bed together, having given Ellen the day off. Scott sat down in exhaustion on the couch, and Jenna lay across it with her head on his lap.

Scott started playing with her hair. "So, what shall we do for the Memorial Day weekend, my love? Sunapee again?" Scott asked her. "Or something completely different? Bermuda's great this time of year."

Jenna groaned. "I can't even think, much less think about another vacation right now," she groaned. He reached down and kissed her.

"We'll talk about it tomorrow."

"Deal."

BUT BY BREAKFAST the next morning, the idea of Bermuda quickly came percolating to the surface as they sipped their coffee. "Enough said," Scott declared. "I'll make all the arrangements."

"I have another idea. How about calling everybody and getting together for a dinner for just the Blacklace family tonight," Jenna suggested. "Friday night was a zoo."

"Blue Skies. I'll make all the arrangements," Scott said affably.

"Another echo?" Jenna laughed.

JENNA'S IDEA WAS inspired. Residual energy left over from Friday night fueled joking and hilarity, on top of all the usual catching up and shop talk. Everyone agreed to go up to Sunapee for the Fourth of July celebrations, which would probably be the only time they could all get together through the summer. Then, before they knew it, Blacklace would be back on the road again.

That thought brought a table full of groans, until Dan succinctly reminded them of the alternative. "Hey, I got this flyer in the mail the other day. From AARP. About rest homes for retired rock 'n rollers. All the amenities: power amps in every room, whammy bars on the beds to call the night nurse. Sounds real cushy, guys." The groans quickly morphed back into laughter.

The sound of a band coming back from break in the lounge filtered into the larger function room Scott had they'd taken for their party. Jumping to his feet, he grabbed Jenna by the hand. "Care to dance, old lady?"

Instantly, the tables emptied and the dance floor in the lounge filled. Anyone who was there that night would talk about it for years.

Chapter 41

✳

THE WEATHER HAD BEEN beautiful for several days before Scott could celebrate spring by finally finding time to take out his Harley. The Tuesday morning before the Friday they were due to leave for Bermuda, he spent all morning getting it cleaned up, then took it for a spin around the neighborhood. Pulling back up the driveway, he found Jenna out planting some flower boxes.

"Want a ride?" he called out to her.

"I want to get these finished before lunch," she said, holding up one of the many six packs of pansies and vincas scattered around her.

"Okay. I'll go throw something together," he said helpfully, then rolled the bike into the garage and headed for the kitchen.

"I should be done in ten," Jenna smiled.

"HEY, HOW ABOUT A quick trip to Newbury Street tomorrow," he suggested as he set out a pair of sandwiches on the kitchen counter. The idea took her by surprise. She looked up at him quizzically.

"You, me and Zach," he elaborated quickly. "And we'll have Georgie drive us – no parking problems. I just want to pick some things up for the trip, and I bet we could find something for you too. And Zach could use a new bathing suit."

"Well – yes! Sure!" Jenna said. She loved the idea.

They'd barely finished eating when Jeremy called to tell Scott that Ben Diamonte, their record producer, had called a meeting at the Boston studio on Thursday. Scott sighed. What had started out as a supposedly easy week was quickly turning into a typically busy one. At least it wouldn't cut into his Wednesday plans.

"Hey, if the weather holds, what do you say we take our bikes into town for the meeting?" Scott suggested. A little fun would offset the grind of business.

"Sounds cool to me, bro," Jeremy agreed. He was always ready to ride, and wouldn't have cared if the weather turned into a full-blown nor'easter.

SO WEDNESDAY SCOTT, Jenna and Zach went shopping. Both Scott and Jenna quickly got in the mood of finding some new fun clothes for their vacation, and they took Zach's bathing suit shopping every bit as seriously as he did. They even sprung for a new floppy brimmed hat to match.

They took a break for lunch, then, seeing how tired Zach was getting, Jenna suggested they might call it a day and head home. "Just one more stop," Scott said, picking Zach up and taking her by the hand. "I'll call Georgie and have him there with the car to meet us," he added, fishing his phone out of his pocket.

Two blocks further down Newbury, he suddenly steered her into Tiffany's.

"Tiffany's?" Jenna said in surprise.

Scott smiled at her, crossed to the service desk and said a few words to the woman in charge, then returned to her side. By now, Zach was sound asleep on his shoulder. Jenna was baffled.

A moment later a man emerged from the back and smiled over at Scott. "Mr. Tenny, it's good to see you again." Jenna could only wondered when this man had last seen Mr. Tenny.

Directing them over to a glass-topped desk, the Tiffany's employee sat down on one side and motioned to them to sit down on the opposite side. Only when they were comfortably seated did he draw a small rectangular velvet box out of his pocket and set it on the desk. He turned it so it was facing Jenna. Then he lifted the lid.

Jenna gasped. Inside were a pair of pink sapphire and diamond drop earrings, set in gold. They matched the necklace from Hawaii that Scott had given her for Christmas.

"Oh my God, they're gorgeous – and a perfect match to the necklace…" She let the thought trail off as she gently touched one of the earrings. The salesman deftly removed it from its velvet backing and held it up to Jenna's ear, indicating with a tip of his head the mirror sitting to one side of the desk.

She bent to the mirror, took in the flash of the pink sapphire against her dark hair and broke into a huge smile. She turned to Scott with an equally huge hug and kiss, then returned to the mirror, slipped out the earrings she was wearing, put the new earrings on and shook her hair back so Scott could see them.

"Oh, babe," he said, bursting with pride. "They look great on you, better than I could have ever imagined. Oh, you're gonna look so fabulous when we go to Bermuda." Jenna was so excited she decided to wear them home.

She kept sneaking peeks at them as they were reflected in the window of the limo, all the way home. As soon as she got in the house, she looked at them once more, then put them away with the necklace.

SCOTT GAVE ZACH his bath that night, then he and Jenna read to him before finally tucking him in for the night. Scott lingered downstairs to watch the news. By the time he got upstairs, Jenna was curled up in bed, her hair spilling wantonly across both pillows. Pulling back the sheet and blanket, he marveled at her beauty, then slipped out of his clothes, slid in beside her and made love to her until they both fell into a deep and tranquil sleep.

He woke up early in the morning, got up without disturbing her and went downstairs to put the coffee on. While it brewed, he tiptoed back up the bedroom, crawled into bed next to her and gently kissed her on the back of the neck. She rolled over to face him as she yawned awake with a beatific smile.

"Good morning, beautiful," he said quietly, then kissed her again. "Want to make love before I leave?" Her kiss told him all he needed to know.

Just as he was about to enter her, he rose up and looked down at her. "Jenna, I love you so much," he whispered. "You don't know how happy you make me. When I thought I was going to lose you, I thought I'd lose my mind. Thank you for giving me another chance."

Jenna smile her sleepy smile up at him and ran her hands up his chest and around his neck, drawing him down and into her. "You've made me so very happy too, Scott. And I love you so much as well. I finally figured it out. *That's* why we're together again."

He entered her then, tenderly at first, then he fiercely brought them both to ecstasy.

SCOTT SHOWERED AND DRESSED, had coffee with Jenna and spent time with Zach till it was time to leave. Finally he got up and went to find his leather jacket which he'd left thrown over the back of a chair in the den two days before.

"Want to bring my helmet out for me?" he asked Zach, but he already knew the answer. Zach knew the drill. He jumped up, ran out to the mudroom room, got the helmet from its peg and came running back with it. He'd been taught great respect for Daddy's helmet. He knew it wasn't a toy.

Jenna and Zach followed Scott outside to wave him off, Zach proudly carrying Scott's shiny black helmet stiffly out in front of him. Holding it carefully, he still managed to jump up and down in time to Scott's motions as he kick-started the Harley a couple of times until the engine caught. Scott opened the throttle, let the motor idle, then smiled over to Zach.

"Come here, kiddo," he said and Zach came running over with his helmet. Jenna followed him over reluctantly. Reaching down, Scott kissed Zach, then opened his arms for Jenna to give her a hug and kiss. She gave him an extra squeeze. Then he took the helmet from Zach and pulled it on. Adjusting it for comfort, he flipped up the visor, then grinned back at his wife and son.

"I love you. You be careful," Jenna said as Scott threw a leg over the bike and settled onto the seat. He smiled at her again.

"I love you too. Even if you do worry too much," he said with a wink, brought down the visor, gunned the motor and took off down the driveway.

Chapter 42

✳

THE COOL AIR OF the May morning slid through the vents of Scott's helmet and put a smile on his face. Thank God for spring, he thought to himself as he cruised the back roads over to Jeremy's.

Jeremy had his '53 Indian Roadmaster out in the driveway and was passing a rag over the bike's brand new red paint job the way a breeder of thoroughbreds runs a knowledgeable hand over a horse's flank. He'd only owned it a year, and it had set him back plenty to buy it. Scott pulled up alongside him and flipped up his visor.

"Sweet!" he said.

"Cherry," Jeremy agreed. "This baby's gettin' nothin' but TLC from here on out. You better believe that paint job cost me." He gave a light polish to the three headlights, then buffed the face of the Indian head fender light. He loved every inch of this extra special bike.

"Worth every penny," Scott decided as he looked the fine old motorcycle over, a rarity, one of the last two hundred fifty Indians produced as the company staggered through its final year of business. "The guy you got it from had to be fuckin' colorblind –that shade of blue he pimped it up with was just plain painful to look at. What was he thinkin'?"

"This is what she's supposed to look like."

"Well, into the saddle, cowpoke. We're gonna be late," Scott said.

"Right," Jeremy said as he picked his helmet up off the ground, kicked the motor into action and jumped on the bike. The fringe leather trim on his saddlebags picked up in the wind as he headed down the drive and out onto the open road.

THE TWO TURNED HEADS as Route 3 fed them onto I-93. No one could know who was under the helmets, but the fringed leather and heavy fenders of Jeremy's Indian set it apart from every other bike on the road, and Scott's gleaming black Low Rider with all its original equipment and understated, vintage-looking red pin-striping spelled serious class.

Traffic was moving well this late in the morning. Scott was cruising to the beat of the Allman Brothers "Ramblin' Man" on his headset. Jeremy's voice cut through on the two-way radio, just as Dicky Betts was settling into one of his classic riffs. "Big-ass rig flyin' up on us in this lane. Let's get over one."

"That's a 10-4," Scott keyed him back, and the two, riding side by side, slid over into the open lane to their left in what looked like the perfectly choreographed precision of the Blue Angels, and the guitar work of Dicky Betts wailed on.

THEY WERE THE LAST to arrive at the studio, and the last to leave after several hours of fine tuning songs with the studio engineers. Getting everyone to agree that they were pleased with a studio version of a song took the patience of a delegate to the United Nations.

Scott might be going through what their recording engineer, termed a 'mellow phase,' but Scott was only one of many who had to give Paulie's work the thumbs up. Scott was usually so impossible to please that the others, out of sympathy for Paulie, rarely bothered voicing their opinions unless something was really critical. This time around, everyone had opinions. Paulie found himself almost missing the old take-no-prisoners version of Scott.

Scott and Jeremy came out of the studio and into an afternoon that had turned brisk and breezy. As they got suited up and ready to ride, Jeremy, checking his pockets, discovered he'd left his gloves inside. "Fuck. I tossed them on the table when I came in. Dammit to hell, I knew I shouldn't have done that," Jeremy chewed himself out.

"I'm gonna get rolling, bro," Scott decided. "I told Jenna I'd be home before five, which probably won't happen anyway, even getting going now."

"She'll forgive you," Jeremy said as he turned to go back inside.

"Talk to you along the way," Scott said, then jogged down the steps to the parking lot and started up the Harley.

Looking around, listening to the satisfying roar of the Harley and taking in a deep breath of spring air before subjecting himself to the less fragrant air of the interstate, Scott realized he felt more at peace with the world than he could ever remember feeling. Riding that bike, especially after a session, was one of his greatest passions, right up there with sex, he'd admit to anyone who'd ask.

JEREMY, WHO ENDED UP leaving the studio only minutes after Scott had roared off, was pleased to see that they had still managed to beat the afternoon rush as he glided up the south-bound on-ramp onto 93. He keyed the two-way radio. "I'm on yer tail, bro."

"10-4, 'n many more," Scott's voice crackled back. He released the two-way button and settled in for the ride, but this time opted not to fill his ears with canned music. His mind was still rehashing the songs they'd been working on all afternoon. One in particular, the bridge of which was still bugging him, kept playing over and over in his head, over the muted sounds of highway noise and the Harley.

Jeremy, with a local rock station for background music, was cruising along thinking about recording an album of his own. He had more than enough material at this point. It was time to just buckle down and do it. Jeremy was quick to admit that he'd always preferred the shared responsibilities of performing in a group. Answering to others provided a momentum that got work done. Working solo required far more personal discipline.

A mile south, traffic slowed, then abruptly came to a halt. Damn, thought Jeremy, looking around him. The gas tanks told him he was only in Dorchester.

Threading his way slowly through the parking lot he'd suddenly found himself in, he couldn't help thinking how Led Zeppelin's "Dazed and Confused" in his headset provided the perfect soundtrack to this madness. To his further annoyance, a traffic alert cut in, confirming what was already abundantly clear. An accident at the Dorchester tanks. A serious one. Involving a multi-vehicle pile-up – and a motorcycle.

Jeremy hit the two-way button again. "Tenny?" No answer. "Tenny. Scott. Speak to me." Silence.

Leaning on the horn, hard, he started forcing his way through the maze of cars, trucks and SUVs as quickly as he could. Drivers had started opening doors and stepping out to see what they could see, making his forward progress difficult.

A quick glance to the right made it clear that the breakdown lane was no better – Bostonians were legally entitled to turn it into yet another driving lane during rush hour. Working his way across to the left, he bounced up onto the median, where it existed, and back down onto the highway where necessary. He reached Scott before the first ambulance.

"Scott," he screamed, finding the mangled body of his best friend sprawled awkwardly on his back across the curb and into the breakdown lane. Kneeling down beside him, he carefully popped open the face shield on Scott's helmet. "Scott." Scott's eyes opened, unfocussed. It was clear he'd heard his name. "Tenny, man." Jeremy choked back a sob.

Scott's mouth moved. "Jer," he gasped. "Jer. I – you…" He coughed blood. "Jenna." Summoning everything within him, he continued, "Tell…Jenna…I love…" He shuddered and fell silent.

"Outta the way," yelled a paramedic, pushing Jeremy to the side. "Let me through. There's nothing – oh, my God, it's Scott Tenny," he bellowed behind him, then looked up at Jeremy.

"Yeah," Jeremy said. "It's Scott Tenny."

"And you're – oh my God –" The paramedic just shook his head, turned to unpack his gear and went to work on Scott with expertise and focus that comes from far too much experience.

Jeremy grabbed the paramedic by the shoulder. "Where are you taking him?"

"Carney. Dorchester, just off Gallivan."

"I'm getting his wife. I'll bring her there. You just keep him alive, right?"

"Right," the paramedic grunted. "But make it quick." Jeremy pushed his way through a growing throng, jumped back on his bike and raced south down a now eerily empty highway.

JEREMY PULLED UP AROUND the back of Scott and Jenna's house with the heaviest of hearts but the greatest of urgency, now blind to the beauty of the day and the spectacular seaside setting that normally stopped him in his tracks.

Hitting the doorbell twice, he let himself in as he always did. Ellen barely looked up from fixing supper for her young charge. She was just pouring him a glass of milk.

"Hi, Jer," she said with her usual friendly greeting.

"Where's Jenna," Jeremy asked without preamble.

"In the playroom, with Zach," Ellen answered. "How are –"
Jeremy cut her off. "Ellen, I need you to come with me and get Zach." He hurried down the hall and burst into the playroom.

"Jeremy!" Jenna smiled broadly, but as she took in Jeremy's ashen face and stricken look, her countenance transformed from delight to dread.

"Jeremy?" He moved to her as Ellen went to Zach.

"Come on with me, baby," Ellen whispered and quickly gathered up several action figures that had Zach's total attention.

Jeremy took hold of Jenna's hands and held them tight. "Jenna, I need you to come with me. Scott's been in an accident. It's – bad, Jenna. We need to get to the hospital. Right now."

Seeing fear in his face, Jenna began to panic. "Tell me he didn't break his leg again," she started to say, then stopped. "Right?" Jeremy shook his head.

"It's – worse, isn't it." Jeremy nodded.

"Hurry," Ellen said. "Don't worry about Zach. I'll stay as long as you need. Go."

REPORTERS AND NEWS CREWS crowded the sidewalk, jockeying for position as Jeremy and Jenna pulled up to the emergency entrance of Caritas Carney Hospital. News of the crash had spread like a wildfire driven by the Santa Ana winds of Jenna's southern California youth.

Jeremy pulled to the curb, cut the engine and jumped out. Hurrying around to Jenna's door, he wrenched it open with no regard for the first of the reporters who now surged around them. Cries of "Jenna! Jenna!" came at her from every direction.

"Out of the way. Let her through," Jeremy shouted angrily, opening a path for the two of them like a pro linebacker twice his weight.

Once inside, Jenna grabbed the first person she saw in scrubs. "My husband. Where is my husband?" Jeremy put a protective arm around her and gently steered her to the admitting desk.

"Scott Tenny. This is his wife," he said succinctly to the on-duty nurse.

"Take a seat," she said. "I'll be right back." She motioned them to a bench, then hurried down the hall, returning almost immediately with a doctor behind her.

"Mrs. Tenny? Dr. Aguire." Reaching to shake her hand with his right, his left quietly covered and held it. "Your husband, Mrs. Tenny, has sustained severe internal injuries." He paused to let that much sink in. Jenna nodded nervously. "And massive head trauma. It – it doesn't look good," he finished softly.

Taking her by the elbow, he led her into the crowded cubicle where Scott lay, barely breathing, covered in blood. Jenna's hands reflexively covered her mouth as she burst into tears. The doctor cleared a path for her to her husband's side. She leaned over him, touched his hair.

"Scott, Scott, it's Jenna. I'm here, honey. You're going to be all right." She bit her lip as she said the words. Scott opened his eyes and looked straight into hers.

"Baby Blue," Scott rasped out his pet name for the woman he loved. "You're – here. Listen," he whispered, and she bent her ear close to his mouth, his beautiful mouth. "Not much – time."

Jenna interrupted him, "Scott, stop, you have plenty of time. You have to, for Zach, for me. Maybe for another. You know we love you so much."

Scott coughed and tried to grab her hand. She took hold of his and held on to it for dear life. He started to speak again, stronger now. "Jenna, baby. I love you more –" he gasped, "– than anyone. You know that. And Zach, too, our son, our boy. Jenna – take care of – our boy. Tell him about me. And – if we did – manage –" Another spasm of coughing wracked his body. "Tell them everything. Tell them I love – them."

He gasped several times. "Jenna – hold me," he finally was able to say. Jenna wrapped her arms around him and held his blood-stained body close, tears streaming down her face. "One more – kiss," he breathed.

She brought her lips to his, kissed him long and hard, then moved her mouth back to his ear. "I love you so much, you crazy man. You've made me the happiest woman in the world. I love you so fuckin' much," she murmured, then pulled back to smile down on him in spite of her tears. He broke into a crooked smile and managed to hold it as he faded away.

And then he was gone.

Chapter 43

✳

"NO, NO! SCOTT!" Jenna cried out. "No! Don't leave me. I need you. I love you so much. You can't. No!"

Hearing her anguish, Jeremy ran into the room. Without a word, the doctor and nurses made way for him and stepped out, giving the two privacy.

Jenna was holding Scott, rocking him in her arms, sobbing. Holding her shaking frame, Jeremy could hear her "I love you" repeated over and over, a mantra of grief. When her shaking had subsided a bit, Jeremy rubbed her arms, trying to bring her back to the moment.

"Jenna," he said. "Jenna, honey. Let him go. You gotta let him go now, sweetie," he urged her, putting his hands on hers and helping her lay Scott's head back down on the pillow. Then he put his arm around her. "Come. Come with me," he said gently, moving her away from the bed.

She took three steps, turned and looked at Scott one last time, then allowed Jeremy guide her out into the hallway and into the waiting arms of almost the entire Blacklace family. The word had gone out; everyone was either there or on the way. They'd face Scott's death the way they did everything – together.

Carrie came over and took Jenna from Jeremy's arms, replacing his with her own. "Jenna, Jenna, precious Jenna," Carrie crooned, rocking her as she did. "Get her a chair," she called over her shoulder as Jenna, overcome afresh, almost collapsed. "Dan, call Joe and Linda. We've gotta get her outta here. We'll take her to our house."

"No," cried Jenna. "No, I'm going home. I've gotta go home. Zach…"

"Ellen's got Zach. I'll let her know," said Jeremy. "She'll stay the night."

"That's – my home. That's where Scott and I lived and – loved. I want to be there, with our son. I have to be there."

"Okay, if that's what you want, Jenn, but we're coming with you," said Dan. Everyone quickly agreed. "At least till the family can get here. No way we're leaving you alone, hon. Come on now. I was able to reach Georgie. He's brought the car around. Everybody, just leave your cars wherever you parked them. We can come back for them tomorrow."

WITH GREAT PATIENCE, Georgie had eased the band's limo up to the hospital's emergency entrance through the mass of humanity who'd been instantly drawn to Carney by the dreadful news. Georgie wasn't going to put the limo in park until he'd guaranteed that Jenna and the rest would have the shortest possible gauntlet of reporters and fans to run. Slowly, slowly, he kept easing forward until he was satisfied.

As Jenna emerged, head down and clearly crying, supported by both Jeremy and Dan on either side, the crowd hushed and parted out of respect. For once, reporters stood mute, fighting back tears to their own, as Jenna passed and Jeremy handed her into the limo.

Jeremy slid open the window separating the passenger section from the front, reached through and squeezed Georgie's shoulder. "Thanks, man. That really helped."

Georgie turned to Jeremy. "Sure, man." Then he softly called back past Jeremy's shoulder, "Jenna, darlin', you've got my thoughts and prayers, honey. God's makin' a stage ready for our boy. It's gonna be one helluva show." Jenna looked up, profoundly moved.

"Bless you, Georgie," was all she could choke out before retreating into herself between Jeremy and Carrie.

As Georgie eased the vehicle back out through the crowd and onto the street and started to pick up speed, Jenna turned and looked behind her until the building where Scott lay – dead – vanished from sight. Her tears flowed once again as she turned back to the front and started rocking and whispering Scott's name, over and over. Carrie held her and when Jenna finally collapsed into her friend's arms, stroked her hair.

"I just want you to know, the family's been called, honey," said Jeremy. "They'll get here just as soon as they can get flights. Jenn –" he hesitated, then brought up what was on everyone's minds. "Do you want help with the funeral arrangements?" The catch in his voice made it clear: he too was hurting, badly. Jenna didn't respond.

"She's in shock," Carrie murmured. "Give her time, babe."

THE LIMO MADE the final turn to the Tenny house. "Oh, my God," breathed Jenna, emerging somewhat from her stupor. Friends and strangers, neighbors and fans by the hundreds, lined both sides of the street, waiting silently in the waning sunlight, gathered in respect and their own grief. Many held flowers, and more flowers lined the road and the fence on either side of the gates.

Watching the crowds carefully, Georgie made the turn into the driveway and waited while the gates opened. Then he slowly pulled the car up to the front door. Tim jumped out and Jeremy handed Jenna out to him as Georgie came hurrying around to help. The three had to practically carry her inside.

"Mommy, Mommy!" Zach came running the minute he heard the commotion at the door. Before Ellen could catch up with him, he'd wrapped himself around his mother's legs. Choking back her tears, Jenna picked him up and held him tight. "Where Daddy?" he asked her.

"Honey, baby," she sighed, brushing the long blond hair out of his eyes, hair he wore just like his daddy's. He reached up, wiped tears from her cheek and looked at his wet hand in amazement.

"Mommy crying?" he asked, puzzled. "Don't cry, Mommy. It's okay," he crooned, just as she did whenever he came crying to her.

"Everyone, settle in. Zach and I need some time. Ellen, give us ten minutes, okay, hon?"

"Sure, Jenna. I'll knock." Burying her head in the little boy's curls, Jenna carried Zach upstairs to his bedroom.

JENNA REMAINED UPSTAIRS for the better part of two hours. She didn't come back down until she had felt she had some degree of control over herself.

By the time she did, Bella and Eddie Strang were conferring with each other in a corner. Bella, it happened, had been two blocks from Penn Station in New York when she heard to news and had been able to get right onto an express train to Boston. She hadn't even taken her coat off yet. And by now, the entire Blacklace family was assembled as well. Jenna kissed them all, accepted everyone's condolences, then drew the group around her.

"Bless you all for being here with me," she began. "Where would I be without −" She cut herself short, gulped, took several deep breaths and went on with what she needed to say. "I am going to wait for the family to arrive before I make any plans. We'll all do it together. That's how we handle family matters − and you guys are all family. Scott would have wanted it this way. I want you all at my side along with everyone else."

Everyone sat quiet, thinking their own thoughts. Bella finally broke the silence. "Honey, I hate to have to bring it up, but there's never going to be a good time, so it might as well be now. The press is down at the gate. Better you deal with them before the family gets here. They don't need to be subjected to that."

"Right," Jenna said with a sigh. "Right." She looked around at all assembled. "I need you all by my side. I can't do it without you. Can you do this with me?" Heads nodded all around.

"You want to change first, don't you?" Bella asked pointedly.

Jenna looked down at the blood on her shirt, then laid her hand on the stains. "No, Bella, I don't want to change first," Jenna said fiercely. "I'm going out there just the way I am. I don't care what I look like. I'm not on stage performing."

Tears started to flow again, but she quickly choked them back. "I just lost the only man I have ever loved. Who loved me. His blood was part of him; part of me. I can't give it up yet. It's all I have left of him." She turned, squared her shoulders and strode toward the front door.

Reporters and photographers had staked out an area to one side of the gates, setting up a make-shift podium in anticipation of the family's statement. Jenna stepped up to the microphones, surrounded by her musical family. Silent, she looked out at faces both familiar and unknown. "Hi, Janice," she said quietly, singling out the Entertainment Seven reporter, who acknowledged her with a look of painfully genuine sympathy. She nodded to a few others, then looked down, pulled herself together yet again, raised her head high and addressed them all, reporters, photographers and fans alike. Her words came slowly, each chosen with care.

"I want you all to know that today we lost a great man, musician, husband, son, brother, grandfather and father. I for one don't know how I'll go on without him. We're here to let you know that we understand how you all feel." She paused, took a deep breath, then continued.

"Scott was the love of my life and we shared so much together – in so little time. I know many of you want to be a part of his final journey. We plan to do the best we can in order for you to be part of that closure. However, in return, we ask your understanding of our grief as a family, and hope you will respect our privacy as we lay Scott to rest."

The last thought proved too much for her. As a sob tore through her, Jeremy stepped in closer, put an arm around her, and took over. "Arrangements will be announced in due time," he said, leaning across Jenna to speak into the array of mikes in front of her. "The band is already talking about holding a memorial service, open to the public. You will be informed as to the time and place. We welcome you to pay your respects then. Until that time, please pray for Scott. Thank you. Thank you all."

Jeremy led Jenna away from the microphones, up the driveway and back into the house. When she entered the living room, her exhaustion was fearfully apparent. Carrie came to her and held her quietly. "You need to get some rest, Jenn," she said.

"In a while, honey," Jenna whispered. "Right now – I need to be alone. I'm going over to the studio." She slipped from the room.

SCOTT'S STUDIO IN THE old barn was his refuge. Out of moments of quiet contemplation came his songs, ready for the band to show up and develop into the predictably heady brew that had become Blacklace's stock in trade.

The studio wasn't just for composing and rehearsing, though. Jenna would just as often find her husband simply sitting on the couch, staring into the farthest reaches of the silent space, usually in those cases with something on his mind that he couldn't put into words. She'd help him and they'd find the words together, often ending these difficult journeys making love on the studio's thick shag carpet and drifting off to sleep in each other's arms.

NOW IT WAS JENNA'S turn. Sitting alone on the couch and staring into space, she heard echoes of Scott's music, echoes of the guys rehearsing, the guys arguing, the guys laughing. She thought about how Blacklace had accepted her so graciously when she came into Scott's life, had accepted her singing with them. The air was alive with it all.

Jeremy came through the outer door and quietly entered the room. He stood at the door for a moment, then came, sat down beside her and took her hand. "Oh, Jenna," he said mournfully. "I wanted to think I'd find you and Scott on the floor when I came in the door. I won't get to walk in on that again."

Jenna tried to keep the tears inside, but she couldn't. It all came pouring out. Jeremy held her close, rocking her as he spoke. "Everything will be all right. We'll all get through this," he whispered into her hair, though he had no idea how things could ever be right again. "I know Scott believed that there was a reason for everything. God, I want to know what the reason for his dying now could possibly be."

Jenna curled up with her head in Jeremy's lap and cried herself to sleep. Jeremy extricated himself without waking her, covered her with a blanket and went back to the house.

BY MORNING, THE ENTIRE family had arrived. It had only been a matter of weeks since they had all last been there. The last gathering had been a jubilant celebration of Scott and Jenna's reunion and love. This gathering was intensely, sadly somber. Zach was oblivious, for the most part, but even Luka understood the gravity of the occasion, and tried his best to help Zach understand too.

"No running," told his little uncle more than once. "We should be quiet." Each time, he took Zach by the hand and led him off to the playroom. There, he seemed to know, it would be okay for both of them to be their usual exuberant selves. Their laughter escaped into the rest of the house easily enough. In many ways, it helped.

With Jenna's blessing, Joe and Linda took charge of the funeral arrangements. Numb with pain, Jenna managed to make all the motions and answer all the necessary questions, to breathe in and out, to eat a little, to walk and talk, to give Zach all the attention she possibly could. When she couldn't, Ellen was at her elbow to step in.

Kristin barely left her sister's side. Jenna had passed the first night on the studio couch, unmoving, curled in upon herself in a fetal position, but the second night, when she was practically comatose with exhaustion, she asked Kristin if she'd be willing to sleep with her in the bed that had been hers and Scott's. The two sisters who had never known each other as children fell asleep like children, hand-in-hand.

The following morning, rising before Jenna, Kristin found the airline tickets for Bermuda on Scott's dresser and went down to the kitchen to call and cancel the reservations. She came back upstairs and told Jenna what she'd done.

Jenna got out of bed, went to her closet, brought out her jewelry box and set the sapphire and diamond necklace and earrings Scott had given her on the bedspread for Kristin to see them. "Oh, Jenn. They are so beautiful," Kristin said, touching the necklace almost reverently. Jenna sat down beside her and cried until, once again, she had no more tears to cry.

On the fourth day, the family held a private ceremony at St. Brigid's by the Sea, under the mournful gaze of the Madonna to whom Jenna had once turned for solace.

THE FOLLOWING WEEK, when everyone had finally left, her mother last, Jenna found herself drawn to the studio constantly, at all hours of the day and night. Sometimes she went with a purpose, to make an effort to sort things out, to make a stab at making sense of the chaos into which she'd been plunged. Sometimes she just went out there for the solitude it offered, to cry.

Sometimes she found herself humming a snatch of a melody, but the moment she realized that she was, she lost the power to hum. She found she could pick out the bare bones of tunes on the guitar, but only sad songs, in minor keys. She couldn't make herself approach the piano. Scott's presence was far too powerful on that empty piano bench. The loneliness of sitting on it by herself would crush her.

At one point, as she listlessly tidied up a pile of loose papers, she came upon the lyrics to the song she and Scott had still been working on, the one he'd started writing for his then unborn son. At that, Jenna sat down and started to cry her heart out, just as Jeremy came in the door. Going quickly to her side, he sat down beside her and put his arms around her. She turned into his chest and sobbed.

When she could, she pulled herself together enough show him the song, which she'd held clutched to her breast as she cried. "We were –" She had to stop and start over, but on her second try she was able to get all her words out. "We were writing this together," she said painfully. "He started it when…" She couldn't finish the sentence.

Jeremy took the paper from her hand and smoothed it out. Looking at it, he put his arm around her again, and again she cried. He found a box of Kleenex and pressed several in her hand.

When she'd calmed down enough, he finally said, "It looks like you'd finished the lyrics, am I right?" She nodded. "Had you come up with anything yet for a tune?" Jenna shook her head miserably. "We'd tried all sorts of things. Nothing was working," she choked out.

"We could do it, you and me and the rest of the band" Jeremy said tentatively. "I'd really like to, and I know I can speak for the rest of the guys. For you. For Scott. And because it would be such a fine legacy for him to have left for Zach. What do you think? I'll happily help make it happen, if you want me to. Let's make it happen?"

"Do you really think we can?" Jenna asked, wiping away the last of her tears. "You're right – it would be a fantastic legacy for Zach. Scott loved his son so much."

"I know we can," Jeremy said vehemently.

"All right, let's do it." And she smiled, if painfully, for the first time in what seemed like an entire lifetime.

By the middle of June, the song, "Child of Mine, Child of Thine," was finished and recorded. It was released in July, topping the charts within a few weeks. By October, the Grammy nominations were announced; Blacklace was once again nominated for Song of the Year.

Chapter 44

※

THE SAME WEEK "Child of Mine, Child of Thine" was released, a memorial concert for Scott was simulcast worldwide, originating from the stage of the Boston Garden. Admission at all the venues that night was a five dollar donation to any of a list of worthy causes, Jenna's shelter among them.

As Jeremy told the world at the opening of the evening, "this stage was Scott's playroom. The night we first performed on this stage, we thought we had made it to the top. We had."

The evening was a sensitive montage, including an opening prayer from Father Bob, who told the audience that, yes, he had had the privilege to marry Scott and Jenna, but that he also knew Scott, well. Unbeknownst even to Jenna, Scott had been going to Father Bob with his problems for years. "Scott was a monumental person, and he had monumental problems," Father Bob told the hushed crowd and the world-wide audience it represented, "but he faced his problems head on and he beat them, with God's help. He knew how to ask for help. Let that be a lesson for us all. I like to think that, now, he's getting to discuss his problems directly with his maker."

Between film clips of Scott and Blacklace as they came up through the ranks, performers all over the world offered both their spoken tributes and their own renditions of Blacklace songs.

The night ended with Blacklace, Jeremy taking the lead – singing "Into His Life." Jenna had come out onto the stage with them, but as Jeremy said as he introduced the song, "This is a song Jenna wrote and recorded soon after she and Scott had become seriously involved. I know there's nothing more that she'd love to be able to do than to sing it herself, and she will again. But for now, we'll sing it for her."

He held her hand through the entire performance, while a montage of images filled the giant screen behind them, four years of Jenna and Scott together. Jenna turned and watched them as they sang.

If there was a dry eye anywhere the show was being seen, it belonged to someone with a hard heart indeed.

"TO INTRODUCE THE SINGER of the next song nominated for a Grammy," intoned a voice over the loud speakers, "please welcome Jeremy Sandborn of Blacklace."

"Dear God, help me," Jenna prayed, as she as she awaited her cue in the wings before stepping out onto the stage of the Staples Center. Even though she knew almost by heart what Jeremy was going to say, she still had to steel herself while he did.

Acknowledging the warm applause, Jeremy cut it short, signaling for quiet, and the house immediately fell silent. Hankies appeared in a number of very well-known hands.

Jeremy got right to the point. "Ladies and gentlemen, before I introduce Jenna Tenny, indulge me for a minute and let me say a few works about our beloved Scott Tenny, whom we all deeply miss." He had arrived at the podium with his prewritten speech, but at this point Jeremy stopped, quietly folded it up and stowed it in his pocket. Looking heavenward for inspiration, he instead trusted he'd find the right words in his heart, and he did.

"Scott and I went way, way back, and I guess I may know Scott better than just about anybody on the planet. At several points in his life, Scott could have sworn he had everything he could ever want in life. He had fame, he had fortune, he had love and glory. After a torrid courtship with booze and drugs, he lost it all, but that didn't stop him. He fought his way back to the top – we all did – and once again he achieved success.

"Scott's biggest achievement, however, wasn't until he met the only thing missing in his life. Jenna Bradford. It was only then that he became *the* most fulfilled man in the world. Jenna loved him unconditionally. Under her influence, he became the most popular, talented and beloved front man of any band in the world, a world that sorely misses this warm, caring, compassionate and loving man today. And surely nobody can miss him more than his family, and the members of Blacklace, but most of all his son, Zach, and his beautiful Baby Blue, Jenna B. Tenny." Still silent, the crowd rose to its feet, holding its collective breath, knowing how very difficult the next several minutes would be for Scott Tenny's widow.

STANDING AT THE PODIUM, the members of Blacklace arrayed around her, Jenna Tenny looked out across a sea of famous faces. She'd performed for far larger crows than this. She'd performed at the Grammys, both as a winner and a presenter. She was an old hand, but what she had to do tonight, in honor of her beloved husband of four short years – *for* her beloved husband of four short years – was going to be the hardest thing she'd ever done. Tonight – right now – she would perform the song Scott had started but never finished, the song that she and Scott had worked on together, and that Jeremy had helped her finish for him, the song that was up for this year's Song of the Year.

The guys in the band had come to her, not sure if they should ask. "You know you're the only person who can do this, Jenna," Jeremy had said, speaking for all of them. "I certainly can't. You've got to. For Scott. For yourself. For Zach. For us. But mainly for Scott."

Quietly, Jenna took off her scarf and tied it around the microphone. With that one gesture, the crowd went wild. Jeremy lingered over a deftly drawn-out chord. Jenna took a deep breath, brought the mike to her mouth and poured out her pain.

"Child of mine, child of thine…" Drawing out the final word of the phrase, holding it like the last time she'd held Scott's hand, she took possibly the deepest breath of her life, let go and plunged on.

> *I wish for you, my son, a life so unlike mine.*
> *I wish for you, my son, a life as fine as mine.*
> *I wish for you, my son, child of mine, child of thine…*
>
> *I wish for you, my son, a sister, a brother.*
> *I wish for another child to have you for a brother.*
> *I wish for you, my son, child of mine, child of thine…*

Her mouth produced the words, but her mind raced back to a place she could only imagine too easily, to an overpass, a twisted Harley and a sight she never saw but would never be able to stop envisioning, the vision of the only man she'd ever loved, laying in a pool of blood.

She knew as she sang the second verse that, as passionately as they had tried, there would never be a brother or sister for Zach. And as that thought hit her, her eyes rose to the upper balconies of the Staples Center and she let herself be blinded by the lights beaming down on her from there. And in the light, she saw Scott's face, also beaming down on her.

Epilogue

※

SCOTT TENNY'S ASHES were spread over the ocean near the home he loved. By now, they have followed the ocean's currents around the world several times.

After the funeral, Scott's will was read. He had more then provided for each of his children, his grandson and his father. He had left a sizeable amount to his sister, niece and nephew and a list of people who were longtime, loyal friends and workers. The bulk of his estate he left to Jenna. She had no idea what do with it. She accepted Jeremy's offer of help with the business end of things.

JENNA SPOKE WITH Laurel and Missy about the house in Sunapee. Both shared her own feelings: she couldn't bear the thought of keeping it. There was no reason to go there now. It was the place where she had shared the most intimate moments of her life with Scott. There she had gotten pregnant three times; they had called it their pregnant place. Jenna decided to sell it.

She would keep the house in Miami for winter trips for any of the family. She and Zach would continue to live in the house they had shared with Scott; Zach would grow up in this house. As for the studio, she would use it for herself and her band if and when she decided to sing again. And, of course it went without saying that Blacklace could continue to use it any time they wanted to.

Blacklace had one more year on their current contract with Sony and had no choice but to honor it, with or without their front man. Jeremy, Dan, Jeff, Tim and Ryan came to Jenna and asked her if she would be an official part of Blacklace until the contract ran out. All they knew was that they wanted to finish what they – and Scott – had started, and they wanted Jenna to be a part of that. For Scott.

She thought about it for several days before deciding. The bottom line was that, before his death, she had come to a place in their relationship and in her heart where she would do anything for Scott, and this was no exception. Jenna agreed.

Their final production as Blacklace was a three-CD set, a compilation of all the fragments of Scott's unfinished work they could find and develop in his memory. The title was *Unfinished Business*. Like so much of Blacklace's best work, it too garnered a Grammy.

They announced their official breakup as they accepted the award. "We will continue on our own paths," Jeremy told the quiet audience," but Blacklace – the real thing – required Scott Tenny. We have no desire to foist a reproduction Blacklace on the world."

JENNA STARTED SEVERAL scholarships in Scott's memory. He had been so involved in the community and had given so much of himself, she couldn't let it go because he was gone. She also kept his ownership in Blue Skies. Fans would continue to come to what became a shrine to the memory of Blacklace and Scott Tenny. Jenna felt an obligation to his partners and to his followers to keep his memory alive. Besides, they'd had their wedding reception and had shared so many other wonderful occasions there. Holding on it was as much for Jenna as anyone, at least for now.

Jenna flailed about for some time, barely singing, mostly throwing her energies into the shelter. One of Scott's bequests had been a new wing for the hundred-year-old house, its first. Planning for that was as much a gift to Jenna as to the shelter. Had he known how lost she would be in the months and seasons that followed his death?

She had lost the most important person in her life. Scott had loved her to no end. He had taught her how to love and make love. He was her best friend, lover, husband and father to her son They had forgiven each other for everything. Truly, they were two of a kind.

Since they had gotten back together their relationship was stronger than it ever had been. Now everything was gone. She was alone except for their son.

TIM TOOK HIS MASSIVE set of drumming skills to That's *John* Straw to You, a solid rock band on the rise, also based in Boston. Dan, Jeff and Ryan were in the process of forming a new band, as yet unnamed, when Jeremy released his long-deliberated over, long-anticipated album, which he simply titled *Solo*.

Jenna and Carrie threw themselves into planning a huge release party for him at Blue Skies, which was in full swing, guests jammed into its furthest corners, when Jenna turned around and found herself face to face with Matthew Caine. She practically dropped the glass in her hand.

"Hello, Jenna," he said, his half-grin bearing both sympathy and pleasure at the sight of her.

"Matthew! What are you doing here? How did you know...?" Her question trailed off at his wink.

"It's my job to know, little lady."

Printed in the United States
206888BV00002B/1-93/P